Sudden Death

Rachel Lynch is a million-copy bestselling author of crime fiction, best known for her gripping DI Kelly Porter series as well as several standalones and the Major Helen Scott military police thrillers. Born and raised in Cumbria, the haunting beauty of the Lake District seeps into every story she tells. After teaching history in London and living across the globe as an army wife, Rachel eventually returned to her greatest passion: writing. Travel and the shared human experience comprise the fabric of her work. She explores the darkest corners of humanity with empathy and edge, weaving gritty realism with unforgettable characters. Alongside multiple standalone novels, she now brings her stories to life in a whole new way, through her podcast *The Killer Storyteller: A Podcast with Rachel Lynch*, where she unpacks every twist and turn, book by book.

Also by Rachel Lynch

The Rich
The Famous

Helen Scott Royal Military Police Thrillers

The Rift
The Line

Detective Kelly Porter

First Act (prequel)
Dark Game
Deep Fear
Dead End
Bitter Edge
Bold Lies
Blood Rites
Little Doubt
Lost Cause
Lying Ways
Sudden Death
Silent Bones
Shared Remains
Cruel Truth

RACHEL LYNCH

SUDDEN DEATH

First published in the United Kingdom in 2022 by Canelo

This edition published in the United Kingdom in 2026 by

Canelo Crime, an imprint of
Canelo Digital Publishing Limited,
20 Vauxhall Bridge Road,
London SW1V 2SA
United Kingdom

A Penguin Random House Company
The authorised representative in the EEA is Dorling Kindersley Verlag GmbH.
Arnulfstr. 124, 80636 Munich, Germany

Copyright © Rachel Lynch 2022

The moral right of Rachel Lynch to be identified as the creator of this work has been asserted in accordance with the Copyright, Designs and Patents Act, 1988.
All rights reserved. No part of this publication may be reproduced or transmitted in any form or by any means, electronic or mechanical, including photocopy, recording, or any information storage and retrieval system, without permission in writing from the publisher.
No part of this book may be used or reproduced in any manner for the purpose of training artificial intelligence technologies or systems. In accordance with Article 4(3) of the DSM Directive 2019/790, Canelo expressly reserves this work from the text and data mining exception.

A CIP catalogue record for this book is available from the British Library.

ISBN 978 1 83598 300 3

This book is a work of fiction. Names, characters, businesses, organizations, places and events are either the product of the author's imagination or are used fictitiously. Any resemblance to actual persons, living or dead, events or locales is entirely coincidental.

Printed and bound in Great Britain by Clays Ltd, Elcograf S.p.A.

Look for more great books at
www.canelo.co | www.dk.com

Chapter 1

Kelly Porter adjusted her seatbelt. It felt tight. Too tight. But she knew that this was just her imagination. It wasn't that she'd put on weight; though Christmas was just around the corner, she hadn't over-indulged just yet. It wasn't that the belt, or her seat, had changed position in the night. And it wasn't that she was wearing the wrong coat. It was none of those things.

She just felt off.

At forty, and a new mother, she could've blamed hormones, baby weight, and any manner of minor irritations, but she didn't. She knew full well what was going on, and she pulled the driver's mirror down, for the twentieth time, to check her make-up. Millie, her nanny, had arrived early this morning, to take care of Lizzie. Today was a big day, and Millie knew it, but they didn't discuss it. At just over four months old, Lizzie was blissfully unaware of what lay ahead for her mother today, though it was tempting to use her as a sounding board, safe in the knowledge that she wouldn't understand a word. But one day she would, and Kelly knew that kids repeat what they hear at home. She'd been a copper for enough years to know that. It's how they caught many parents who happened to be criminals; or were they criminals who happened to be parents?

She kept her chat with her daughter to gurgles and playful squeals. In itself, this drove her to the worrying realisation, at times, that she thought she was going mad. The absence of adult conversation at home, except with Millie when she arrived for her shift, and when she handed over at night, or her stepdaughter, Josie, studying for her A levels, bothered her. It was different at work of course. As the gaffer of the serious crime unit for the northern Lakes in Cumbria, she enjoyed plenty of chat in the office, but it wasn't really the kind of exchange she craved. It was all statistics, case files, and people doing horrible shit to each other. What she really needed this morning was someone to tell her everything would be okay when she faced Johnny in court. Her ex-boyfriend, and Lizzie's dad.

As she sat despondently in the car, willing herself to start the ignition and begin her journey to the crown courthouse in Carlisle, her mobile rang, as if on cue. It was Kate Umshaw. Detective Sergeant Umshaw was her right arm, and her second in command. The woman she couldn't live without. Their friendship had grown from the necessity of being colleagues, when she'd turned up in Cumbria, fresh from the Met in London, six years ago, tail between her legs and eyes wide shut, to the close bond they had now. They'd been through much together, and Kate was about the only person on the planet who understood what she was facing today.

'Hey,' Kate said.

'Hey,' Kelly replied. 'It's so good to hear your voice.'

'How you feeling?' Kate asked.

'Shit.'

'Obviously. Are you sure you don't want me there?'

Kelly had told her that she'd rather face today on her own. It wasn't because she didn't want or need Kate by her side, it was just that she had to concentrate on shutting out the noise. It was a paradox that to get through one of the hardest days of her life, she'd have to purposefully focus on being quite alone. Of course she wanted Kate there. Kate had been there, in Highton prison, when it all kicked off. Kate had seen what Ian Burton was capable of. But most of all, Kate knew Johnny. It wasn't that Kate couldn't face him – quite the opposite, in fact; she'd been arguing that life was too short to hold grudges. It was testimony to her emotional maturity that her 2i/c liked the man, but disapproved of his behaviour.

In court today, the defence team was wrapping up. Yesterday had been the turn of the prosecution, and Kelly knew the case inside out. It was her case. She'd lived the details for months, from the moment they'd found Jack Bell's body to the moment they'd finally given the Crown Prosecution Service enough to charge the twisted bastard who did it.

What she hadn't seen coming was that the divisions between the defence and prosecution inside the courthouse would tear her love life apart. Johnny had moved out, but it wasn't that they'd fallen out of love straight away, or had a massive messy fight and thrown things, or said stuff that they couldn't take back. No, it wasn't like that. It was simply impossible to live with someone who was a witness for the defence. He'd been Kelly's rock pretty much the whole time she'd been back in Cumbria. He'd helped her pick herself up when her mother died. He'd caressed her in the middle of the night when she woke up sweating, not sure if she could go on pursuing people so sick in their heads that it made her physically ill.

'Of course I want you there, but it's better if I do it on my own. It's selfish of me, but I think I'll keep it together better if I'm on my own. Besides, I don't want you facing Ian Burton,' she told Kate.

'Oh, Kelly, you know I'd love to face Ian Burton, on my own, in a cell, with a rusty piece of metal,' Kate replied.

'That's what I mean,' Kelly said. They laughed. 'We're looking good. But I've said that before,' she added, alluding to the fact that, in a courtroom, the truth didn't always prevail. She took the conversation back to the case. They'd all seen bastards walk free, or get shorter terms than they deserved. Equally, they'd all seen Mrs Miggins get three years for fuck all. It made no sense sometimes, police work. Mrs Miggins was police jargon for busybodies who stymied the whole criminal justice system. They brought 10 per cent of criminals to trial, and most of those didn't get what was merited. As soon as an investigation left the confines of the office at Eden House, in Penrith, and was passed to lawyers and barristers, crime took on a new life form. It turned into an entirely different beast, and it was out of their hands.

For her lover of almost five years to travel so far to that side of the law made her blood boil. But they shared a child. And she missed him. That was what really disturbed her today.

'Just remember my ex is a dickhead too. We all have one.' Kate's ex-husband, Derek, had left the family home after twenty-odd years.

'Did you see the papers this morning?' Kelly asked.

'Yup, absolute bollocks,' Kate said.

The headlines had run with Johnny's noble commitment to PTSD charities and how Ian Burton had dedicated his life to the military, for queen and country. The problem was that the prosecution, in going after a soldier who suffered undoubtedly with mental health issues, came across in the media as unfeeling twats. The fact that Ian Burton was warped in the head before he ever touched a uniform was irrelevant. If they even suggested that Ian Burton was damaged goods, then the human rights card was played, and plastered all over the news. It didn't really matter how loudly they argued that not all ex-soldiers damaged by war turned into serial killers. Whichever way you looked at it, Ian Burton was a victim and his targets were scum convicts, so who cared?

It was the first time that Kelly had been in the news and targeted by journalists on a personal level. They'd raked up her history from the Met and got soundbites from so-called ex-colleagues about the botched Coryn Boulder case that wasn't even her fault. It was years ago, in London, when a material witness jumped off a roof, being pursued by her unit. But no one cared. This was a classic case of coppers going after the innocent. What could she do? Her team had been put on trial by social media, and lost. Her face was all over the news and journos had camped outside her house for weeks. Which was why she parked a few streets away, and went out the back, across her terrace, exiting the rear gate, crossing a tiny bridge over the River Eamont, and scuttled over the newly unveiled Pooley Bridge, avoiding most of the attention from reporters hoping to get a shot at her.

It was exhausting.

There'd be plenty of them at the courthouse too. The world had gone mad. It was as if no one wanted to remember what Ian Burton had done to his victims, or the organised crime ring run by his father from inside Highton prison. All they wanted was to fight for a killer's human rights because it looked good on social media and influencers got a million more followers for using hashtags such as #freedom and #justice.

Thankfully, inside the court room there was no such circus. In Britain at least, things like that were still unwelcome in the business of judicial proceedings; how long that would last remained to be seen. The way things were going, Kelly reckoned she might not hold her breath. Like the chief constable reminded her: policing wasn't a popularity game and she should keep her head down and do her job, if she still wanted it.

She did.

Even after the media slurs and the stupid things she read on social media about herself, she still believed in her role, and that she made a difference. That was all coppers wanted at the end of the day. They didn't get it mostly, but every now and again they did, and that was good enough. She owed it to the families of the victims.

'Good luck, but you don't need it, you'll wipe the floor with them,' Kate said.

Her second in command referred to the case in general, and not Kelly's testimony, which in fact hadn't been needed in the end, so convincing was the forensic case her team had built. The facts spoke for themselves, so much so that the jury squirmed every time details were brought up of exactly how Ian Burton liked to torture his poor sodding victims. Burton had pleaded not guilty and so subjected the families of those concerned, as well as the public purse, and the poor jury, to a litany of brutality in court. It was criminal in itself, but that was another matter.

'Thanks, love,' Kelly replied.

They hung up. She checked her rear mirror again and caught a glimpse of the hills to the east of Ullswater, and felt a pull that she hadn't experienced for some time. She'd been so wrapped up in hiding from the press, and coping with Johnny's betrayal, that she'd given the hills a rain check. It was as if she lived in any other ordinary town, and not on the edge of the national park, surrounded by wilderness. She knew in that moment that the first thing she'd do after the verdict, whether it went their way or not, was get up there above the snowline, and hike her guts out. The thought gave her renewed resolve and she started the car just as a couple of journalists, grabbing coffee at the shop next to the Crown pub, spotted her and darted towards it.

She sped past them and had never felt so much desire to flick the bird at somebody as she did in that moment. It took all her strength to keep her finger hidden. She drove past them and headed off towards the M6. She gripped the steering wheel so hard that a stinging sensation alerted her to her senses. Her nails were digging into her flesh and she released her grip.

This case was killing her.

Chapter 2

The Right Honourable Lord Donald Reilly held his woollen coat close to his body, as he battled to pull on his leather gloves at the same time. The damn weather up north was confounding. The wind almost blew him off his feet, but one of the pilots gently took his elbow and guided him towards the machine that was to take them back to London. The helicopter, whether modern or a hundred years old, was a certified death trap if ever there was one, and defied physics. A scientist at heart, and by academic award, Donald hated them.

There was something distinctly untrustworthy about the dynamics of the blades and their flimsiness in the face of the slightest gust of wind and covering of grey cloud. The Lake District had both, in spades. He knew that the only reason his associate for the weekend chose to be transported in one, was status. Helipads sounded respectable and impressive. To Donald, though, they rang alarm bells in his head.

He'd flown in enough of them to know. He closed his eyes and said a silent prayer, as he always did before he flew. He'd checked the credentials of the two-man crew, who were both ex-RAF, and they were, as expected, exemplary. However, his sensible brain kept throwing up grave uncertainty, warning him of impending doom. Only Bart could convince him to climb inside a damn metal box that was about to defy logical mathematics, because he had a way about him like that. And Donald had to admit that he was grateful to his friend. Over the weekend, he'd been more than generous. Donald had reached the conclusion that, due to Bart's wealth and confidence, the chances of him chartering a poorly maintained vehicle were slim. He even smiled at his paranoia.

He glanced over at the house which had been his home for three days, and marvelled at the grandeur. All weekend, he'd been treated to a steady stream of the things in life that were the preserve of the rich and powerful. Bart never disappointed. A flicker of guilt wafted through his mind, as if fluttering into the 'copter on the wind, and he thought of his wife and two children, who were technically adults now, for the first time all weekend. He hadn't had them on his mind last night when his friend had served up the entertainment just over the lawn there, in the private rooms of Laurie Fell House. But he reassured himself that his movements were protected and Bart's network watertight. It had to be. As a member of the government, Donald had a duty of care to the nation as, at the very least, an example to them. But that was the fundamental attraction of breaking the law: it was intoxicating and addictive because it was risky.

The jitters hit him once more, as thoughts of betraying his wife and children deserted him. His mind was cast back to his nerves, and again he saw himself facing certain death in an entirely unreliable invention of humanity. The helicopter. He reached for his diazepam, prescribed by his private doctor in Mayfair. That, and the substances he'd imbibed last night, should do the trick, but his hands still shook.

He climbed into the cabin and the fine leather interior beguiled him for a moment. As a peer of the realm, certain privileges were owed to him, and he smiled to himself at the apt nature of his surroundings. He sat back and settled somewhat. It was a short flight after all, and they'd be in London soon enough. He'd told his wife that he was being driven by limousine from Cumbria back to the capital, a long and thoroughly dull journey by road. She didn't expect him until late tonight. However, Bart's last minute idea to fly, though at the time crazy, was a perk Donald's ego couldn't resist, despite the risk of the press getting hold of photos of them together. They'd managed to avoid direct contact in the public eye for a good few years, at the direct intervention of the prime minister. But Donald was confident that Bart was discreet. He'd had plenty of practice.

He reflected on the forty-eight hours that had just passed. This remained their most perfect secret. He trusted his host with his life. They'd known each other a relatively short amount of time, if one counted the political spectrum in the UK as one spanning centuries. Indeed, their friendship had taken up less than a decade. In that time, under-secretaries had come and gone, business interests had shifted and the prime minister had become older and greyer, prematurely, as they all did eventually. Donald had never fancied the top job: it was for show-offs and attention-seekers. Better to be out of the spotlight and able to continue one's indulgences off the radar, rather than have them played out in the gutter press, for all to see and judge. Downfall was rarely as a result of bad performance on the political stage. It was more to do with ancient tweets, personal mistakes and unfortunate gaffes, usually involving sexual miscalculations.

He plopped himself onto the seat and placed headphones over his ears as he was told. The interior might be sumptuous, he thought, but the wind whipping through it made it feel as flimsy as a two-man tent on Dartmoor. He could barely hear himself think as the current of air travelled through the cabin like a knife cutting ripe camembert. The whole machine shook. The blades above his head made a deafening din and the whirring sound induced nausea. Back in the eighties, he'd avoided the machines like the plague, but unfortunately, as an officer in Her Majesty's armed forces, he hadn't had much choice. It was the preferred transportation when in theatre, and in the eighties there was enough deployment around the world to give everyone a ride occasionally.

The headphones gave him some comfort.

The pilots busied themselves with checking charts and finalising their computer-programmed flight plans. He rolled his eyes and said another prayer as he realised that he was probably going to be ferried back to London on autopilot, not even at the hands of a human being. People trusted computers too much these days. He'd skipped breakfast; his nerves wouldn't allow it. He'd dismissed the chauffeur at the last minute, and the driver would be making the three-hundred mile journey now on his own. It was too late to change his mind and indeed, he saw Bart striding across the grass, beaming from ear to ear, and eager to get going.

Bartholomew Kennedy-Craig was the type of companion who could get you to do all the things you said you never would. He was the ultimate salesman. Donald couldn't help smiling as he watched his friend climb in beside him, and some of his charm and confidence rubbed off, allaying his worst fears. Bart produced a quarter bottle of fine brandy from his pocket and winked.

'Party's not over, Donald,' Bart said.

'We shouldn't travel together, Bart,' Donald said. Bart had a meeting in Glasgow later this morning, to discuss the progress of various mining projects for oil and gas. Strictly speaking, fracking – a hideous term – was all but illegal, but Bart was one of the first to take advantage of the government's desperation to wean itself off foreign energy quotas. Bart was always at the front of his game. Flying to London and back again didn't make sense, but then, nothing about Bart ever did.

'I know. Stop worrying, Donald, no one will ever know. I want you to see some of this stunning landscape. My friend, you need to relax.'

Donald took the small brandy bottle and took a swig, studying his friend. No one would guess that Bartholomew Kennedy-Craig had been partying all night. His tailored suit and immaculate camel coat, together with the stench of money dripping from every pore, would reassure even the severest critics about his legitimacy. He smelled of cologne and his smile was that of a man in charge. It hadn't taken much convincing to get Donald to agree to the two of them taking the risk of flying together. In a way, it was as if the weekend hadn't really ended, and this was their last hurrah; a toast to getting away with it all these years: the girls, the deals, and the special relationship. One day, not long off, Bartholomew would be put forward for a lifelong peerage. Donald had already paved the way, with Bart's money, of course.

Donald's face was chilled by the wind and snow was forecast. The nip of brandy warmed him, but also surely contributed to the reddish-purple hue across his face, and he thought of his wife telling him that he drank too much already. Bart was ten years Donald's junior, but in politics and business, age was a mere number. In his early sixties, Donald was nowhere near retirement, and the prime minister relied upon his integrity and longevity, almost as much as he did his own. Last night had given him the little boost he'd needed.

It was the prime minister he'd represented this weekend, and what a triumph it had been. The climate conference had been a resounding success, and local businesses had benefitted hugely, as well as raising the profile of the area, that was in dire need of it. Unemployment in Cumbria was up there with the highest rates in the UK and, apart from tourism, they were desperate for a bit of glory and praise. Images and soundbites had been broadcast all over the world, and the UNESCO status of the area had drawn in the national and international press. It was a glorious backdrop and made even the most miserable attendees look quite perky. And that was the point. It had been Donald's idea in the first place, and he'd been driving for it for two years. As under-secretary to the Department for Environment, Food and Rural Affairs (DEFRA), he'd driven the agenda, and delegates had gone home impressed and satisfied with progress. Of course, China and Russia had failed to send representatives, but it was essentially a bonding exercise for the West, so it was only to be expected. All in all, Donald felt smugly contented with himself. Being hosted by Bartholomew, even though it had to be kept secret, was simply the icing on the cake. Thoughts of the protesters outside the hotel, and the feeling as the egg had slammed onto the top of his head, subsided as he controlled himself and focused on the positives.

A sudden change in chugging made his stomach leap and he reached out for Bart's hand absent-mindedly. Bart laughed.

'Oh, Donald, relax. It cost me seventeen thousand quid to rent this thing. The pilots are excellent, and they like my tips. Believe me, they want to get home to their girlfriends tonight too.'

Donald had panicked about every detail when Bart had suggested he go back to London on his private chartered helicopter. That included questioning leaving the helicopter out overnight in freezing temperatures, but he'd been assured that with the proper protective equipment and de-icing first thing, everything was in order.

'Ex-RAF eh? Good job,' Donald said.

The pilots indicated that they were ready and the bird lifted a little off the turf. Donald looked over at Bart, who was like a small child peering out of the window. He had to admit it was a luxurious model. The interior was all tan leather and mahogany tables, seating a capacity of at least fifteen. What a waste of money, Donald thought, but that was the point with Bart. The upholstery smelled new, and at least the opulence gave him some sort of comfort. From their elevation, Donald could see the housekeeper's car returning from dropping off the girls. He felt his groin stir, and that was the problem with clandestine lasciviousness: it was intoxicating. Like the first time one tastes sugar: a desirous seed is planted and grows stronger and stronger until the passion for it exceeds all sensibility. But that was the thing about money: it had the power to transcend all boundaries.

'I've asked them to fly over Scafell Pike,' Bart gushed.

'What?' Donald asked in horror.

'Oh, don't worry, Donald, you'll love it.' Bart patted him on the knee and the contraption rose steadily further up into the air, until it nodded to the sprawling stone estate of Laurie Fell that had been their home for the weekend, before spinning round and up over Lake Ullswater, which he could see snaking away like a lazy fat serpent. For a moment, Donald forgot his fears: this was no Iraq or Kuwait. He held his breath as the mountains came into view and the vista mesmerised him into silence. The brandy helped, and the memory of the two girls.

Scafell Pike was to the west, and, like all the high peaks at Christmas time, covered in snow. The sky was bright blue and Donald felt his heart leap as he took in the views, committing them into his memory bank, in order to tell his wife.

It had been a damn fine weekend.

Chapter 3

Kelly parked in the multi-storey next to the shopping centre. It was away from the courthouse and she knew the way around the back from there. The press would be all over the place and waiting for her to turn up, and she could barely handle it as it was, without having to face them as well. It was a sensational story.

> …Female copper limps home to Cumbria after being implicated in a fuck-up in the Met, tries to become superwoman, lording it up back home, but never quite fitting in, and then falling flat on her face again. Oh, and dumped by her boyfriend too, the great Johnny Frietze, decorated ex-army officer, mountain rescue legend and champion of PTSD. What a bloke…

What a loser she was.

That's how it had played out in the papers. And she could do nothing about it. Reputations and lives could be ruined by one story, and she had dozens about her in circulation. Sometimes it was too much and she sat in her office chair and put her head against her desk, just for a moment, looking for some respite from all the unfairness. A breather.

In those moments, she heard her mother's voice. 'You're doing everything you can. You always did.'

She wished Wendy could be here. She'd died too young. Her mother belonged to the generation that didn't kick up a fuss if you weren't feeling too well. By the time they found the cancer it was too late. Kelly sat at the wheel and called the only person that she could think of. Her only place of safety.

'Dad,' she said.

'I'm at the courthouse,' Ted said. He had good reason to be. It wasn't that he was there because he was protecting his daughter from the press, though he wanted to do that. He also happened to be the senior coroner for the northwest of England, and he'd followed the trial keenly, giving evidence as the prosecution's main expert witness.

'Can you meet me in the usual place?' she asked.

'I'm already waiting for you.'

'Journalists?' she asked.

'None yet. You're clear.'

Ted finished the call and she gathered her things. She carried a small handbag. Usually, her work uniform would be more casual. If she wasn't attending to relatives of the deceased, or making an appearance at mind-numbingly tedious meetings at Carlton House with her chief constable, then she opted for comfortable trousers and a T-shirt, under a loosely tailored jacket, with pumps. Always ready to run. She carried a backpack full of kit she might need, should she have to move at short notice. But the legal team had instructed her otherwise for the duration of the trial. They told her to dress up. Look the part.

She felt foolish but had got used to the tight skirts and silk blouses, as well as the tiny handbag. She wore more make-up and brushed her hair. The first time she'd gazed into the mirror looking like the perfect prosecution witness, she'd laughed out loud. Millie said she looked like a ball-breaker. Josie, her teenage stepdaughter, said she looked hot. Lizzie giggled.

She felt like a twat.

Her heels clicked on the pavement and she rounded the final corner which led to the back way into the courthouse. She was almost at the door when a journo spotted her and ran after her.

'Kelly Porter, can you forgive your partner for betraying you?' A mic was shoved in her face. It was sensationalist bullshit. She rounded on the woman.

'Fuck off.'

She got to the door and pressed the entrance code rapidly into the keypad. The door buzzed and she went in, slamming it behind her and breathing heavily. She prayed that the journo had spotted her unexpectedly and hadn't got her recording equipment ready in time. Oh Jesus. She'd just done, on the final day of the trial, what the legal team had forbidden her to do for two whole months.

'Are you all right?' Ted asked, coming towards her.

'I just told a journalist to fuck off,' she said.

Ted sighed. 'Well, it was only a matter of time.'

'Thanks, Dad.'

They walked together to the stairwell leading to the courthouse and he held the doors open for her.

'Is he here?' she asked as they approached the lift.

Ted nodded. 'I saw him earlier when I went to get coffee.'

'Fuck.'

He faced her and put his hands on her shoulders. 'Look. Sometimes the truth isn't what people want to hear in this world, Kelly. That's all you do and you do it well. Don't let anyone else's agenda sway you. Johnny made his own decisions, and so did Ian Burton. He's guilty as hell, that's a given. The verdict and sentencing will reflect it, mark my words. This will all die down and you can get on with your job. You're a fine detective, Kelly. And I don't want to work with anyone else.'

He smiled at her and gave her a cuddle, which she so desperately needed.

'You know when I saw your mother at Wasdale Hall, over forty years ago, she looked radiant. In her green dress, she looked as though she could do anything, talk to anyone, and achieve anything. She was a fighter, Kelly, and so are you. Come on.'

—

Upstairs, the waiting area outside the courtroom was rammed with people, and Kelly thought she might turn and run. Ted squeezed her hand.

Then she saw him.

She'd faced him on plenty of occasions when he collected Lizzie, or she dropped Josie off at her dad's to spend the night. But not like this. Not as enemies, on opposite sides of the judicial system. It was as if an ocean was between them, not just some cheap plastic chairs and a coffee machine. He smiled at her and waved, as if nothing was out of the ordinary. Before she knew it, Ted had waved back and Johnny was making his way over. Kelly turned away. Her heart raced and her cheeks burned. Thank God no photos were allowed inside the courthouse.

'Morning, how's Lizzie today?' he asked.

Kelly couldn't answer. He wore a suit, and a tie, with a crisp white shirt, and was about as at home in it as a fish out of water. She moved her mouth but nothing came out. Ted did it for her.

'She's great.' Ted and Johnny shook hands.

Kelly could smell him. His familiar body scent took her back to a memory that dripped with regret.

'Suppose everyone will get what they want today. And then we can all go back to normal,' he said.

Kelly bit her tongue and willed herself to look at him. She spotted a defence barrister behind him, who took his arm gently and asked him to join them. He eyed her suspiciously, as did the whole defence team, as if she were a smear on their campaign, and Johnny gave his apologies.

She breathed again and Ted placed himself in front of her, blocking her view of the defence team.

'Coffee?' he asked. She nodded. They were standing right beside the machine and Ted leant over, putting his credit card against the reader and punching in codes for a cappuccino. Finally, she spotted the prosecution barristers and they approached her through the crowd. Suddenly she was with allies. She wished she'd let Kate come. The feeling of being outnumbered was overwhelming – anyone would think she was attending a high-profile retrial, or some kind of controversial case where a huge miscarriage of justice was about to take place, not a murderer getting what he deserved.

An announcement signalled that the court was ready, and a rush of pushing and shoving ensued. The public gallery had been packed to bursting every time she'd been in: vultures circling over the details of death. It made her question everything about what she did. She had staff going off sick all over her department, the strain of too much work and too few resources was pinching them all so tightly that they struggled for air. The reputation of the police in the press had reached an all-time low; morale was in tatters. Maybe it was time to get out.

But this was all she knew. Her gut told her what to do and always had.

They took their seats and watched the jury file in, and then stood for the judge to enter. At least in here she was able to breathe because no fucker was allowed to talk apart from the poor bastard in the stand.

Ian Burton never took the stand. He kept his secrets with him, and she knew he always would. She'd met enough serial offenders to know that he was the type who loved the power of withholding information. She drained her coffee and wished she'd got another, if only for something to do with her hands.

She felt a burning sensation in her neck on the right side and realised that Johnny was staring at her. She turned her face to meet his as they all sat down. She kept her eyes on his and continued to look at him as he sat. There was no way she was looking away first.

He did.

She turned back with satisfaction. It was childish, she knew, but it felt good.

Chapter 4

At this time of year, just before Christmas, and indeed throughout winter, it was quite normal to experience dramatic cloud inversions across the national park. It was something to do with geography, a subject Donald had studied at A Level, at Eton College, and he explained this to Bart, who wasn't really interested, but Donald needed to talk through his anxiety, as the helicopter flapped about on the wind like a new-born fledgling, clumsy and vulnerable to predators.

'It's really a temperature inversion,' Donald droned on. 'Ordinarily, air is colder the higher it rises, but in an inversion, the opposite is true and a blanket of cold air gets trapped underneath. Look, it's sticking to the layer below it like glue.' Donald pointed as the big metal bird lost a little altitude. 'Jesus, I'm going to vomit,' he said, grabbing the seat.

Bart smiled.

'Good God, Donald, think about that young Sasha riding you, tits everywhere and screaming your name.'

Donald shot him a look and his eyes widened. This time it was out of embarrassment, not fear for his life, because he thought the pilots might have heard what Bart had just said.

'The mics are one-way, they can't hear a thing. For example, if I said that I snorted the finest grade cocaine out of Chloe's arse cheeks, they wouldn't even flinch, look.'

The pilots carried on, oblivious to the conversation going on in the back. Donald relaxed a little and smiled. 'Jesus, Bart, you kill me.'

'In fact, that valley over there, well, let's just say it reminds me of something,' Bart said.

Donald guffawed heartily. 'It is beautiful, though, I'll grant you that.'

Bart stared out of the window, knocking his friend's arm with his elbow as he swigged brandy.

The early morning cloud looked as though it was being sucked downwards, snagged between cliff edges. It was as if it was snared across the valley, an ethereal net laid by farmers the night before to catch some mystical animal that threatened the fells. The fluffy carpet couldn't quite reach the high peaks; so adhered was it to the valley floors that it looked like an ocean, with the mountain tops like islands protruding through it. So if one was in the lucky position to be at the top of one of the significant summits at such a time, or in a helicopter, then the clouds would be beneath you, benign in their beauty and beckoning in their allure. It was quite something, and Donald's breath was simply taken away. It helped to remove the premonitions of impending death. Or the vision of what he'd done to a girl half the age of his daughter last night.

'That's Helvellyn dead ahead,' one of the pilots pointed out.

It got their attention. There were only four or five peaks projecting out of the cloud ahead, and Donald picked one out and remembered the name. He'd heard of it, but wished he'd paid more attention to that particular aspect of geology. He was more interested in the great volcanoes of Hawaii, or the vast and awesome heights of South America. The Lake District seemed paltry by comparison, but the vista before him now was stunning.

The machine vibrated and shook. Donald reached for his briefcase, into which he'd put a bottle of water for the journey. Suddenly he was irritated with Bart for showing off. This silly diversion was unnecessary and all about his companion's ego. 'Look what I can do!' It was so Bart. He splashed cash around because he had so much of it that the boredom drove him to purchase mindless trinkets of stupidity. However, the annoyance was short-lived, because he knew that it was that aspect of Bart's character that kept him supplied with his playthings too.

'It's clearing,' the other pilot said, jerking Donald from his judgement of his friend. He concluded that he simply felt guilty for cheating on his wife. Again. If serial addiction to underage girls could be classed as anything so benignly common as cheating.

'Perfect timing,' said Bart. 'I even control the weather,' he added.

Donald looked at him. He was one lucky bastard. Everything he ever coveted fell into his lap. Just like that. Bart was one of those fellows who attracted everything that was worth having in the universe: girls, money and power. It was like a cycle of the best hors d'oeuvres in the most exclusive restaurant on the planet: the platters kept coming and swirling round and round, offering titbits of ecstasy. When he was with Bart, nothing was off the menu, and he grinned as the machine soared over the mountains.

Chapter 5

High on Scafell Pike, England's highest mountain, runners in competition vests sweated and panted their way up an incline gradient of almost twenty degrees. Low cloud was the worst weather to race in. It made everything slippery and screwed with the balance of the contestants because it compromised visibility. But then it levelled the playing field too. It had been bitterly cold when they set off this morning.

It was a serious fell race; for the heavyweights only. Glynn Cortantes was one such young man. He had a pleasant, agreeable demeanour, and this was his secret weapon: it disarmed his competitors. Everybody thought he was a pussycat, until they raced next to him. His body's ability to process oxygen, to feed his hungry muscles, when they were screaming halfway up a scree run a thousand feet in elevation, was off the chart. He was half Spanish, half mountain goat. Thus his race name: El Cabro. But he was no kid. At thirty-three, he should have been considering retirement, but he had years left in him yet. He was only just beginning to smash the records he'd dreamed of his whole life. The UK Lake District races weren't the highest, but they could be some of the most challenging because of their incessantly unpredictable terrain, and the weather.

The lifting of the cloud was a blessing and a curse. It would open up the field. Well, the field behind Cortantes, that was. He was way ahead. The Scafell Round was a winter highlight on the circuit. It took in five peaks, and was unique in that one had to rely upon climbing equipment to get from Scafell to Scafell Pike, via Mickledore and Broad Stand. It was a delectable piece of topography for those who were turned on by that sort of thing. They were on the final leg, having dumped their equipment behind them on the eastern edge of the pike.

Cortantes had won the Scafell Round for four years straight. The cloud seemed to bow to his command as it enveloped him and then cleared ahead, as if he were Moses of the mountains. He pounded his way up a stage that was a path, and some might think that these were the easier parts, but they'd be wrong. The man-made trails laid in stone were killers on the knees and ankles. He dug in and never slipped in his rhythm.

Fell racing attracted athletes from all over the world, but little press coverage. The landscape prevented it, but also the funding. It wasn't as sexy as the big sponsorship events such as football or track and field. Cortantes was patronised by many sports labels, and made over 2 million euros per year in endorsements alone, but you wouldn't find his name in the papers, or on the front of flashy magazines. It enabled fell runners to stay humble and lead fairly private lives. Even the best ones.

There were few spectators, and certainly not on the top of the fells. A few fans waited in the cold on the Lingmell Col with flasks of hot chocolate, and they cheered him on, but it was mostly family and friends. There was no TV coverage. Somebody sent the occasional drone above him to post the footage online later, and he'd got over a million views for one of them, but it was a niche sport, and he liked it that way. He settled his breathing and came off the path onto soft grass. It made his calves scream but at least it stopped the pounding in his bones. Occasionally he peered behind him, but rarely, because he could tell by footfall that he was alone.

He looked up ahead as he heard the chopper. It disturbed his concentration because it was a sound that sent shivers through anyone truly involved in the mountains. It usually meant that somebody was being rescued by the MRT. It certainly wouldn't be a TV crew: they weren't interested in grey days in Cumbria. Fell runners weren't Usain Bolt and couldn't command that type of hype or following. He looked up and saw it through the clouds. It was low and he shook his head: it wasn't the normal red or yellow of a rescue craft and he assumed it was a sight-seeing trip; they'd surely get a good photo of him from that distance. He'd look them up later on. It would be a damn good photo. A group of people emerged from the misty remnants of this morning's cloud inversion and they clapped for him, but stopped when the helicopter caught their attention.

It was coming up the valley, over Wast Water. Cortantes almost stopped when he looked back and saw the view. It was about as good as it got: the area's deepest lake curling around between two magnificent geographical wonders; it was spectacular. There were some mountain ranges that made your heart stop in your chest and simply commanded your time, and this was one. The tiny Lake District in England. He laughed to himself. He'd competed in the Himalayas and there, the locals would see these fells as tiny mounds of dirt, not even making up the foothills of the mighty 8,000ers.

Steam escaped from his body as perspiration evaporated around him and the temperature rose with the parting cloud. It was a steady nine degrees, and the snowline had got higher this last week. It was better for running but not for photo opportunities or tourists who spent Christmas here hoping for snow.

He witnessed the next two seconds in slow motion and dived sideways, to the ground, as his brain was overtaken by what was unfolding above him, and instinct took control of his large motor skills. He saw the machine slow down and the tail blade come off first, and he watched as it floated silently down towards the lake. Then he stood helpless as the rest of the helicopter seemed to slow dangerously and then hover, and then it began to rotate dreadfully.

There was a screaming whir as it spun faster and faster, and descended towards the racers behind him, who didn't know what was happening until they looked ahead, at him, and then skywards, and in the half second before they were crushed by the metal missile, they'd been distracted by why the great Glynn Cortantes had stopped running.

He could see in their eyes that they momentarily thought they could catch him, now he had stopped, unaware of the true reason he'd thrown himself to the ground. He became aware of the pain in his shoulder, and realised he had hit it on a rock. He hid his head in his hands as an explosion rocked the mountainside behind him. His knees came up to his chest and flying debris rushed past his body as he curled tightly into a ball, placing his arms as far around himself as he could to protect his organs. In the moment before the fireball subsided, and the rush of air sucked every sense of feeling out of his ears, he realised that if a piece of metal belonging to any part of that helicopter hit him, neither his hands nor his T-shirt would save him. He braced himself for impact. But it never came.

Then silence.

Chapter 6

Major Lance Tatterall breathed deeply, and took in as much of the pure mountain and lake air as he could, willing himself to remember this moment forever, to cherish and take back with him when he had to return to his ordinary life, which he kept running from.

He was holidaying in the Lake District, a kind of mental break, some decompression from the demons in his head. He'd spent the last twenty years flying helicopters; mainly Apaches. Now he'd made the dizzy heights of promotion to chief instructor for the Army Aviation Centre in Middle Wallop in Hampshire.

He'd come here alone. It was time to reflect and make decisions on whether he wanted to remain in the army or divorce it, after a painful twenty-year romance. The same was true of his marriage, but the Lakes had at least given him the space to park that to one side of his head, and embrace the peace and quiet.

That serenity had just been blown apart by something up on the mountainside, and he stood stock still, trying to work out if it was a trick of his imagination.

He'd come down to the lake from the Wasdale Inn, where he'd been staying. He'd enjoyed some fine walks in this most quiet section of the national park. He came every year, and each time he left feeling more positive and recharged. It was a cold day, and the mountains above had been covered with cloud until the last few minutes, when it had cleared to reveal their majesty. That was why he'd been peering up, and seen the snaking line of coloured vests, and remembered that a fell race was on today. Jock, at the inn, had told him.

Up there, everything was silent, apart from what he'd heard just a couple of moments ago, and even that was a mere echo travelling down the mountain path towards him, dissipating as it reached his ears, and further puzzling him as to whether it had actually happened.

The thing was: he knew helicopters.

The one he'd seen hurtling down the lake was a private charter.

It was an AgustaWestland 139, recognisable anywhere in the world, but particularly so in a wilderness like this. They were fucking expensive: 10 million dollars and upward. Sleek, with the nose of a shark, with wide, extravagant windows for passengers to enjoy their surroundings. This one was white with a blue trim, and Lance almost wished he was up there flying the damn thing. He knew instantly that whoever was in it had to be in possession of stacks of cash. They were a dream to fly.

Which was why he questioned, again, if what he had just seen was a dream.

He did calculations in his head and his mind flipped back to weeks in the Apache simulator, showing students how *not* to fly, and what to do should a catastrophic error occur. Torque forces, yaw axis ratios and air flow indications over the blades all fought in his head, which was full of questions.

He was getting ahead of himself – but then he saw the smoke.

What he'd witnessed was genuine, and the calmness of the last couple of days left his body as he realised that a helicopter had just come down.

The uncontrolled spin was authentic. The debris he'd seen fly off with violence towards the deep lake was real, and in all probability was the tail rotor. The savage revolution that had ensued after the piece of metal had spun off was textbook. One of the most basic elements of helicopter mechanics was the role of the blades. The main rotor spun clockwise, and the tail rotor was designed to offset this power, with its own orbit, thus balancing torque. What he'd just seen was a spectacular failure of this beautiful relationship.

He had no time to think; his body was already moving towards the path up the side of Scafell Pike from the Wasdale car park, and he sprinted towards it with vigour, calculations and scenarios whirring inside his head. Whatever had happened up there, he knew that the AW 139 could carry fifteen people, as well as two crew, and a spin like the one he'd just witnessed, followed by the crash, was in all likelihood not survivable. But he had to try. He'd done enough disaster training to know that the first people on the scene were crucial to the survival rate of those on the ground. The emergency services and the MRT wouldn't be alerted yet, and they certainly wouldn't be able to get up there any time soon.

His nerves jangled, but turned stress chemicals inside his body into a steely determination to help as many people as he could.

Then he remembered the fell race.

As he went through the first couple of gates on the slate path, his lungs heaved deeply and he knew it would be a hard slog. Jesus, the best fell runners took forty minutes to get up England's highest mountain and he wasn't that fit. As a major, he'd had too many desk jobs and too many boozy nights out to compete with that level of fitness. But he had to try. If it took him two hours to get up there, at least the emergency services would have another pair of hands.

He stopped and took some water from his bottle and was grateful that every time he went out around here, he always packed like a soldier. He had everything he needed: layers, water, whistle, compass in case the cloud came down again, and his mobile phone, which he'd already used to punch in 999. But down in the valleys of the national park, phone service was abominable, and so he kept trying, hoping that somebody on the mountainside had already dialled it in.

Chapter 7

As expected, Kelly's investigation was being pulled apart by the defence in their summing up. They'd moved to dismiss on the grounds that they lacked evidence several times during the proceedings. It was common, but it still made her blood boil. All she could do was listen, as each point was elucidated, to the horror and gasps of the gallery. She watched the jury. There were six women and six men, of all different ethnicities, ages and backgrounds. Gone were the days when lawyers could get their heads together and kick a few off the final line-up, now it was in the hands of the jury service. Contrary to common belief, judges could sway trials easily. The standard perception was that the judge simply sat and umpired, and made sure everybody did their job. However, in his (or her) summing up, he regularly and easily was able to influence the ordinary men and women sat watching and eager to get home and out of the circus, particularly if it was a trial that attracted a lot of attention, and this one had. Of course it had; it was multiple murder, and it was Cumbria.

Kelly wondered which way the judge would go. She was a wizened old bird: white, Caucasian, no doubt heterosexual, a few kids, stereotypically standard in her politics, and part of The Firm. The prosecution expected her to go with them.

She did.

She was spectacular in her bias against Ian Burton being stitched up, as the defence had continually argued, as much as anyone could be in a democratic and fair legal system, with her tongue firmly in one cheek. Kelly could tell from the facial expressions and tics emanating from the jury bench that they had them on side. She glanced over to Johnny, who was grimacing every time the judge reminded the jury about Burton's crimes in detail, which was her right, inside her courtroom. Behind the thick glass of the dock, Burton sat expressionless. The prosecution barrister sneaked a look behind her towards Kelly and smiled.

They had him.

The defence's summing up had been brutal, but thankfully brief. It was all about reducing Ian Burton's sentence, rather than placing doubt in the mind of the jury over whether he was guilty. The defence knew it, but they were dangling as many loose ends as they possibly could to get a life sentence reduced to, say, twenty years, out in ten.

Ted reached across and squeezed her hand.

They were done. Now they just had to await the verdict. The judge stood up and so did the rest of the court, and she glanced at Johnny, who reached into his pocket to take a call. She watched his brow knit, then her phone went off too. She glanced around the court at the journos and realised that their phones were buzzing too. Silently vibrating, it would seem, across the packed court. Something serious was happening. Jesus, it didn't take long, she thought. But, then when she answered the call, she realised with surprise that the news everybody was clamouring to spread was not about the trial at all.

A chopper had come down on a fell race high up on Scafell Pike and the emergency services had been alerted. The whole county, it seemed, was being summoned, and anyone with advanced first aid was on their way up the mountainside, because no ambulance could make it up there, and there was nowhere obvious to land a helicopter except maybe the Col, but that would depend on the weather.

She stood listening to Kate on the other end of the phone, and her eyes met Johnny's. She knew he was talking to the desk at mountain rescue HQ in Keswick. Given the magnitude of such an accident, they'd be calling everyone they could reach, on or off shift. She read his eyes and he nodded to her.

'What is it?' Ted asked.

She held her hand up slightly and indicated that she'd fill him in as soon as she could. The judge left and members of the public gallery began to file out. Only journos and the legal teams stayed behind, and half of those were on phone calls just the same as hers.

'Somebody videoed it and it's been uploaded onto YouTube already,' Kate said.

'Jesus, casualties?'

'A lot,' Kate replied.

'Who's been mobilised?' Kelly asked.

She knew that in any scenario like this, it would be a race to the mountain, given the location of the valley and the inaccessibility. It wasn't a case of following the rule book and sending a couple of ambulances and a squad car to take statements. They were facing potential huge loss of life and anybody with any kind of relevant training was heading up there as fast as possible. The police would take charge of the multiple agencies who could get onto the mountain, but in the meantime, it was a mess, and someone was needed up there to keep things calm.

'Surgeons are being flown from the Penrith and Lakes. They're going to try and land them on the Lingmell Col,' Kate said.

'How long ago did it happen?'

'Twenty minutes. The wreckage is still smoking. Police have been sent from Egremont, Whitehaven and Millom. Lancaster is sending helicopters, mountain rescue have five teams going up.'

Kelly hung up and filled Ted in briefly.

'Jesus,' was his response, and there were a lot of confused stares among those left in the courtroom echoing his sentiment.

Then Johnny was beside her. She looked at him and knew what he was thinking. They looked at each other's clothes.

'I've got running kit in the car,' she said.

He nodded. 'Let's go.'

Chapter 8

People use the words 'disaster' and 'emergency' too often. When it actually happens no one really knows what to do. Decisions aren't made as the catastrophe unfolds; rather, training undertaken over many years kicks in and instinct takes over, for those who have it. Those who don't stand by helplessly and, more often than not, just get in the way. Dozens of race watchers scrambled up to the top of the mountain at the head of Wasdale, but few who reached the wreckage in the first hour actually knew what to do. On the mountainside, those who witnessed the crash couldn't even get to the twisted metal, though they could hear screams.

It was too hot, too smoky, and too terrifying. Who ran towards danger? Only a psychopath. The families, friends and fell runners on the mountainside weren't psychopaths; they were ordinary people. A small number of the folk on the tiny paths and tracks possessed simple first aid skills but those consisted of clearing airways on test dummies and positioning fully intact models on their sides in the recovery position. Real trauma was something that required high-level practice. In any scenario such as the one unfolding on the slopes of Scafell Pike, those who knew what to do took time to arrive, and meanwhile, people were dying.

Black smoke mingled with low-lying cloud, pieces of twisted metal and body parts, which were strewn everywhere. Spectators of the fell race, who were dotted along the whole route up Scafell Pike, screamed and ran in all directions, panicking and shaking from the adrenalin flooding their bloodstreams, becoming disorientated and making terrible decisions. One man ran along the Lingmell Col, which led down the Corridor route off the mountain, but he took a tumble down the cliff face towards Piers Gill, one of the most dangerous spots in the whole of the national park. It had been covered in cloud one minute and the next displayed in all its horrific glory as a gaping rocky ravine with sheer drops and terrifying rocky edges, only leading to the bottom. No one saw him disappear over the edge.

Shouts and moans floated on the wind, punctured by moments of absolute silence, as victims lost their grip on life.

The helicopter itself had come down just below the Col, on boggy ground, and the wreckage was fairly intact, apart from splinters of metal that had shot away from the main body on impact, and during the ensuing explosion. The main fuselage was burning, but in one piece. It was impossible to tell how many runners were underneath the machine and its blades, which, as the bird came down, ripped up the bog and took bodies with them.

Suddenly, the sound of voices calling 999 pierced the eerie quiet.

Glynn raced back down the route and was on the Col in a couple of minutes. The mist clung to him and his skin glistened with sweat. Others joined him and he quickly took charge. He assessed victims and spotted those who were still alive. Some of them barely clung to life; they were the ones he began working on. He ripped off his shirt and made crude tourniquets, tying them around the ragged remnants of limbs, attempting to stem blood loss. Other runners watched him and did the same, but some couldn't move for fear. Their brains had shut down in horror. Some people tried to treat the dead and Glynn ignored them.

'I'm a medic!' he heard someone shout through the cloud that was rising and falling as if taunting their efforts.

'Here!' Glynn shouted. A man rushed to his side and he showed him what he was dealing with. The man's head was gashed deeply, and Glynn had roughly bandaged it with what was left of his shorts. He had no clothes left, apart from his underwear. The medic began taking clothes out of his bag. He also had a simple medical kit. Glynn left him and made his way to the 'copter, which was on its side, but became more accessible as the flames died back. He knew he shouldn't approach it because it could explode again, at any moment. He smelled aviation fuel. But he could also see that somebody inside was still alive. An old man was staring at him through the cabin, which was crushed and twisted, as if painted by Salvador Dali, Glynn's hero. They were both Catalan. As Glynn got closer, the heat was intense around the cabin, and he saw the remains of the pilots. One was decapitated and the other had metal melted into his body, making him look like some kind of transformer machine, part human, part helicopter. Movement caught his eye and another man, behind the older of the two, moved as well. He stared into their eyes and assessed the situation. Flames rose where they hadn't been before and inside Glynn's heart, he knew the fate of the two men was sealed. Even if he could get to them, he could see that they were stuck on their sides.

It would take him long minutes to get them both out, and already he could see that the flames had reached their bodies. He locked eyes with the older of the two, who seemed strangely calm. It was the younger one who flailed about, screaming and pulling at his clothes.

Glynn made it to the cabin and never took his eyes off the older man as he tried to find something to try and break into the doorway, but it was unrecognisable as a passable space, and he couldn't find any way in. The heat burned his breath. The screams pierced his brain. The smell of burning electrical circuitry mingled with flesh and he felt himself being dragged backwards. It was the medic.

'You can't go in there!' he shouted at Glynn at the top of his lungs. 'Get back!'

Glynn put his hands up to his face as the heat got too much and he felt the skin on his face begin to tingle as he bent over double in a coughing fit. The older man was weeping.

The screams of the other man stopped.

Glynn dropped to his knees and realised that the wet boggy grass was a welcome sensation on his charred skin. The medic slapped him on his back. 'Well done, pal, you did what you could.' Then he was gone.

Glynn stopped coughing and turned away from the helicopter. From his position on the ground, he could see three or four bodies underneath the cabin, and none of them showed signs of life. He moved backwards, on all fours, and his foot hit something hard. He stared at it before realising that it was one of the helicopter blades. It was stuck out of the ground, like a great knife which had cut through the landscape angrily. The cloud lifted and he saw it was fully intact, and it was enormous.

He shuddered. Then he heard more moaning. A child was face down, pinned by some wreckage that he didn't recognise. It wasn't a blade, but it didn't matter. Thoughts of blades cutting down whatever was in their path flew through his head but he ignored them and pushed them away. His recognition of helicopter parts at this precise moment in time really didn't matter, and he almost laughed at his own wild thoughts. The child whimpered. She was seriously hurt and he crawled to her and held her hand. He lay next to her and tried to assess where she'd been hurt. She was covered in blood and dirt, but he had no idea where her injuries were.

'Look at me. What is your name?' he asked her. Her lips trembled and her face was screwed in pain. He smiled and stroked her hair. Her legs were stuck in the earth. He had no idea how they'd got like that but they just disappeared into the mud. He held her.

'What is your name? Mine is Glynn,' he said.

'Andrea,' she said.

'I'll stay with you, Andrea, don't be afraid. Help will come soon, I promise,' he said.

Chapter 9

'My car is closest,' Kelly said.

Johnny didn't argue. Now wasn't the time to question who might drive, and which route they might take.

The crash was all over the news already, but Kelly had real-time access to the police radio and the events unfolding as they happened on the mountainside. The media was way behind. No one from the emergency services had managed to get up there yet and, as in any disaster scenario, they'd rely on civilian actions before anyone with training got to the scene. It would be hell up there.

'Let me drive, you get changed first,' he said.

She nodded. Rushing to the boot, she grabbed what she'd need for an afternoon, and potentially a night, on Scafell Pike. It was crazy. They were miles away. But they both knew that they had to do something. They were both trained in high-level first aid, one step down from a paramedic, and it would be vital to get as many helping hands up there as possible. Landing helicopters in such conditions was a tricky affair, but the local Great North Air Ambulance crews were supremely talented.

'Lancaster is sending help and there's a naval vessel sending a Sea King from the Solway Firth. There's two surgeons on board.' Johnny had been listening intently to her radio.

She jumped into the passenger seat and Johnny started the car. Kelly flicked on the blues and sirens and Johnny manoeuvred his way out of the city centre. Journos stood agape at the spectacle. Two major witnesses in the Ian Burton case, on opposing sides, fleeing the scene using police sirens; it would make a great story. They just so happened to have a child together, too.

With Johnny driving as though he was escaping rebels in Basra, they were on the M6 in under ten minutes. Kelly was fully changed and checked her kit.

'Route?' she asked.

'Put my phone on speaker,' he told her.

'Officially, I need to take over the driving,' she said, doing as he asked. She pressed the recall button for the Keswick mountain rescue.

'Johnny, we've got eleven on their way so far, we're sending shuttles up there by helicopter and three teams have gone the long way road and will approach from Wasdale Head.'

The Wasdale mountain rescue team was one of the most critical in the national park. It served the mountains around England's highest peaks, and dealt with some of the most serious accidents. Usually people thought they could bag three or four of the summits by hopping from one to another, not realising that it was impossible on some routes without ropes. 'But they looked such little mountains!', they were often told. Unpredictable weather always scuppered the best plans. Johnny knew the Wasdale team well, and they were all fit and prepared to face what was unfolding. It would take them perhaps an hour to get to the Lingmell Col. Johnny had done it in forty-two minutes. Kelly in under an hour. But today wasn't the time for records. They already knew that there were fatalities up there.

'There was a fucking fell race on. It came down on competitors,' Kelly said.

Johnny shook his head. 'I'll pull in here, you take over the driving,' he said. They were halfway between Carlisle and Keswick, and had another twenty minutes to drive.

'I've still got a kit bag for you, it's on the back seat,' she said. She'd got it out of the boot when she got hers. She'd never got round to returning it to him. He looked at her as he indicated to pull over to the hard shoulder.

He stopped and she ran around to the driver's side while he grabbed the bag. She set off and traffic parted for the vehicle as Johnny changed clothes in the passenger seat. Mountain rescue told them to go to the Keswick helipad. As they drove, more details of the disaster filtered through and Kelly began to piece together a picture in her head. They knew that the helicopter had come down on its own at least and no other airborne vehicle was involved. There were countless witnesses, thanks to the fell race. They knew there were multiple casualties. The priority of getting as many hands as possible up there was to keep people alive. A tourniquet, or some CPR, could be the difference between life and death. Minutes and seconds mattered, and the emergency services, with all of their skill and training and the best will in the world, wouldn't be able to mobilise properly on top of a mountain for maybe hours. Triage on the mountainside was vital. It's all they thought about as they turned off the M6 on to the A66 towards Keswick, lights still flashing and traffic moving to the side of the road for them.

By the time they reached the Air Ambulance helicopter, waiting in the field opposite Hope Park in

Keswick, by the lake, they were fully prepared. They parked in the car park, grabbing their bags. The Keswick mountain rescue was situated at the lake, and they headed there. It was the quickest way across to Scafell Pike, over the mountains and valleys preventing road access. Teams from coastal towns were proceeding along the road beside Wast Water, but it would take them hours to reach the casualties. Helicopter evacuation was vital. The chopper had already made one journey to the site, with as much fire extinguishing equipment as it could carry, and the Wasdale MRT had already begun their ascent to the new aluminium stretcher box up on Sty Head pass, on the Corridor route. The news was grim. Johnny got the okay from the team to jump in the next helicopter with Kelly, and they headed to the metal craft, its blades already whirring slowly around.

The horrific accident was an example of why she hated helicopters: they were death traps. The Air Accidents Investigation Branch (AAIB) had already been alerted and a thorough investigation would take place, but first the scene had to be secured, and medical aid given to those who were still alive.

They took off and the 'copter swung south, over Derwent Water, heading for the Borrowdale valley, and from there it would begin its climb to the Lingmell Col. She had little time to think about her fear of flying in a machine that defied physics. Modelled on a bumble bee, and an attempt to mimic Mother Nature, the craft was a clumsy excuse for a working aircraft. But the benefit was that it could move up and down, unlike a jet. The craft banked and she caught her breath. Derwent Water was a perfect oval from above, and she stared at the islands made famous by the literature of the past: *Swallows and Amazons* jumped into her head and the tales of Benjamin Bunny and Squirrel Nutkin. But today she wasn't heading into the cosy backdrop of a fictional idyll. Soon, the cluster of hills to the south-west grabbed her attention and she saw the great peaks of Pillar, Kirk Fell and Great Gable in the distance. The western fells were black with sheer rock and scree, and some of her most exhilarating climbs had been achieved there, but it was fairly inaccessible and kept the summer tourists, who were more interested in ice creams than proper walking, at bay.

It was a privilege to be flying over them, and Scafell Pike loomed ahead, the highest of them all. They could see plumes of smoke billowing on the wind. The cloud cleared at some points, and Kelly's stomach knotted as the unusual sight interrupted her adoration for the views. They weren't here to count peaks.

'Jesus,' Johnny said. 'It must have been full of fuel. Do we know who was in it yet?'

'No,' Kelly replied. 'I've got people working on it. It must be a private charter. We've contacted Carlisle airport for a list of private aircraft requesting permission to fly over the national park, as well as submitted flight data and plans.'

'Probably some rich guy from down south holidaying for a few days,' he said.

Kelly agreed. It was likely that, if Carlisle airport hadn't approved the take-off from their own turf, then it must be a private charter. There were plenty of private homes with helipads in the Lake District. It was a millionaire's paradise, with huge modern and traditional homes using vast swathes of land for privately chartered journeys. For those who had no patience for the M6, it was a fun option, if expensive.

The pilot talked to air traffic control, who informed them that the Sea King was on route, and they'd be the second craft to arrive. Weather on the Col was favourable, though the wind was picking up, and the last group had been able to disembark without much issue. They'd be on the mountainside now, administering first aid, and trying to spread some kind of calm, as well as extinguishing any fires. Kelly rarely carried her radio out with her but today she had, because she wanted to stay in contact with the emergency services. They'd be some of the first personnel on the ground, and Kelly's body was overrun with adrenalin. Sounds became background wallpaper, and her focus was entirely on scrambling up the mountainside to coordinate a rescue effort – if there were any survivors. They had no idea what to expect.

Chapter 10

Donald opened his eyes. He'd lost all recollection of where he was. He appeared to be upside down, and then it hit him: the pain. And the smell. And the heat. His senses screamed into life and an agonising piercing along the length of his leg jolted his memory into action. He'd been in a crash. Was he alive? It would seem so. He smelled aviation fuel, and he felt the heat. Then he saw Bart, who was on fire, and screaming. That was what had woken him up.

His head throbbed and his vision wasn't clear but the pain told him that it was so: he'd survived a crash. A helicopter crash. Elation soon gave way to terror when the smell of fuel threatened to overwhelm him. He tried to move, but his belt was stuck tight against his chest. He couldn't lift his right arm, but his left arm was free and he desperately tried to recall where the belt mechanism was located, so that he could undo himself. His leather gloves gave him no assistance in locating the belt fastening, but he couldn't get them off.

The smell of burning upholstery, a mixture of sickly sweet smoke and thick toxic waste, was becoming stronger, and he figured out that it was coming from behind him. In the mangled wreckage, he couldn't see either of the pilots. He guessed, from his view of the ceiling beneath him, and the wires hanging all over the place in a higgledy-piggledy fashion, that he was still inside the body of the craft.

He heard a voice and peered towards where he thought it came from, and he realised that he could see out of the window that had once been beside him. It was now crushed against the ground and he could smell the earth. He saw feet ahead. Then he saw a man running towards the craft, and others behind him. They wore athletic-type vests, with numbers on them, and he remembered that as they neared Scafell Pike, the pilots had pointed out fell runners ascending the route. They'd joked about what fools they were, but Donald had admired them and wished he'd kept up his fitness from his twenties. He'd let himself go. His wife's cooking and the stress of life had convinced him to side-line his health and he'd stopped training, growing portly and out of shape. It was just as they were watching the runners struggle up the steep incline that the pilots had lost control. He recalled a loud bang and ungodly grinding sounds, and the pilots shouting; and then the machine plummeting quickly to earth. He'd hung on, thinking of nothing but the impending impact and how his body would be crushed under a pile of metal.

How long had he been here?

The heat behind him grew more intense. And Bart's screams more sporadic. He didn't have the strength to keep turning his head to see his friend, and he couldn't imagine the pain he was in. He remembered they'd had a full fuel tank for the journey to London. Donald knew how this could end, but he didn't want to burn alive.

'Help,' he rasped.

'Help!' he shouted louder.

The man in trainers was kneeling and Donald noticed that he was naked from the waist up, wearing only underpants, and for a moment it distracted him from his intense pain.

'I'm going to get you out,' he yelled. Then the man was crawling inside the wreck and Donald knew that he was looking for his belt. He could smell the man's flesh, and it was the same smell that his son exuded when he'd been out for an early morning run: he smelled fresh and sweet, like the air. The man's breath came in clouds and for a moment he felt at peace.

'Shit!' the man cursed. And Donald knew then that it was hopeless. The stranger couldn't work his hands around his huge fucking cashmere coat. He heard the *crinkle crack* of flames devastating fabric and black smoke quickly filled the tiny space. The man disappeared.

'I'm sorry,' the man said. He was in tears. Donald could hear his sobs of anguish.

'*Lo siento,*' the man said.

Donald closed his eyes as he felt the first licks of the flames against his legs that were trapped underneath his seat. Dear God, the pain. *No, no, no. Lord, don't let me die this way*.

More shouts of sheer distress followed and he saw more feet, with trainers on, stomping around the smashed shell.

'Help me get him out! Over here!'

Now the heat of the flames came in swirls around his legs and Donald knew he was on fire.

He thought of Elaine, and when their son was born. Henry had been such a large baby that Elaine had torn badly, but her pain had melted away as soon as she took him to her breast and he began to suckle. Henry's face, now grown into a man's, filled his memory and his love for his family wrapped around him like a blanket, wishing to shield him from the inevitability of his present circumstance.

Henry at Christmas, introducing his fiancée. Elaine's tears at her realisation that she was about to lose her son to another, younger, woman. His reassurances that Henry would forever remain theirs. His daughter, Abigail, and her double First from Oxford. Her face when he bought her first car. Her judgement when she learned his secret. Maybe they'd be better off without him.

His body began to shake and the pain seemed to subside, but then return, in waves of nausea and blistering agony. His clothes were alight now. His hand in front of him twisted like a shape shifter, and he realised that it was melting. The calm that overcame him, and the cries of somebody in terrible torment, which, he realised, were his own.

The hull of the 'copter moving with what he assumed was the wind, or perhaps it was the men trying to shove the thing off him. Their last efforts would be forever his comfort. The terror and the damn heat.

He couldn't breathe, but he didn't want to.

Then a coolness that he understood as God accepting him as his true son, taking him into the gates of heaven. The sensation of being forgiven.

The white clouds enveloped him and it was wet and sticky. The sound of high pressure squirting. No. This wasn't right. They were trying to save him. The cold was water and the white clouds were foam. A man's face close to his, telling him to hang on. The flames disappearing.

In his confused and trauma-fuddled mind, he was surprised at how baffling dying was. He hadn't known what to expect, because what live human thinks about death and how it feels? But now he saw it as messy, noisy and very wet. If the flames didn't kill him off soon, then the water of his maker surely would.

A hand around his waist. The relief across his chest as his belt was released.

Then blackness.

Chapter 11

From above, the scene was about as close to hell as they'd both expected. Kelly and Johnny stared wordlessly from the helicopter, as it circled over the crash site and prepared to set down on the Lingmell Col. They descended, and Kelly scoured the landscape for casualties. She noted that many of the people she saw kneeling and helping others wore running tops, with competition numbers stuck to their chests and backs. She didn't have time to consider the generosity of humans in a disaster zone, but she had no doubt that this was what she was witnessing. The closer they got to the ground, the more distinct grew the cries. People shouted instructions, begged for help, ordered this and that, and then some were silent. The smoke from what was left of the helicopter was subsiding and she saw that a man had been pulled from it, covered in fire extinguisher foam.

Their helicopter touched the earth and she and Johnny sprinted to the crash site. An MRT climber had taken charge of the rescue of the man covered in foam and was applying tourniquets and dressings to his wounds. He looked unconscious. She and Johnny didn't need to speak. They began at the impact site and circled outwards, assessing casualties to determine those still alive and requiring treatment.

'Dead.'

'Wounded.'

'Priority.'

Johnny got to work on a lady who was probably a spectator to the race. Her leg was missing and she was convulsing. But she was alive.

Kelly worked outwards from the hot zone. There were so many people in different states of dress, and it was as if she'd walked onto a film set. Some wore running vests, others were almost naked. All across the Col, voices pierced the wind and she did her best to assess priorities. She rallied those who were not wounded and asked them to look for survivors, or to stand back and remove debris from the helicopter landing site on the Col to make way for further landings. If they couldn't stomach the casualty work, then they needed to get out of the way.

She and Johnny had brought advanced medical equipment with them on the flight for stabilising trauma victims, and she assessed a runner. She shouted at anyone who'd listen that the emergency services were on their way, and to stay calm. She directed walking wounded to an area behind a pile of slate providing natural shelter from the wind, which was threatening to turn into a gale. They'd checked the weather before they set off and knew that the nearer they got to nightfall, the worse the weather was predicted, with the darkness forecast to bring freezing low fog and rain. It was almost three p.m. and they had about half an hour of sunlight left.

A man told her he was a doctor and his son was competing in the race. He hadn't found his son yet but he'd been in second place, behind Glynn Cortantes, when the craft came down. She squeezed his shoulder and thanked him for his efforts. She looked skyward and willed the Sea King to get here, with surgeons on board. Another 'copter from the Penrith and Lakes hospital was also on its way, and she scoured the valleys for its blades. No sign yet. She had a fleeting vision of a flock of geese, which fly in arrow formation, the leader exerting all of its strength to lead the flock, until it tired and then was relieved by the next goose, and so on, so the group stayed together. If any of them fell behind or were injured, then two geese would always wait behind until the group came back, or accompany it up until its death, before joining the group once more. She didn't know whether to laugh or cry that this was how she saw the helicopters: flying in to save one of their own, and not giving up until the group was back together. The smashed vehicle was forlorn on the ground and she saw a trail of debris perhaps one hundred foot long, leading down to the valley floor, and to Wast Water below.

Whatever had happened was catastrophic and had begun mid-air over the water. She glanced back to the 'copter and realised that its tail was missing. A story of destruction began forming in her head, but now was the time for emergency thoughts only and she assessed another body. She directed those who said they had the stomach to help to check for signs of life in those who were lying on the ground.

'Apply pressure to wounds, keep them talking, keep them warm, clear airways. Cover those who are deceased,' she said.

She ran towards the 'copter and assessed which piece of wreckage should be where. She knew enough about them to realise that the cabin had broken in two. The man who'd been dragged out of one section was being attended to by Johnny. She quickly spotted the other section and ran to it. A few people stood in silence, and others cried.

They were rapidly going into shock and needed to be removed from the mountain. She speedily evaluated the spectators and approached them, showing her lanyard ID to reassure them that the authorities had the situation in hand.

'Please help the walking wounded to the Col, over there,' she said as gently as she could. She didn't possess the calm manner of a trauma specialist but she gave it her best shot. She'd attended a few disaster sites in her time, but had never been in charge. Until they could evacuate the critically injured and those still clinging to life, she was running on adrenalin. She shouted into her radio and gave an update to the emergency response team that had taken charge of coordinating the rescue effort on the ground.

Her priority, after identifying who could be saved, was not counting the dead but stabilising the scene. It seemed callous but there was no point dealing with corpses when the living could still be saved. She began creating a human chain from the crash site to the Col, so the volunteers could pass items along when needed, and when the stretchers arrived, they could pass survivors too. There were two stretcher boxes in the area and the one at Mickledore was the closest. Two members of the first team at the site had headed off to collect its contents: stretchers, first aid kits and blankets. The new one at Sty Head was sturdier and larger but further away, and a team carrying its contents was almost at the Col. She'd liaised with the professionals present as soon as she and Johnny had reached the Col, and she received information via radio every couple of minutes and knew that several helicopters were nearby and ready to evacuate critical victims. Seventy-two MRT members were on their way up various routes, and would evacuate those stable enough to walk.

'We need more than four surgeons,' she shouted into her radio. A commander at an emergency response pod in Keswick had been appointed and was coordinating the emergency services.

'I'm sending as many as I can get up there.'

She knew they'd try their best, and she knew it wouldn't be enough. Many would die up here tonight. She watched as the man who'd been pulled from the wreckage was administered CPR by the doctor she'd met briefly. Johnny had gone to help others. The whole scene chilled her soul. Then she heard the familiar shouts of command from MRTs and saw groups of climbers emerge from the fog, which had descended once more. Their red and blue clothes were distinctly welcome at that moment, and she ran across to the Col to give a situational report. If there was one priority for scene stabilisation it was that one person needed to call the shots, otherwise time would be lost, confusion would rule, and people would die.

She'd assumed that role and the more people that knew about it, the better. They listened to her instructions and her summary of casualty priorities, and set to work. Everywhere she looked, ordinary humans were helping those in their most critical time of need. They were buying time until the wounded could be taken to hospital and there was a strict order of priority. The man who'd been pulled from the wreckage would go first and a stretcher was taken straight to him.

Kelly noticed a group making their way up from the Wasdale side, carrying large bags. They heaved with exertion and wore minimal clothing despite the time of year. Kelly knew that they'd carried up vital equipment provided by ambulances from all over the national park, and they'd likely volunteered, knowing exactly how hard it would be to haul the kit up to the Col. She recognised a couple of those carrying kit as members of the Wasdale MRT. She and Johnny had enjoyed a pint with several of them, in happier times. She guessed that two figures carrying little kit, and struggling with the exertion, were medics, and she was right – better than that, they were consultant trauma surgeons from Carlisle University Hospital. She directed them to the worst casualties and they retrieved drips, sewing equipment and monitors from the huge rucksacks that had been carried up for them. They still gasped for air themselves but got straight to work.

Then the mighty Sea King glided into view, surprising everyone with its majesty and manoeuvrability. It swung above the Col, emerging from the fog on the Corridor side, and prepared to land. Her radio informed her that three navy surgeons were on board. The beast could take five casualties and Kelly quickly assessed that, along with the man who'd been pulled from the wreckage, four competitors on the ground would be going too, barely clinging to life, but worth trying to save. More people arrived from the Wasdale side and they carried blankets, flasks and basic first aid kits. Dozens needed warmth, hydration and minor wounds dealing with, and many members of the public got this done without even being asked.

'I've found the pilots,' Johnny said to her. He'd come from behind and startled her somewhat.

'Alive?'

He shook his head. 'There was another passenger too, still strapped to his seat, and he didn't make it. As far as I can make out, the other seats were empty, or at least they are now. Eleven dead so far,' he added.

'Jesus.'

But their work had only just begun.

Chapter 12

By seven p.m., Kelly still hadn't had a drink or anything to eat, and she was freezing.

But what she did now know was who the passengers were. A paper log book found on the mountainside had been handed in by a member of the public. It had obviously been blown out of the fuselage on impact. It told her what she needed to know and also provided some measure of relief that the accident could have been much worse. There were two passengers and two crew. It hadn't taken long to establish that the names of the two travellers were going to make headlines. One was a DEFRA minister, and the other was a wealthy Tory party donor. It had been confirmed that the man pulled alive from the wreckage was the DEFRA minister, who'd been attending a climate conference in Glenridding for the weekend. The other passenger had been confirmed dead, along with the two pilots.

Johnny walked over to her and offered her a blanket and a small flask cup of something hot. It steamed against the bitter air of the now black night. The moon was bright above the fog and cast eerie shadows across the crash site. Lights had been erected over an area of hundreds of square feet and generators kept medical holding tents warm and fully functional. She'd lost count of how many helicopters had landed on the Col. A makeshift landing pad had been denoted out of red lanterns and three MRT members with RAF experience directed landing crafts. The critically injured had all been airlifted and the surgeons had gone with them. All of the spectators had gone home, either carried down or on foot, and the mountain was quiet.

Those left on the Col were covered in mud from kneeling and carrying, and exhaustion was setting in. Dead bodies were still strewn across the most inaccessible parts of the mountain, but those treatable had all been evacuated, and the medical tents were quiet. The last of the medics were being evacuated and she looked around, satisfied that this was now a secure site ready for investigation when morning broke. Nothing more could be done now. The names of competitors in the race, as well as spectators, and the passenger list and flight path from the helicopter had all been submitted and they'd done their best to account for everybody. Just two runners were still missing and it was suspected that they were underneath the wreckage. They wouldn't know until it was removed, and that could take days. The AAIB would be up here first thing in the morning and until then, Kelly had done her job. The site was secure and she could get one of the last rides home to start writing her report.

What a start to the week. Yesterday, she'd been cooking a roast chicken for her family and today, well, here she was, covered in mud, numb with cold, and surrounded by dead bodies. At least she'd been able to finish her chicken last night, along with a few glasses of red wine with her father.

She spotted the young fell runner who'd caught her eye because of his unfailing resilience and the aid he'd given in the first few hours, when he was truly needed. She approached him and offered him a sip of coffee. He took it gratefully. He was wrapped in a blanket, but looked chilled to his bones: he'd given most of his clothes to casualties in need of makeshift bandages.

'You need to get home now. What's your name? You've been absolutely bloody amazing,' she said.

'Glynn,' he replied.

He had a slight accent and his deep brown eyes told her that it wasn't just English blood running through the veins that ran along his arms, bulging with vascularity. He was a typical fell runner: like a streaky piece of bacon, zero per cent body fat and long, lean muscles. But he had a warm face and he'd impressed her.

'Where were you trained to handle such situations?' she asked.

'I wild hike a lot and so you have to be prepared. Sometimes I volunteer with the MRT. I keep up to date,' he said.

He spoke quietly and Kelly liked his unassuming manner. He wasn't showy or arrogant, and he displayed no signs that he was likely to brag about what he'd done on the mountainside this afternoon.

'You saw everything?' she asked. She figured she might as well begin her interviews now, so she could pass on to the AAIB any witness testimony that was fresh. Besides, she wanted to hear how it happened.

'I was over the Col and halfway up to the Pike. I heard the helicopter across the valley, but you hear them sometimes and I didn't stop to look at first, I was aiming to smash a personal best. But then I knew it was struggling. The cloud was low, but it was clearing, and I saw it smash into racers behind me. It happened so fast.'

'Of course. It'll take a while to ascertain what happened. Are you okay with being called as a witness? We'll need your statement in due course.'

He nodded. 'That's fine.' He looked down.

'You knew a lot of them?' she asked.

He nodded again. 'I think the two runners who are missing are under there; they were behind me,' he said, pointing at the main part of the wreckage. The medic who'd given so much aid to the victims still hadn't found his son, who'd been in second place.

It was as good a confirmation as she could get, and she gave Glynn her sympathy. Poor bloke. To witness such a thing was awful, but to see two of your fellow racers crushed to death would be traumatic for anyone.

'You did amazingly today, you really made a difference,' she said. 'I'm Detective Inspector Kelly Porter, by the way.' She held out her hand, which felt silly, given what they'd both just been through. It was so polite and proper, and the opposite of the chaos that surrounded them. He shook her hand.

'Glynn Cortantes.'

'Cortantes? The Goat? I've heard of you,' she said. The runner was a bit of a local legend, and anyone who followed local races heard his name all the time. Johnny talked about him when he competed. Cortantes looked embarrassed – even in the dark she could see it.

'It's an honour to meet you,' she said. 'And thank you, there are lots of people who've left this mountain today in a better state than they would have been because of you,' she added.

'I just did what I thought I should,' he replied.

Johnny approached them and she turned to him. The three of them looked as though they'd been mud wrestling for hours. They must look ridiculous.

'Johnny, this is Glynn Cortantes, he's been a real hero today. Glynn, this is Johnny Frietze, a member of the Keswick MRT. I'm surprised you haven't worked together,' she said.

Johnny took the man's hand and grasped it hard. Kelly knew him well enough to know that he was a little star-struck and it made her heart warmer, if not her appendages.

'I follow your success. I'm a bit of a fan,' he admitted sheepishly. It was a touching addition to a crazy afternoon.

'I'm not a hero,' Cortantes said.

'Accept it, mate, I watched you. You were a valuable asset in a shitty situation,' Johnny said.

Cortantes put his hands on his blanket and pulled it around his body, shivering.

'It's time to go. I'm good to walk down,' Kelly said. 'It'll get my heart pumping, Eden House has sent a car for me to the Wasdale Inn. You can both grab a lift if you need it?' she asked.

They both agreed and Kelly went to hand over to the police cordon, who'd stay here all night, for their sins, guarding the crash site. It wasn't all bad. They were fresh, well clothed, and warm, with plenty to eat and drink. They'd set tents up, and part of Kelly wished she was camping on the mountainside tonight, if only to pay respects to those who hadn't survived. She felt a weird connection to the site, but she knew that it was a passing folly: her emotions processing the adrenalin-fuelled rush of the day. Tomorrow, waking in her own bed and fresh from sleep, she'd have a clearer head. The descent from the Col was just over an hour for three fit individuals. They gathered their things and Kelly radioed to Eden House that she was done for the day.

'Two casualties just passed away at the Penrith and Lakes hospital. The three airlifted to Manchester are stable.

Lord Reilly is still critical,' the operator informed her. Two of the bodies stuck underneath the fuselage had been freed, deceased. That took the total to fifteen dead and seventeen wounded. It would be huge news and the police were struggling to keep journalists away. They'd already turned away reporters posing as climbers, but nothing could stop video footage and photographs leaking online. That was how it was.

'Ready?' she asked her two walking companions. They nodded. The steep hike down was all paved and it made for hell on the thighs and the knees. But the three of them were used to their leg muscles screaming. Kelly was thankful for her base fitness level, thanks to hiking these hills since her return from London, six years ago now. The exercise settled her mind, and her body, and it distracted her from the fact that she was facing motherhood essentially alone, at forty. There was something about connecting with nature and the outdoors that soothed the demons that told her she was a failure. Now, as the punishing slate pounded her feet and the reverberations vibrated up her weary body, she knew that she'd keep it up. Her body felt stronger than it had in ages. Was it true that those in love let themselves go a little? Of course it was. Comfortable in romance, eyes were quickly seduced away from the other little necessities in life. It had certainly happened to her, and then she'd been pregnant. Her body had been through so much in the last year; it was enjoying being treated well again. She was no longer breastfeeding, having given it up recently, and she was eating good regular meals, thanks to Millie, who insisted on making her packed lunches before work. She smiled to herself. Maybe she'd never needed a husband at all, but a wife.

Chapter 13

Vivienne Kennedy-Craig was helped out of the Bentley outside a smart white building in the middle of Mayfair, just round the corner from Le Gavroche restaurant, a stone's throw away from Grosvenor Square. The family owned the whole building, but were surrounded by flats and lawyers' premises. Nowadays, full townhouses in the London borough were difficult to find, but Vivienne insisted that she didn't want to live in a penthouse, despite it being the best real estate on the market. She didn't care. Her five-storey Georgian townhouse in the middle of Mayfair was more desirable to her than any modern pad overlooking the Thames, or top floor of a new-build, like a lot of their associates rented these days. She was old-fashioned and enjoyed the feeling of pulling up to a front door: *her* front door, and owning the lot. Just recently, a foreign businessman had had the temerity to knock on the door and ask the butler if the owners would be willing to part with their home for 20 million sterling.

'Fuck off,' she'd instructed Terrance, her butler, to tell them. They weren't for sale.

It was late, and the London streets were teeming with people looking for restaurants and bars, even on a Monday night. She was used to the stares from random tourists wandering through the city's most exclusive neighbourhood, as she was escorted from the car by the driver.

She ignored them. Terrance opened the huge oak front door, decorated with a fantastic Christmas wreath from Harrods.

'Good evening, ma'am,' Terrance purred.

Vivienne shivered and the door was closed behind her.

'Good God, it's freezing, I hope the fire's on, Terry.'

'It is, ma'am, and a glass of Faiveley red is by your chair. Ma'am, just one thing,' he added.

She turned to him as he took her coat and gloves. The driver had brought her shopping bags in and Terrance would deal with them in good time. She turned to him.

'The police are here, ma'am. They want to speak to you about something very important,' he said.

'Oh God, what has Fabian done now?'

Fabian was her and Bart's only child. At twenty-four, he still caused them to suffer headaches and emotional turmoil over his life choices. He didn't seem to understand the difference between right and wrong, and Vivienne blamed herself, like all mothers do, but that led to more indulgence and mollycoddling, and so the vicious cycle went on. What he really needed was to be cut off, or so Bart said, so he could discover who he really was, but Vivienne wouldn't have it. It was one of the many things they argued about, but didn't all parents do the same? Whatever he'd done, Vivienne would end up supporting him and Bart would shout and bang about, ruing the day he'd been born.

'No, ma'am, I don't think it's about Fabian,' Terrance said.

Vivienne knitted her brow and went into the drawing room, where the fire burned brightly, surrounded by a giant stone hearth, also decorated by Harrods for Christmas. Two uniformed officers stood by the fire, warming themselves, and stood to attention when she came in, as if she were royalty. She was used to it. Money did that to people: made them feel inferior. She went to the table beside her armchair and took the glass of fine red wine from the Bourgogne, downing its contents in one. She sat down.

'Officers, it's late on a Monday evening, what could you possibly want? You look very serious, if I may say so. Mince pie?'

They both declined. They introduced themselves and gave their instantly forgettable names. Vivienne waited. They were deferential and awkward in her presence, but Vivienne had that effect on people. It was as if she were some elderly matriarch when, in fact, she was only in her mid-fifties, but her lifestyle was from a different era, and means.

'Mrs Kennedy-Craig, we have some terrible news.'

Vivienne placed her glass down and looked at Terrance, who was loitering. She didn't need to ask him to fill her glass. It was done. She braced herself. The officers looked awkward.

'Is this to do with my husband? He's not here, he's in the Lake District,' she said. 'I'm afraid that's all I can tell you. He's a busy man, and I don't follow his every move.'

The officers looked at one another.

'Your husband's helicopter came down in bad weather over the Lake District. It crashed. We have no news on the cause as yet.'

'What?' Vivienne didn't know what to say. 'The what? What was he doing in the sodding helicopter? Terry, did you hear that?' she laughed.

Terrance coughed.

'Mrs Kennedy-Craig…'

'For God's sake, call me Vivienne!' she snapped.

'Vivienne, your husband didn't survive. He's dead. We're so sorry.'

Vivienne didn't know what to do. She looked at Terrance, who equally seemed lost, and he asked her whether she'd like a mince pie. Why was he asking that? She went to grab her glass but her hand knocked it and it fell to the floor, red liquid making a puddle on the fluffy cream rug, as if death itself was taunting her. Terrance, thankful for something to do, ran from the room to get cloths.

'Have you just told me that my husband is dead?' Vivienne asked.

'Yes, Vivienne, that's correct. He was in a helicopter flying over the Lake District when it crashed. He was killed. There were two pilots and a second passenger who survived; he's in a critical condition in the local hospital close to the crash site.'

'Another passenger? Who was he with?'

Terrance came back in the room and busied himself with the mess on the floor.

'A gentleman called Donald Reilly, madam.'

'Lord Reilly?' she asked.

The officer nodded. 'I'm so sorry, madam.'

'Christ.' Her hand flew to her mouth. 'What the hell was he doing with Donald? I mean… But Christmas… His mother. Oh my God; Fabian! I need to tell Fabian. How can I do that?' she asked Terrance, who stopped rubbing and looked up at her. Everything seemed to slow down, like an old movie which was dubbed badly.

'I can't breathe,' she said suddenly. One of the officers went to her and knelt in front of her. He said something but she had no idea what it was. All she knew was that panic had begun to spread across her body and she no longer seemed in control of it.

'This isn't happening, it can't be happening,' she said. That sounded right, she thought. 'No, it's not happening, you've made a mistake, how do you know? What was Donald doing in the helicopter, for God's sake?' Her voice was becoming pitchy and the officers looked awkward.

'We're part of the family liaison team, Vivienne, and we're expecting another colleague along shortly, who'll be able to give you some more information. You've had a shock. We're here to stay as long as you need us.'

'Need you? Why would I need you? Terrance, tell them to go away. I can't breathe.' She tried to stand up.

The officers nodded understanding to Terrance, who escorted them out to the huge hallway, also decorated for the season. He ushered them into another reception room and left them there, while he went back to his mistress.

'Terry, did I just hear that right? Have they gone? Why did they come here?'

'Ma'am – Viv – you're in shock. You need to take a sedative. Here.' He opened a box on the mantelpiece and took out a couple of pills, giving them to her with another refill of wine.

'I'll call Fabian. He'll be here as soon as I can get him.' He knelt in front of her and held her as she fell forward. Her breathing was shallow and erratic. Her body shook.

'I'm here, Viv, I'm here.'

'Oh my God,' was all she could repeat over and over again, until the drugs kicked in and she went a little limp. He laid her gently back and placed a blanket over her.

'Terry,' she whispered. He turned and went to her, taking the glass from her hand.

'It's all right, Viv, everything will be okay,' he said.

'Call George,' she said.

'Of course. Now, you rest.'

He left her and went back to the waiting officers.

They looked as though they did this sort of thing all the time, but equally, they gave the impression that they cared.

'I'll try to get hold of their son,' Terrance said.

'Any more siblings?' one officer asked.

'No, Fabian is their only child.'

Terrance went into the kitchen and closed the door, taking his phone out of his pocket. But he didn't call Fabian first, he called George Fellows.

Chapter 14

By the time Kelly and her two companions reached the Wasdale Inn, their thighs were shaking with exertion and they couldn't feel their feet. Their bodies had begun to shut off for the night, after the adrenalin had left them wasted and whacked. The inn owner was a burly Scot who knew Glynn, or so it would seem. He came from behind the bar and shook his hand, peering at the state of all three of them.

'Jesus, look what the cat dragged in. You three been helping up there?' he asked.

Glynn nodded and introduced his two new acquaintances.

The proprietor went behind the bar and reached up to the top shelf, taking down a fifty-year-old single malt.

'Can I use your bathroom to clean up?' asked Kelly.

'This is what ye' need,' he said, beaming from ear to ear, reaching for glasses. 'The place is full of people off the mountainside,' he added. Kelly looked around and saw that many of the drinkers were unusually quiet, for a fireside pub in the Lakes. It was quite obvious that many of them were survivors and witnesses. She recognised couple of them from their efforts on the mountain. One man in particular stood out, she'd been told he was military, and she made a note to thank him personally.

'I turned off the TV, all gloom and doom, the last thing we need,' Jock added.

Kelly nodded appreciatively. She reckoned the proprietor had been handing out whiskey all afternoon. She also figured he had perhaps sunk too much of the stuff himself, given the redness of his cheeks, but she was grateful for a wee dram. He poured four.

'Folks, these guys right here are heroes, been on the mountainside all afternoon helping those poor souls,' he announced.

Kelly felt uncomfortable as punters came up to the threesome and congratulated them, offering them drinks and asking for news. The gossip from the mountain crash had been the only thing on people's lips.

She excused herself and took her backpack to the ladies' toilet where she changed quickly into clean clothes. She took off her boots and carried them back to the bar, where Johnny and Glynn had taken seats adjacent to a roaring fire, and Kelly listened as Glynn regaled the audience. The landlord had given out blankets and Kelly was reminded of the unity of people when under duress. The Goat was a natural: not too showy, but engaging enough to satisfy his audience. She felt Johnny's eyes burn into her. She hadn't seen him in any other capacity but as Lizzie's father in two months. Now she could feel herself wondering what he'd been up to, and the question that plagued her every day popped uninvited into her head: did he stand by his testimony in support of Ian Burton?

Her cheeks burned from the heat of the fire, and her belly smouldered with the whiskey. The other drinkers hung on Glynn's account of the afternoon, and at one point she caught Johnny's gaze. She looked away.

'So the' say one's in the hospital in a critical condition – one from the 'copter itself, some Lord or other, fancy bloke from London. PM's made a statement an' all,' the landlord said.

Murmurs of concern.

'He was at the climate summit,' a female hiker chipped in.

Kelly already knew from the helicopter passenger list that the man who chartered the private helicopter wasn't Lord Reilly, but Bartholomew Kennedy-Craig. It wasn't unusual for Tories to jaunt around with millionaires, but why this one, she wondered. It would be looked into, of course, by the AAIB, as part of their inquiries. Kelly's part in the drama was thankfully over. Her curious nature wanted to know the answers, though. Helicopter crashes were fairly rare but the damn things were death traps, and Johnny had reiterated this. No one in the army trusted them, but that was probably more to do with their rival corps that flew them: the RAF. One had to be a pure-bred lover of thrills to learn to master one. The pilots would be looked into as well, and she felt thankful again that it was out of her hands. Lord Reilly had a wife and two grown-up children, who'd flown in to Carlisle to be with him at the Penrith and Lakes hospital. She hoped the old guy made it. There were two sides to every investigation: finding out the truth, and the human tragedy that unfolded after the event. Apparently, Lord Reilly had suffered burns to 90 per cent of his body and was being cared for on a bed of specially designed material that supported his delicate flesh with air pads, so the wounds didn't adhere to material. It always amazed her how advanced medical technology was, but behind all the learning and techniques was a litany of misery. The thousands of ways a body could be burned was just the tip of the iceberg.

She settled back into her wingback chair, noting the fuzzy feeling spread through her body. She never wanted to leave, but she knew that some poor sod had been tasked with driving her home tonight and she dragged herself up, excusing herself, to go and check on her ride.

The air outside was bitter and she thought she felt snow on the way. The lights from the inn lit the surrounding area, but beyond that there was just blackness, except for the tiny twinkle of lights on the mountainside. If she didn't know better, it could have been some night hike for Christmas lighting up the crags, but the sad fact was that it was a terrible scene up there. She put her hand out to feel the air and a few crystals of ice melted in her palm. If it snowed tonight, it would hamper the clean-up effort. She walked to the only police car in the parking area where a young lad sat in the driving seat. He put his window down as she approached and she introduced herself.

'Hi there,' she said, smiling widely. 'We're just warming up inside, why don't you join us? I saw a coffee pot on the go, though admittedly, I think that's about it for non-alcoholic offerings. You must be freezing,' she said.

'It's all right, ma'am, I'm happy to wait. I knock off at two in the morning and I want to get you back to Penrith safe,' he smiled. He must have been in his twenties. She'd never seen his face before, though he could have been pulled from any station in the national park. The county and surrounding areas had pulled together this afternoon and they should all be proud of themselves. She'd write it up in her report, and she knew that the chief constable would share her pride.

'We won't be long,' she said, and left him to go back inside. Tiredness hit her like a wall, and she yawned. She went back to the fire, where there was quite a crowd around the heroes now. She noticed that Glynn and Johnny had refilled glasses.

'Sorry to be a party pooper, but we'll need to get going. Glynn, where can we drop you?'

'I'll ha' none of it,' the landlord said. 'The Goat is staying here, I've just had beds made up. You're both welcome, too.' He looked at Johnny, who shrugged.

'I'm just about whacked. I think I'll stay,' he said to Kelly. He looked at her and she recognised the desire behind his eyes. It took her by surprise. She'd missed his body in her bed, there was no doubt about that, but she also knew that it wouldn't be right to go to that place so soon after the ice between them had started thawing – if indeed it had at all. Disasters had a terrible habit of making people fall in love, even if they'd fallen out of it very recently. But then, she wasn't sure if she had.

'Well, it's a lovely offer, but I'm afraid I'm needed early in the office tomorrow.' She used a convenient truth. It would have been easy to stay, and argue that she should be here to survey the site tomorrow. After all, she had no idea when the AAIB would get here. However, she also knew that to jump into Johnny's arms now would be its own disaster. Besides, she missed Lizzie. She'd already spoken to Millie, who'd assured her that she could stay the night and not to worry about what time she made it home, but Kelly was itching to get back.

Glynn stood up. Somebody had lent him a thick jumper and it would have looked comical over shorts on anyone else, but he somehow managed to make it look natural.

'It was an honour to meet you, Kelly Porter.' He held out his hand for her to take. Something in the way he said her name made her think that he knew something else about her, other than what he'd seen today. Whatever it was, it made Johnny burn with jealousy and he, too, stood up.

'I'll walk you out,' he said firmly.

She almost laughed. She'd never seen Johnny in the primitive protector role that he was presently assuming, and it didn't suit him. He was green with envy, and well might he be. Glynn 'The Goat' Cortantes was a handsome man, with endless eyes and a beautiful smile.

'I can see myself out, thanks,' she said.

Johnny's face dropped, but she wasn't about to become the focus of some testosterone-fuelled duel. She thanked the landlord and drained her whiskey glass. God, it tasted good.

She walked out into the cold once more and climbed into the back of the squad car, which was lovely and warm.

By the time they pulled into Eden House car park, Kelly was fast asleep, and it was gone midnight.

Chapter 15

Elaine Reilly was escorted through an army of press and ushered into the critical care unit at the Penrith and Lakes hospital. The prime minister had extended his sympathies in person. Donald was an outstanding minister and a great man... Blah, blah, blah. Yes, she knew all of that. It was frankly irrelevant when she had to tell her children what had happened to their father. They'd flown in to Carlisle airport to join her, and they held her hand as they were shown through the stuffy, smelly corridors, reminiscent of when Elaine couldn't afford private health care. She hadn't been treated by the NHS in years.

Away from the flash of cameras, the corridors were gloomy and quiet. It was clear that they were being given VIP treatment, because no lay person would have an army of doctors and nurses tending to their every need, without a fee. A consultant actually asked if she'd like a coffee. She accepted. She was parched. He scurried off. Didn't he have other patients to attend? She supposed it wasn't every day that a cabinet minister was airlifted for surgery here in the middle of nowhere. Only the daylight of the morning would confirm how dreary this place was. Donald had told her over the phone how grim it was in the towns, and bitterly cold. But he'd also told her of the stunning beauty of the rural Lake District, somewhere they'd never actually taken the time to visit. As minister for DEFRA, this was indeed ironic, as he should be visiting farming hubs like this as part of his job, chatting to common farmers and forest rangers as a matter of course. But he didn't. He relied on an army of civil servants to give him the common touch, and she wasn't interested anyway. Four years ago, she'd agreed to stay married to him for the sake of his career.

He'd never mentioned his intention to meet Bart Kennedy-Craig.

Before the news sent shivers down her spine, she hadn't worried particularly that she hadn't been able to get hold of Donald since Saturday morning. She'd simply assumed that the conference was in full swing, and left him to it. He'd call her back when he was ready, she'd thought. It wasn't as if it was important: simple Christmas arrangements, that was all. If she'd known who he was really with, she would have accompanied him herself and made sure it never happened. Bart's violent and sudden death was all over the news, and ordinarily she tended to ignore such tittle-tattle, but now she couldn't help herself googling the story every five minutes. Gossip and sleaze was already emerging about why Lord Reilly might be on a very expensive private helicopter with a staggeringly rich businessman like Bart. She felt sick to her stomach. What they were doing together was something that sat heavily on her conscience. Whatever it was, it wouldn't be good for her marriage or his career, if he survived the night. The press had already begun to ask questions about why a cabinet minister was accepting rides in a helicopter from a millionaire who funded the Tory party under a cloud of controversy, due in part to his business affairs. It wouldn't take long, under this scrutiny, for the press to dig a bit deeper.

It looked bad.

But that really was the least of Donald's worries right now. He could die tonight.

And that was what her children needed her for right in this moment: to be their mother. The other stuff could wait. But she fully expected a shitstorm. The PM's office had already approached her delicately on the subject. They wouldn't remain delicate for long. Sensitivity would shortly turn to robustness before Donald could be turned in his bed, she was damn sure of it. But she had nothing to tell them. She'd had no idea that Donald was meeting with Kennedy-Craig this weekend. A knot sat in her stomach. She knew he was up to no good, though. Bartholomew always was.

The entourage approached ICU and their voices hushed. It was explained to her that they were allowed no further than the viewing windows for relatives. They'd waived the rules on one visitor per patient, and were allowing the whole family in. The consultant came back with her coffee and she gulped it. Jesus, it wasn't made by anyone who knew what they were doing, but she forced herself to smile gratefully. There was a fabulous coffee shop a stone's throw away from their Westminster apartment, where she bought her coffee for her power walks around St James's Park from her favourite barista, Morris from the Isle of Man. She was forever spoiled after that, and coffee would never taste so good anywhere else. But it was wet and warm, as her mother used to say.

They went in.

The ICU was deathly quiet and she chided herself for comparing it to a bloody tomb. She hated hospitals. Nurses wandered around looking earnest and relatives stared at their party, instantly knowing that they were somehow more important than any of the other patients. Maybe some of them were already aware from the news that a lord was being treated here. Her children were distraught, bless them, and well might they be; Donald was a good father, he was just a shitty husband. But that wasn't their fault.

They came to the correct window and somebody had positioned barriers around it, so they could enjoy their privacy. It was a touching gesture. Then they saw him. Abigail, her daughter, let out a heart-wrenching sob. She was a daddy's girl. But it wasn't just her. Henry was in tears, too.

Donald was suspended above the bed, his whole body under an array of sheets. Only his head was visible, and that was full of tubes poking out of it, making it look like the alien from the film. It was truly shocking and Elaine turned away.

'I'm sorry, I know it's a shock,' said one of the consultants.

Suddenly Elaine was claustrophobic. She felt weak and hot and one of the nurses must have noticed because a chair was pushed behind her. She sat gratefully. Henry and Abigail continued to cry.

'Can we be left alone?' Elaine asked.

'Of course,' said a consultant, who began to clear everyone away from the tiny area. Suddenly, they were alone. Now Elaine could hear the bleeps from within the room, and she guessed that they meant Donald was fighting for survival. As long as those machines made noises, she figured, then he was clinging on to life. His prognosis wasn't good, she could tell.

'Do you want to sit down?' she whispered to her children. More chairs had been set out for them and they nodded. They sat in a row, like lost strangers waiting for an audition: terrified and ill-prepared. They were grown adults but now, in here, faced with the end of their father's life, they regressed to small innocents, looking to her for guidance.

Elaine took her phone out of her bag and scrolled through her contacts list. Somewhere, from long ago, she reckoned she just might have Vivienne Kennedy-Craig's number saved. It was a long shot but it was something to do.

Chapter 16

Kate Umshaw had waited at Eden House for her boss all day.

'God, Kate, don't you need to be home?' Kelly asked. But she was thrilled to see her friend.

Kate was in her forties, and divorce suited her. She had three grown-up daughters, with Millie, Kelly's nanny, being the youngest. Kelly and Kate had become closer following a prison riot two months ago, during which Kate had been caught inside. She'd come close to being beaten to a pulp by a gang of inmates. The atmosphere of testosterone-fuelled, sex-denied men presented with a woman like Kate had made for an explosive stand-off. They'd wanted to take the woman who'd dropped into their world, and use her to their satisfaction. It was a horrific situation. Kelly had been on the outside with the negotiating team and she knew that if it hadn't been for several of the inmates and the civilian teacher inside with Kate at the time… well, she dared not think what might have happened. Kelly knew her friend had faced things she'd only shared with her, yet Kate had insisted on coming back to work straight after the riot, despite HR begging her to take time off to decompress.

'Decompression, my arse,' Kate had announced abruptly. 'What I need is to catch more bastards.'

Kelly could hardly have agreed more, knowing full well that if it had been her, she'd have been throwing herself into work too. She'd approved her second in command carrying on her duties. It was soothing, having her by her side.

Kate had been busy all day, coordinating information from the crash site, whipping multiple agencies into shape and dealing with the press office.

'Prime minister's office is breathing down the constabulary's neck,' Kate said.

'No surprise there, then,' Kelly said. 'The cabinet minister is in bad shape, I heard from pub gossip at the Wasdale Inn, at least. And the press are having a field day. The deceased, Bartholomew Kennedy-Craig, is getting an absolute bashing.'

'The lord is hanging on by a thread,' Kate agreed.

'God, what a day.'

'What was it like up there?' Kate asked.

'Horrific. Bodies everywhere. Some of the runners were amazing, I have to say. One in particular was standout. They call him "The Goat". He's a famous fell runner... well, famous in the fell running world at least, and he's gorgeous,' Kelly said.

'Tell,' Kate said, perched on the side of a desk in the incident room. It was empty apart from the two of them. Eden House was busy downstairs, as it was always, but shift work didn't apply upstairs, where the serious crime unit was based. Kelly tried to make sure that her team kept their hours. Night work was only encouraged when chasing leads that couldn't wait.

'He's called Glynn Cortantes,' Kelly said.

'Cortantes... now there's a name! He sounds sexy already, I'm imagining brown eyes and rippling muscles.'

Kate closed her eyes and gave the impression she was picturing the young Spaniard in his running kit.

Kelly slapped her playfully. 'Johnny came with me.'

Kate opened her eyes. 'Oh?'

Kelly nodded wearily and yawned. 'Awkward. We were in court and everybody's phones went mad, so we headed over there together. He looks well.'

'Of course he does. Any feelings of regret?' Kate asked.

Kelly shook her head. 'He suggested I stay with him at the Wasdale Inn. I think he was a bit put out by El Cabro.'

'El Cabro?'

'It's Spanish for "The Goat". Get me, I'm virtually fluent.'

They laughed.

'Have you spoken to Millie?' Kelly asked.

'Yeah, she's fine, she adores that baby of yours. She's put her to bed and is sleeping in the spare room.'

'Thanks, Kate. You should head off,' Kelly said.

'I'm plugged into the coffee machine, I'll go when I've updated you. I'm fine, don't worry,' Kate said.

Kelly took off her coat and sat down at the computer Kate had obviously been working on. 'Right, what have we got?' They had other work to catch up on as well as the crash.

'Local scumbag beat up his girlfriend, two squad cars were sent over this afternoon, called in by a neighbour. There's clearly a controlling situation. Tiny flat, three kids under five. Social services are aware. He's a dickhead, it's all on bodycam. He's known to us. Paul Edderbridge. The partner is in the Penrith and Lakes. He's a nasty violent man and currently in a police cell downstairs. We're trying to get the girlfriend to press charges, but she's terrified.'

'Can't keep his hands to himself. His days are numbered.'

Kelly's brain switched from disaster zone to her bread and butter: people breaking the law.

'It took armed response to convince him to surrender,' Kate added.

'Jesus, what a piece of work. Armed response have got better things to do than arrest arseholes.'

'Exactly.'

'Anything else?'

'Thank God it's been a quiet day. Everybody has been on the crash. Any preliminaries on what caused it yet?' Kate asked.

Kelly shook her head. 'They're bloody death traps as it is. Apparently, Lord Reilly was attending the climate conference at the Glenridding hotel in Ullswater over the weekend, and some millionaire from London was hosting him. I get the impression that's what's bothering the authorities, because Bartholomew Kennedy-Craig is a shady character, and you don't really want a cabinet minister hobnobbing with millionaires. And you can't really preach holier than thou morals about global warming when you're taken on a jolly sightseeing over Scafell Pike. The government is embarrassed. But, you know what? It's not our problem.'

'Yeah, I got that impression. The press office has been going mad. The Home Office has forbidden any statements on it, apart from sticking to the facts about the crash, and saying that the casualties are being attended to,' Kate told her. 'So, who's Bartholomew Kennedy-Craig?'

'A very dead Bartholomew Kennedy-Craig was founder and CEO of Tactika Enterprises. It's a global company, into all sorts – and not all of them legal, according to the press. His next of kin have been informed. The two pilots were locals, ex-RAF, very experienced, apparently. I reckon there are two bodies under the wreckage, both runners. Glynn knows both of them.'

'So, it's Glynn, now?' Kate teased her.

Kelly rolled her eyes. 'It's not my investigation. The AAIB people will be there in the morning. So, what have we got on nasty violent man? Has he been processed and interviewed?'

'No, he's hammered. Sleeping it off.'

'Right, I'd better write my report to give to the chief constable tomorrow, the AAIB team will need it. I've got to say, I was proud of how the agencies all came together today. Fire, medical, police, and civilians, they all did a superb job. The death toll is horrendous. It was tough day.'

'Coffee?'

Kelly nodded and turned to her computer to begin the tedious task of filling in an incident form. This one would be longer than usual. She'd already chatted to the AAIB and told them everything they needed to get started. How the hell they were supposed to lift a helicopter off the top of Scafell Pike was beyond her, and it could take weeks to get the right equipment up there. The human tragedy of the day hit her and she fell silent as she filled in the information. Names, ranks, actions all had to be accounted for in the event of a public inquiry and, given that one of the casualties was a cabinet minister, she couldn't leave anything out. This story would run and run.

Kate came back into the room with two mugs and placed one next to her. She yawned again.

'So, is Johnny staying up at Wasdale?' Kate asked.

Kelly appreciated her friend trying to keep her awake. She nodded and sipped her coffee.

'It was weird. We didn't really talk, but it was like we were still together. You know, we acted like a team. It was comforting in one way, but in another, so fucking irritating. I think he felt as though he'd proven something to me.'

'Like you can't live without him?'

'Or work without him.'

Kate rolled her eyes.

'It was his decision to work with the defence team. From what I saw inside Highton prison, there's no excuse for what Ian Burton did. He and his father controlled everything inside that prison, and to suggest that Ian did it because he was traumatised makes a mockery out of people who really suffer with PTSD. Soldiers don't go around killing people just because they're pissed off with what they saw in Iraq.'

Kate's anger bubbled up to the surface and Kelly realised that if she ever took Johnny back into her life, it would be very difficult to explain it to her friend. It was helpful to have friends who were so sure of their morals. Kelly and her second in command rarely disagreed about human beings. Sometimes good people did bad things. Everybody made mistakes. But that was why the law accounted for the difference between murder and manslaughter. What Ian Burton did to his victims wasn't accidental, and he wasn't insane.

Chapter 17

Johnny was becoming intoxicated and he liked it. He'd matched the landlord, drink for drink, out of some foolish bravado, and his body wasn't used to it. The old Scot was clearly built for booze and the poison barely had an effect. Contrastingly, Johnny was becoming hammered. The young fell runner was more sensible and it made Johnny dislike him even more. The guy was solid, funny – and he'd caught his girlfriend's eye. Correction, his *ex*-girlfriend's eye. He still couldn't work out how the break-up had happened, but that was what men did, he conceded: they went along with situations without seeing the signs behind the warnings. Kelly had tried to talk to him about his PTSD work and he'd shut her out. Every time.

He'd been arrogant. He'd not wanted to listen to what she had to say because he didn't want to accept that she might know something about human behaviour. She'd witnessed plenty of coppers go off the radar because of trauma. Some had even killed themselves over what they'd faced. Only last year, three members of the Cumbria Constabulary had taken their lives, and it was on the increase. He'd underestimated what the police faced, and he'd pompously assumed that only military combat could produce severe trauma in individuals. He felt a dickhead, and seeing her today, working so closely with her, had made his guts turn over. Not only was she beautiful – he knew that with every fibre of his body, and the haunting dreams he had about her face – she was intelligent, and more than that, she knew people. She read them every day in her job. But it was also her passion that drew him to her. His ego had made it impossible for him to back down once he'd given a statement to the defence team, and then it was too late. His stubbornness had reared its ugly head. He'd resigned himself to another failed relationship. He'd thought Kelly was the one; he'd never felt calm like he did when he was with her, and he couldn't believe his luck when they moved in together. Josie had fallen for her, too. Now, Josie would rather be with Kelly instead of her own father, and he got it. Kelly always told him that it was his lack of conceit that had attracted her to him. It was a cliché, but she told him he wasn't like other guys. He guessed they all said that. But he'd dared believe her. Now, after their first major disagreement, he'd blown it, and his own obstinacy had led to where they were now. It had just got worse and worse, until they agreed he should move out. It was the same bloody-mindedness that had led to the collapse of his marriage.

He should have known better, he told himself. He wasn't built for long-term relationships. Deep down, he knew that was just a pathetic excuse to explain his loss, but it was all he could hang on to. His stubbornness had also enabled him to support a murderer. Of course he knew what Ian Burton had done, but if he went against his statement, for Kelly, then it would undermine everything he did.

But he bitterly regretted it.

Besides, Lizzie was better off with her mother.

The booze was making him maudlin and self-indulgent, and El Cabro wasn't helping, with his stories of greatness on the mountainside. To be fair, the young lad wasn't bragging at all, but the alcohol was playing tricks on his mind and he knew it was time to go to bed. The landlord had prepared a four poster bed for him, and he'd wanted nothing more than for Kelly to climb in beside him, but he'd have to sleep alone tonight. Again. He chastised himself.

'Your missus not happy with you, mate?'

Johnny looked at the hiker, who was sitting at the bar. The stories had turned to the army, and the guy who'd rudely interjected on his personal life had taken an interest. He was seated next to a pilot who Johnny recognised from helping on the mountain today. He was regaling those who'd listen on the mechanics of helicopters. There were plenty of ex-army people in the MRTs across the Lakes, and Johnny was well known. So, it seemed, was his personal life.

'What's that supposed to mean?' he asked. The air turned prickly.

Glynn watched and listened with interest. The pilot next to him stood up, ready for trouble.

'Pal, it's maybe time to go to ye' bed,' the landlord said to the hiker, who was wasted. The pilot agreed. But Johnny wasn't ready to let it go.

'I meant nothing by it. I just thought, you know, you and Kelly Porter were a thing,' the man said.

'What do you know about Kelly Porter?' Johnny said. Groups of drinkers around them fell silent. Everybody waited for the answer.

'Well, she's famous around here, and you're on the opposite side of the fence in the Burton murders. I meant nothing by it.' The man was back-pedalling and trying to appease Johnny. But the damage had been done. Glynn watched him, and Johnny felt foolish. His head spun.

'I reckon that accident wasn't all it seemed,' said a man's voice.

The words made everyone change their focus away from Johnny towards the man who'd spoken: the pilot who'd been talking about helicopters. It distracted everyone. Attention was turned to the pilot, the same one who'd been a legend on the mountain.

Johnny was willing to take him seriously because he was a fellow army man, and that meant something, and he saw that the pilot wasn't intoxicated, like the rest of them.

'What the fuck are ye' talking about?' the landlord asked, echoing everybody's sentiments.

'I was watching the race from the lake. Then I saw the 'copter. I watched the trajectory of the thing. It wasn't normal, then the pilot lost control. Catastrophic mechanical failure isn't common in helicopters – I know, I know what everybody says about them, but it's weather disorientation that brings most of 'em down, that and enemy fire.' He laughed. No one joined him.

'Ye' should write fiction stories, pal,' the landlord said.

But Johnny wanted to know more. Nobody on the ground had been interviewed officially yet; the rescue effort had taken up the whole day. Nobody had asked those witnesses in the surrounding area what they had seen, apart from to acknowledge that they'd watched a helicopter come down. Sure, the fog bank had been low, thanks to an earlier inversion, but at the time of the crash, the clouds had lifted, ruling out spatial disorientation. Johnny knew that part of the investigation would involve checking the pilots' medical records, and their blood for drugs and alcohol.

'Wait a minute, how can you tell the difference?' Johnny asked.

'I'm not saying I know for sure, but only some kind of catastrophic mechanical failure would cause a 'copter to behave in that way, and force an uncontrollable spin. I watched it; it should be non-survivable.'

'Isn't that the same as an accident?'

'I made a few phone calls this evening, and I asked around. I knew the pilots, and that helicopter was less than three years old.'

'Johnny Frietze.' Johnny held out his hand. 'Ex-Light Infantry.'

'Lance Tatterall, Army Air Corps.'

Chapter 18

Lizzie's cries woke Kelly with a start and she had no idea if it was day or night. She groaned and rolled over, expecting her arm to connect with Johnny's back, but it wasn't there. This awareness was followed by the same sinking feeling that she'd had every morning for the past two months on waking and realising anew that he just wasn't there anymore. She sighed and put her pillow over her head, and then she heard Millie padding along the landing to her daughter.

'I love you, Millie,' she whispered to herself.

She reached for her phone to check the time, knowing that it would be difficult to get back off to sleep now. It was still fully dark but she was startled to learn that it was gone seven o'clock in the morning. Dawn wasn't until eight o'clock but the false sense of security given to her by the shadows set her mind going, and she knew that she'd have to get up. A strong coffee and some eggs would set her up for the day; she could make Millie some, too. At nearly four months, Lizzie had tried eggs. Most of it had ended up on the floor but, mixed with lots of butter, she'd loved it. Mushed-up local black pudding was next to try. Current advice was to wean at six months, but Lizzie was a hungry, healthy baby who'd weaned early.

Kelly flopped back onto the bed and read her messages. Her phone had gone mental during the night and there were several from Johnny.

> We need to talk.

For God's sake.

About the crash. Another one read. This got her interest. They were inextricably linked now in a way that she hadn't foreseen. He could access her at any time about Lizzie, and to chat about joint childcare, but now he had another excuse: the crash, and she didn't know how she felt about that. He'd been up late. She noticed that the text was sent at two a.m. But in the early hours, she'd ignored it, thinking it could wait. Had he been drunk? Johnny wasn't the type to lose control after a drink. It was an important point, because so many people she knew let their hair down and became outrageous on booze. Not Johnny. She wondered if he'd always been like that. No one is perfect, she reminded herself. From the text, she got the impression that he'd been a bit tipsy.

It was good working beside you today

Her stomach did flips and she got out of bed to avoid having to face the wave of feeling washing over her. In the dark, she ran the shower and stripped off her T-shirt and pyjama-shorts, as well as her woolly socks. She'd turned into a cliché: the woman just out of a relationship wearing unflattering and unsexy, but bloody comfortable, attire to bed, instead of wanting to impress their partner. The same was true about lazy Sunday afternoons. She rarely left the house, apart from perhaps to take Lizzie out in her pram. She much preferred to sit in front of the fire and watch a Netflix series. But the novelty was wearing off and the vision of the mountains yesterday afternoon had made her realise that it was time to get off her arse and get organised. Keeping fit was one thing, but organising long walks in the outdoors, just for pleasure, was something she'd put off doing alone. But she wasn't alone. She had Lizzie, and Josie, and Millie. And Kate. She realised that she had all the company she needed, and it helped her process the texts from Johnny. Of course she missed him, but that didn't mean she was going to jump straight back into bed with him, like he'd intimated last night – or was that because he was jealous of Glynn Cortantes?

Or at least that's what she told herself.

She stepped into the shower and the hot water woke her up. She didn't want to get out. The heat massaged her aching muscles. Yesterday had been like a twelve-hour shift on a building site, and she hadn't paused to question her body. Now she ached. She stretched her arms up and back in the shower and rinsed her hair. Reluctantly, she turned off the water and stepped out, taking a fluffy towel from the rail. She dried her hair loosely and wrapped the towel around her body. She threw open her curtains and saw shadows of faded purple and orange were slowly replacing the darkness. There was enough emerging light from outside to find what she needed to wear for the day. She had a feeling that she might be called to the mountainside by the AAIB. One never knew; it would be just her luck should she wear a smart skirt suit to be called up there, so she chose easy trousers and a polo top, over which she threw a Norway sweater from the shop in Keswick. It would be below freezing outside, and she shivered to think of the bodies on the mountainside over near Scafell Pike.

She left her hair to dry naturally and went out into the hall. Josie's door was firmly closed, as was expected of any decent upper sixth form student; only rising when absolutely necessary. Kelly had helped her fill in her application for the universities of Warwick, York and Durham. That had caused an issue between her and Johnny, because he felt snubbed by his daughter. Surely he should be used to that? she'd told him. It didn't go down well, and to be fair, it had been a low blow.

The lights were on downstairs and she could hear Millie singing to Lizzie. Kelly wanted the girl to have aspirations to leave the Lake District and follow her dreams, but every morning when she saw her with Lizzie, she realised that Millie's dreams were right here, looking after a baby, and who was she to criticise? Just because she'd gone to the bright lights of London as soon as she passed her initial police training, it didn't mean everybody followed the same path. And look how that had ended.

She went into the kitchen and made faces at her daughter, who giggled and screamed in delight.

'Thanks for yesterday, Millie, you're a life-saver,' Kelly said.

'I bet it was horrible, are you all right?' Millie asked.

The kitchen was clean and tidy, and Millie looked as though she'd lived here all her young life. Kelly would struggle without her. She knew that Kate had hoped that her daughter would go to university, but she'd put it off for at least a year. Kelly felt guilty but she wasn't about to kick Millie out.

'Don't even ask if I can stay all day today, of course I already am. I know enough now to know that when a big case starts, you have your hands full,' Millie said.

'Well, the crash will be dealt with by the accident investigation people. I won't be involved apart from as an aid, but I'll probably go over there today. Eggs?' Kelly asked.

Millie nodded.

Kelly put on some toast and carried on reading her texts. One was from her father, Ted, asking how yesterday had been. Christ, he'd be busy with the bodies this week. Half of them would be sent to the Penrith and Lakes, and the other half to Carlisle. She worried about him. Not because he wasn't up to it, but because she knew he wouldn't stop. He wasn't getting any younger, but at least she'd convinced him to hire a few more assistants, which wasn't hard because he was a damn fine teacher and university hospitals were chomping at the bit to send their students to the eminent Ted Wallis. Kelly flicked on the radio, which was essentially part of her job on cases like this: to check what the journos were saying. It was all about the helicopter crash.

'Detective Inspector Kelly Porter was at the scene, the same detective who was only hours before giving evidence at the Ian Burton trial…'

'Mummy's famous,' Millie said to Lizzie.

'So far, the cause of the crash is unknown, but it is too soon to rule out sabotage, considering that Lord Reilly was attending the controversial climate summit over the weekend…'

'That's what the press would like,' Kelly said. 'The more drama to report, the better.'

'Lord Reilly was the victim of an egg-thrower over the weekend…'

This caught Kelly's attention and she flicked on the small TV on the kitchen countertop. Sure enough, the news was all about the crash, as was expected. They showed Lord Reilly from archive footage, as well as the egging incident over the weekend, and the man who'd been arrested for it: Neil Hardy, a known climate activist who'd been arrested for violence towards fox hunters and capitalists over the years. He was a serial protester.

She buttered toast for herself and Millie and plopped an egg on top of each slice. She finished making her coffee and sat down. Her phone began to buzz and then didn't stop. She sat, coffee in one hand, and toast dripping in egg yolk in the other, and watched as messages flooded onto her phone. They were all telling her the same thing. The duty sergeant at Eden House, Kate, the press office, and her father: all were asking her if she'd seen the news. Something was going on, and she flicked channels, coming to one which had an up-to-date report.

Word was circulating that the crash wasn't an accident. Some punter at the Wasdale Inn was claiming he was an expert, and a helicopter instructor, holidaying in the Lake District. That was what Johnny must have been bothering her about.

She dialled his number and drained her coffee.

Chapter 19

Lord Donald Reilly survived the night.

Elaine had refused to leave the corridor outside his room. Now she was allowed inside it. She'd convinced her children last night to go to the hotel booked for them by the prime minister's office. They were chauffeured there and had called her this morning at five a.m. She promised them she'd slept but she hadn't. Her mind wouldn't let her rest. But at some point before dawn, which was now breaking outside, she'd dozed off against a machine next to one of the chairs, and her neck had gone into spasm. She rubbed it and for a moment forgot where she was, until she saw her husband and heard the bleeps. She sighed.

She stood and went up close to him, as close as she dared, fearful of causing some kind of alarm to go off or some such emergency, and it being all her fault. His face was somewhat peaceful, but the lines around his eyes and mouth seemed deeper, and he looked older. He must have been terrified. She knew he hated flying, and didn't trust helicopters. How had Bart convinced him to get in it in the first place? She dared not touch him, but she couldn't help thinking that a warm loving touch might help. But her heart had been broken before and she couldn't bring herself to do it. She reached out a hand, as if in response to some kind of instinct, but stopped short of stroking some stray hairs out of the way of his left eye. He didn't move and the bleeps didn't change.

She stood back and stretched deeply, feeling grubby and tired suddenly. She went to find a nurse or anybody who could at least get her a coffee, even though it was ghastly hospital piss. The ward was deathly quiet, and she realised that she was surrounded by desperately ill people, and that those in hospital uniform padding silently around were trying to save lives. She felt a humbling respect for them and decided to leave the ward to find her own sustenance.

There was a police officer outside the door.

'Morning, ma'am, I've been asked to make sure you don't—'

'What? Am I not allowed to get a coffee and stretch my legs?' she snapped.

She regretted it instantly; she was used to having police protection. Donald had his fair share of death threats like any cabinet minister, especially from climate activists, but she never took them seriously. Now they'd almost succeeded in killing him, and the PM's office was obviously not taking any chances. She calmed her active imagination; the cause of the crash was yet to be determined but Abigail had sent her footage of a helicopter instructor, on holiday in the Lake District, being interviewed, and saying he thought it wasn't an accident. It sent shivers down her spine.

'I'm sorry for being cranky,' she said.

'It's all right, ma'am, what would you like? I'll radio my colleague,' the uniform said to her.

'Anything. Coffee, sugar, pastry, you know, that sort of thing? Something to keep me awake.'

He radioed into his shoulder and she checked her phone. For want of anything better to do and to avoid going back into the ward, she tried Vivienne Kennedy-Craig's number again. During the night she had tried three times, each time leaving a message. This time it was answered straight away.

'Hello Elaine.'

The response took Elaine by surprise. She hadn't expected it and had concluded that Vivienne was avoiding her.

'I expected your call, but don't expect me to give you any answers about why they were together. I had no idea either. I don't exactly keep tabs on Bart. I'm sorry I can't help.'

Vivienne was as blunt as ever. The two women had never spoken directly about the relationship between their husbands. They simply knew they should be kept apart. Vivienne's response was an emotionless barrage of blandness and Elaine put it down to shock. She mustn't forget that the woman had just lost her husband, regardless of his questionable morals. Bart hadn't been as lucky as Donald, though Elaine couldn't help wondering if Donald might believe he was better off dead when he finally woke up, if he ever did. She knew that the headlines would hurt deep. Donald had always been sensitive.

'Nice to talk to you too,' Elaine said.

'Let's not pretend we have any catching up to do, Elaine. Or is there another reason you're calling?'

'Well, I thought you might have heard…'

'What?' Vivienne asked. 'I know as much as you. In fact, I'm sure you know more. My husband is not the priority here, is he? The cabinet minister – and his reputation, of course – is what everyone is worried about. My husband is dead, and I'm sure you're relieved about that, because no one will ever know what he was doing up there for sure. Goodbye, Elaine.' She hung up.

Elaine stared at the mobile in her hand and back to the policeman, who stared forwards, as per his duty.

'I'll go and get my own breakfast,' she said. 'I need some air.'

Chapter 20

Johnny had sounded rough over the phone, but whatever he'd been consuming the night before didn't stop him from answering Kelly's call on the second ring.

'Long night?' she chided him.

'You could say that. Jesus, I feel like shit. Jock had me up half the night sampling his top shelf,' Johnny said. The real name of the landlord of the Wasdale Inn wasn't Jock, but that wasn't the point.

'I'm sorry I didn't see your texts until this morning, I was working late at Eden House and then I slept through. Christ, I ache,' she said.

'Me too, I've just tried to move,' he laughed.

'It's all over the news, Johnny, that an instructor is staying there, at Jock's, and he's waxing lyrical to anyone who'll listen that the crash was sabotage. Is that what you were getting in touch about?'

'Yep. He's convincing, Kel,' he said. The use of his term of endearment for her sat awkwardly, but she let it go.

'What's that mean?' she asked.

'He's been a helicopter pilot in the army for decades, and now he's an instructor at the Army Aviation Centre in Middle Wallop, in Hampshire. Even I know that helicopters are simple machines, there's only so much that can go wrong. They're like tanks in that sense. He saw it come down.'

This was news to Kelly. 'He watched it?'

'Yup. He also told me that he knew the pilots.'

'Jesus, I need to speak to him. Is he still there?'

'I haven't ventured downstairs yet. I did tell him to hang around though, and he said he would. He was planning to go up Great Gable, but obviously there's no climbing round here today. Listen, Kelly, about last night...' he added.

'Don't, it's fine,' she said.

'I got carried away, you know? The emotion of the day and all that.'

'You didn't actually ask me to sleep with you.'

He sighed. 'I wish I had. That's all I want every night, Kel. You must know that. I didn't want this.'

It was her turn to sigh. 'I know, I'm sorry.' She was instantly angry at herself for apologising and she paced up and down the terrace. She'd come outside to make the call, so she wasn't distracted by Lizzie. It was freezing but fresh. Her breath came in clouds out of her mouth, but it still didn't mean that her words made sense. They floated away on the crisp morning and she didn't know what to say next.

'Can you get him to call me as soon as he can? What's his name?' Kelly was assuming her role as lead investigator until the accident people took over.

'He's an Army Air Corps major. Lance Tatterall. He's the chief instructor of Apache pilot training.'

'Was he the military guy helping out last night?'

'Yes.'

'Are military helicopters that different to civilian ones?' she asked.

'No, not at all. He's adamant that it was an uncontrolled spin due to the tail rotor coming off. He saw it spin off before the crash. He teaches this shit all day long, and he said mechanical failure that would lead to that sort of thing is rare. The 'copter was also newly ordered.'

'How the hell did he know that?'

'He's a bit of a nerd and models like that are like the Rolls-Royces of the helicopter world. He looked it up. He took the N-number.'

'The what?'

'It's an ID number on all military and commercial craft.'

'Like a number plate?'

'Exactly. He saw the tail rotor come off, but when he got up there, the tail section itself was amongst the debris. He said he teaches about recovering spins all the time. Anyway, I won't bore you with the mechanics.'

'No, please do, I think I can follow,' she said.

'Sorry, I didn't mean that. I know you can, I didn't think you'd be interested.'

'It might be fundamental,' she said.

He explained everything Lance had told him about torque forces and the role of the tail rotor, and what it would take to render it useless, and bring down the 'copter.

'He said that at high speeds, a skilled pilot might be able to control the spin and accomplish an emergency counter force. Of course, flying over Scafell Pike doesn't really leave much room for a smooth emergency landing. Google it. I have. It sounds lame, but it's all over the news about the cabinet minister.'

'I know, I haven't spoken to the chief constable yet but I'm guessing there'll be a summons from him by the time I get to Eden House. Whatever the outcome of the accident investigation, this now throws doubt over the cause of the deaths, and so there'll be a police investigation opened.

Suspected criminal intent can't be ignored if this guy's observations can be verified. It's not lame, by the way. I believe you. What's this Lance character like?'

'He's a good bloke. I actually know some people who've worked with him.'

'How did he know the pilots?' she asked.

'It's a small world. They were both ex-RAF.' He paused. 'I'm guessing you'll be chosen to lead it, the investigation I mean, given you were up there all day and night yesterday.'

She knew he assumed correctly. He knew her institution well. The police was akin to the army in terms of procedures. Her name was already being linked with any future investigation on certain news channels. Of course she'd be tasked with the job. But she wanted it. Having seen the carnage on the mountainside and the extent of suffering caused, she already felt involved, and now there was the possibility that the crash had been sabotage, there was no chance she would want to walk away from the case. Her mind was already whirring with questions.

'Thanks, Johnny, and thank you for yesterday. Getting so many people up there so fast saved lives.'

She'd slipped back into official mode and he noticed. It had the effect of making him withdraw, and he'd just opened up to her for the first time in two months, possibly longer, given how guarded they'd been over the whole Ian Burton investigation. She'd blown it. He'd said he missed her in his bed, but did that mean that he loved her, or just that he missed sex with her?

Right now, she had other priorities, and they hung up.

She went back into the house and found Ted there.

'Dad!' she went to him and gave him a hug. She needed it and it was comforting to be in his arms. He held her tight and then stood back, giving her that look that he took on when he was concerned about her. He couldn't help himself. He was seventy, but still vital. His broad shoulders and tall stature showed no signs of diminishing, and his eyes sparkled. His grey hair was almost gone, but his smile never wavered.

'How are you? It must have been rough up there,' he asked.

Millie came through with Lizzie and she kicked and hankered for her grandfather.

'Darling!' he cried, holding out his hands for the baby. Millie handed her over.

'You'll have a packed week, Dad. Have you seen the casualty figures?' Kelly asked.

He nodded. 'Yes, I know. I've got plenty of students to help me. That's why I popped in to see you. I'm on my way to the Penrith and Lakes now. I'll keep you updated. Of course, the priority will be ruling out sabotage and human error, so bloods will be a priority; pretty standard stuff, really.'

'Have you got time for coffee?' she asked, walking to the kitchen. She needed another one before she set off for work.

'Always,' he said, following her, still carrying Lizzie.

'I might have more of a role in this than I first thought,' she said. 'Looks like, due to the VIP on board, I might be involved in the investigation. Also, it's being reported – unverified at the moment – that it might not have been an accident.'

Ted raised his eyebrows. He was experienced enough to appreciate a cool head when theories were thrown around in the press. 'Well, they'll be lucky to have you on board,' he said.

She made him coffee and he sat down, resting Lizzie on his knee.

'How's Johnny?' he asked. He always did.

She had her back to him and paused before answering.

'He was a great help up there yesterday.'

'I thought I saw him on the news. You two are a great partnership.'

He did this. And he did it well. She could never argue with his summary wisdom. She also couldn't dictate his relationship with the father of his only grandchild.

'It's true, Dad, we work very well together,' she agreed.

'Just work?' he asked.

She turned around and smiled at him. His eyes twinkled. 'Dad, if there's a reunion on the cards, you'll be the first to know, but right now, I've got a helicopter crash taking all my time.' It was a tad melodramatic but it sent a clear message for him to change the subject.

Chapter 21

Chief Constable Andrew Harris called Kelly on her way to work, as she sat in traffic on the A66 towards Penrith. It was just as easy to turn off to the circular route around the town and head to Carleton Hall, to see him face to face.

He was an old-school copper and Kelly had much affection for him. Their relationship had been solidified over the prison riot inside HMP Highton in the autumn. Her best friend also happened to be dating him. Kate and Andrew had felt instant attraction when he'd taken over the position in the summer. They were both divorced and available, and they both shared a wicked sense of humour. It was a second chance for both of them. The HR department was aware. They'd been informed on Kelly's advice, considering the difference in rank between the two officers. Relationships in the force weren't banned, but when potential influence was concerned, for example over promotions, favouritism and the like, then one had to declare it. They had. Kelly could see that they were besotted with each other and wanted to protect them, which was why she never took Kate to Carleton Hall any more. They needed to be professionally distant.

The headquarters was a 1960s extension of a nineteenth-century pile, and it sat in splendid isolation on the outskirts of Penrith, surrounded by rolling fields and ancient woodland. It was peaceful and rather beautiful, and a welcome retreat on days when Kelly needed to get her head together. Her shoes crunched on the gravel as she headed to the main entrance and showed her lanyard, signing in for an hour. She was asked if she wanted coffee and accepted one gratefully. It was becoming her new bad habit. She'd never felt the effects of too much caffeine, but her intake had definitely climbed up. Not since her days at the Met had she consumed so many stimulants. Sod it; it was going to be one of those days.

She was shown straight into Andrew's office, where she found him peering at his computer.

'Hi Kelly, sit down, please. Good to see you,' he said.

They swapped pleasantries. They never discussed his relationship with her second in command, but she was envious of them: their freedom, their freshness and simplicity, and the fact that Kate had a warm body waiting for her at her lover's house. No bloody wonder he was smiling. Had Kate gone over there last night? She knew that Kate would be in a great mood all day too, lucky buggers.

'You can imagine how much heat is on me right now,' he said.

She sat down and nodded, taking off her thick walking coat and gloves.

'Let's make sure we're together on this. What are our priorities?' he asked.

'Sir, are you assigning this as a new case? I guessed it would be made official, but I've had no confirmation,' she said.

'Ah, yes. I was tasked by the Home Office late last night. We both know that it's the involvement of Lord Reilly that's driving this, but it's the other passenger who's actually making everyone nervous. If we can rule it as an accident and move on then that's all well and good. It should only take a matter of weeks to get this thing done and dusted then we can all go back to our normal jobs,' he said.

Kelly felt a little deflated. The driver behind the intense scrutiny given to this particular accident was the importance of one passenger, and the only one who'd managed to survive. It wasn't fair. She wondered whether she would even be involved if Bartholomew Kennedy-Craig had been the only victim last night?

'I've informed the AAIB that you are my choice of commander,' he continued. 'I need all agencies working together on this. You'll coordinate all the inquiries and report directly to me. I need answers fast. You have the support of the Home Office and so your purse strings are very healthy compared to what we normally have. Also, your scope includes all armed forces, so get in some RAF experts if you wish, as well as emergency services. The Penrith and Lakes and Carlisle University hospitals are aware.' He sat back.

'Right, sir.' Kelly's head spun.

He waited. He knew her well enough to know that she needed a bit of time to process new cases, not because she didn't know what to do first, but, quite the opposite; she wanted to get her ducks in a row and decide on a strategy. It was a huge responsibility.

'Sir, have you seen the news about the Army Air Corps instructor who gave an interview to the press about the crash being as a result of sabotage?'

'Indeed I have.'

'I think I'll start there,' she said. Major Lance Tatterall had been interviewed by a lone reporter who'd caught him outside the Wasdale Inn, and, it would seem, in a moment of remiss. The poor guy had been ambushed, and all of his training to say fuck all had gone out of the window. He'd simply gone outside to think, and they were there. Or that's what Johnny told her. She sensed an affection from her former lover towards the pilot, and that was a good sign for Kelly. She could forgive him a stupid comment to the press; anyone would be freaked out by watching a helicopter crash and then spending all day on the mountain helping the rescue effort. Kelly wanted to thank him in person.

'Be careful with that one, Kelly. It's common for witnesses to dramatise events in these situations. Concentrate on getting the AAIB report wrapped up,' he said.

The coffee arrived and she took the sugar bowl and added a spoonful to hers and stirred.

'You have my full support,' he said.

'Thank you, sir,' she said, looking over her cup.

—

The drive over to Eden House was peaceful and straightforward. If ever there was anything that could be deemed a rush hour in Penrith, then it was because of a build-up on the M6 and not because thousands of commuters were choking the city. It was mainly a tourist town, with winter walkers milling about, and most of them looking for taxis and buses west into the mountains, which could be seen from everywhere in town. They seemed untouchable from here, with their snowy, arrogant peaks.

Her first task in the office would be to get her team together. She needed all of them. From today, all information would be coordinated through her, until they got some answers. There was still plenty to do on the mountainside, not least evacuating the bodies of the deceased. She'd checked with Ted before she left that they had capacity in the two mortuaries they were using for the incident. They had space. It would be tight, he'd said, but they'd manage. Ted planned to prioritise the autopsies of the pilots and the dead passenger, Bartholomew Kennedy-Craig.

Meanwhile, she wanted to know where the helicopter had taken off, because she already knew that it wasn't from Carlisle airport.

Chapter 22

The man who'd been arrested last night for domestic violence charges and was being held downstairs in the Eden House cells had apparently sobered up, and had been interviewed under caution in the early hours of this morning.

Detective Constable Emma Hide had prepared the transcript. Kelly greeted her team and everybody in the room stopped what they were doing. They were all aware what their boss had been up to for most of yesterday, and that she was once again in the news.

Kelly noted their grim faces and knew she had to rally them today. It was a welcome diversion, if a short one, for her to recharge and reset. They sat round a large table set up in the centre of the roomy space, and each was ready with a laptop, but also a good old-fashioned pen and notepad. The room was warm and coffees were distributed generously. There was no time for pleasantries, other than a cordial greeting. Kelly would have liked to have asked everyone's plans for Christmas, already knowing that Kate was planning to introduce Andrew to her girls. But it wasn't really the time. DC Rob Shawcross, her money expert, looked drained, as he had done since the day his son was born just over a year ago – in fact, they'd had cake in the office to celebrate the milestone. His wife was pregnant with number two. His Christmas would be full of nappies and cheap plastic toys, as would Kelly's. Kelly had come into the office early on several occasions to find Rob asleep on a few chairs pulled together, covered with coats, and she understood how he saw the office as a calmer place to be than home.

DC Emma Hide sat next to DS Dan Houghton, as they did frequently and openly now. They manoeuvred themselves on to the same jobs but, to Kelly, this wasn't a professional problem, because they worked together so well. But she was well aware that the two were lovers as well, despite Dan being married. Her eye was firmly on their corner, in case the relationship spilled out into the work environment. It happened. Sometimes detectives spent so many long hours together that they became the job. Kelly had done it herself, back in London with her boss, somebody she'd taken years to forget. Relationships were complicated, she should know. But she was no marriage guidance counsellor.

Her team was solid, even if they didn't really want to talk about Christmas.

'Emma, can you give us an update on handy man downstairs?' Kelly asked. Anyone who hit women – and they came across a lot – was referred to as 'handy'; it was a derogatory slur just for the office, but everyone knew who she meant. The man – Paul Edderbridge – was already known to local police, and he'd been gobbing off at the authorities since primary school. The fella was angry and needed to take it out on somebody. His old man had been in and out of prison his whole life, and Paul had grown up with no rudder, watching his mother beaten to a pulp most nights of the week by the men who filled his father's shoes. Behaviour like that left a lasting impression on young lads' brains, and they often, contrary to what one might think, became violent abusers themselves. It was depressing, and working with domestics was like trying to divert a tsunami with a beach spade.

'Is it any different this time?' Kelly asked. They all knew the score: man beats woman, woman spends a few nights in hospital, man says he'll change, woman presses no charges. It was about as frustrating as it got – that and people beating babies and denying it. Everybody at the station hated domestics, not because they weren't huge crimes but because few women, and even fewer abused men, would ever press charges. It was the bane of proactive policing.

Emma shook her head. 'She's been interviewed in hospital and she's already sworn he did nothing. She slipped, she said.'

'Again? What about the kids?' Kelly asked.

'Social services are on it but they've got no concrete evidence they're in danger.'

'Until one of them "slips" too,' Kelly said, exasperated. 'How long have we got?'

'He can be released in two hours, and we've got nothing.' Emma confirmed what they all knew. Paul Edderbridge's girlfriend was taking him back, even as she was being helped out of her hospital bed. That was the power of an abuser. It wasn't the woman's fault; his girlfriend wasn't weak, and it wasn't just about that. Kelly had seen it herself a thousand times. It was as if they were under a spell. The abuser menaced the victim in all sorts of ways, until, gradually, they believed they were worthless. Usually, the threats involved the kids, and that was the Holy Grail for a mother; she'd almost always sacrifice herself for her kids. The irony, that her children would be safer without the abuser in their lives, never came up.

'Okay, release him,' Kelly said with resignation. They all knew that he was guilty as hell, but there was no case without a willing victim, or a dead one. They had to let it go.

'Right, thanks, Emma. So, on to yesterday's crash. I thought I would be handing over to the AAIB today, but surprise, surprise, and I can confirm that this is strongly to do with the cabinet minister being a passenger, I'm opening a new investigation based on a question mark over the cause of the crash and suspected criminal intent. We have to rule everything out. So, let's get to it.'

She tapped keys on her computer, and slides appeared on the whiteboard at the head of the room.

'This man, Major Lance Tatterall, is the chief instructor for the Army Aviation Centre at Middle Wallop in Hampshire. He was staying at the Wasdale Inn and saw the 'copter come down. He's saying it didn't look like an accident. I'm going over there to interview him officially. I need to get my head around how these death traps fly, or don't,' she said. 'I've already spoken to the RAF about the pilots' records; they're exemplary. In fact, the instructor staying at the Wasdale Inn, our main witness, knew both of them.'

Eyebrows were raised and notes jotted.

'It's a tinder keg in the press. A cabinet minister and a rich Tory party donor together on a privately chartered aircraft; it looks bad. We need to cut through the bullshit. That's not to say I want to ignore what's being reported – we can use it to our advantage, but keep an open mind. Kate, I'm putting you on the Reilly family. I want to know as much about the Right Honourable Donald Reilly as you can dig up. Rob, you can work with Kate on this, and look into the dead passenger, Bartholomew

Kennedy-Craig. Why were they together? What were they up to at the weekend? Lord Reilly was attending a climate conference in Glenridding, see what he did there. He was egged, we know that much. Find Neil Hardy, and bring him in again. Arrange to interview all family members. I believe most of them are in London, though Elaine Reilly and her two children are here at the Penrith and Lakes. And Rob, apply your silky skills to the Kennedy-Craig family company, Tactika Enterprises, will you?'

Rob had a nose for business, and had he not gone into the force, he'd have been a high flyer in the City. Or a money-launderer for a drugs cartel. Thankfully, he was on their side. He had a knack for hunting out any foul play, especially when it was well hidden, and the press were having wet dreams over the reporting on Kennedy-Craig's questionable practices around the globe, which was why the PM was embarrassed. Kelly wanted to know why.

'Dan and Emma, I want to know by the close of play today everything about the pad on Ullswater where Kennedy-Craig was staying. Was it rented? Or did he own it? And where the 'copter took off. Look at the pilots. What were they doing the night before? Toxicology will come back in due course. Who was allowed near that helicopter? I'll liaise with the AAIB people and try and get an answer out of them ASAP. Any questions?'

It was pretty clear what each of them had to chase and, at this stage, they stared at their sparse notes on their pads. Filling in the gaps would be the hardest challenge.

'Right, good. I'm getting a sodding lift by helicopter over to Wasdale,' she said.

'Woah! Boss, what?' Rob chipped in helpfully.

'I know.' She raised her eyebrows. 'It's the quickest way. I'm putting my faith in the Mountain Rescue Team. They're still removing bodies from up there, and the navy has sent another Sea King.'

'The pictures on the news are horrific. I know loads of runners in that race,' Emma said. She was a keen fell runner herself and Kelly and Kate had both noticed that Dan had become interested in the sport recently too.

'Do you know El Cabro?' Kate asked Emma. Kelly shot her a withering look.

'Of course. Everyone knows him; he wins every year. But he's okay, isn't he? I saw it on the news.'

'Yes,' Kelly said. 'He was a legend on the mountain yesterday.'

Kate smiled, but only Kelly noticed the wickedness behind it.

Chapter 23

Kelly left her car at the Keswick MRT car park and went in to the stone headquarters building to introduce herself. The last thing she wanted to do after yesterday was to climb into yet another helicopter, but to drive to Wasdale Head would take her an hour and a half via the coastal route, and she simply didn't want to waste that amount of time on the road. It was Johnny who suggested the helicopter. The teams across the national park were still busy on the mountain, collecting evidence and frozen body parts. She'd been informed that the AAIB was now in situ, and they were making full use of local people power to begin their investigation. She'd be there in twenty minutes.

The MRT hub was an unexpected vision of calm. Radio contact with the teams was constant, and Kelly heard the low controlled hum of instructions and information flowing both ways. She was put immediately at ease. People who came and went smiled at her as they heaved equipment in and out of the sheds. She looked at the photographs on the walls as she waited. There were framed news articles about the team's successes, and generally saving people's lives. She watched as members gathered their familiar red jackets and white helmets, ready for another long day, though perhaps not as frenetic as yesterday. It was the worst disaster ever seen in the Lake District.

'Right, Kelly, let's go. Here's a helmet. I'm expecting Johnny to come back with us, how long will you need?' one of the team asked her. It was a woman in her mid-fifties and the exchange left Kelly in awe of the people who risked their lives to bring people safely off the mountains, day or night, in their own time. Their experience and skills were impressive and she felt small and insignificant in comparison.

'A couple of hours?' Kelly asked. 'I've got to conduct an interview at the Wasdale Inn too.' The woman nodded, leading her out to the road between the building and Crow Park, where the coast guard helicopter could land. It was a lovely open green space right next to Derwent Water, and it was quiet at this time of the year. Most tourists stayed away for the Christmas season, and Kelly thought to herself how much bigger this job would have been had it happened mid-summer. Only dog walkers and the odd family frequented the grassy area, and they stood with gaping open mouths as the helicopter landed. Everybody knew that it would have something to do with the accident on Scafell Pike, and people stopped to watch.

Kelly watched the spinning blades as they got closer, and her nerves got the better of her and made her stomach do flip-flops. She had no time to pull out and she followed the woman blindly, until she was being ushered into the back and her seatbelt fastened. She was handed headphones, and the woman got into the front seat next to the pilot. She listened to them discussing the carnage on the mountain.

'It's a mess up there. More bodies to come down. The weather is coming down too,' he said.

Oh great, Kelly thought. That was all she needed. She closed her eyes as the engine whirred louder and louder until they hovered slightly off the ground, before pitching steeply towards the lake. She concentrated on all the equipment inside the craft: a few stretchers, body bags and lots of containers with labels, as yet empty. There was nothing she could spot that indicated that they were on a mission to retrieve people who were still alive. This was the work of the dead: tidying them up and getting the mountain functioning again. It was a grim realisation. She was flying to a potential crime scene.

Her stomach lurched and she thought she might throw up as suddenly the helicopter banked and accelerated like a fairground ride. She reached out her hand absent-mindedly, wanting to grab on to something, and all she found were black plastic body bags intended for human remains to be brought back to the Penrith and Lakes hospital, for her father to examine and report on. They flew over Cat Bells and soon she could see the range of mountains comprising the eastern fells, the highest of them being Scafell Pike itself. However, she realised with concern that the cloud was gathering over the hills, sticking to them, darkening by the minute. Sure enough, as they flew on, south-west, the visibility changed dramatically, and by the time they descended over the Lingmell Col, she could only see pockets of the hills around. The 'copter dropped rapidly to the Col and Kelly held on for dear life as the machine lowered against all natural laws, to Kelly's mind anyway.

The view distracted her.

As they descended, Kelly saw the fuselage of the 'copter, broken in two, with the N-number clearly readable on the tail section. Daylight changed her perspective.

Detritus and carnage was spread across the mountainside for hundreds of metres. People in climbing gear were trying to access the most dangerous part of the crags to retrieve bodies or bits of the craft, possibly vital in the investigation, and volunteers made a human chain down the mountainside to Wasdale, passing to and fro items crucial to the effort. It was a wonder of human resilience and dedication and Kelly felt humble. Thoughts of her own imminent death subsided and she jumped out and joined the chain to help fetch and carry.

Then she was led to the woman in charge of the AAIB investigation.

The woman, a civil servant, was dressed oddly for the terrain, in a trouser suit, over which she wore a huge coat, and a white MRT helmet on her head. She was youngish, in her thirties, and shouting orders. Kelly waited for an opportune moment to introduce herself and held out her hand.

'Kelly Porter, SIO,' she said.

The woman eyed her, sussing her out, and eventually took her hand.

'I'm Zoe.'

'Great, why don't you bring me up to speed and I'll head down to interview Major Tatterall,' Kelly said.

'Lance Tatterall?' Zoe asked.

'The same,' Kelly said. 'You know him?'

'I sure do, I was working with him last week. He's your witness? The one who's saying it wasn't an accident?' Zoe asked.

Kelly nodded.

'Well that changes things. Usually I dismiss such conjecture as gossip, but I'd like to hear what he has to say. Where is he?'

'Down there,' Kelly pointed down the mountain towards the Wasdale Inn. 'It'll take an hour to get down, but it's steep and hard on your knees,' she said, looking at the woman's feet. She'd at least had the sense to wear walking boots.

'What the hell is he doing here?' Zoe asked.

'Don't know, holiday, I guess,' Kelly said.

Zoe looked at her watch, presumably calculating if she had time to leave the site. She changed the subject.

'It's very unconventional, you know, for the AAIB not to have full jurisdiction, but orders are orders,' Zoe said. Kelly cringed inside. This was the last thing she needed, some power-hungry thruster.

'It's the sheer amount of agencies involved,' Kelly said. 'Somebody needs to coordinate them all. I won't tread on your toes. You're simply delivering information to me; I won't interfere.'

Zoe looked at her again and nodded.

'Fair enough. Let's go over there, where our heads won't be blown off by this fucking helicopter,' she said. Kelly warmed to her a little more. She liked straight talking.

Zoe filled her in on the operation so far. She was arranging for the helicopter's main body to be airlifted to a hangar in Penrith. They'd managed to free the two last runners trapped underneath, and they'd been confirmed as deceased and transported to the mortuary at the Penrith and Lakes. Kelly watched as Zoe pointed out various groups working on evidence and packaging boxes to be transported to the hangar, so the machine could be reconstructed. There were thousands of pieces to bag and tag, for painstaking work later. Kelly reckoned it was like a typical crime scene but a million times larger and more complex.

'Personal effects?' Kelly asked.

'We've retrieved six mobile phones, I think, so far.'

'Six? For four passengers?' Kelly asked.

'Indeed. I guess that's your job,' Zoe said and smiled.

They walked side by side and Zoe checked in on her staff wearing AAIB bibs, trawling through evidence bags. Zoe picked something up; it was a clear bag containing a small bottle of brown liquid.

'Brandy, found in the cockpit,' Zoe told her.

'Oh dear,' Kelly said. They carried on, Zoe replacing the bag in the evidence box.

'Something ripped the tail rotor off,' Zoe said. 'It was found near the lake, down there,' she added, pointing down the valley.

'You must know a thing or two about helicopters?' Kelly asked. Kelly didn't. Except what Johnny had briefly shared with her. She was terrified of them. However, even in her ignorance, the image of something coming off a tail, from anything meant to fly, sounded devastating. 'Apparently Lance Tatterall saw it come off,' she added.

'I'll come with you when you're ready and finished up here,' Zoe said, and walked away. Kelly appreciated the candour and the freedom to wander around the site and get a feel for the destruction. She walked towards the Col and stopped short of the sheer drop. A team coming up the Corridor route had reported a body on the other side, which still hadn't been retrieved. She chatted to various teams who were busy bagging evidence and logging debris ranging from the tiniest fragments to whole sections of the helicopter. It would take weeks to write the report, and longer to publish. She had to release her mind from the pressure she was under and start at the very beginning.

When she was satisfied that proper evidence handling procedures were in place, she went to find Zoe, and told her she was ready to trek down to the Wasdale Inn.

On the way down, Zoe didn't complain once, or ask to rest, and it was a demanding descent. Kelly pressed on and by the time they reached the bottom, her knees were screaming. Twice down the gruelling path in less than twelve hours wasn't something she'd recommend. They arrived at the Wasdale Inn before eleven o'clock.

Johnny was sitting with a man at the bar and they were drinking coffee. They turned to greet her. Johnny introduced the Major and they shook hands. He greeted Zoe warmly.

'Zoe! They've got the best, I see.' Lance turned to them and began to explain how they knew each other. Kelly watched him. She liked his manner.

'I never expected to be working on a practical case study with you so soon after your excellent theory delivery,' Zoe said to Lance. Gallows humour, just like the police.

'Not the walking holiday you expected?' Kelly said to him.

He smiled. 'So who wants to talk to me? The police or you lot?' he asked Zoe.

'I do,' both women said in unison.

'Major Tatterall,' Kelly said. 'This is a joint investigation and I'm the investigating officer, but Zoe is the expert. And you, of course. Can you kick off by telling me exactly what you saw, and explain the technical terms to me. Zoe has her own questions, obviously.' She waited. She could have sworn that Johnny puffed out his chest a little. Zoe smiled. Kelly liked her.

'Let's start with you talking us through exactly what you saw from the first time you spotted the helicopter,' she asked Lance. 'Zoe, can you jump in when you want to? Please use lay terms when you can, I'm afraid I'm a novice on how these things work.'

Chapter 24

Terrance knocked lightly on her bedroom door and Vivienne knew that it meant her son was home. He'd caught the first available flight from Argentina, where he was part of the sponsorship group for the national polo team. Fabian was the horse-lover in the family, and the one who'd convinced Bart to invest. It must have been a long flight, given the news she'd burdened him with before he boarded. She'd had no choice. It was all over the news. It was one thing keeping a story out of the Argentine press, but quite another once he boarded first class and read any choice of English newspaper handed to him. The headlines about his father were disparaging, and frankly harrowing to read.

What was cabinet minister doing with the King of Dodgy Cash? Read one. Another announced: *Lord Reilly in intensive care after crash with Mr Cash*. A higher-end publication announced: *Minister hitches doomed ride home* and *Questions asked after cabinet minister critical and billionaire dead*.

The last one caught her attention. She was unaware that they were billionaires, she considered, tongue in cheek. But on a more sobering note, she felt for Elaine, a little. Donald was a dithering old-school fool, but he was also a terrible husband and so deserved to be caught out. That was a tad uncharitable, but she honestly believed

Elaine was better off without him and that, in time, the children would agree, if the old goat didn't pull through. It didn't look good, from what she'd read, and Elaine had sounded shell-shocked when she called. So she might; the stupid woman had actually believed that her husband was going to stay away from Bart for good. Vivienne knew hers better than that. Elaine was still concerned about appearances, like they all were when they were caught with their pants down.

She felt protective towards her son, who would have read all of the loathsome and offensive headlines about his father. She felt the familiar rush of burning anger in her body and knew it was a reaction to the sheer fact that it was all so bloody unfair. The press had got their teeth into a new scandal, and the story would run and run. Meanwhile, her husband's legacy – and the father of her son – was being side-lined and diminished, as if he didn't matter at all. And her name was being dragged through the dirt with him. However, she realised that this could work to their advantage. Taking a little heat off Bart's death in the press might be just what they needed.

She sat up in bed and called for Terrance to come in.

He opened the door and she noted how old he'd become. They'd been together for twenty years, on and off, and he was a loyal servant. She often wondered what made men faithfully attend others, but she guessed it was consistent employment, and the fact he was able to reside in a most sought-after postcode, in the middle of the vibrant capital: her favourite of all of them. Always immaculately dressed, Terrance smiled at her and stood in the doorway.

'Fabian is here, madam. Shall I tell him you'll receive him shortly downstairs? I have the fire going.'

It was gone midday, but Vivienne had stopped caring what time it was years ago. She could do what she damned well liked.

'No, he can come in here. I can't be bothered to get up. Has he been fed?' she asked.

'He's not hungry, ma'am.'

She nodded. She was still well turned out, even in bed, and she was fully dressed, with make-up and jewellery in place, so she was more than decent to welcome guests. She knew that her mid-fifties was too young an age to take to one's bed – without a lover at least – but she disliked the outdoors. It was too full of people who thought they knew what was good for you. She put down her book, a mindfulness tome about retiring not expiring. Bart turned his nose up at her self-help books, but then Bart wasn't in possession of emotions like other humans, she'd decided long ago. And now he was gone. Just like that. Burned to death in a crushed lump of metal. She felt nothing. It had been hard work pretending to be the mournful wife in front of the police, but they didn't know what she did. She was fully prepared to turn it on when she had to. Of course there'd be an inquiry because there was someone important riding with him in the helicopter. A lord, no less. Stupid fool. He was probably showing off.

They'd lived separate lives for the best part of a decade. Vivienne had married too young, but Bart had been persistent. Still, she looked on the bright side: she was soon to have all of his money. Her favourite home was this one, where she stayed as often as she could stand the inclement weather. When she wanted sun, she flew to their estate in the Caymans. It was easy to avoid one's husband if one could afford it. It suited them both. Bart could indulge his perversions and she was left alone to read, post blogs, tend to her only child – not that he needed it any more – and volunteer for acceptable charity work. She took Terry with her wherever she went.

His hand touched hers as he took in her morning tray and she grasped it for a few seconds, squeezing it and smiling up at him.

'I'm ready,' she said.

Terry nodded and left the room, closing the door. Vivienne heard voices, and footsteps on the stairs. The door burst open and Fabian waltzed in. He was handsome, but then every mother says that about her son. He was also tall, like his father. He had a generous full head of auburn hair, and deep dark eyes, framed with shiny chestnut brows. His skin was tanned – of course; it was the Argentine summer – and his face was fresh, though the dark circles underneath his eyes gave away a night of restless sleep, despite the luxury of his cabin. He rushed to her and sat on the edge of her bed, thrusting himself onto her and throwing his arms around her neck. She cradled him, though he was twenty-four years old, and it never ceased to amaze her how much she remembered the first time she held him, like she did every time they were reunited. That feeling, she supposed, would never go away. She felt his body relax but she knew that he was crying.

'Darling, I'm sorry,' was all she said.

She'd tried to keep the reality of his father's darkest nature from him, but children see everything and Fabian had never really warmed to his father. Equally, Bart had never fully embraced his son, seeing him as a weakling. It broke her heart, but that was years ago. Bart's struggles with his masculinity were something it took her a long time to work out. Vivienne knew that all men of power struggle with male offspring, it was something that was part of being a ruthless bastard. They all expected them to come out just as determined and gifted as them, and it never happened. But they were from different worlds. Bart had crawled up from nothing, whereas Fabian was born with it all. How could they possibly have anything in common? Bart's success was as a direct result of his shitty upbringing, whereas her son was gentle and kind and sweet, and had no desire to make money. He also lacked the capability. He didn't understand the intricate world of business and so Bart was constantly disappointed in him and happy to ship him off to corners of the world, away from attention, where he couldn't do him any damage by losing deals and shaving millions off share prices. Fabian simply wasn't possessed with a business mind. Which was why she was Bart's sole heir.

But now, with her son in her arms, she realised that a father can do his worst, he can be absent, abusive – violent, even – but he will still be loved by his child.

It was so pitiful.

But now wasn't the time to tell Fabian that everything was for the best. She'd have to tread carefully, and appear at least a little destroyed at the loss of her love. Her priority right now was protecting him from the vileness in the press.

He gathered himself and looked up at her, but to her shock, he was smiling.

She thought it might have been a trauma response, like when people laugh at tragedy and pain, and so she gave him a moment.

'Fabian?' she asked, not really knowing why.

His face changed, as if he realised how it was set, and he straightened his grimace and wiped his face.

'Are you all right, Mummy?' he asked.

'I don't think it's hit me yet, darling,' she said. 'I'm sorry for cutting your trip short,' she added, for want of anything else to say. She felt awkward and hadn't expected it.

He sat back, and sighed. 'Well, I'm here now. What are you doing in bed in the middle of the day? You can't let yourself get down. I'm going out. I've arranged to see a few people.'

She looked at him warily. 'Whatever for?' She panicked suddenly and thought he might turn to drink, or drugs. Maybe he already had. There'd been that time at school when he'd been caught dealing marijuana. She fully expected the press to rake it up now. Every scrap of indignity was in the public domain and there for the taking, and she was sure that while Lord Reilly lay reliant upon the dear NHS for survival, so Bart would be, and already was, vilified as the corrupt and depraved party who'd led the peer astray. She couldn't shield Fabian from any of that, but she had an army of lawyers who could fire some warning shots. If the press went too far then she'd sue their arses, just because she could. She'd already been on the phone about the articles she'd read insinuating Bart's business history was less than legally clean, and worse, that he was some kind of morally rotten influence on legitimate partners. She wouldn't have it. Bart was a shithead, and all manner of other things, but she wouldn't have her name, and that of her son, hauled through trial by newspaper, just because it sold copy. She would use her extensive contacts to encourage articles that might serve to distract the press from Bart's more lewd pastimes. That much was imperative. At all costs.

She hoped Lord Reilly pulled through, not because he was a decent chap, or even for Elaine's sake, but simply because then the circus surrounding the crash would die down.

But she also couldn't help wondering why Donald had met with Bart in the Lake District in the first place. She knew it wasn't for afternoon tea. There had to be more to it than that.

Maybe it would be better for all of them if Lord Reilly never woke up.

Chapter 25

Lance drew a diagram for Kelly.

'You can imagine what happens to any chunk of metal when five blades above it are turning at 290 revolutions per minute.'

'It spins,' she said.

'Exactly. That's where the power comes from. It has to have a counter force, and that's what the tail rotor provides.'

'But it's tiny,' Kelly said.

'Think tug boat. It's just physics, it works,' Lance said.

Zoe was being very patient.

'What might cause the tail rotor to fail?' Kelly asked.

'Hydraulics leak, something mechanical like nuts and bolts being poorly maintained, wear and tear. But all of these things should set off the appropriate alarms and give the pilots a viable picture to work with so they can stabilise the situation.'

'Unless it's catastrophic,' Kelly said.

'Exactly. And that's what our focus is on,' Zoe interjected. 'I've got people examining as much as they can related to the tail up there.'

'I don't know how you can work your way around a mess of wires and metal,' Kelly said.

'They know exactly what they're looking at,' Zoe said.

Kelly believed her. 'I'm sure they do. How do you rule out sabotage?' she asked.

'By ruling something else in. It's a painstaking process of elimination and might take time, but it's all we've got, unless we get lucky.'

'Whitehall is breathing down my neck, I haven't got the luxury of time,' Kelly said.

'Tough, they'll have to wait. You can't rush an accident investigation,' Zoe said.

'I agree,' Lance said. 'But you could start with the things that would rule out sabotage,' he said.

'And that's what I instructed before we left the mountain, Kelly.' Zoe turned to her. 'There are certain places to look for patent tampering, but if it wasn't an accident, then I doubt it'll be made obvious.'

'How skilled would somebody have to be to pull it off?' Kelly asked. 'And could the pilots have been in on it?'

'Not unless they were suicidal,' Zoe said. 'It's something we'll look at – their mental health. Lance, you knew them?'

'I taught them. But what I've learned is that you can never predict somebody's mindset,' he said. 'They can appear the happiest of people on the outside.'

There was silence for a few seconds as the four of them let this sink in. It was a touchy subject for Kelly and Johnny: what the human mind is capable of when it's damaged. A suicide mission, if enough money had been promised to the deceased's family, for example, was one thing they had to consider.

'Suicide would make sense if it was flown straight into the mountainside. No one could pull off that spin on purpose,' Lance said. 'Look.'

They watched him type something into his phone and he showed them video footage of a particularly horrendous helicopter spin as a result of tail damage. It was simulated, of course, but the graphics were convincing.

'Have you ever seen this before?' she asked.

Lance looked at Johnny and nodded.

Kelly knew that this meant that he had and that it had been in the theatre of war. Of course, she thought to herself sadly. War makes excellent military instructors. The best.

He told them about what he'd seen and Kelly heard enough to convince her that these incidents were catastrophic, and virtually unheard of in a new Agusta AW139. Zoe agreed. But that didn't prove anything. Zoe, like Kelly, was an investigator, and their first consummate rule was to assume nothing.

'We've got a lot of work to do,' Zoe said. 'Have I got to climb back up that thing?' she asked Kelly, meaning Scafell Pike.

'No, there's helicopters going up and down from behind the Wasdale car park, on a stretch of land that's flat. They're still taking up equipment.'

'So why did you make me walk down?' Zoe asked.

'They were in between flights at the time, and I thought you'd appreciate the fresh air.' The women smiled at each other.

Zoe excused herself as her phone rang. She wandered off to take the call and Kelly stretched. Her whole body ached. She caught Johnny staring at her, but then she remembered Lance. She flicked her eyes towards him to see if he'd noticed the frisson that had passed between her and her ex, but he hadn't. He was staring down at his hands.

Kelly knew that the guy had demons of his own. She recognised the look, and the sloping shoulders. Or it could have been trauma from yesterday. Not likely. He'd seen worse. She knew it.

Zoe came back.

'That was one of my investigators. Ladies and gentleman, we've got a cut hydraulics line up there.'

Chapter 26

Ullswater was what was technically known as a ribbon lake, so called because of its finger-like formation left behind after being sloughed by a huge glacier, or in this case, three, between hard rock formations. It was actually a Z shape and easily the most glorious and peaceful lake in the whole park, though some might disagree. It was the perfect drive for two lovers, and not perhaps two coppers tasked with finding out where the late Bartholomew Kennedy-Craig had spent his final night, presumably hosting a member of Her Majesty's government. Either that or he'd got there very early to take the flight back to London. A check with the Glenridding hotel, where the climate conference attendees were staying, had established that Lord Reilly was checked in there, but did not stay on Sunday night, or any other night.

Dan and Emma had accepted the brief gladly, and had already discovered that Kennedy-Craig regularly rented the sprawling estate of Laurie Fell, hidden behind the sloping hills, and had done so for the whole three weeks running up to, and including, the climate conference. Unsurprisingly, he hadn't been invited to that, however Lord Reilly had attended. It was their job to find out why the two had met and how the minister had ended up hitching a ride in a helicopter with the CEO of Tactika Enterprises. Now Kelly had informed them of the latest development on the mountain, it was vitally important that the last movements of the pair were looked into.

Emma stopped for coffees in Pooley Bridge, midway between Eden House in Penrith and Laurie Fell, halfway along the A592, which bordered Ullswater's northern shore. Real estate here was premium, and holiday lets were clustered mainly around the hiking hubs of Glenridding to the west, Pooley Bridge to the east, and a few campsites along the way. The steamers chugged up and down all year round, though less so in winter, and compared to somewhere like Windermere, it was a quiet and serene lake attracting those wanting to get away from it all. It boasted a smattering of well-hidden five star rentals, and a few of them had helipads.

Laurie Fell was one of them.

It had taken a phone call to Kennedy-Craig's PA to find it. She had clearly not wanted to hand over the particulars, but it was amazing how you could change your mind about withholding information when your boss was dead. It turned out that Laurie Fell was rented by Tactika for most of the year. The owner was a lady called Nellie Lowther, who was an ex-teacher at a local school in Keswick, but recently retired two years ago.

'Why didn't he just buy it?' Dan had asked. 'He could clearly afford it, if we are to believe what they're saying in the press.'

'God, Dan, when do you ever do that? Besides, this way, he paid less in tax, and the owner won't sell,' Emma told him. She'd been the one who talked to the PA.

'The owner is also the housekeeper, I guess she likes to keep an eye on the place. She lives in a private residence on the estate, and she keeps the main house ready for whenever Kennedy-Craig fancies using it,' she told Dan as she concentrated on the winding road, and he looked out of the window.

'More money than sense,' Dan said.

'Obviously,' Emma agreed.

'How the other half live,' Dan said.

'Any more clichés?' Emma asked. 'Are you just jealous?'

'Damn, yes,' Dan said in his broad Scottish accent. 'Why don't we get invited to stay in plush pads along here, eh?' he asked.

'Because we're not important enough, I guess.' She concentrated on her satnav, which wanted to take her down a dirt road, but she ignored it and relied on good old-fashioned map-reading skills instead. She'd looked on Google Maps before leaving Eden House and she knew that it was one of the turnings near Aira Force, but they were all tucked away. And that was the point. Privacy cost money.

'The owner is expecting us, then?' he asked.

'Yes, she was a bit shaken. She said she'd known the man for the best part of a decade.'

'Good, she should be able to enlighten us, then. Did you ask her if Lord Reilly was a regular guest?'

'I was saving that little nugget,' she replied. 'Officially, all the delegates for the conference were checked into the Glenridding hotel,' she reminded him, 'but of course he wasn't there Sunday night, and he seems to have stayed elsewhere for the duration of the conference. Are we heading over there?'

'After we've finished here,' he said, as Emma turned off and drove between two stone pillars, and the trees opened up to a clearing with a stone wall, and a stop sign next to an intercom. There was barbed wire on the surrounding fences and cameras too.

'Exclusive,' Dan noted. 'Those cameras might come in handy,' he added.

Emma put the car into park and got out to walk to the intercom, pressing the bell. A female answered and she recognised the voice as that of Nellie Lowther, whom she'd spoken to on the phone. A buzzer sounded and the metal gates opened slowly. She went back to the car and drove through them, as they closed behind the car. The road wound further for about two hundred yards and then the trees opened up once more and Emma pressed the brake.

'Jesus.' They both looked at the huge, castle-type mansion.

'I'll have to ask them how much it is for a night, and we can check in,' Dan joked.

'I don't think we could afford an hour,' Emma said.

'Is that an offer?'

She hit him playfully. She parked the car in front of the massive double-fronted entrance, which was draped in the leftovers of what must be dramatically impressive creepers and climbers in the spring and summer. Even the gravel looked well-tended. They got out and examined the place. It was like turning up to a high class wedding when one nominally knew the bride and groom, but felt out of place.

One of the giant oak doors opened and a small woman appeared, wringing her hands. She looked all of her sixty years, wearing a knitted cardigan and looking as though butter wouldn't melt, like someone's granny. She was slight, with a full face of make-up and an old-fashioned pinafore tied around her waist. She didn't look like the type to own a palatial pad like this. It was quite a leap from English teacher to landowner.

Emma held out her hand and greeted the woman. Her hands were freezing and her handshake was stilted, but Emma put it down to shock. Dan introduced himself but kept in the background. Always on the lookout for information, but with an open mind, both coppers were sussing her out, but they equally got the impression that they were being assessed too. Kelly had given them specific instructions not to get swept away by the media view of Bartholomew Kennedy-Craig, in other words: a sleazebag. They were to gather particulars pertinent to their inquiries regarding the start of the helicopter's journey, as well as the nature of the relationship between the two men. Unfortunately, humans judged as a matter of course and there was a distinct frostiness to the tiny woman, after they'd accounted for the grief, and both coppers felt it. It was of note because it was unnecessary.

They were shown inside. The place smelled of cleaning products.

The enormous doors were shut behind them and Emma wondered if there was a side door which would have been less formal. Before either detective could kick off any questions to set the tone, Nellie had disappeared and Dan and Emma quickly followed her so they didn't lose her. They walked though pristine hallways, decorated richly and adorned with fresh flowers, and past lots of closed doors, until they came to a wide open kitchen. Dan tried a few door handles but they were locked.

In the kitchen, they were told they could sit at the table and Nellie plonked herself down too, wrapping her knitted cardigan around her body tightly. Her well-painted lips remained tight and Emma decided to jump right in.

'It's terrible news about Mr Kennedy-Craig, Nellie. You must be in shock. There must be numerous staff members for this huge place of yours, have they all been informed? I mean, those who were working over the last three weeks, while he was here.'

'Just me,' she said. Far too quickly.

'You do everything? Cooking, cleaning, bed-changing, entertaining, gardening, admin, and the like?' Emma asked.

Nellie nodded.

'Fair enough, keeps costs down, I suppose.' Emma smiled, but it wasn't reciprocated. 'Let's start at the beginning. We're investigating the cause of the crash, and we'd like to get a picture of Mr Kennedy-Craig's last few days. Lord Reilly, as I'm sure you're aware, is currently in a critical condition in hospital. Was he a guest here?'

'He might have been, I don't pry into the chief's business,' Nellie said.

'The chief?'

'It's what I called Bart.' Nellie looked down at her hands and Emma was touched by the affection.

'Did you see this man?' Emma asked, showing her a photo of Lord Reilly.

'No.'

'Can you show us where the CCTV cameras feed into? We'd like to check them.'

'Bart set those up.'

'You don't know where they are?'

'No.'

'Right, who arranged the helicopter?'

'The chief.' Nellie looked down again.

'You were close?' Emma asked.

'He paid my wages, as his housekeeper, and he doesn't – *didn't* – like the word "boss". Tea?' Nellie got up and busied herself at the range, fiddling with cups and taking milk out of the fridge. Dan and Emma stared at one another.

'With respect, did you need the money?' Emma asked.

'It wasn't about the money. What I meant was that I respected him as the chief around here, that's all,' Nellie said.

Emma was confused. 'But you own this place?'

'So? I need a little help with the business side of things, that's all. Bart helped. I was left this place by my papa when he passed. I was a school teacher,' she laughed. 'I don't know what to do with a place like this.'

'Fair enough. So, he stayed here on his own for three weeks, and then chartered a private helicopter, and at some point must have invited Lord Reilly?'

'Must have.'

'Did you meet the pilots? Make them a cuppa?' Dan asked.

Nellie shook her head.

'Can we take a look around?' Emma asked.

'Have you got a warrant?'

'Erm, not right now…'

'No, then. The chief is a very private man. *Was* a very private man. Sorry, I…' Nellie got a tissue out of her skirt pocket and wiped her eyes. She set a tray down on the kitchen table and poured three cups.

'I appreciate he was the only visitor here for some time, but it's your property, Nellie, you get to say if we have a look around or not.'

'And I've said no,' she said forcefully, in between sniffs. She placed three cups on saucers and tea spilled over the edges. Dan took his gratefully and sipped, watching Nellie closely. Emma knew he was thinking that this woman was a loon; she was as uptight as a coiled spring, displaying more irritation than bereavement.

'All right, we'll secure a warrant later today and we'll leave you to it. Thank you for the tea. Just one more thing – can you show us where the helicopter took off?'

'I can do that, follow me.'

They went outside. Nellie showed them the rear of the property and it was even more spacious than the front.

'I read the news, you know. Have you got anyone yet?' she asked.

'What do you mean?' Dan asked.

'Those protesters. They broke into the grounds and left graffiti. Look over there,' she said, pointing.

Dan and Emma looked to where she was indicating. At the back of the property, and on the side of the house, was a message scrawled in pretty basic street art style, probably with spray paint: *Tory Scum*.

'Nice. You see anyone?' Dan asked.

Nellie shook her head.

'CCTV working?'

'Bart checked and they weren't on it,' she said, too quickly.

Dan was getting the distinct impression that Nellie had rehearsed some of her answers.

'And when was this?'

'Sunday night,' Nellie said, then marched them across to a landing pad that was denoted by its flatness and a small rectangle of concrete. Emma took a photo of the graffiti. They looked around. There were plenty of huts and outbuildings close by and most of them were locked shut. They could also see that the property wasn't overlooked by any others from here – or anywhere, for that matter. The lawn stretched down to the lake, and it boasted a boathouse and private jetty.

'Did Mr Kennedy-Craig use the boats?' Dan asked.

'Sometimes,' Nellie said.

'Are there cameras in there too?' he asked.

She shrugged. 'I don't go down there.'

She stood with her arms folded, waiting for them to throw what they had at her, and she was unflinching in standing her ground, utterly defensive. Some people reacted like that to the police, and rich people tended to employ people who were aware of how important their privacy was. Nellie was clearly used to keeping her mouth shut. But they needed a picture of her chief's final movements. And she wasn't giving them anything. And Emma was convinced that it wasn't just because of nerves.

'Were you here when it took off?' Emma asked.

'No.'

'Don't you work full time when the chief is in town, so to speak?'

'I was busy cleaning.'

'Did you hear it take off?'

'No, I listen to music when I clean. Besides, I stay at my place over there,' she said, pointing to a bunch of trees about three hundred yards away from the main house.

Dan wandered off, he'd had enough of the woman pretending she didn't know who stayed in her own God damn house.

'Oi! Where do you think you're going?' Nellie shouted at him. 'I said you can't look around without a warrant, now buzz off, both of you!'

Dan strode over to the patch of concrete used by the helicopter and looked around. He noticed several storage sheds in the vicinity and marched towards them. Nellie scuttled after him and Emma was surprised at the woman's agility. Damn, she moved quickly for an older woman, she thought. She had zest in her; that was for sure.

Dan threw open the door to a barn, looking inside. Emma had no idea what he was looking for. Nellie shouted at him, but he was already quite apart from them, and when he eventually turned around to listen to the woman, he explained that he hadn't heard her, and apologised profusely.

'What are you looking for?' Nellie asked.

'Where did the pilots fly in from?' he asked.

'I have no idea,' Nellie said, 'How would I know that?'

'They're rotor covers.' He pointed to a large bundle inside one of the sheds.

'Are they?' Emma asked breathlessly, having followed them to the barn.

Dan winked at her. 'Helicopters must be hangared if staying overnight before flight in freezing temperatures, to avoid the build-up of ice on the blades, or they've got to be protected and heated. Look, they're the type of heaters that might be put inside the cabin to prevent ice. I'd wager the 'copter was kept here overnight. We need to find the log.'

'I said you couldn't look around! You haven't got a warrant and this is private property!' Nellie was desperate to get rid of them.

'With respect, we've been granted permission to investigate the buildings and holdings of Tactika Enterprises, including long-term leases,' Emma said. It had nothing to do with a warrant but Nellie wasn't to know that. Emma betted on her misunderstanding. They'd had phone calls with Tactika HQ in London, who'd agreed to cooperate, but again, Nellie wasn't to know that. Emma waited.

Nellie glared at her. 'Tactika Enterprises don't own this property, I do. Now get off my land.'

They walked around the property to Emma's car, followed by the owner, who watched them leave all the way down the drive and out of sight.

'Jesus, touchy,' Dan said as they pulled away.

'How the hell did you know all of that about rotor blades and stuff?' Emma asked.

He shrugged. 'It's all on Google,' he said.

A trip to the Glenridding hotel confirmed that Lord Reilly had been booked to stay all weekend, but it didn't take long to find the maid who cleaned his room every day, and to establish that he hadn't spent one night there.

Chapter 27

'Are they gone?' George Fellows asked Nellie, when she returned to her cottage to tell him what the coppers had said.

'For now, but they'll be back. What the hell am I supposed to say, George? They know I'm not being cooperative, it's bloody obvious.'

'Calm down, Nellie. Look, I know you're upset but we've got to pull ourselves together. The family will look after you, don't worry, but we have to tidy up. You know what I mean, don't you?'

Nellie nodded. They were stood in the modest living room of her private cottage.

'The police have to snoop around and ask questions, because Bart was such an important man,' he said. 'The fact that Lord Reilly was with him has brought scrutiny. Did Bart mention anything to you about planning a helicopter ride?' he asked.

Nellie shook her head. 'It was last minute, typical Bart. He wanted to take Donald sightseeing. I think he thought it was funny that Donald was so scared of the helicopter,' she said.

'Jesus. Well, it's done now. I'm relying on you, Nellie. Don't let the family down.'

George looked away. The woman's lack of courage unsettled him. He suspected she might turn out to be a weak link, but his orders were clear. They had to distract the press away from this place. For the sake of the family.

'I just didn't expect them to come knocking this quickly. Some expert up on the mountain yesterday has put it into the minds of the investigators that the crash was no accident,' he said.

'I saw it on the news, I just don't believe it,' Nellie said with indignation.

George went to her and placed his arms on hers. 'It was just that, Nellie, a terrible, terrible accident, but you know what the press is like. If they get wind of what Bart was doing here with Donald, then it's all over for all of us and that includes you. Jesus, why did he have to put us in this position?'

'It was an accident, wasn't it, George?' she asked meekly.

'Of course it bloody well was. And Donald wasn't even supposed to be on that goddamn helicopter. Why didn't you stop him?'

'Me?' Nellie wailed.

'Nellie, I didn't mean to blame you. We're all just shocked. But why did he get on it with Bart?'

Nellie wiped her eyes and blew her nose. 'Bart insisted. He gave Donald brandy. You know how he was. Very persuasive,' she smiled and sniffed. 'Bart was like an excited boy,' she snuffled.

'Well, it's in the past now, we can't change it. Look, the investigation will die down. It was an accident. Maybe it was my fault. I should have checked out those pilots myself, but he'd used them before. I don't know what happened. I'm no expert on these things. The important thing is, this place must be cleaned and tidied for the next time the police come knocking, do you understand?

Because they'll have a warrant next time. We'll deal with the press.'

Nellie nodded.

'Good God, it's bloody freezing in this place. I should've stayed in London, like Bart should've too,' he said.

'You don't like the Lake District?' she asked, trying to change the topic a little to distract herself more than George. 'Bart loved it,' she said, and the tears came again.

'I know he did, Nellie, but I doubt it had anything to do with the bloody scenery. Give me the names of the girls,' he demanded.

She jumped at his abruptness. She handed over her phone to him, and her hands shook a little.

'They're just schoolgirls, wee things, they won't say a word,' she said.

'Well I need to make sure of that, don't I?' he said. 'Bart's dead now, and my job is to make sure that he doesn't take the rest of his family down with him. I've wiped the CCTV, anything else you can think of?'

'No, I've told you everything,' she said.

'Good. I can count on you, Nellie?' he asked.

She nodded.

'And, Nellie, don't ever use my private mobile number again.'

He'd only just met the woman who kept the place going for his ex-boss. And he wasn't impressed. His job was to find holes in leaking ships and this one was like a fucking deluge.

Chapter 28

Fabian Kennedy-Craig slammed the newspaper down on the occasional table. It knocked the china cup containing his Earl Grey tea with milk, and it spilled onto the carpet. He put his head in his hands and got up to pace towards the window, out of which he stared at the London street beyond. A tear rolled down his cheek and he wiped it away. A fire raged in a grand hearth, making his cheeks burn. His father's name was already muddied in the press, but this was a step too far. A respected broadsheet had published a piece only this morning about his involvement with fracking and greenwashing, intimating that his helicopter had been brought down by environmental fanatics.

He scuffed the carpet roughly with his stockinged feet, then paced back to the newspaper and looked at the name of the journalist scum who'd probably wet his pants when he'd made the front page.

Lord Reilly's helicopter brought down by climate fanatics? It asked, with the sub-heading: *Questions asked this afternoon of PM: Was Tory-funding climate denier, CEO of Tactika Enterprises, a target too?*

It was a crass headline for the highbrow rag and he made a note to phone the editor in person, who his family had put through fucking college.

Fabian had put his distant father on a pedestal all his life. His desperate need to impress him had got him nowhere, but that didn't mean he'd stopped trying. And now he had to clear his name. He didn't give two fucks about Lord Reilly or what he was doing with his father; all he cared about was making sure the investigation got to the bottom of why his father had ended up ploughing into a mountainside. He didn't trust anyone. It was quite obvious to him that his mother had given up, but he never would.

He stared at his phone. Over the years he'd been allowed to glimpse the inner workings of his father's business interests, and shown the ropes. Tactika was a giant, and he was just getting started, but nevertheless, he knew enough of his father's contacts to begin the fight back for his name. Donald being on the helicopter was a problem, of course, but there was no point moping about it and becoming self-defeating. His mother could do that on her own in her bed, waited on by the butler she was fucking. But of course, he wasn't supposed to know about that. Neither was his father, but all that would be dealt with in good time.

He scrolled through his phone, tapped a number, and waited.

It rang out.

He paced up and down, frustrated. George was supposed to be on hand any time of the day, according to his father.

'You have a problem, you go to George,' he'd said. Fabian knew that his father took George everywhere with him. And that would have included the Lake District. So, why wasn't he picking up?

Next he found the direct number for the editor of the broadsheet that had published the article. It went to voicemail.

'Quentin. Call me. It's Fabian Kennedy-Craig. If I don't hear from you in the hour, then I'll start digging out my father's files on you, before we gave you a new name. Hope you're having a great morning!'

Fabian pressed 'end call'. It felt good just doing something. He vowed to spend every minute he had clearing his family name in the press. Then, and only then, could his takeover begin in full. He felt alive.

There was a light knock on the door and Terrance entered with a tray of breakfast things. Fabian used to love the ceremony and grandeur of such routines, but now it felt hollow. The tray was huge and silver, and on it were delicately cut pieces of toasted bread in a basket, jams and preserves, solid silver cutlery – slightly tarnished – which was intricately carved; as well as napkins, orange juice, pastries and tea. The smorgasbord jarred him as something that was served to the living. The contrast between this luxurious sustenance being brought to him and the treatment his poor father's lifeless body would be receiving hit him in the gut. He knew that his father was awaiting further humiliation at the hands of a pathologist in the arse end of nowhere in some poxy local NHS hospital. The police had already informed them that the body would be released after examination.

And so would begin the official cover-up. The minute it had been reported in the press that his father's passenger was Lord Reilly, Fabian knew they'd never get to the truth. The institution looked after its own interests, at the expense of anybody in its way, and the truth was always the first casualty. The PM, a dithering Old Etonian wanker, would do anything to save his own skin, and distancing himself from Tactika money, Fabian knew, would be a priority. He couldn't trust anyone with ties to the British government, including the NHS hospital holding his father, or the police investigating the case, who were only there because of Lord Reilly.

He eyed Terrance, who looked a little too smart for a butler, in a tailored three-piece suit and, he noticed, a rather expensive watch from his mother's favourite Swiss dealer. Terrance bowed, as was customary, and retreated.

On that note, his phone buzzed. It was George Fellows.

'George,' he answered.

'Fabian, I'm so sorry about your father. Am I right in thinking that your phone call is perhaps something to do with that?'

'You guessed correctly, George. I don't care how much it takes. Name your price. I want to know what happened to my father, and I want to know why Lord bloody Reilly was with him,' Fabian said. 'I assume you're still there?'

'Indeed I am,' George said. 'I've already started to look into it.'

'Good man. I'll be in touch with a phone number to use from now on. You talk to nobody else, especially my mother,' he added.

Fabian heard George suck in his breath a little.

'George, she's been through enough, and she's emotional. I don't need that. I want a clear head on this. Please promise me,' he asked.

'Done,' George said.

'I'll arrange for payment to be left at the usual place. Send me a box number.' They hung up.

George Fellows was paid by leaving a shit-ton of cash in Amazon delivery pick-up points around the country. Fabian would hear soon where to leave the first instalment. Private investigation didn't come cheap. George would need travel and living expenses, as well as potential bribes and unexpected costs. Fifty thousand should be a convincing initial remuneration. But he knew that George was loyal. Employees were always easier to control when you had personal dirt on them. George Fellows had lost custody of his daughter to his ex-wife, and he wanted her back. Their family could pull strings in social care. George Fellows would do anything for them. But George was also a violent man, and the hope of seeing his daughter again was something that Fabian realised could keep him dependable a little while longer. Desperate people had loose boundaries and that was just what he needed right now.

The call left him buoyant. Adrenalin shot through his body; his father would approve. *'Don't think, Fabian, do!'*

Now he fully understood. All the lost years, missing his father, knowing he was building his legacy for his only son, left a pain which tore at his heart. They'd never had chance to get to know one another and here he stood, with all the money in the world at his fingertips, but no one to guide him. He wiped his eyes and buttered some toast. Was he ready? He was about to find out.

His phone buzzed again and he recognised the number as the private office of the editor of the newspaper.

'Quentin! Good morning. Tell me why you would pay a freelancer climate freak nerd to trash my father in your newspaper, did the education we paid for teach you nothing?'

Chapter 29

Kelly read the headline of one of the numerous news articles on her phone. It was the age in which they lived. Public opinion mattered. Social media could destroy cases; it could also lead to stunning leaps forward in investigations. She'd grabbed another coffee from Jock, who was already pulling pints of Stella, despite it only being midday or thereabouts, and had taken it outside to open the attachment on her phone, sent by Rob.

The sky was clear blue and it was the type of day in the Lakes when all you wanted to do was jump in a lake or run up a hill. She could do neither, and it was also fucking freezing. Her breath blew in clouds about her head. Activity on the mountain was still frenetic and she saw helicopters taking off and landing, as well as MRT members coming down the path with evidence bags, to be collected by the AAIB at the Wasdale car park, which had turned into an incident camp. From there, evidence was driven to a hangar in Penrith, where the AAIB would piece together the fuselage and begin their painstaking work of figuring out what happened up there. Their priority was finding the cockpit voice recorder and the flight data recorder which, Zoe had told her, on these models was a combined digital unit called a CFDCVR. Unfortunately, it would take some digging out, as it was stuck in about three feet of boggy mud up there.

She spoke to Rob on the phone.

'So, the article was written by a freelance journalist who, it appears, has made it his life's work to expose Tactika Enterprises, amongst others, as a giant climate destroyer, in bed with powerful US companies. They pour billions a year into anything that will discredit scientific research into global warming. They create companies with names like "Eagle Freedom" and "Friends of the Hedgehogs" and filter funds through them, ostensibly producing papers on green issues and diverting attention away from the carbon footprint of their real enterprises.'

'Friends of the Hedgehogs?' Kelly asked.

'I made that one up,' Rob replied.

'I get the idea. And fracking?'

'So currently Tactika fund fifteen fracking explorations around the UK alone, several of them in Scotland, which was where Kennedy-Craig was heading after the Cumbria conference.'

'But the flight plan was to land in London,' Kelly said. The flight log had been downloaded digitally by Zoe, as soon as her team had been able to locate the port on the badly damaged control panel. Kelly was amazed at how robust these automated machines were, but at the same time, not quite enough to protect human flesh and bone.

'I know, and from there, he'd chartered a flight to Glasgow the same afternoon. Why take the shortest route when you're so rich you don't have to?' Rob asked.

'Quite. So it makes sense that he was taking his friend on a sightseeing trip over the fells. That might explain why it looked as though Lord Reilly's name was added last minute to the passenger list; it's in different writing and untidy, like an afterthought. It also corroborates what Vivienne Kennedy-Craig said when she was first told of the accident; she was shocked that Lord Reilly was a passenger, he shouldn't have been on that flight.'

'Have you seen the footage I sent you of the conference?' he asked.

'No, I've been talking to the helicopter instructor over here, and the head of the AAIB investigation,' she said. 'She's a strong addition and doesn't mess around. Is it the footage of the egging?' she asked.

'Yup, we've got it from several angles from a dozen journalists, and there are a few characters I've looked into. Turns out several of them have travel bans and public disturbance orders against them, including Neil Hardy, who was charged and is awaiting sentencing.'

'Is it such a big leap to helicopter sabotage?' she asked.

'Well, we'll soon find out. I've got them being rounded up and interviewed. Turns out Neil Hardy, the one who threw the egg, is a coordinator and leader figure, and he's still in the area. We should have him in here soon,' he said.

'Good. If nothing else, he'll be willing to talk to avoid a hefty fine, or, given his previous, time inside for the assault.'

'I was going to call the journo as well, the one who wrote the story. He's a nerd like me and we speak the same language. It's actually a very good article,' he said.

'I'm sure the family won't agree with you, and it's something the Home Office won't want linked to party funds. Talk to him anyway, see if he's been pressured either way,' she said. 'The AAIB have found a slit hydraulic line on the 'copter.'

'Does that mean anything? The g-force of the crash could do that, no?'

Rob was a natural sceptic and that's why he was a worthy addition to her team. He needed proof, like she did.

'Zoe told me, and the pilot instructor agreed, that wear and tear presents as erosion on hydraulic lines; they're thick reinforced tubes, made of some clever amalgam of plastic and metal on modern helicopters like the AW139, or so I'm told. It's not chafed, it's cut, and it would have to have been done pre-flight. It would have leaked fluid slowly and could either cause a fire from the vapour, or lead to loss of pilot control on the cyclic stick and yaw pedals,' she said.

'Jesus, Kelly, you sound like a techy! Welcome to my world.'

'I got a crash course – excuse the awful pun. They said that the pilots would have been frantic trying to press the yaw pedals and pull the cyclic back and forth trying to straighten her up, and it would have been horrendous for the passengers. The flight data record should show us; it's all computerised on these models, all they have to do is download the programme.'

'Like on *Air Crash Investigation*?' Rob asked.

'Kind of, it's in an orange box, if that's what you mean. It's a combined unit and is to be flown to their HQ at Farnborough airport, not far from where Lance Tatterall works. Zoe's got him working with them, so I'm confident we'll get a complete report as soon as it's ready.'

'Did you ask her if you'd have to be an expert to know how to cut a hydraulic line?' Rob asked.

'Of course. She said that, with instruction, anyone could do it, which is why we need to know who had access to the helicopter in the hours before it flew, so I'm giving that job to you. Examine the contracts it had in the week before the crash.'

'I already know the answer to that. It was rented by Kennedy-Craig for the whole weekend. I just need to find out where it was hangared in between flights, because it wasn't at any locations I would expect. For example, Carlisle airport isn't far away, they could have used that but they didn't. There are a few others dotted around, but so far I don't have it at any of those.'

'So, where the hell was it?' Kelly asked.

'No idea,' he said.

Chapter 30

'Are you getting an airlift back to Keswick?' Kelly asked Johnny.

Lance Tatterall had disappeared off with Zoe. They had work to do. They were technical and professional soulmates, and now they had a mission. Kelly couldn't help feeling that Lance had come alive when it became clear that Zoe wanted him to work on the AAIB investigation with her, as a key witness, but also a fellow expert. It was a match made in heaven, as far as investigations go. She got the impression that Lance had been up here, on his own, climbing to get away from something, and now he had a purpose. She parked the thought and looked up at the mountain. They were standing in the makeshift incident camp at the foot of the Scafell Pike path and hoping to hitch a ride home. Her work here on the mountainside was done; she could add nothing else and Johnny was still nursing a hangover. She'd rarely seen him in such a bad way. He'd clearly off-loaded in some way last night and he'd needed it.

'Come to mine for some dinner and spend some time with Lizzie?' she offered.

He looked at her and nodded.

'Does Josie go today?' he asked about his eldest daughter. She was about to go off to complete her gold

Duke of Edinburgh award, wild camping in Borrowdale for three nights, without a phone.

'She should have left by now. She gets back on Friday,' she told him. She thought she discerned a little trepidation in his question, and it quickly turned to relief when she replied. It was no bad thing, she thought, for a man to be held accountable by his daughter.

They walked to the landing site and chatted to the MRT member coordinating flights in and out. They could get on the next one.

They walked over to the dry stone wall, probably there for a hundred years, and Kelly leant on it, peering towards the lake. Wast Water was the most dramatic lake in the national park, or so she believed. It was the Scot, John Wilson, who'd described it as *'The cradle of the storms … Where poets fear their self-created forms…'* and Jock, at the inn, had the words engraved above the bar. Of course, Kelly thought, he'd never promote English Romantic poetry, so he found a Scot. Good on him, he was a proud man. But, now, looking across the water, she knew that he was right. The deep glorious lake, in mocking silence, made you question your existence.

'How you feeling?' she asked Johnny.

'Like shit,' he replied.

'You needed a blow-out?' she asked.

'Guess so.' He glanced in the same direction, as if the lake would help his hangover. 'Look, Kel. The trial. I gave them what they asked for, under oath.'

'I know. You want to talk about this now?' she asked.

'Why not? We've got nothing else to do apart from wait for a helicopter ride. Maybe we can discuss it without arguing. The outcome wasn't changed by what I said in court.'

'Yes, it was. It could influence the prison term he gets. Everyone knows he's guilty as hell, but the press love a good story, and the squabbling between the lead detective and her lover was more important to them than the actual trial. It was unhelpful,' she said. She fixed her stare on the mountain screes, unmoved by their bickering. 'And now this.'

'You're a local legend,' he said.

'Oh, please,' she sniffed.

'You are. If anything, I've served as the baddie, alongside Ian Burton. You've come out a champion of righteousness and now you're the right person for this task, too. The press will be on your side.'

'It's not about sides. And I've never wagged my virtuous finger over you.' She felt herself getting angry and was reminded of why she'd asked him to leave home. This wasn't about who had the upper fucking hand, it was simple: it was about right and wrong. End of. She turned to him, her back against the uneven wall.

'He's guilty of murder, and he was of sound mind when he did it. You saw horrendous things in Iraq and Afghanistan but you never cut people up because of it! Jesus Christ, Johnny, this is about character. Ian Burton is an adult with choices and that's all I care about. Sometimes good people make bad choices, but Ian Burton isn't a good person and he needs to be off the streets.'

'I agree,' he said simply.

'What?'

'I agree with you. Look, I didn't realise that this would mean so much to you—'

She went to interrupt him.

'Kel, just listen, for God's sake. Let me finish. I felt as though I was doing my bit to protect those who no one cares about. The people who, as you call it, fall through the cracks and get left behind.'

'Ian Burton didn't fall through the cracks; he had everything.'

'What? A pathologically criminal family? Yeah, that set him up nicely in life. Look, all I'm saying, and I know you believe this too, is everybody deserves a fair trial. We don't lock people away and throw away the key any more, we're not barbarians. He'll go to prison for a long time, I just wanted his people to have a voice.'

'His people?'

'People who are fucked up in the head because they made shit choices or shit choices chose them, whichever way around it is.'

Kelly looked at him. She was overwhelmed, but not with anger, with something else. How could she argue against such compassion? Wasn't that what she fought for every single day? Fairness? Voices of the unheard? She was in check-mate and it felt fucking terrible. They turned to the lake again. She was about to embark on championing the truth for a potentially corrupt businessman and his peer pal who'd enjoyed his hospitality. Ethically, it was the right thing to do, but morally, it could be seen by some as reprehensible.

'I think you're amazing,' he said quietly.

A few rogue clouds threw shadows over the landscape and it changed colour, like looking through a kaleidoscope.

Her phone buzzed. It was a text from Kate.

Ian Burton got life, with a minimum sentence of nineteen years, it read. She held it up for Johnny to read. He said nothing. The sound of helicopter blades disturbed their thoughts and they looked overhead. Kelly had seen enough helicopters in the last twenty-four hours to last her a lifetime. A navy Sea King was coming in today to lift the wrecked fuselage of the AW139 off the Lingmell Col. It would be taken to the hangar in Penrith along with all the other thousands of pieces, to rebuild and form the basis for Zoe's report.

The final verdict could take weeks, and the report a year, but Zoe and Lance were on their way up the mountain to look at the slit piece of hydraulic line. They'd call her when they'd assessed the likelihood of it having caused the accident. For now, she had enough to carry on with the inquiry on the basis that the deaths it had caused remained unresolved, and thus suspicious. In her world, there was no such thing as natural death, and Kelly wondered if she wanted to kill off the only thing in her life that was a source of good: the relationship with the father of her child.

Chapter 31

The vibration of her phone shook Kelly's hand, which she held on to for dear life. She was being dramatic, she knew, but that wasn't the point. She hated helicopters, and she'd seen first-hand what an accident looked like. The journey was short, and not enjoyable. She reckoned that even if they flew over all Seven Wonders of the World, she'd never enjoy another helicopter ride. She'd yet to discuss the casualties – or what was left of them – with her father. It wasn't just the blunt force trauma, or the way human bodies were torn apart during accidents with all manner of vehicles, it was more the horror of what their last moments would have been like. Since having a baby, Kelly had felt her emotions soften a little – not too much; she wasn't going rogue and feeling sympathy for criminal bastards, not just yet, it was more a pause before she judged, and a visceral need to protect the innocent. The death toll had crept up overnight to seventeen. To think that somebody might have caused this carnage on purpose was sickening.

She watched the footage sent to her by Rob on her phone, on repeat, to deafen the imaginary noises in her head of how the rotor blades would have pulled and pulled in the wrong direction without the tail rotor, exerting unsustainable torque pressure, ripping the cyclics out of the pilots' control. They would have been pinned into whatever position they sat in, watching the earth race towards them, until impact.

The climate conference had been held at the Glenridding hotel and attended by dozens of delegates from all over the world. Climate change activists had gathered in the local village, choking it and angering locals. Scuffles had broken out and it was footage of this that she watched on her phone. Rob had sent her several videos as well as stills of known activists; the ones who turned up wherever there was trouble, no matter the cause. Attached were files on the main players, and their histories, and what they might have been doing in the area. The one she watched, to take her mind off the dips and sways of the helicopter's trajectory, was taken outside the hotel. It had been posted on Twitter; Rob had been going through the footage from the weekend, sent to him by a contact at the security team, which had been tasked with managing the delegates' safety. A delegate from Italy had been giving a press conference and things turned ugly when a member of the crowd threw an egg. It was clear to Kelly that Lord Reilly was the main target. He'd been standing behind the Italian delegate, and the egg had glided over the speaker's head, breaking on the head of the peer. Kelly couldn't help admiring the accuracy of the perpetrator's aim. Shortly after, a struggle ensued and a couple of security men in dark suits descended on the man who threw the egg: Neil Hardy. He was wearing the usual mob attire: khaki trench coat and jeans. She watched as he was wrestled to the ground, then the video clip ended. She played it again and Johnny nudged her.

She looked out of the window and saw they were flying over Derwent Water, and the landing site in the park was now visible. They would be on the ground within minutes. She put her phone away. The machine descended and her stomach lurched. Finally, they were down and she unclipped her belt. If she'd been religious she might have said a silent prayer of thanks for her survival as she hopped out of the thing and ducked from habit until she was well clear of the rotating blades. Johnny followed her to her car and they got in.

'What was that on your phone?' he asked.

'Footage of the conference, where Lord Reilly was egged by a protester.'

'Poor bloke. I'd never be a politician if you paid me.'

'Well that's the point, contrary to the democratic history of our great country, politicians don't need paying because they come from the class that don't need it.'

'Ouch, cynical,' he commented. She smiled and started the car.

'Why don't you drop me off at home and I'll spend the afternoon with Lizzie, and I'll have something ready for you coming in,' he said.

She noted his use of the term 'home', and nodded. She had a few things to do back at Eden House, and her dinner invitation, though flippant at the time, had not been forgotten by Johnny.

'Don't worry, I'll go back to mine after,' he added, as if reading her mind.

She turned off the main road and entered the small village of Pooley Bridge. Pulling into her road, she saw it was packed with journalists.

'Of course,' Johnny said. 'They've just heard the verdict.'

'And we're together,' she said. She turned off at the next junction and swung around the back of her row of cottages, keeping their heads down. They had to climb over a fence and hold on carefully, but they managed to reach her back terrace and congratulated one another like conspirators. Lizzie screamed happily when she heard her father's voice. He took his daughter into his arms and threw her up in the air. Kelly looked at Millie's confused face but the girl was wise enough to mask it. She looked genuinely happy to see Johnny in the house and got on with her other chores while he rolled around on the floor with the baby.

'Right, I'll see you later, then,' Kelly said.

'Bye, Mummy!' Johnny said, and Lizzie mimicked him in her own unique four-month-old way.

She went back out through the terrace, watching her footing as she made her way back to her car, hidden from the crowd.

She didn't have to sleep with him, she said to herself. It's only a meal and time with his daughter. She drove away and headed towards Penrith.

Her first stop was the hospital, where she was due to meet her father who was working on the bodies of the casualties. He'd be looking for evidence of foul play, searching for things like unusual burns, possibly indicating an explosive device, or toxicology anomalies. It was an excuse to see him and let go of some of the angst she felt over Johnny. She felt a pang of regret that she couldn't talk to her mother. When she'd been alive, they hadn't exactly had a close relationship, but she missed her warmth and her ability to bring reason to any tricky situation. Ted had become her anchor. He was a great listener and had a knack for making her feel better about herself when she was riddled with doubts.

Going to the hospital was also an opportunity to visit the Reilly family, to see how Lord Donald was doing.

He'd been unconscious when he was brought in last night, and was still unresponsive so far. His brain activity had slowed extensively but it was too early to ascertain if parts of it had been damaged permanently. The priority right now was keeping him alive. He couldn't breathe on his own, and all tests on the Glasgow scale had been worryingly low. The examination was performed on all coma patients in the ICU and was a scale of awareness assessing basic responses. Lord Donald Reilly was in a bad way. On the drive over, she rang Kate on hands free for an update: it was still grim news.

'They're treating his burns, and testing his brain activity every hour. The family is with him; he's got two kids, and his wife is called Elaine. I popped over there this afternoon to talk to her. She's a tough nut to crack. They're showing all the expected signs of a family concerned for a loved one,' Kate said. It was customary to discuss things like this when the injuries of a victim were potentially suspicious. In this case, they had no idea yet whether or not Lord Reilly was a target, or if the crash had been caused by sabotage. When assessing a family's responses, they expected several patterns of behaviour and it sounded as though Elaine Reilly was presenting suitably as a worried spouse.

'Did you ask her about Bartholomew Kennedy-Craig?' Kelly asked.

'Well, I mentioned him, and the tragic circumstances of his death – gently, of course, but she definitely stiffened at his name. Given the press reports about their relationship, I should imagine she's embarrassed.' Kate said. 'Rob updated me on the hydraulic cable,' she added.

'It doesn't look good,' Kelly said. 'Any news from the Laurie Fell estate from Dan and Emma?' she asked.

'Sounds like Dan's on to something. He reckons the AW139 could have been hangared there in the open elements. There is equipment in one of the sheds for such an eventuality, but the owner was a cold fish, and she basically kicked them out,' Kate told her.

'What's she hiding? Surely she'd want to help find out what happened to her only tenant,' Kelly said.

'Dan reckoned she was protecting Kennedy-Craig's privacy, but she wasn't exactly helpful,' Kate said. 'She called him "the chief". Odd, don't you think?'

'Nothing as queer as folk,' Kelly said. 'So, did the pilots stay over too?' she asked.

'The owner didn't say.'

'Strange. That stinks to me,' Kelly said.

'Me too,' Kate agreed.

'I'll mention it to Ted; he should have done the toxicology on both of them by now. If they were guests overnight then they might have drunk too much,' Kelly said. 'That could explain her reticence.'

'One more thing; Dan said there was a boathouse, and it looked in use. He asked about CCTV but she zipped up again. We'll have to wait for a warrant.'

'To get to the north shore from anywhere on Ullswater you'd need to moor a boat at Glenridding or Pooley Bridge; check their jetties,' Kelly said.

'Sure thing,' Kate said.

'I'm at the hospital car park now, I'll see you later.' Kelly ended the call. She parked in the multi-storey and took a ticket, and made her way to the mortuary.

Chapter 32

The steel interior of the Penrith and Lakes hospital mortuary looked like a chop house. Gurneys were wheeled in and out at a rate of a handful every hour, and Ted felt as though he was deluged with body parts and reports. Every limb, crushed vertebrae and mashed skull needed recording and examining, and matching to any other body parts that were brought in in separate bags, then meticulous DNA testing would identify them in time. Whole intact corpses were few. The bodies of the pilots and Kennedy-Craig were complete, though badly burned. His work was to try to collate as much information as possible to identify every casualty so they could be returned to their families for a last farewell. As well as to confirm how they all died.

Specimens, in various states of integrity, were at different stages of examination all over the mortuary operation room. Assistants, dressed in green scrubs, gloved and masked, worked silently and diligently, and to some kind of process, though it wouldn't seem obvious to anyone off the street.

It might seem manifestly plain to rule that they had all passed away as a result of a tragic helicopter accident; however, it was Ted's job to find what nobody else could: anything out of the ordinary that might solidify the case in the coming weeks, and Kelly knew he was thorough.

He'd worked on major accidents before. Road traffic pile-ups were the worst. The injuries were pretty predictable, but occasionally he came across something that could only be explained by human culpability.

He had several students from Carlisle University Hospital working with him all week, because there was nothing quite like the opportunity to learn from a disaster, such as war or an accident; it was where most leaps in medical knowledge had been made through the ages.

Kelly walked into a hive of activity that looked like the back stage of a horror movie set. She scrunched her face and wrinkled her nose, sniffing the Vicks she'd smeared under it. She spotted Ted and went to him. He looked up and nodded his greeting, stopping speaking to a group of three students to introduce her.

'Everybody, this is Detective Inspector Kelly Porter. She's in charge of the inquiry into this tragedy. She also happens to be my daughter.'

Kelly blushed under her mask. There was a rumble of interest around the room and she said awkward hellos to the strangers staring at her. She even gave a small wave, which she instantly regretted.

'Sorry, I'm so proud of you,' Ted whispered to her.

She patted him on his back and squeezed his shoulder. 'How you doing? It looks awful in here,' she said.

'Yes, I'm sorry about that. This is what it looks like, I'm afraid. I worked on the Omagh bombing in '98. You can't imagine,' he said.

Kelly knew he'd worked in Northern Ireland during The Troubles as a resident pathologist, and she couldn't conceive what it might have been like. He'd seen all manner of injuries, and the depths to which humans can sink when they want to hurt one another. She bowed to his supreme experience in matters of trauma and surveyed the scene. He clearly had everyone working to a methodical set of procedures in the most extraordinary and calm way.

'So, the thing is, Kelly, I've got very little for you. I've seen everything I would expect, and not a lot of what I wouldn't. Ninety per cent blunt force trauma. Multiple fractures consistent with high speed impact, mainly facial bones, skulls, thorax and pelvic bones, as well as tibias. We've got plenty of lacerations and burns – that hydraulic vapour is evil when it catches, and the 'copter had full fuel tanks.'

Kelly had smelled the aviation fuel as soon as she walked in.

'It's all over everything,' he said. 'Then you have the damage to all major internal organs. It's a tsunami at the moment. We're trying to send DNA testing off for every sample, trying to match up whole bodies for the families, patching them up as best we can, to send back to the families.'

Kelly nodded.

'We've had a breakthrough,' she said.

'Already? That's good, isn't it?' he asked.

'They found a slit hydraulic line. And those things are tough. The helicopter was under three years old, so wear and tear is ruled out.'

He stopped working, and held a limb with his left hand, and a scalpel in his right, waiting.

'They're trying to confirm if it fed the tail rotor, which came off over Wast Water.'

'Dear God.' He put the appendage down on a steel slab. 'Sabotage?'

She nodded again. 'Toxicology?' she asked.

'It'll take time.' He turned to her, hands in the air, covered in blood, scalpel still in hand.

'The AAIB discovered a bottle of brandy in the cockpit,' she told him.

'Oh dear. Well, the pilots are done. Their results should be first, you'll be pleased to know.'

'What about the passenger?' She referred to Bartholomew Kennedy-Craig.

'Yes, we've done him, so you should get the results you want in twelve hours, for those at least.'

'Thanks, Ted. They're the important ones, really. If you know what I mean.'

'You don't have to excuse yourself to me, Kelly; I do this every day, and my priorities might seem callous to those who don't understand. Sorry I haven't more to tell you. Looking at this lot, I'm frankly flabbergasted that one survived the impact.'

'Yeah, the AAIB reckoned he must have been cushioned by something, perhaps upholstery. Also, they told me that where he was sitting would have been significant when the thing came down. Luck, I guess.'

'How's he doing?'

'Not good. I'm on my way up there now to meet the family. It's not just the impact trauma to his skull that's worrying the docs; he's brain-damaged too, but they can't tell to what extent yet.'

'Dear God, it makes you question if you'd want to survive something like that.' He said what she was thinking.

'I suppose you've read the papers?' she asked.

'What, about my superstar daughter, and Ian Burton's jail term?'

'No, Dad, about Lord Reilly's connections with Bartholomew Kennedy-Craig.'

'I'm playing with you. Of course I have. Politics and money. The oldest toxic relationship. I don't envy you piecing this one together. Climate change activists? Surely they don't have the resources to pull this kind of thing off?' he said. 'It's not their style, is it? They usually egg people and set off fireworks.'

'True. It would help if I knew who the target was: Lord Reilly or Kennedy-Craig.'

'Or both. Or neither, if the pilots were the worse for wear.'

'Yes, it's a mess.'

'Well, Kelly, I don't envy you this one.'

'Thanks, Dad. I'll pop in to say bye before I leave, if you've time for a cuppa?'

'I'll see. This is only half of them; the others have gone to the university hospital in Carlisle,' he said.

She left him to it and took off her overalls as she went through the swinging metal doors leading to the changing rooms. She took a deep breath and inhaled Vicks. She rubbed it off with her hands before washing them, trying to rid herself of the stink of body parts.

Chapter 33

'Look, Fabian, I know you're angry…'

Quentin St John, pronounced 'Sinjin', the editor of one of the most prestigious broadsheets in the UK, was trying to tell Fabian that he understood how he was feeling. Fabian's neck glowed red. Quentin was a name chosen after much thought, to make the working class boy sound as if he came from good stock. He didn't, and occasionally, his actions showed it. Tactika had a generous scholarship scheme which his father had insisted upon, which awarded prestigious university places to those less fortunate. It was his father's way of helping gifted people out of the mire, so they didn't have to fight like him. Fabian thought some of them should be more grateful, and loyal.

'Listen to me,' Fabian said in a low voice. Quentin went quiet. Fabian let his rage vent. It probably wasn't fair, but life wasn't fucking fair, and the buck had to stop somewhere.

'This scrotum sack, what's his name? The freelancing scumbag.' Fabian grasped the newspaper in his free hand and searched for the name at the bottom of the article. There was a photo, too. It was his minute of fame, and it made Fabian seethe even more.

'Who is he? I've got my people on him. He sounds like he's some woolly Russell Group dropout searching for dirt. Why did you pay an amateur to bring my father's name into disrepute?' he screamed down the phone. Perhaps he shouldn't have called until he'd calmed down a bit. Every time Quentin tried to respond, Fabian launched another tirade.

'Are you that desperate that you can't even pay your own any more? You sniff around for scraps like the gutter press? Jesus! Do you know the damage you've done?'

'Fabian—'

'Shut the fuck up. How much did my father pay for your degree in the end? Including trips abroad, your secondment to *Le Monde*, and your access to Sky News? Jesus, what kind of turncoat are you, Quentin?'

'Fabian—'

'Are you being paid by the Labour lobby?'

'Fabian—'

'Do you know how much damage you've done? Now you've risen to the dizzy heights of editor, you don't need us, is that right? You selfish, immature, ungrateful bastard. Our shares dropped by thirteen per cent this morning. Greenwashing! How fucking dare you!'

'Fabian—'

'You can kiss sweet goodbye to any more money. All the perks and holidays and timeshares, Quentin, wave goodbye, you fucking traitor. I can tell you for nothing that we have everything on you, still, in a rather large envelope. My father throws nothing away, and now I'm sole heir, by God I'm going to destroy you.'

'Fabian, shut up and listen to me!'

Fabian stared at the phone in his hand and words failed him. They stuck in his throat and simply wouldn't go any further. It was as if someone had put a sock in his jaws. He put the phone next to his ear again.

'Fabian. Go talk to your mother. I published that article on her suggestion. She approved it.'

The line went dead.

Chapter 34

Kelly approached the ICU.

Compared to the rest of the hospital, it was dark and quiet, as if death had already visited to take her quota for the year. Nurses shuffled about like automatons, covered in blue robes and masks, as well as head gear, making them look like they were battling some kind of contagion. She went to the desk and introduced herself, showing her police lanyard.

The nurse behind the station nodded and removed her mask.

'Sorry, we're always trussed up like turkeys in here.' She held out her hand and Kelly took it.

'Mrs Reilly is expecting you, and I've set up a room for you. The waiting room is often empty because the relatives in here are either taking breaks elsewhere to get away from the tension, and taking a walk, or at the bedside.'

'Thank you,' Kelly said.

'Let me show you,' the nurse added.

Kelly followed her to a room at the end of a corridor, passing closed doors and vast windows glowing with the lights from machines. She had no idea which one was occupied by the Reilly family. The nurse took her into a room which was sparse and no more lit than anywhere else on the ward. There were a few chairs, but she remained standing. The nurse disappeared and Kelly sighed. This was the worst part of her job: dealing with the damage left behind by tragedy. It was a delicate skill and she was better suited to being out there catching the fuckers who caused the pain in the first place.

The nurse came back, followed by a woman who was introduced as Elaine Reilly. She was alone and Kelly was thankful. She knew that Lord Reilly had two adult children and sometimes kids had a way of muddying the waters when emotions ran high. She wanted to talk to them, but not right now. Elaine attempted a smile and Kelly felt for her. She couldn't imagine the stress of watching a loved one in a coma. It was bad enough being reminded of her mother dying of cancer, in this very hospital. The silence. The lack of hope. The nurses offering you endless cups of tea. The lack of sleep. The burden of the anguish, its incessant grip on all of your senses.

Elaine Reilly looked knackered.

'Should we sit down?' Kelly asked.

'If you don't mind, I'll stand. I've been sitting next to Donald all night and all day.'

The woman stretched. She was well presented, and so she should be as a cabinet minister's wife. She wore immaculately applied make-up, and her hair was coiffed. Kelly thought she'd seen her in the paper alongside her husband at some point, and she carried that air of a senior politician's wife: a combination of purgatory and privilege.

'How is he?' Kelly asked.

'To be honest, I have no idea. They test him every ten minutes, or so it seems,' Elaine said, smiling weakly.

'He's in the best place.' She instantly regretted her facile comment. 'Sorry, what I mean is, this hospital's critical care history is excellent.'

'I'm sure you know all about that in your line of work,' Elaine said respectfully.

Kelly liked her. But she was yet to delve into why someone might want to bring down her husband's helicopter, or why he was rubbing shoulders with somebody like Kennedy-Craig. She had to tread carefully. Elaine Reilly could easily be a sheep in wolf's clothing. Politicians didn't get to the top of the slippery pole without a ruthless spouse by their side.

'I'm going to ask you some direct questions and some of them might not seem relevant, and others, well, frankly impertinent,' Kelly said.

'Fire away, I've known the PM for twenty years; you can't scare me.'

Kelly smiled. 'There were some disturbances at the climate conference, did your husband discuss this with you?'

'Yes, he had an egg thrown at him. Par for the course in his work, I'm afraid.'

'Any other incidents we might not know about? Threatening letters? Stalkers? That kind of thing?'

'Not that I know of.'

'Did he discuss why he decided to catch a lift with Bartholomew Kennedy-Craig, rather than be chauffeured home like the other delegates?'

'No. I had no idea Bart was up there.'

'Bart? You know him personally?'

Elaine looked away. 'Unfortunately, yes. He's a prick. Excuse me.'

'No problem. Expand, please. I'm interested.' She saw that Elaine was studying her, measuring her up. Kelly saw some of the fire that was fitting for a member of the elite inner circle of government, and she knew she was about to get a glimpse of the true woman.

'I'm sorry, these questions, which I am more than happy answering, of course, they're making me feel as though my husband is under some kind of investigation. I thought you were being sent to me today to get a picture of Donald to help the Home Office counter the claims in the press.'

'Ah. No, I'm in charge of the investigation into the helicopter crash.'

'Investigation? It crashed.'

'Yes, it did. But we don't yet know why.'

Elaine stared at her. 'Why it crashed? You're telling me it wasn't an accident?'

'No. I'm not. Due to the delicate nature of the passenger list, there needs to be a thorough investigation to rule it out,' Kelly said.

Andrew Harris had told her that Elaine had been briefed over the phone. Clearly this was massaging the truth a little, or Elaine hadn't been listening.

'You're a detective inspector?' Elaine asked. She eyed Kelly's lanyard more carefully.

'I am.'

'And you're in charge of this investigation? Not the Air Accidents Investigation Branch?'

Elaine knew her processes.

'No. They're reporting to me.'

'I think I'll sit down now.'

Elaine sat. Kelly remained by the window, and took off her coat, suddenly warm.

'You were telling me how you knew Bartholomew Kennedy-Craig,' Kelly said.

'No I wasn't.'

The two women eyed each other.

'But I will. He was a toad. I don't want to speak ill of the dead, but he was. Donald liked everyone, he was a people person, and Bart was a smooth talker. He contributed party funds, but in return he expected favours.'

'What kind of favours?' Kelly asked.

'It's all in the public domain, and I gather you have full security clearance?' Elaine asked.

Kelly wasn't exactly sure what level of security clearance she was referring to. If it was MI6, then perhaps that was pushing it, but she knew she was on to something, and played the game.

'Yes. It's my investigation, I need to know everything,' she said.

'He was after certain things being kept out of the press – like his environment problems, for example. The conference was something Donald felt strongly about. He knew Bart ran thousands of small companies whose environmental record wasn't great, but there are ways to keep it legitimate.'

'Greenwashing?'

'Exactly.'

'Was your husband open to such pressure?' Kelly asked.

'I thought not, detective, but it would seem that he might have been after all. Why else would he spend the weekend with Bart? I called Vivienne, his wife. She brushed me off. She said she doesn't know anything either.'

Kelly did a quick catch-up in her head and realised that Elaine was talking about Vivienne Kennedy-Craig, Bart's wife, like they knew each other.

'You're close?'

'No. But I thought if anyone knew why Bart was up there, she would. So, she's either lying or he told her about as much as Donald told me.'

'I get the impression you have your suspicions about why they were together,' Kelly said.

Elaine looked at her and sighed.

'How much of this is to be used in the investigation?' Elaine asked.

Kelly realised that the woman was used to dealing with civil servants who not only massaged the truth for the public, but also decided what to feed them.

'This is a different game to politics, Elaine. I want to get to the truth.'

Elaine laughed. 'The truth! Who are you? Joan of Arc? The government won't allow one of its own to be smeared; you'll be used to bring solutions to the table, and that will be all. You must be incredibly naïve to think otherwise.'

Kelly was taken aback. And rattled.

'If there was a crime committed here, then I need to discover the motive in order to find out who was behind it. I assumed you'd want to know the truth.'

'This isn't about what I want, detective. It's about making sure whatever my husband was up to with Bart is kept to a minimum damage potential. Do you understand?'

Kelly nodded. 'Give me your worst case scenario.'

Elaine sighed, and Kelly thought she was about to open up to her, but instinct and years of being a Whitehall wife caught up with her.

'You strike me as the go-getter type, Joan. You figure it out.' Elaine got up and went to the door.

She turned as she opened it. 'For the record, I doubt it was climate protesters. In my experience they're a bunch of halfwits who love yelling, but have no balls. You're much more likely to find your truth if you look at Bart's businesses. If you'll excuse me, I have some difficult conversations to have with my children.'

'Wait, do you know where your husband stayed on Sunday night?' Kelly asked.

'I thought he was in a fancy hotel, but if Bartholomew Kennedy-Craig was throwing a party, then Donald would have been at it.'

She left.

Kelly was torn between admiration for the woman, who put duty before herself, and downright disgust that she was blatantly withholding information that could potentially help her investigation.

Joan of Arc… Bitch.

Chapter 35

Fabian burst into his mother's room, closely followed by Terrance.

'Sorry, madam, I tried to stop him,' Terrance whined.

'Fuck off,' Fabian barked, and slammed the door in his face.

'Darling, what irks you?' Vivienne purred.

She was sitting in bed, propped up by several pillows, her silver tea tray discarded on an occasional table, with the remnants on it of an afternoon pick-me-up. She put down her reading glasses and folded a newspaper.

'Jesus, Mother, you're fifty-five, not seventy-five! Why are you hiding in here?'

She cocked her head to the side and waited to find out what he really wanted to discuss.

'I see you've read it, then.' He nodded to the newspaper. 'I've just spoken to Quentin. What have you got to say about that?'

'Darling—'

'Don't darling me, Mother. Why the holy fuck would you approve such a thing?' He stood at the foot of the bed and ran his hands through his thick auburn hair. He was dressed in joggers and a grey hoodie.

Vivienne smiled at him and patted the bed. 'Come and sit down, and don't use foul language with me.'

'Mum, the profanity that falls out of your mouth would make any self-respecting twenty-four-year-old like me blush, and you know it. Don't change the subject,' he said. But already he was defeated by her charm. He trusted her as a mother, but not as the captain of this particular ship that his father had left in his care. As soon as the will was read, she'd know, and he could get on with his life. Being in the same room as her simply made him feel better because it was the only security he'd ever known. But soon he'd be on his own, as his father had intended. However she explained herself, he knew he'd accept it. He just wanted to hear it. He went to the bed and sat as he was bid.

'How is Quentin?' she asked.

He laughed. 'Mum, you're up to something and I want to know what it is. I'm absolutely gobsmacked that you would let such a respected newspaper trash Dad like that.'

'They're not trashing Dad, they're trashing Tactika, which is completely different. It's diversionary.'

'Diversionary?' he asked.

She held out her hand and took his. Her palms were warm and for a moment he felt relief. The strain of taking on his father's empire in its entirety, as his sole heir, weighed heavy on his shoulders, like a great burden. His mother had the skill to alleviate it, so he wanted to listen. That was why he'd come in here; to get some reassurance. Panic had engulfed him and he, as was his character, had allowed it to take over, and he'd spiralled down a negative-thinking hellhole. He listened.

'You are Tactika now. And I believe in you, my love,' she soothed. 'Dad's will is to be read first thing in the morning. The lawyers are coming here. They'll take their cut of course, as they have to, just for turning up, the blood-sucking bastards. However, when all's said and done, everything is ours and you have a lot to learn. In time, I will hand the reins to you. Your father's death will be overshadowed by other distractions in the media, I promise you that; it's already begun, so we have two choices. We can ignore it and allow it to rocket out of control. Or, we can manipulate it and try to lessen the damage.'

He overlooked her comment about his father's will. It wasn't going to go the way she planned, but he'd deal with that when the time came. His father had in recent years made plans, in private, for him to take over, albeit when he was ready. As for the other issue, he could see his mother's logic, although the thought of any criticism of his father in the press was hard to stomach. The idea of accepting one style of slander to avoid another was exasperating. But money could make many things go away, or morph into something unexpected, and Tactika had fingers in a multitude of media pies.

'It's all a game, Fabian. And you need to learn to get ahead. Think of any sport,' she said. 'Take skiing. You choose your turn before you get there, don't you? You place your pole in the snow way before your body even rises to sway you around it. Cricket. You watch the way the bowler runs, how he raises his arm before he lets the ball loose. You're reading if it's going to be long or short even before he's halfway down the area, trying to predict where it's going to land and where to place your bat. Business is the same, my darling. So is politics. Let them all have their say on your father. Success always comes with enemies, otherwise it wouldn't be an elite sport, would it? The secret is to predict what your enemies will do next, and get there first.'

She continued stroking his hand. Her words, as always, connected the dots in his mind. She was right. He had to hold his nerve. He knew first-hand that his father had many business ventures that, if exposed, could bring them unwelcome scrutiny and loss of confidence. Letting idiot conspiracy theorists to espouse a little, in a controlled way, could work to their advantage.

'But he called Dad a fraud, and a cheat,' he said. 'He's not even buried yet.'

'I know. But they're just words. Sticks and stones…'

'Oh for God's sake, Mum. We're not in primary school; we're talking about billions of dollars.'

'We're talking about people, and adults remain stuck in that school playground. Where do we learn to fight? And to survive? And to win?' she asked him. 'And as for news, my God, it lasts a day. By the time your father is buried, this will all have blown over. Quentin is publishing another article this afternoon about your work in South America.'

'What?'

'People who don't bother finding the facts for themselves and rely on a daily fix of news are lazy, Fabian. Give them the faults first, then show them the philanthropy behind it, and forgiveness follows very quickly. Besides, it was your father who might have made a few mistakes. His heir isn't going to be like him. Give him a chance. Forgive past blunders. That's what people love to do. Let them lambast the dead, what does it matter? We know who your father was and that's all that deserves our energy. The shares will be back up by this afternoon, you watch.'

He smiled. 'I hate them talking about Dad like he was some kind of heartless hustler.'

'I know. But there is so much worse they could be saying about him. You should feel sorry for the family of Lord Reilly. Now there's a family who is about to fall spectacularly from grace. He's being demolished in the press, and he might survive to read it all. He'll lose his job, his credibility, and possibly his family.'

She took the newspaper and opened it at another page. One that he'd missed in his vision of red mist that had skewed his every thought. He hadn't seen the article on Lord Reilly. She gave it to him.

'Hypocrite has to go.' He scanned the article. It was a damning diatribe on Lord Reilly's track record of accepting perks from private Tory investors, like his father. When he came across his father's name, he winced, but he forced himself to finish it. *'How can he remain the face of tackling climate change when in private, he's in bed with the biggest producers of fossil fuels?'*

'It's called survival, darling. Damage limitation is just that: you have to accept a little bit of water in the lifeboat, and it's worrying and annoying, but what you need is to make sure not too much gets in to sink it. Then you sail off and start again.'

His mother had always spoken in analogies, allegories and stories. It was her style. When he was a kid, he'd thought her poetic and goddess-like. She had a way of making even his shittest days at boarding school seem manageable, and it was as if he grew up in a fantasy world with the friends and legends she'd created in his mind. Now, though, as an adult, he saw her for what she really was: a ruthless fucking bitch who always won. Maybe that was why she stayed in bed all day, like a vampire, preserving her energy for her next kill.

'And did you have a little chat to Quentin about this article too, Mother?' he asked.

'Of course, darling. And there's plenty more where that came from, should the noise around your father not subside quite as quickly as I'd like.'

'Why was Dad with Donald up there at the conference, really?'

'We'll probably never know, darling. Let's not think the worst.'

'It can never get out,' Fabian said.

'It won't,' she replied.

Chapter 36

Kelly walked into the incident room at Eden House, and went straight to the coffee machine. They'd clubbed together to buy a fancy De'Longhi model that frothed milk as well as made the best coffee. Between around fifteen of them who worked at the serious crime unit full time, it had been a bargain and worth every penny. The only problem was that there was always someone stood waiting. It was that good. The other problem was that now Kelly drank around five cups of coffee per day. She'd started using sweetener instead of spoonfuls of sugar, though.

'Boss, I think we need to think about placing a cordon around the Laurie Fell estate. A video has been posted online, showing some kind of party there over the weekend, and some journos have begun gathering there.'

'Really? Can I see it?'

'There are loads of them,' Rob said, swinging round on his chair. 'This will really stick in the knife. The Kennedy-Craigs are getting sick of reporters outside their residence in London too, and Downing Street, as well as the hospital,' Rob added.

'That bad?' Kelly asked. The coffee machine was free. She grabbed a cup and set it up, slipping in a pod. She always chose the colour she fancied, rather than what combination of roast was actually inside the thing. Today it was red. The milk compartment bubbled and spat.

'Come and have a look. It's on Instagram, Facebook, and Twitter. Lord Reilly has over one hundred and fifty thousand followers on Twitter, and Kennedy-Craig, though no Alan Sugar, has a healthy two million. There's a holy battle raging, and all the Facebook Karens are taking their bras off.'

Kelly hit him playfully round the head.

'Keyboard warriors?' Kate chipped in. It was a joke, but carried with it a heavy dose of caution. Opinions online, hate and rage, could swing public opinion. Especially against the police. They knew that first-hand. Words, even digital ones, out there in the ether, were now as dangerous as knives. Monitoring social media was something that Kelly did on every case now, as a matter of course.

She grabbed a chair with her free hand and sat next to Rob, who started a video clip. It was taken from the shore of a lake, and the filming was directed towards a large house. She could tell it was large because all the windows were lit, and there were dozens of them. It looked clandestine, as if the taker of the phone footage wasn't invited to the party.

'Dan and Emma have seen it and say it's definitely Laurie Fell. The house that sits on Ullswater, where Kennedy-Craig was staying,' Rob said.

Kelly looked across at Emma, who nodded.

'Housekeeper's a cow,' Emma added for good measure.

'I've got a present for you,' Kelly said to her. 'The warrant came through on my phone. It's yours.'

'Result,' Emma said. 'Ready?' she asked Dan, who stood up and grabbed his coat. Kelly turned back to the screen and sipped her coffee. It was delicious.

'Guys, before you go, come and show me the layout,' Kelly asked. Emma and Dan made their way across to Rob's desk, leaning over it.

The footage showed Laurie Fell and whoever was filming moved closer, paying particular attention to the low thud of music seemingly coming from one room on the ground floor. The people filming began to giggle, and a figure was seen dancing on the grass in front of the phone. Then it ended.

'Quiet night, just the two of them talking global warming, then. This won't look good at all, will it?' she said. 'Though it's not exactly a capacity rave. Play it again.'

Dan and Emma peered over Rob's shoulder. Dan leant over and paused the film, as the vista appeared at its fullest. He pointed out the back of the house and the wooden storage facility where he'd identified equipment for the helicopter.

'It's not a hundred per cent clear if Lord Reilly was there, though,' Dan said. 'The housekeeper was giving nothing away.'

'Why would she feel obliged to hide information like that?' Kelly asked. 'It's too late for the Reilly family anyway. The public have already decided he was there. What I need to establish is if the two pilots were also there. We need to bring the housekeeper in under oath, and formally interview her.'

'Here's another one,' Rob said, clicking some keys on his computer.

They huddled around and watched as a video taken from Snapchat showed two young figures in the grounds of the Laurie Fell, dancing in front of the camera. Teenagers had a handy habit of typing a strapline across everything they posted and this one read: '*Wasted Sunday night!*' It seemed intentionally vague but it confirmed the location and date.

'Do we know whose accounts these are being posted from?' Kelly asked.

'I've got two names.'

'Locals?'

'Yup. Teenagers.'

'Right, pick them up for questioning,' Kelly said. 'Anything else?'

'The girlfriends of the pilots were interviewed earlier today,' Kate said.

Kelly turned around. Kate was standing behind them, holding several printouts. The inquiry was countrywide, though the investigation was based here in the Lake District.

'One of the girlfriends lives in Holloway and she's a student nurse. The other lives in Peckham, she's a teacher. She was sent some WhatsApp messages by her boyfriend on Sunday night, bragging about where he'd been put up for the night. She didn't know what it was called but my guess is that it's some kind of swanky residence here in the Lakes.'

'Right, have you got the messages?' Kelly asked.

Kate nodded.

'Let Dan and Emma have a look. Familiar?' she asked them.

Dan and Emma flanked Kate on either side and stared at her phone. Sure enough, the images showed one of the pilots giving the thumbs-up beside an enormous bed, then the view from his window. It was of Ullswater. They judged it to be the same stretch as could be seen from the Laurie Fell estate.

'That's as good as a positive for me,' Kelly said. 'I want the housekeeper brought in under caution. I imagine the family will provide a lawyer, if they haven't already.' She referred to the Kennedy-Craigs. If the housekeeper was in their clutches, as she seemed to be, then it was expected that she'd be protected.

'I took the liberty of tasking a constable to trawl through these social media accounts responsible for the footage,' Rob said. It was a good move, and a standard one. Kelly nodded. She sipped her coffee.

'Right, we have lots to work on. I want all social media posts from the weekend connected in any way to the Laurie Fell estate, collated and traced to real people. Let's pick them up and get a picture of what was going on there, particularly on Sunday night. Meanwhile, I've got a telephone call with a station in Manchester who've managed to pick up our egg-thrower. Several protesters were arrested at the scene but released. However, the ones in the photos were recognised as usual suspects at protests like these. They seemed to pack up and go home pretty quickly, which I guess is standard behaviour for climate conferences – cause trouble and piss off – but we'll get what we can anyway. The toxicology hasn't yet come back from the bodies of the pilots, but it's quite obvious they weren't resting, like pilots should the night before their flight.'

'Boss,' Rob said.

They all looked at him. Emma had her bag slung over her shoulder, ready to run a marathon if needed, Dan two paces behind her, in a padded coat, replenishing their takeaway cups with coffee.

'Look at this,' he said, peering at his screen.

They assembled around his screen once more and watched as he played a video posted by a social media account belonging to somebody called @Sasha4, late Sunday night. It showed two girls, barely eighteen, if they were even that old, walking across the gravel towards the entrance of Laurie Fell house. They weren't trying to hide, indicating they were supposed to be there, unlike the other videos. Their faces were smothered in make-up and they wore sparkly earrings and furry coats. The video was taken as a selfie and it wobbled with the taker's unsteady hand. Each girl could be seen to be carrying a large bottle of what appeared to be alcohol, and both smoked cigarettes. They beamed into the camera. The strapline read: '*Going at it hard. $$$Bills*'.

It was crass, cringe-worthy, immature and off-putting, but that wasn't the point. It was evidence that at least two people were invited to the grounds of the Laurie Fell estate on Sunday night. And they weren't pilots or politicians.

Chapter 37

The not-so-young activist who'd thrown the egg at Lord Reilly was a professional troublemaker. The report on Neil Hardy's background revealed that he'd started his protesting career in the nineties with the poll tax riots. Since then he'd been arrested at football matches, various industrial strikes at the Barrow shipyard, and a car plant in Essex, making his way steadily up to hunt sabotaging. There was a wealth of information on him, and he'd been arrested for affray and assault a total of fifteen times. His arrest for egging Lord Reilly would likely land him a prison sentence.

A small group of journalists had got wind of the video online and had begun the trial by public opinion, which always ended badly. They jumped on the egg-thrower outside the station and he'd arrived pleased with himself that he'd got attention for his cause. He was cocky and reckless.

Two detective constables were tasked with his interview held in a station in the centre of Manchester. Kelly watched by video link, and had the ability to direct the questioning. Her job was to watch him and interfere as little as she could, giving her an impression of the man who'd caused Lord Reilly the very open and widely reported embarrassment during the conference. Whether or not the same man could have been involved somehow in the bringing down of the aircraft remained to be seen.

Kelly watched him closely. He bore the expected swagger of somebody who'd enjoyed five minutes in the overt limelight of being a civil nuisance. It might not end well for him, given the charges, and the fact that his last sentence was a suspended one. Regardless of the outcome of the interview, it looked like Neil Hardy was going back to prison. She sighed at the game these petty criminals played. Her Majesty's penal system, if one landed in a category C institution, was not onerous, and could be seen by some as an acceptable way of life. There was no deterrent against that. The prison system was full of them.

Neil Hardy's address was given as a squat in the centre of the city of Manchester, near Centrepoint, on North Parade. A legal aid lawyer sat next to him and the two DCs began the interview. He was under caution and so his rights were read to him. The CPS had approved the charges in record time. The inquiry into Lord Reilly's death had sent ripples around the country, and the two detectives were happy to do their bit to take a scumbag off the streets. However, all interviews had to be approached with a certain grace. If they wanted to get anything out of the suspect, they couldn't go in there threatening and getting in his face. Those days were gone. They were on tape and being recorded. It was their brief to find out what else Neil Hardy had been up to over the weekend. If anything. Kelly's hunch was that he had nothing to do with the helicopter accident, but she wasn't ruling it out. If he was involved then her first impressions of the man was of a follower, not a leader. Egg-throwing was probably the height of his activism on behalf of democracy. Terrorism?

She doubted it. She studied him with interest on her screen.

'Were you in the Lake District for business or pleasure, Neil?' one detective asked. The lawyer sat staring at her notes, as they usually did. They were there for the record.

Kelly noticed Neil fidgeting. He asked if he could smoke. Kelly rolled her eyes.

'No, Neil, we became a no-smoking constabulary over ten years ago. You know that.'

Kelly watched as he smiled and put a fag behind his ear. He carried on fiddling.

The lawyer nodded to her client and Neil prepared to speak.

'I was at the conference to bring attention to this government's appalling record on climate change,' he said defiantly. 'I'm no murderer,' he added contemptuously, to which the lawyer shuffled uncomfortably. This was a good sign, it showed that Neil Hardy was in the habit of going rogue. Kelly had already emailed over the questions she wanted asking, and the detective constables were doing a good job. Hardy denied being in Cumbria to bring serious harm to Lord Reilly.

'I didn't rightly care who the egg hit, mind. I was glad, though, when it hit him.'

'So you weren't aiming it at him?' the constable asked.

'Nah. I'm not a good shot,' Neil winked.

'Were you aware of any other plans to sabotage the climate conference?'

'No.'

'Were you aware of any associates of yours who were planning to cause serious harm to Lord Reilly?'

'No.'

And so it went on.

'So it wasn't an accident, then?' Neil asked.

Kelly acknowledged his intelligence. He wasn't as stupid as he looked. She rubbed her eyes and continued watching the merry dance, feeling sorry for the two officers.

'Do you know something that would indicate that it wasn't an accident?'

'Nice try. No.'

'Where did you stay during the conference?'

'In a campsite in Patterdale, just down the road. We all did.'

'Names of those you travelled with?'

Neil gave them willingly, though they might not have been legitimate. They'd have to check them all out.

'Any newcomers to the party, Neil?' The officer referred to Neil's established network of protesters. It was the same at every gig; the same punters turned up, caused trouble and pissed off. Kelly wanted to know if he recognised all of them.

He sat back in his chair. He looked at his lawyer, who nodded again. Kelly paid attention.

'Neil?'

'Well, there was this fella. A local arsehole, excuse my French. He was bragging about bringing down the government. He was slaughtered, man; I mean he was proper off his head. I reckon he'd done some serious gear. He was on his own, talking to anyone who'd listen. Trying to provoke us, like.'

'What do you mean, provoke?'

'He said we didn't know what we were doing, said we were amateurs, all the lads and lasses saw it. Ask them, I've given you all the names.'

'Can you describe him?'

'Sure. What do I get?' he asked.

Kelly pressed her mic and spoke to one of the officers, telling him that negotiating his sentence for affray and assault this time was in the hands of the court judge on the day, but they could file with the judge the fact that he colluded with the police in an important inquiry. It might make a difference, no guarantees.

The message was relayed to Neil Hardy.

'You'd have to give us something that made a difference to our inquiry, Neil. Why did he stand out? What was he bragging about that we might be interested in?'

'Because he said the way to bring down rich bastards is to hit them hard and fast, like, take them out. He said egging them and shit was child's play.'

Kelly watched him. She could tell that Hardy had been offended by the stranger, whoever he might be, and this wasn't all bullshit.

'Did you get a name?'

'Nah.' Kelly didn't believe him.

'Which campsite did you say it was?'

'The Green Lead Slate Camp, behind the pub on the corner. Not a bad place, cheap. I've stayed in worse,' Neil said.

Kelly knew there was CCTV there, because she'd requested it before, in an old case that sent shivers down her spine. She tapped her pen on her pad.

'Is that where you met him?'

'Yeah, he was hanging about; he was banging on the door of the big white pub, shouting at them to let him in for a lock-in,' Neil laughed at the fond memory. 'He said they should open for him because he had a wad of cash as big as his pocket.'

Kelly spoke to the officers. 'Clarify it's the White Lion in Patterdale that he's talking about,' she said. It was.

The landlord would surely remember a pisshead banging on their door past closing, demanding more booze. They might have CCTV too. It was another lead at least.

She instructed the constables to get a description of the man and press Hardy further for information. He had nowhere else to be in a hurry.

Chapter 38

Kelly called the proprietor of the White Lion pub in Patterdale and spoke to a waitress preparing for evening service.

She said she'd go and find somebody in charge. Anybody who might give her some answers would do.

Finally a woman came on the phone and shouted at it, as if the receiver was hard of hearing. Kelly pulled the phone back from her ear.

'This is Detective Inspector Kelly Porter,' she repeated.

'Oh. The police?' The woman's nature changed instantly. At least Kelly now had her attention. The woman confirmed she was on shift on Sunday night and she did indeed remember a man banging on the door gone midnight, demanding more booze.

'It's not unusual. Are we in trouble? I didn't let him in.'

'No, not at all, all I want to know is if you knew him.'

'Oh yes, he's done it before. It was Paul Edderbridge. Proper dickhead, excuse me. He's a real pain sometimes. He just needs a firm hand, but some of the younger girls are afraid of him.'

Kelly racked her brain as to where she'd heard the name before and then realised that it was the man who'd assaulted his girlfriend on Sunday, and was in the cells sobering up when she came in on Monday night. She thanked the woman and asked her if she could identify the man if she sent over a photograph, and she said she could. Meanwhile, Kelly downloaded the only image they had of Paul Edderbridge, taken the night he was brought in for beating up his girlfriend, and sent it to the two DCs in Manchester, hoping for a positive ID from Neil Hardy. Kelly didn't think that, from what they knew about Paul Edderbridge to date, it was normal for him to be carrying large amount of cash around with him.

Her phone buzzed and she saw that it was Zoe from the AAIB.

'Hi Zoe, any news?'

'Well, we've reviewed the combined flight data and cockpit voice recorder. It confirms there was a catastrophic loss of power to the tail rotor twenty minutes into the flight. That would put them over Wast Water and close to the crash site. They slowed down to watch the fell race, then there was a pull anticlockwise, indicating the tail rotor failed, and they went into an uncontrollable spin. It was harrowing.'

'I'm sure it was,' Kelly said.

'Those pilots were working against unbelievable g-force, and disorientation would have been overwhelming, but they fought, that's for sure. They tried to deal with every warning that sounded, and they had their shit together. They didn't give up.'

There was a silence as Kelly absorbed the terror experienced by the pilots as they fought for their lives.

'And the hydraulic line?'

'Yes, we're working on that as our strongest culprit so far. A steady loss of hydraulic fluid wouldn't have made much difference to torque or power until enough had been leaked, and that coincides with the tail rotor failure, so the timing fits.'

'Coincides?'

'That's the word we use, Kelly. As far as I'm concerned, up to now anyway, that is our working theory. The mechanics who've been examining it all agree that hydraulic lines don't erode in that way, and so our reasonable conclusion is that it was either faulty at manufacture, which is impossible because it has over seven hundred hours of flight, or that it was cut prior to this individual flight.'

'Thanks, Zoe,' Kelly said. It was depressing news. The report wouldn't be ready for weeks, but she still had to investigate the crash with an open mind. 'How's the Wasdale Inn?' Kelly tried to lighten the load.

'I'm moving to a place in Penrith this evening, to be closer to the hangar. It's a nice part of the world. I wish I hadn't been brought here under the current circumstances,' Zoe said.

'Is Lance Tatterall still around?'

'Yes, I'm keeping him up here until we're done. The powers that be at the MOD have agreed. Funny how a disaster involving a senior politician brings all the resources I need to my door,' Zoe replied. 'Any news your end?'

'Plenty to go on. I might need Lance to meet me at the Laurie Fell estate. It's near Ullswater.'

'That means absolutely nothing to me,' Zoe said.

'Of course it doesn't. It's not far from Penrith. If you've got time, let's meet there and you can have a look at where we think the helicopter was hangared over Sunday night.'

'Of course, let me know and give me the satnav, otherwise I may never find it.'

They hung up.

Kelly walked out of her office and over to Rob's desk, perching on the edge. It was fully dark now. It had been a long day. Kelly loved the winter. There were certainly fewer tourists. People chose to spend Christmas with their families rather than climbing, and the towns across the national park tended to be quiet. It was the perfect time to tackle favourite fells for those locals who lusted after the silence and solace the respite provided. Not so now, though. The place was rammed with journalists and reporters. They seemed to be camped everywhere, asking passers-by about what they knew. The car park at the foot of Scafell Pike was no exception. Network teams were living in tents there, in freezing conditions, because Jock at the Wasdale Inn wasn't allowing them to stay, and his was the only option for miles. It made Kelly smile. Not so long ago, when she worked in the capital, she'd been disparaging about provincial attitudes to progress and intrusion, but now she realised that it was a source of comfort. She wouldn't go back to London if her salary doubled.

'This is a printout of Kennedy-Craig's visits to Laurie Fell over the past year. You can see he's a regular,' Rob said.

'Why didn't he buy it? He had enough money,' Kelly said.

'Tax purposes probably; this way he used the expenses to offset tax and avoid the HMRC. He ran an account solely for Laurie Fell, and other places of a similar nature around the country and all over the world. He barely went home.'

'Where's all this from?'

'It's part of the Tactika accounts sent to us by their bank. You just have to know what to look for.'

'It's all just figures to me,' Kelly said, looking at his screen. 'What kind of money are we talking?'

'To be honest, boss, it's more what he spent it on. I've done the calculations and on a one-week visit to Laurie Fell in the autumn, he spent seven hundred grand.'

'What?'

'Helicopter rides, equipment for maintenance, staff, food and wine accounts for over two hundred of that; he had Beluga caviar flown in from London, you know, from the place on Piccadilly near the Ritz?'

'Yes, I know it.' Kelly said.

'There's also a ton of cash changing hands here, and if I was looking at a drug dealer's accounts I'd say he was laundering, but he's not, he's spending it.'

'On what?'

'We'll never know. He's typical of many mega rich business people who carry cash all the time; it's another way to avoid tax in the country of residence and elsewhere. It'll take me some time to work it out, and I'd like to start with the housekeeper. If she was paid in cash then you can bet that others were. The size of the place indicates he'd need many more staff to clean, cook, organise events and the like. It just doesn't add up that he was there for quiet retreat-type stays. It's a blatant lie, I just need to prove it.'

'And Dan and Emma said Nellie Lowther told them she looked after the place herself, and employed no one,' Kelly said. 'And what were those girls doing there? Did the dollar bill signs mean they were making money? I doubt they turned up there for bridge lessons.'

'Exactly.'

Chapter 39

'Have you seen this?' Kate asked Kelly as she made her way to the lift. She fastened her coat and stopped to listen to what Kate had to say. She showed her a newspaper article on her phone.

'Published online about an hour ago,' Kate said.

'More sleaze for the Tories: Lord Reilly was attending sex party' the headline read.

'Oh hello,' Kelly sighed. 'Any legs in it?'

'No idea, you want me to check it out?' Kate asked.

Kelly nodded. 'Walk with me. I'm driving over to Laurie Fell. The forensic teams are setting up tonight. After that, I'm heading home.' She was freezing and her body felt like it was seizing up. It was as if her bones had petrified up there on the mountain and they hadn't woken up yet. She shivered.

'You coming down with something?' Kate asked.

'Hope not.' She sneezed. 'Oh bugger.'

'I'll call this journalist.'

'She won't tell you a thing,' Kelly said.

They both knew it was true. Reporters didn't have to reveal their sources, even to police. However, she might be able to get an impression of what had led to the headline. Rob had called the author of the story that had broken this morning and it was a dead end. The journalist had revealed nothing they didn't already know, though he did say that he'd been trying to get his work published in the broadsheets for years and suddenly, the bigger names had contacted him over this, not the other way around. Quentin St John had called him privately.

Kelly sneezed again.

'Why don't you just go straight home?' Kate asked.

Kelly raised her eyebrows in response.

'I know, you can tell me to fuck off, but you're no good to anyone ill. Maybe a good night's sleep is what you need. You were on the mountainside all day yesterday and I bet you didn't eat a good meal.'

'You're right. I didn't. Laurie Fell is not far from home, I might as well kick them off to a good start; there are certain things I want them to look for.'

'Whips and chains, according to this article,' Kate said.

'Let's have a look, then,' Kelly said. She shivered again and took Kate's phone. The article was written by a freelance journalist, like they all were these days. It reported that Bartholomew Kennedy-Craig was known for his gatherings in exclusively private residences, and the soliciting of dozens of women and girls to provide the entertainment.

'As far as I can see, there's no solid evidence, just lots of soundbites in speech marks to avoid libel litigation,' Kelly said.

'This says it's been going on for years, so why the leak now, I wonder. Who stands to gain from rubbishing Kennedy-Craig? Not the government. Not their families surely. Political enemies?' Kelly asked.

'I'll call her,' Kate said. Kelly finished her coffee and walked to the lift. She'd be back for morning brief nice and early.

Chapter 40

Laurie Fell Estate was almost four hundred years old. Its consummate anonymity was what had obviously attracted Kennedy-Craig in the first place, and Kelly wondered what it must be like to have that much money. They knew that it cost him fifteen grand per month to secure on a retainer. It was a different world and one she needed to understand to get to the bottom of the relationship between Lord Reilly and Bartholomew Kennedy-Craig. After all, it struck her that if the crash was caused by sabotage, then they had no idea who the target was, or if it was both of them.

What was bugging her was exactly how it was done, which was why she'd asked Zoe and Lance to meet her there, with the technical plans of an AW139 hydraulic system.

It was almost nine p.m. What had begun as a light splattering of wet hail had now turned into fully fat snowflakes as she drove along the north shore of Ullswater. They cast a spell on her as the windscreen wipers worked hard to keep them out of her vision. As she navigated the single road and all of its sharp bends, her eyes were drawn to a bright aura of lights above the treeline to the west. As she approached the entrance to the estate, she knew that it must be the lights from the forensic team tents set up around the house. It amazed her that when they were investigating a standard middle-of-the-week burglary or domestic, funds were tight and the machinery of investigation slow, but when a cabinet minister was thrown in the mix, suddenly the resources were infinite.

The long drive swerved this way and that and she finally came to a wide open gravel entrance, flanked by huge pristine planters full of evergreen hardies. The stone facade was impressive, and looked odd being used as a thoroughfare for men and women in white overalls, carrying boxes and bags to and from several vans parked up to the side. She got out of the car and Zoe appeared from the shadows and greeted her.

'I got your text. Lance is round the back looking at where the equipment for the helicopter is stored. There's a lot of stuff, but I get the impression that Kennedy-Craig hired 'copters whenever he was up here. He liked to impress, and he hangared them here for privacy. There's kit for all sorts of maintenance and overnight provisions, as well as de-icing equipment.'

'I read your email. The cockpit voice recorder has them de-icing on Monday for a good hour,' Kelly said, following her.

Zoe nodded. 'It's standard, nothing to worry about. The blades should have worked perfectly well afterwards, and the flight data recorder showed no irregularities that would indicate an icing issue, so we've ruled it out. The question is, who had access to these outhouses on Sunday night?'

Kelly nodded and they continued to walk around the vast property. White tents were erected all over the huge lawn and she could see the jetty and boathouse on the lake where she knew the social media posts had been filmed.

'We've hit our first problem,' Zoe said.

Kelly stopped walking. 'I love your optimism. I can see a thousand problems with this case; so far you've got one.'

Zoe grinned. 'All the CCTV has been wiped. There are cameras at the main entrance, and at the boathouse, as well as a couple on bedroom balconies. The officer in charge is a good egg.'

'That's because I chose her,' Kelly said. 'And told her to cooperate with you fully.'

'Thanks. Well she has. The station that housed the digital CCTV feed is in the basement, and it's completely blank. We don't even have footage from anyone arriving last week. It's gone. Or it never worked.'

'Curious, because the owner told my officers that Kennedy-Craig looked at the CCTV on Monday morning to see if he could catch who had left the graffiti on the side of the house, and it was working then. Will you be able to tell if it was wiped since then?' Kelly asked.

'Not straight away. The equipment was unplugged. I saw them bag it to take away, so when they analyse it they can see when the IP address was last used. If it was Monday then I'd say you have a problem.'

'Where's the owner?'

'In her private house over there.' Zoe pointed to the small cottage behind some large mature trees.

'The warrant doesn't extend to her private residence,' Kelly said. 'Now I know that information I'll request it, but if she was the one who wiped the CCTV then I doubt we'll find anything inside her house.'

'Well if it was her who tidied up inside then she did a shit job, so look at the positives,' Zoe said.

They carried on walking and came to a wooden barn, much like the others around it. Kelly saw Lance inside checking various boxes of equipment. He stopped what he was doing and walked towards Kelly.

'Have you told her?' he asked Zoe, who shook her head.

'Told me what?' Kelly asked.

'This has got to be one of the most badly organised excuses for a maintenance shed we've ever seen. There's shit everywhere. Boxes of tools, stuff left around, wires and spare parts, no paperwork, and I mean *zero* paperwork. I flew with both of those pilots and I have no idea what would make them so casual.'

'Money?' Kelly suggested.

'It's out of character and goes against everything they learn in the forces. They know money can't buy safety,' Lance said.

'People get carried away, arrogant even, complacent at least,' she said. 'They get put up overnight here in a swanky pad, they tell their girlfriends they're being treated like lords, told everything is taken care of, plus they get paid more money than they've ever been paid before. Cushy deal, wouldn't you say?' Kelly asked.

'I just can't believe they would compromise themselves like that,' Lance said.

'I get where she's coming from. Ninety per cent of accidents I investigate are pilot error caused by poor judgement. Humans and machines are not great bedfellows,' Zoe said.

It was Kelly's best working theory that the pilots were wooed so successfully by the good things in life that they simply let their standards slip. It wouldn't be the first time.

'But they wouldn't have cut their own hydraulic line,' Kelly said. 'We have to work on the assumption that somebody got to the chopper on Sunday night when the private party was in full swing. It was posted on social media and so it was no secret, although we're just catching up.'

'It had to be Sunday night or Monday morning because the chopper couldn't have flown more than twenty minutes with that cut in the line, and it didn't,' Zoe said. 'The flight log was computerised, thankfully; that's a huge benefit of these new models. It flew here on Saturday, from a trip over the sea and back, at sunset. Seems like a leisure trip. After that, it was stationary, here, until Monday morning.'

'Show me how easy it is to get to a hydraulic line on one of these things,' Kelly asked.

Lance found a space on a workbench and rolled out some plans, telling her that she was looking at the tail rotor blade of an AW139. It didn't look that technical, in as much as she thought she could find her way around it, if someone showed her how.

'All you would need to be told is how to get into the compartment, and which line to slice, that's it,' Zoe said.

'That's it?' Kelly asked.

'It's like sabotaging a car,' Lance said. 'If you're going to do it, you can do it. Everything you need is under the bonnet. There's no alarm or safety mechanism to deter somebody if that's their agenda,' he said.

'So it wouldn't have to be somebody technically minded or trained at all?' Kelly asked.

'You've got someone, haven't you?' Zoe asked.

'Not yet, I've got a few options I'm looking into,' Kelly replied. 'Good work.' She turned away. Then turned back. 'How long would it take to get in here and cut the line?' she asked.

'Ten minutes,' Lance said.

'Jesus. And they'd be stupid to walk in the front gate... my guess is they came by boat,' Kelly said, peering down to the lake. The moon reflected off the water and she could make out the shape of the boathouse.

'I'll be inside if you need me,' she said and walked towards the back of the house, where she'd seen people coming in and out.

She took a set of overalls and shoe covers, put on plastic gloves and went inside to look for the senior forensic officer. She found her huddled around the kitchen table, speaking to several other officers about what to do with the exhibits they'd collated so far, which were clearly mounting up. They knew one another and had worked plenty of scenes before.

'Evening,' Kelly said.

The officer greeted her warmly, and her eyes crinkled in a friendly manner indicating that she was smiling under her mask.

'Hey, Kelly, I'm glad you made it. You want to see this! Christ, this place is a shrine to fun, fun, fun,' she said.

'What do you mean?' Kelly asked her.

'It's like my son's university halls but twenty times bigger, and I know he'd hate for his mother to know what he gets up to, but I can't leave my job at the door when I'm allowed to visit. This place is set up to entertain, and I mean *entertain*. We've got booze, cameras, music decks, film-making equipment, dress-up stuff, games and so on. Now there's nothing illegal in that, I don't have to tell you that, but there are a few images that we've found that might be concerning. Upstairs, there are seven master suites, and each of them has a collection of items that are quite obviously used for bondage games. Now, the disturbing and possibly illegal bit is that there's a lot of schoolgirl garb up there. Now, when you come across a scene like this, that's standard; these pervs love schoolgirl shit, but this is predominant. Also we've taken several computers – we won't know what's on them until they're properly examined, including the master control for the CCTV cameras, but we found stacks of old-fashioned Polaroids – school-theme heavy – and plenty of them are of girls who look underage. Then there's the drugs swabs – actually too many to give you a figure just yet, it's everywhere. Whoever had the job of cleaning this place, they did a crap job, or they never thought they'd be caught, or they were just stupid and didn't realise what they were doing. There are bags of rubbish everywhere. It's as if somebody was in the middle of tidying up and just gave up.'

Kelly took it all in and looked towards the house lived in by Nellie Lowther. She'd told Dan and Emma that she was responsible for the entire upkeep of the place. In her investigative brain, none of it proved anything, just that there were private kinky parties here, in all likelihood with the owner's consent, but if no money changed hands, then they were frankly legitimate and on private property. Except if the school paraphernalia wasn't just fantasy. Depending on the outcome of the drug swabs, they could have the drug squad brought in and bring charges for that.

'Show me the Polaroids,' she asked.

The forensic officer took her to an evidence bag and handed it to Kelly, who, with gloves on, carefully opened it and looked through the contents. There were plenty of girls in various stages of dress, but it was difficult to tell their ages because of all the make-up and props. She stopped at one of the photographs, and stared at it.

It was of the two young women who'd uploaded a video of themselves at Laurie Fell on Sunday night.

'I need to keep this,' she said.

'Go ahead. Keep it in the bag, though,' the officer said. 'I'd better get on, this is an all-nighter.'

'Of course,' Kelly said, folding the image inside the clear bag. She rang Kate and asked her how she was getting on with the social media hunt for the two young women, and told her about the Polaroid.

'I'm just on it now. I should have full names and addresses for you soon, their privacy settings are shocking – oh and by the way,' Kate said.

'Yes?'

'They're fifteen years old and go to the school where Nellie Lowther used to teach.'

Kelly was beginning to understand why Elaine Reilly might not want her husband's name associated with this place, and why the Kennedy-Craigs were being hauled over the coals in the press. It might also give her a motive for why somebody might want both of them dead.

'That's not all,' Kate said.

'Go on,' Kelly said.

'A boat was stolen from Pooley Bridge jetty on Sunday night. I've requested their CCTV and they're sending it over.'

Chapter 41

Kate packed up her things to leave for the evening. She'd called the parents of the two schoolgirls who'd uploaded a video of themselves at Laurie Fell. Neither had answered, and she'd left messages. It was imperative to make contact with them. Kate had looked at the images over and over again, unbelieving and horrified. As the mother of young women, Kate had a terrible feeling in her gut. Lord Reilly was in his sixties, and Bartholomew Kennedy-Craig in his fifties. There weren't many plausible reasons why two overdressed and made-up fifteen-year-old girls would have got an invitation to spend the evening with them.

Given what Kelly had been shown at the mansion – the Polaroids and the gear that had been found – Kate couldn't help feeling, and Kelly agreed with her, that there might be more than sensationalism to the story in the press about the type of parties Kennedy-Craig enjoyed. She'd found the two girls easily online, from their profiles on Snapchat. They both attended the same school in Keswick, and their ages had come as a shock. Kate had also looked at their Instagram pages and found that they had thousands of followers, and it wasn't difficult to see why. Their uploads were heavy on the selfies and parties, like all teenagers. She should know, especially because her youngest was still in the grips of the obsession with appearance, and the insecurity-driven half-naked selfies, figure-hugging dresses, underwear and boob shots. It was a constant battle trying to get her to tone it down and understand that whatever she posted online would stay in the ether forever, and could never be taken down.

These two girls were no different. What amazed her was the lack of privacy settings on their accounts. Anybody around the globe could access them and see their most intimate photos, captioned with laments of teenage loneliness and vulnerability.

Chloe Tate and Sasha Granger were typical fifteen-year-olds, but that meant different things to different people. In Kate's day, as a fifteen-year-old, decades ago, the quintessential schoolgirl on the cusp of adulthood, raging with hormones, was likely to be found in the same dresses, covered in the same amount of make-up, displaying their desire to be noticed not on an international platform, but down the local pub, trying desperately to get served alcohol. Now the booze was irrelevant. There was a dealer on every park bench and at every school gate, and the attention came thick and fast into your inbox. The neighbourhood bar, with a few perverts hanging about, had turned into a gigantic international market, with no hours, no closing time, no taxi rank and no exit.

She'd trawled through countless images of the two girls advertising themselves as good time party players, ostensibly not caring about who might be watching. Each of their images garnered thousands of likes and messages from all over the world. It was par for the course nowadays that if the police suspected a crime, they could access private data by requesting it from the platform provider. Kate had already done that and discovered that the girls had had conversations with men much older than them, all interested in making a connection. It was a nightmare world which parents failed to regulate because they had no idea it went on. The networks themselves weren't even obliged to watch over activity of minors. Trying to protect kids from crime was like shovelling snow when it was still snowing, and in the Lake District, Kate knew how hard that was. She could see outside against the street lamps that a heavy night of snowfall was ahead and it matched her mood.

Everybody thought it was easy to police this sort of thing, but it wasn't; it was almost impossible. Looking at the profiles of the two girls was frankly depressing and a heavy feeling settled in her stomach. What had they got themselves into?

Now, she received a call from the mother of Chloe Tate. She sounded wary.

Kate explained who she was.

'Chloe isn't here,' the mother said.

'Do you know where she is?' Kate asked.

'Is she in trouble?'

'No, there's nothing to worry about. Her name has come up in an inquiry of ours, that's all. We need to speak to her and her friend, Sasha. Do you know when she's due home?' Kate asked. She'd tried the girls' mobile phones, which was perfectly legal, but they weren't answering.

The mother paused. It was difficult to work her position out over the phone, and Kate decided to jump in her car. The girls both lived a stone's throw away from her place and she was heading home, to avoid the worst of the weather closing in all over the Lake District.

'She's been skipping school. Is that what this is about?'

Kate heard fear in the mother's voice.

'I tell you what, I'm not far away, I'll head over and we'll have a chat,' Kate said. She gave the mother just enough time to utter a semi-response, and hung up. She grabbed her bag and thick winter coat and turned off her computer. Rob was still at his desk.

'You should head home; the snow is settling,' she said to him, aware that he was spending long hours at work, and she understood why. He had a one-year-old at home, and an exhausted pregnant wife. He would rather be here. She got it. She laid one hand gently on his shoulder. He looked up from his work. She glanced at his screen, which was full of numbers and spreadsheets.

'What you up to?' she asked.

'Offshore accounts and shell companies owned by Tactika. He was a clever guy.'

She knew he referred to Bartholomew Kennedy-Craig.

'Legal?' Kate asked.

Rob nodded. 'All of it. Stinks to high heaven, but legitimate. The boss said that the data from the phones retrieved from the crash site is ready to go through first thing; maybe it will shed some light on what's missing in this lot,' he said.

'What do you mean?' Kate asked.

'He's cleaner than clean, despite what the press is saying. The boss said there were six mobile phones in the helicopter. Who knows who they belonged to but it's my guess that anyone with an empire this big would have a couple at least.'

'And with a bit of luck we might find out why they were together in the first place,' Kate said. 'You going to be long?'

'I'm on a roll. You go,' he smiled at her.

'You know a couple of weeks ago, it was snowing like hell, like tonight, and I was working late, I thought I might get trapped here and have to stay. I brought a sleeping bag and pillow in,' she said.

He looked up at her and waited.

'They're under my desk, just in case,' she added, and walked to the lift.

Chapter 42

Kelly drove slowly towards her house in a long queue of traffic. People were making their way home all over the Lakes to wait out the snow storm for the grit lorries that would give them a hope of venturing out tomorrow, but at this rate, it was looking grim. The journos had given up in the bad weather and her driveway was clear. She pulled in and answered a call from Kate. She kept on her heater and sat watching the windscreen wipers fight against the barrage of white flakes.

Kate updated her on the conversation she'd had with the mother of Chloe Tate.

'I was heading over there but I've just made it home and to be honest, I'll be lucky to get my car back out,' Kate said.

'Agreed, don't bother, you'll get stuck. No reply from the other girl's mother?' Kelly asked.

'Not yet. I've been through their social media accounts and you'd think they were single good-time girls in their twenties,' Kate said.

'Jesus. What the hell were they doing at Laurie Fell?' Kelly asked.

'Well, if the tabloids are to be believed then they weren't there for extra lessons in maths.'

'Did you call the journalist?' Kelly asked.

'Yep. Sources protected of course, but she told me that they were watertight. She also told me that every single one of her contracts had been cancelled since the article broke. She's bang out of work.'

'Frozen out of the industry?' Kelly asked.

'Exactly. The article has now been deleted.'

'Well, well. That is some power there. There's no point dedicating hours to it. It's quite obvious who'd want articles like that out of the press. I've just arrived home. I'll see you in the morning, if this eases up. Did Rob tell you the phone data was ready?' Kelly asked.

'Yes. I reckon he'd already made up his mind to stay at the office tonight,' Kate said.

'You gave him the sleeping bag and pillow?' Kelly asked. She'd taken it in for that purpose but hadn't wanted to make it obvious to Rob that his boss knew he was sleeping there.

'Yes. I think he believed me but whatever, at least he'll have a comfy night,' Kate said. 'Jesus, this is heavy. Millie said Johnny drove her home earlier,' Kate said.

Kelly allowed the question to sit momentarily.

'We talked,' she said.

'Good, positive?' Kate asked.

It was a warmer response than Kelly anticipated. 'Kind of. I said he could come over for dinner, but now this weather is going to force my hand, isn't it?' she confided in her friend.

'Well, you do have a spare room,' Kate reminded her.

'I know. I'm sat in my car outside. I'm actually nervous to go in, can you believe that?' Kelly asked.

'Yes. That's why I know he won't spend the night in the spare room,' Kate said.

Kelly wanted to argue with her friend, perhaps to admonish her, but there was no point. There was only warmth in Kate's voice. 'I'll see you in the morning,' Kelly said, and they hung up.

Kelly gathered her things and went inside. The short walk from the car saw her covered in snow by the time she walked into the hallway, and a wall of heat from the fire and the smell of roasting meat in the oven made her shoulders relax. Johnny was doing everything to charm her into believing that everything was back to normal and she hadn't quite made up her mind how she felt about it. He came out of the kitchen and helped her with her things.

'Wine?' he asked. She accepted a large glass of red and took a sip, savouring the body of the vintage – not that she knew much about wine, but she could tell when he'd spent money on a bottle.

'Long day?' he asked.

She nodded, putting her glass down to take off her shoes. She went straight to the living area of the open-plan space and sat down on the huge sofa they'd chosen together, and held her glass close.

'Lizzie in bed?' she asked.

He nodded.

'What's cooking?' she asked him.

'Chicken.'

She sneezed and sank onto the sofa, curling up and tucking her feet underneath her body. He sat down next to her and put his hand on her leg, and she closed her eyes. For just a second it was as if he'd never left. She was tired. Weary of pretending that she was all right without him, and that Lizzie didn't need him. She missed moments like this, when the world outside was freezing over but inside her space, safe and warm, she could forget the case she was working on. Like the helicopter remains on the mountainside being slowly covered by a blanket of snow, she allowed her worries to submerge beneath a heady mix of open flame and red wine. She'd face what was left of it all in the morning. Johnny sat close to her and she moved for him to sit back, so she could lie on him.

They didn't need to talk. Chatter would ruin the moment and perhaps pour doubt onto it. She sipped her wine and Johnny stroked her hair. She stared into the flames and allowed herself to be coddled by the perfect stillness of the house. The lamps cast an orange glow over everything and she felt herself drifting off. He smelled good, and even though she was beginning to feel the symptoms of a cold, she could still recognise her favourite scent on him. He kissed the top of her head and she finished her wine.

'How long has the chicken got?' she asked.

'Another half an hour,' he said. 'I'll wake you when it's ready.'

Chapter 43

Kelly woke to the sound of her daughter gurgling. She felt as though she could stay in a bed for two weeks and not emerge until this case was over. She'd slept soundly and as a result, her chest was heavy and her nose congested. She reached over for a tissue and sat up to blow her nose. Her bed was empty but ruffled where Johnny had slept. She reached out to his side and touched the sheets. She heard Lizzie giggle from along the hall and looked at her phone. It was gone seven and she got out of bed and looked out of the window, over the River Eamont and towards the lake. The snow had stopped for now, and the surrounding mountains and low-lying hills were covered in a thick white coating of perfection. It made everything look pristine and as if they lived in a world without crime and death, if only for a second. She put on a robe and went to Lizzie's room, where Johnny was getting her up and ready, and tickling her. It wasn't the time to question whether she'd done the right thing welcoming him back into her bed last night, and she put it to the back of her mind and told herself to enjoy the moment. She'd done that a lot in the last couple of months since she'd had room to figure things out.

The radio was on in the background and the newsreader announced that the main roads were clear. The efficiency of gritting lorries in the Lakes was impressive and they'd been working through the night to clear the main roads. If she could get her car out safely then she'd be able to get to Eden House. She knew that any work on the mountainside would have stopped, though. Zoe had told her that the fuselage had been scheduled to be lifted yesterday afternoon, but the snow had stopped that and it would lay there now until the operation could proceed safely. It would cause huge delays. She was thankful that she'd instructed the forensic team to take moulds of obvious shoe prints and tyre tracks surrounding Laurie Fell last night before she left the estate. In the snow it would have been impossible. Johnny had already told her that he wasn't on call today, and so he could look after Lizzie all day, and she could head to work, not having to rely on Millie. It was a weight off her mind.

'Eggs?' she asked. 'They're Lizzie's new favourite.'

He nodded and she left them to it. A fleeting thought crossed her mind as she went to her room to shower and change quickly before fixing breakfast for the three of them: was this it now? Was he back with them? She forced herself to let it go. There was no time limit on these things. They'd have to talk later. Last night they'd both said they loved each other, but she had yet to work out if it was because of the gap of loneliness being filled up, or if it was real. She didn't know.

She tied her hair up and ran the shower and stretched her aching body. Running around the mountain on Monday night had taken its toll, but a decent meal last night and a good sleep seemed to have given her a boost. That and the attention. The steam from the hot water began to clear her nose and she felt a little refreshed.

Downstairs, she started coffee, having bought a replica of the machine in the office because she realised she couldn't live without it, and cracked eggs into a bowl. The kitchen was tidy and a load of dirty baby clothes and linen spun in the washer. Johnny really was trying his best to get into her good books. She smiled.

Notices began popping up on the team WhatsApp, which was kept to the five of them in her professional circle. All of them were able to get to Eden House this morning, despite the snow. She knew that Rob had slept there, and that Kate was in Keswick so the A66 would be clear. Emma and Dan were less specific and Kelly couldn't help raising her eyebrows. Emma had mentioned a hotel in Penrith.

She popped in some toast and scrambled the eggs in butter. By the time Johnny came down with Lizzie, she was ready to finish her coffee, share a quick breakfast and go. She kissed them both and headed out.

'I dug some tracks for the car,' Johnny said.

She stared at him. 'When in hell did you do that?' she asked.

'Lizzie was awake at six. I didn't want to disturb you,' he said.

Outside, her feet crunched in the deep snow and she could see cars were queuing already to get across the bridge. She got in and set up her hands-free unit. If it was going to be a long journey, then at least she could catch up before the brief at Eden House. First she called Kate, who updated her on the two schoolgirls.

'It would seem that both mothers assumed they were at the other's house. Until anyone checked, they were both happy to believe that, even though it's a school night and they have a history of bunking off,' Kate said.

'So where are they?' Kelly asked.

'No one knows. I've filed two missing persons reports but if they don't want to be found because they're at some party or just avoiding being questioned, then it'll make our job a nightmare,' Kate said.

Teenage girls went missing all the time, and often they turned up having got on a train to the other end of the country 'to think' or take time out, or whatever they needed to do to off gas. It was common. But in this case, they were potential witnesses to an event that might be important to a criminal investigation, and so not only were they vulnerable because of their ages, they were also potentially in danger.

'What are the parents doing?' Kelly asked.

'Both mums are on their own, with other kids to look after.'

'No clues as to where they might be?'

'No. They gave the impression that both girls run their own lives, pretty much,' Kate said.

'God, that's just fucking wrong,' Kelly said.

'I guess it's just easier that way,' Kate said.

'Phones?'

'Yep, we've got their mobile numbers and the technical team are trying to trace them, as well as keeping a close eye on social media activity, of which there has been none on either of the girls' accounts since yesterday afternoon.'

'Do we know where that was from?'

'A park in Keswick.'

'Okay, at least they could still be close by. With the snow last night and the cancelled trains, they can't have got far. I'll send a squad car to the school to see if we can get any clues as to where the girls hang out,' Kelly said.

Her next call was to her father. The heating inside the car had relaxed her shoulder muscles and she'd taken painkillers from her handbag for the classic flu symptoms. Light snowflakes began falling again and the outside temperature gauge read minus three degrees.

'Good news; the pilots' toxicology came back and there were no traces of alcohol or drugs in their systems,' he told her. 'However, the same can't be said for Mr Kennedy-Craig. His plasma cocaine levels were sky high, and that tells me he was a regular user. He was also intoxicated with ethanol, and so he must have had a pretty heavy night.'

'Then there was the brandy on the flight,' she said. She reckoned she could do with a nip of the strong stuff to ease her congestion right now.

'But he wasn't flying the thing so he hasn't broken the law – if you discount the cocaine, of course,' he said.

'Thanks, Dad. Where are you?' she asked.

'I stayed in a bed and breakfast near the hospital last night,' he said. 'The breakfast was fabulous, though now I've got indigestion. Did you make it home?' he asked.

'Yeah, Johnny cooked a gorgeous meal and…' Too late.

'Johnny? That's nice.'

Kelly could see his smile all the way across the M6.

'We spent a lot of time together on the mountain on Monday, Dad.'

'Is that why you sound as though you've got a cold?' he asked.

'Probably,' she said.

'You working things out?' he asked.

'I don't know yet. It felt right, but how do I know? How could I be so sure two months ago and then not now?' she asked him.

'Well, if you want advice from an old goat like me, follow your heart. Don't listen to your head, it's too noisy.

Keep it simple. I bet Lizzie was pleased to see him,' he said.

'Of course she was. They're spending the day together. He dug my car out so I'm on my way to Penrith now. If you're stuck there, let's catch up. I can't go far today in this weather, and the investigation on Scafell has stalled. Don't spend another night in a B&B, come back with me tonight,' she said.

'I'm sure it'll clear by tonight, though,' he said.

'Doesn't look like it. I think we're in for another dump. I'm sure you'd love to see Johnny and Lizzie,' she said.

'I don't want to interfere,' he said. 'But if you insist, then I'd love to come over,' he said.

'I'm hoping to get Kennedy-Craig's son up from London today, so I might see you at the hospital. Is the body ready?' she asked.

'The technicians have done a decent job, considering how he came in,' Ted said.

'Great, I'll see you later,' she said, and they hung up.

The traffic ahead cleared and sped up as she hit the A road, and her journey onward was smooth. She listened to the radio and sure enough, the news was about Lord Reilly and his critical state, as well as questions over his connections to Kennedy-Craig. It had overtaken the trial of Ian Burton and its outcome, and for that, at least, she was grateful. She felt for Elaine Reilly, and wondered how she lived in such an exposed world. It took guts, but also foolishness perhaps? Then she thought about Vivienne Kennedy-Craig and the statements she'd read from the officers who'd attended the family since Monday night. Kelly had asked why she wasn't making plans to come to the Lake District to fly home with the body of her dead husband. No one could give her an answer. What she had learned, though, was that Vivienne Kennedy-Craig's use of language on the night she'd been informed of her husband's death was curious. She'd specifically said that Lord Reilly wasn't supposed to be on the helicopter, and it bugged her.

She wanted to talk to the woman who'd also shut down the formidable Elaine Reilly. Maybe she could shed some light on the man who'd partied the weekend away with fifteen-year-old girls and not paid too much attention to who had access to his helicopter. On the plus side, the son, Fabian Kennedy-Craig, was planning to fly up to the Lake District. Better late than never, she thought uncharitably.

Town was quiet; though the roads were relatively clear, more snow was forecast for later today. Zoe had told her that even though the main body of the helicopter wreckage hadn't been airlifted by Sea King to be examined yet, as it had turned out to be a bigger job than at first assumed, they'd tested many of the crucial mechanical elements of the craft in situ. The engines were in perfect working order. The yaw pedals were functional, the main rotor blades were fully functioning before they were ground into the marshy mud, and of course the data from the CFDCVR all pointed to one thing: catastrophic mechanical failure caused by a leaking hydraulic line. Zoe and Lance had stayed in a hotel in Glenridding last night, and were heading back to Laurie Fell today. Nellie Lowther had hidden away in her private cottage and hadn't been seen once by the forensic officers, after letting them into the main house.

As Kelly reached the office, she read confirmation on her phone, via email, from the detectives in Manchester who'd interviewed Neil Hardy, that he'd positively identified Paul Edderbridge as the man bragging in the pub in Patterdale on Sunday night. Kelly walked into a warm office, and a mug of coffee was placed in her hand by Rob, who she thought looked fresher than he had in weeks. The team was assembled and ready to go, and Kelly sorted her notes out ready to collate. They now had two missing minors, sober pilots, a functioning helicopter and a house set up for a private sex party, which wasn't against the law, unless it involved minors. It would be a tough pill to swallow for the families, not to mention the Home Office, but something told Kelly that neither would be surprised.

Now she had to fill in the gaps by leaning on Nellie Lowther, who was due in at ten a.m. with a lawyer provided by Tactika; bring in Paul Edderbridge; and find two missing girls. She'd faced worse days. She stood in front of her team and took a gulp of coffee. Kate had updated the software programme they all shared on their Toughpads, with information on Chloe Tate and Sasha Granger. They studied it and took it in. School photographs of the two girls came up on the white screen on the wall.

'Kate, do you want to start?'

'I'm ashamed to admit that my youngest daughter follows these two on Instagram. So I spent last night looking through their private stories. The post from the park was the last one from Sasha Granger's Snapchat. You can see they're in school uniform. Officers are at the school now, taking statements from friends and classmates, and their photos have been released by the press office,' Kate said.

'It's vital we find them, and quick,' Kelly said. She pressed keys on her keypad and the Polaroids from Laurie Fell popped up on the whiteboard behind her.

'These are Polaroids seized at Laurie Fell, showing numerous young girls in various states of "dress up", shall we call it, taken at the main house. They've yet to be verified and dated. As you can see, they are heavy on the uniform of this particular school, and Nellie Lowther retired as head of English there two years ago, because she inherited her father's estate. I want to know her connection to the school now, and if she has a discipline record for inappropriate behaviour towards minors. Somebody introduced these two girls to two considerably older rich men looking for underage girls.'

She studied the two schoolgirls on the whiteboard. Their faces were round and young; they had the glow of youth that can't be bought with wealth and she guessed that was why older, rich men liked them. Their skin was smooth and plump, and their make-up was jarring as it sat unnecessarily on such pristine faces. Though their smiles were wiser than their years, they were still kids, and vulnerable. They looked as though they had all the swagger to insist they made their own choices, but that wasn't the point. At fifteen, they couldn't.

Chapter 44

George Fellows made a call to Vivienne Kennedy-Craig on a phone purchased from the Tesco Express at the services on the M6. He kept another phone for his calls to young Fabian, which were fewer, but kept the young heir sweet. The speed of the investigation into the crash had shaken him. That and Nellie's call to his private number. It was only a matter of time before the trail led to him. Thus his panicked buying of new burner phones every day. As a private investigator to the Kennedy-Craig family for almost twelve years, getting the job done was George's priority. He was an ex-copper, who'd become disillusioned by the red tape that prevented real criminals from being caught. Flitting between masters wasn't his style and he answered only to Vivienne now. She was his paymaster, but he was acutely aware that power was fickle, and Fabian could take the upper hand at any moment. But for now, she was the one who had connections to the social care board deciding the future of his daughter's situation. And that was his number one priority. He took Fabian's money, but that too came from his mother. The cash promised by Fabian had been deposited in the Amazon drop box at Penrith train station, but what Fabian didn't know was that he'd been in the Lake District since last week, on Vivienne's instructions. The last time he'd spoken to Bart was Monday morning, when the businessman had told him that he was diverting on a sightseeing trip for a friend, on the AW139 he'd hired to play with for the weekend.

Fate was a fickle thing, and now he had to pick up all the pieces. The problem with plans was that they never survived contact with actual people. He should have seen it coming. Reilly was never supposed to have been on the fucking helicopter. But there was little he could do now.

Vivienne spoke tersely, meaning she wasn't alone.

'Busy?' he asked.

'I'd love to do tea soon!' she replied.

George stood pacing from foot to foot in the freezing snow, having not packed appropriately for the Lake District. He got the gist: she was with her son.

'It's all in order. Things are progressing the way we discussed,' he said simply.

'Marvellous, darling,' Vivienne purred.

They hung up.

George looked around and took in his surroundings. Like any migratory mammal, he scanned for any imminent risk and quickly made decisions on where and when he was safe. However, unlike the habits of more social beasts, his were solitary, and the key to his success was remaining unattached. He pulled his wool coat around his body and tightened his gloves and straightened his wool hat over his brow. It was fucking freezing. And it was still snowing.

He looked up as he walked out of Penrith station, and calculated where all the CCTV cameras were, to avoid them. He thrived off being indistinctive and wore grey and brown most of the time. He was clean-shaven and wore contact lenses rather than spectacles; nothing to make him memorable and likely to provoke interest.

He fitted in, as a gentleman perhaps visiting his family for a mid-week lunch, or even a businessman home from London. Walking to the taxi rank, he tucked a newspaper under his arm and got into the back of a cab and gave his temporary address for as long as he had to stay in this wilderness. He missed the city. Any metropolis afforded him anonymity in a way that was routine to him; however there was merit in the rural landscape too. It lacked all the pitfalls of the modern urban sprawl: CCTV cameras, large police forces, busy traffic and traceable taxi rides. Black cabs were the worst. Here, in the arse end of nowhere, cabbies were over-friendly but also erratically employed and so one never got in the same one twice, if careful. It was better than driving one's own vehicle, which left a footprint not only on traffic cameras, but also by way of petrol filling stations, insurance, tax and rental records. His police training was still firmly ingrained in him and that was why Bart had trusted him, but he'd discovered quickly that Vivienne wore the trousers in the marriage. Bart's Achilles heel had just eliminated him in the most spectacular way, and now he had to hold Vivienne to her promise.

The cab dropped him off at a block of flats in the centre of town. He paid over the fare, but not too much, not wanting to be memorable. The sky had been dark when he woke up this morning and it remained so: it was grim up north, he thought unfairly. He found his keys and let himself into the entrance, taking the stairs to the third floor and unlocking the apartment he'd rented for a couple of weeks. Once inside, he shivered and threw off his coat, slapping his hands together and checking the heating to see if it was on full. He heard the TV in the next room and went to check on the girls.

They lay on the double bed, glued to the new iPads he'd provided for them, predicting they'd get bored quickly. They were sullen and ungrateful, but their eyes lit up when they saw the new equipment. He was sure that if he ever got his daughter back, he would teach her humility. He'd confiscated their phones for obvious reasons, having turned them off near their school, storing them in another room. They had everything they needed: food, drink, a hot shower and Netflix. He'd also promised them a lot of money.

They peered over their screens as he came in the room and Sasha rolled over onto her back, speaking to him from an upside-down position, which reminded him of his own daughter. Every time he looked at them he was jolted by their similarity and it hurt like hell, but also served to justify some of the more suspect choices he had made on behalf of the Kennedy-Craig family.

'Hey, George, when can we go home?' she asked.

'Like I said, when everything blows over you can get back to your lives, and once you've got your stories straight.'

'George,' it was Chloe's turn. 'We're not stupid; we can remember instructions. We're not going to rat,' she said.

'That might be a bit difficult with you all over the newspaper,' he said, holding up the rag.

Both girls stopped gazing at their machines and sat up, looking at the paper in his hands. It was a story about their social media posts.

'Two missing fifteen-year-olds has made big news and now I don't know what to do with you,' George said. 'If you go back to school and get picked up by the police then they're going to grill you about what you were doing at that house.'

Chloe got off the bed and grabbed the newspaper from him, and squealed. 'Oh my God, we're in the paper!' she beamed.

George rolled his eyes as Sasha joined her friend in the celebration. 'Let me see!' Sasha demanded. They read the story together. George seethed; these girls were confounding and predictably immature.

'Shit, we've been reported as missing,' Chloe said. 'I told my fucking mum to say I was at yours,' she said to Sasha.

'Me too,' Sasha agreed.

They looked at George.

'Can we see our Insta? George, please! I bet we've got, like, thousands of likes,' Sasha pleaded.

'Hundreds of thousands,' Chloe added.

George ground his teeth. 'Look, both of you, sit down. Jesus,' he added. The girls did as they were told, and gave a hint of their young age. They were suddenly behaving like the innocents they really were, and George felt the desperate gravity of his situation. Controlling teenage girls was about as reliable as betting on the Grand National, and he regretted not talking Vivienne out of it. But the damage had already been done. He told himself that, in the long term, he was protecting the Kennedy-Craigs' family name. Once the accident blew over and the investigation was closed then everyone would have forgotten about the sleaze allegations and the two girls. These things disappeared out of the news quickly, he told himself, and Vivienne agreed.

But two missing schoolgirls. He had to find a way to minimise the impact of the headlines without causing so much fuss around the girls. He knew from the inside of investigations like this that missing minors would cause a stir in the local police department, and attract heavy media attention.

'I've bought phones for you both,' he said.

They squealed in unison.

'Dear God,' he said, holding his ears. 'Can you not actually do that?'

'Sorry, George,' they said.

'They're burner phones, not iPhones, so don't get excited. They're simply for you to call your mothers and tell them to stop worrying. Tell them you've gone to Leeds shopping, or some other stupid excuse. Get the police off your backs. We need to send them a photo or something, and tell them you lost your phones.'

Sasha and Chloe looked at each other and giggled. They looked like two young girls on an adventure, and that was exactly what they were, George thought. What they did for money — what he could only guess happened inside Laurie Fell — framed pictures in his head that he found difficult to shake, and it galvanised his need to get his daughter back. On one hand, he marvelled at how these two girls seemed unaffected by what they did. But then he knew that underneath, they were just like his daughter: vulnerable and exposed. At least, for now, here with him, they were safe. And that was how he justified confining them. He opened his bag, took out two new phones and threw them over to the girls, along with two SIM cards. They squealed.

'Tell them that you bought the phones because you're having fun, and you don't want to have to come back yet. Laugh and joke and act natural,' he added.

'My mum won't be bothered anyway,' Chloe said.

'It'd be more normal to have an argument with her,' Sasha said.

'Right, do that then,' George said.

The girls unpacked the phones and placed the SIM cards inside and turned them on.

'Do we do it now?' Sasha asked.

George nodded. 'As good a time as any, I suppose,' he said.

Chloe rang first. Her mother picked up on the second ring and Chloe looked shocked. George mouthed 'act normal' to remind her and she nodded.

'Mum, hi, it's me.'

Sasha and George watched as it became clear that Chloe's mother was upset. The girl calmed her and George encouraged her; she was doing a great job and he silently clapped his hands to applaud her.

'Mum, I'm fine. We came shopping to Leeds, but I saw my picture in the paper. It's such a fucking joke, tell them to leave us alone!' she shouted.

George accepted that this was how Chloe always spoke to her mother because Sasha didn't look up.

'I'm not using my phone because I know what the pigs are like; they'll trace it. I'm not stupid, Mum!' She didn't mention George, or the fact he'd banned them from any other contact, or using social media, bribing them with cash.

The conversation went on and George indicated for her to hurry it along.

'I don't have to tell you why I went to a party, it was just a thing. No, I don't know an old man who died in a crash,' she said.

George slid his hand across his throat in warning and stood in the middle of the room, animated and stressed, like a half drunk dad on Christmas day playing charades. Chloe got the message and said her goodbyes.

'Well done,' George said to Chloe. 'Right, Sasha, not as long. Don't give away details, just act normal, and if that means having a shouting match, then so be it, but no details,' he said.

Sasha nodded and called her mother.

It was a similar exchange, and George watched the youngster take control of her mother over the phone. It told him more about the girl in a short minute than anything he could have read in a school report or by looking at her social media. These girls were used to going it alone. They were survivors; independent, and learning what it meant to be alone far too young. He thought about his own daughter again and how innocent she appeared next to these two girls.

Depressingly, they both did an excellent job.

George knew that what he was doing was simply a holding exercise. It wouldn't keep the authorities away for ever, but it was all he could achieve under the circumstances. Should things get out of hand and Vivienne's plan not work out, and Bart's name didn't disappear out of the press, then he knew that Vivienne might change tack, and he was undecided, as yet, how far he was willing to go to protect her. But, equally, he knew it might be taken out of his hands. He looked at the girls as they took apart their phones, having been instructed to do so. He'd tried his best not to connect with them as human beings. He'd tried his hardest not to engage with them as real people, but it was impossible.

Secretly, he admitted to himself that he was developing a kind of paternal protective attitude towards them, and every time he asked them to do something for him, he cared more. They were surprisingly good company, and for the first time in years, he felt like something approaching a real father, and he dared not think of what Vivienne might ask him to do next.

Chapter 45

The last will and testament of Bartholomew Kennedy-Craig was read in the library by his lawyer, in the presence of Vivienne and Fabian. The grand room, with tall ceilings, was covered in bookcases, bespoke to fit the sometimes awkward spaces around fireplaces and the like. The wood was a mixture of cedar and oak, and Fabian had no idea what the vast majority of titles were about. A lingering smell of linseed oil, from Terrance's efforts, made the space seem clinical, but Fabian was still impressed every time he came in here, and had been since he was a child. But he associated the private room with his father, and that hurt. When his dad was home in London, he spent hours in here on his own with the fire blazing, sipping brandy and speaking on the phone.

Now it was silent and gloomy, despite the sun streaming in from the largest window in the house. The sunlight caught particles of dust floating in the atmosphere and Fabian watched them to take his mind off why they were there. His mother was serious in her manner and dress; she'd put on a suit for the occasion, and her jewels sparkled in the brightness. Fabian had never known his parents not wealthy. He was used to large chunky gems on her fingers and exclusive watches on his father's wrist. The cars, the staff, the first class travel and the tailored clothes were a part of his life, and he'd grown up with all of it.

By comparison, the lawyer looked pedestrian in his worn shoes and ordinary spectacles. Fabian's father always told his boy that he could smell money, and Fabian wondered if this was what he meant. The lawyer wasn't rich, and it made him uptight. He was clearly uncomfortable in such lavish surroundings, which were normal for Fabian. But that didn't make him an enemy, just different.

He sat at Bart's desk and fiddled with envelopes, papers and pens. He looked nervous. Fabian couldn't work out if that was simply because they paid his wages, or he was just like that as a human: highly strung and edgy. He coughed. Fabian cradled a coffee and sat in an easy chair, reading titles that were a revelation to him. There were first editions of classic novels, as well as great encyclopaedic tomes, and current crime thrillers. They mesmerised him, and also killed the time.

'So, let's begin, shall we?' the lawyer spoke.

'Please do,' Vivienne told him.

Fabian gazed at his mother who, he could tell, expected a straightforward process. Everything would be left to her and so it would go. A minute pang of irritation caught Fabian off guard and he wished that he'd discussed such matters with his father long ago. But why would one do that? Why would he invite calamity by being so morbid? What would he have said? *'Dad, by the way, are you leaving everything to Mum when you die?'*

None of them had seen it coming.

The sound of the lawyer slitting the envelope with a paper knife cut through him and made him sit up. He finished his coffee and placed the cup on an occasional table for Terrance to collect later.

The lawyer scanned the document and Fabian thought he noticed slightly raised eyebrows and a fleeting glance towards his mother. Maybe he was mistaken.

'Get on with it,' Vivienne said.

Fabian threw her a look, sure there was impatience and... something else in her voice. Fear? Arrogance?

The lawyer read the preliminaries and legal terms and then the guts of the contract.

'I leave my entire estate to my son, Fabian Kennedy-Craig, who, I trust shall take the proper care...'

Fabian didn't hear the rest. All he could focus on was the noise in his head caused by his mother's outrage.

'What?' she demanded.

She stood up and went to the desk, and Fabian was convinced she was going to get a revolver out from a secret compartment under it and shoot the lawyer dead, her rage was that palpable.

'Mother!' he exclaimed.

She swung round. 'Be quiet, Fabian, there's been some mistake,' she said, glaring at the lawyer.

'No mistake, madam, Mr Kennedy-Craig discussed all of this with me shortly before he died. And with his son.'

'What?' she seethed.

Fabian stood up and put his hands on his hips, for want of anything better to do. He hadn't imagined it would go this badly.

'What do you mean? Shortly before he died? He changed it?' Vivienne asked.

The lawyer nodded.

'Why?' she demanded. Her voice was growing desperate and Fabian watched the exchange, trying to melt into the background.

'Mum, it's all right. It isn't like you think, Dad just wanted…'

She cut him off.

His mother turned to him and eyed him suspiciously. 'What? My rightful inheritance?' she thundered.

'What I mean is it really doesn't matter what it says, I'm not exactly going to kick you out, am I?' he said.

Vivienne swallowed hard and Fabian could see the blood vessels in her neck expand. The lawyer said nothing.

'Is that it?' she rasped. 'You knew and you didn't tell me,' she raged.

The lawyer nodded. 'The entire estate and all assets are in Fabian's control now. There is, of course, a generous allowance for maintenance…'

'Why did he have it changed? Surely that's not legal!' she ranted.

Fabian watched her and grew embarrassed by her outburst. Why was she doing this to him? What difference did it make, anyway?

The lawyer began packing away his papers but Vivienne walked to the desk and with one swoosh of her hand caused all the documents to fall to the floor, fluttering with a noisy whisper and then settling around her feet.

'Mother!' Fabian said again. But she wasn't listening. She was incandescent with fury and Fabian was taken back to other times in his life when she'd shamed him in front of people in authority, whether it was school housemasters, or his father's associates. He went to the desk and knelt down, trying to gather the papers, helped by the lawyer.

'I'm so sorry,' he said.

They looked up at one another when they heard an almighty bang and realised that Vivienne had stormed out and slammed the huge oak door as hard as she could.

Chapter 46

Nellie Lowther gave the impression of a meek and weathered older lady, with all the innocence of a charity volunteer, or a school dinner lady. She dressed plainly, in dated prints, and wore a cleaning pinafore under her coat. Her hair was tightly curled as if recently coiffed and she smelled of Estée Lauder. Kelly reckoned that, if she was trying to pull off the harmless granny approach, then she was doing a cracking job. The woman had taught English at the school attended by Chloe Tate and Sasha Granger, and she was ticking the boxes for that stereotype too: stuffy, straight and staid.

'Thanks for making the trek today; it's treacherous out there,' Kelly said. She knew that the woman had been hiding in her cottage at Laurie Fell, because Zoe had told her.

Nellie smiled nervously and held her coat close around her body. Nobody wanted to attend a police interview, it just set all the alarm bells off: fight or flight. Bar none, everybody hated it. Like insects under a microscope, they squirmed and wriggled, trying to get free. The only people who didn't were kids. They told the truth, plainly, because they had yet to learn to lie.

Police interviews were a game, and part of a copper's training was learning to play. The outcome was always more satisfying if it ended in some kind of confession

These days, without forensics, the CPS wasn't going to fork out for a costly trial unless the case was watertight. A seasoned witness could scupper the whole thing. Kelly had yet to work out which type of witness Nellie Lowther was. Would she surprise them?

So far, Nellie's demeanour was that of a person who was terrified, and this could work to Kelly's advantage. At the end of the day, all she wanted was the truth, but that was the precise thing people didn't want to give.

Not the whole truth, anyway.

Potentially, Nellie was a gold mine of information about what went on inside Laurie Fell when Bartholomew Kennedy-Craig was there, and that could give them a clear picture of who might want him dead. All of her information pointed to Lord Reilly's presence on the craft not being widely known about, so they had to assume, until they discovered otherwise, that Kennedy-Craig was the target.

Nellie had arrived with a Tactika lawyer. No doubt they cost an arm and a leg and it indicated that the family and the company was wary about what Nellie knew. The last thing Kelly needed was a barrage of 'no comment' offerings, but more often than not these days, that was all they got before any charges were brought. The onus was all on the police to prove a case. Gone were the days where criminals understood the scope of the law and could be intimidated into making mistakes. Not that she saw Nellie as a criminal – yet – but after talking to Dan and Emma, they had to question why Nellie had not wanted to cooperate with them when they visited Laurie Fell.

They began.

Kelly got on with the formal process of identifying the witness and recording her date of birth and the like.

'Nellie, I want to make clear that this meeting is a fact-finding exercise about the last known movements of Bartholomew Kennedy-Craig, as part of the inquiry into his death.'

Nellie looked at her lawyer, who nodded.

Kelly proceeded. 'What was your relationship to Bartholomew Kennedy-Craig?' she asked.

'He rented my property. I made sure it was ready for him when he wanted to stay.'

'And I believe you have no other tenants?' Kelly asked.

'No.'

'How did you two meet?' Kelly asked.

Nellie sighed and brought a tissue from her pocket – her emotional response in direct contrast to how the way Dan and Emma had described her reaction when they'd visited Laurie Fell after the crash.

'Mr Kennedy-Craig was visiting holiday lets, many years ago, and he fell in love with Laurie Fell. I showed him around. That was when my father owned it. It was my idea to rent it out; my dad needed something to do, he couldn't live in that massive place on his own.'

'You didn't live with him?'

'He gave me the cottage years ago. I lived there.'

'And how did that work? Mr Kennedy-Craig was your only paying guest, but it's still advertised on websites?' Kelly asked.

Nellie smiled and looked at her lawyer, who nodded.

'It's common practice. In all honesty, I just never got around to removing it and to be honest, I always thought I might change my mind, for the right client.'

Kelly didn't like it when witnesses used phrases like 'in all honesty' and 'to be honest', especially twice in one sentence. It made her hackles raise, like it did now.

'We've got a problem with the guests you allowed to use your property whilst Mr Kennedy-Craig was in residence,' Kelly said. 'Were you aware that he invited underage schoolgirls to attend your property with him and his friends?'

'I knew nothing about that,' Nellie said.

'Schoolgirls who attend the school you taught at until your retirement two years ago.'

'So? How is that important? I took early retirement because my father left me Laurie Fell in his will.'

'But you still have ties with the school and you must be familiar with a lot of their pupils. You at least know the uniform well. You're there at the house the whole time, on your own, by your own admission. Didn't you question the various props he liked to have lying around – such as the school uniforms? Given your old career that would flag up a huge problem for safeguarding, would it not?'

Nellie didn't answer.

Kelly spread out the photos taken by the forensic team, for clarity. She pointed out the bags of rubbish and the various items left half packed away.

'Did you tidy up after the weekend or employ somebody to do it?' Kelly asked.

Nellie didn't answer.

'Whoever it was didn't do a very good job of it, judging by what was left out. I know the families of your two guests would be surprised to learn that this was the kind of thing they were using over the weekend,' Kelly said.

'I was shocked. I didn't know... I tried to tidy up but I was just so taken aback by what I found,' Nellie said, picking at her cuff and looking down at her hands.

'So, for clarity, none of the items that are shown in the photos here belong to the property, or were inside the property the last time you were inside these rooms?' Kelly asked.

Nellie stared at the photographs and her cheeks burned.

'Because you refused entry to my detectives, we had to get a warrant to search the property and this is what we found. Do you recognise the items? And I'll remind you that you're under caution, so if you rely on anything in court that contradicts what you tell us now, then it could affect your position,' Kelly asked again, repeating herself. She could see that Nellie was dumbstruck and struggling to place herself inside the situation she'd found herself in. That was normal. Kelly waited.

'Why should my client be relying on anything in court?' Nellie's lawyer asked. 'Is she charged with an offence?'

'She's helping with our inquiries, and as an ex-teacher she must be concerned over the welfare of two minors. Recognise these two girls?' Kelly asked, spreading out the Polaroids of Chloe and Sasha.

'No.'

'We advise that your client answer carefully. We're investigating several potential criminal acts. One is the sabotage of a helicopter hangared on the property on Sunday night. The other is sexual acts with a minor, or minors. Both are grave and as you'll be aware, and by her own admission, your client is the sole proprietor and caretaker of the said property. If she knows anything about the helicopter being hangared in the garden, then we want to know now. Next week or next month is too late. Similarly, these two girls are missing and were last seen at the property owned by your client. Again, if she knows them, or saw them on Sunday night, or any other night, we need to know urgently. They're vulnerable girls, and we need to find them.' Kelly placed images from the girls' social media accounts on the table. 'As an ex-teacher, I would have thought that their safety would be of paramount importance to her.'

Nellie stared at her lawyer.

'The helicopter was sabotaged?' Nellie whispered.

'The cause of the crash is as yet undetermined,' Kelly said.

Nellie covered her mouth with her hand and shook her head. Kelly couldn't work out if it was an Oscar-winning performance, or genuine. A knock at the door gave her a welcome reprieve.

The door opened and Kate poked her head round it. Kelly stopped the interview and allowed a break, and left the room. She closed the door behind her.

'What is it?' she said to Kate.

'The mother of Sasha Granger just called asking us to drop the missing person status of her daughter. Sasha called her and told her she's safe and shopping in Leeds, with Chloe Tate.'

'What?' Kelly asked, puzzled and instantly suspicious.

Kate raised her brow.

'But we need to speak to them urgently,' Kelly said.

'I know, but first we have to find them, and the mother says she knows nothing.'

'Isn't she concerned?'

'Didn't sound too fussed. It appears the two girls do this a lot, and get away with it. It's normal behaviour, and a waste of resources for us, officially, if we spend time looking for them.'

'We still need to speak to them.'

'I told her that; she told me to find them myself.'

'What about parental disinterest? Surely we can proceed on the grounds of neglect.'

'Exactly, which is why I've left their status as missing. Should I reiterate that to the press office?'

'Yes, do that now,' Kelly said. 'Have we got any results from the computers and hardware seized from Laurie Fell yet?' she asked.

'I'll chase them on it. Rob was definitely expecting something today.'

'Thanks, Kate.'

'How's Nanny McPhee in there?' Kate asked.

'Like wading through treacle. About as helpful as a chocolate fireguard.'

'Thought so. Have you dropped the bomb yet?'

'Not yet. Get it out that we need to speak to Chloe and Sasha as a matter of urgency.'

Kelly turned away but her phone interrupted her again and she saw that it was Zoe calling.

'Have you seen the news?' Zoe asked.

'Not at this moment, I'm in an interview. What's up?' Kelly asked her.

Kate stopped and hung about, listening.

'The Kennedy-Craigs are launching a civil action against the AAIB and running their own investigation.'

'On what grounds?'

'That the AAIB investigation is compromised by leaks to the press, and the resulting media storm is litigious.'

Kelly considered the irony of a family who at once used and abused the power of media. 'And you heard about this in the press?'

'Exactly.'

'Is it a stunt? They can't touch the investigation while it's ongoing,' Kelly said.

'Yes, but they are entitled to run their own. It undermines us. If it was sabotage, which we all agree is looking likely, then any insurers won't pay out. I guess it's about money,' Zoe said.

'Well they can't change that.'

'But they can slow things down,' Zoe said.

'How?' Kelly asked.

'Just by being awkward.'

'Right, well, it doesn't change anything as far as I'm concerned. I think what we've got is a family in denial. Mrs Kennedy-Craig is on my list of people to speak to. I'll get on to it this afternoon. Just crack on with what you're doing,' Kelly said. 'Has the snow storm affected you?'

'Not really. We'd already airlifted enough to the hangar to complete an investigation; what's left on the mountainside is just a shell. We've got the electrics and major mechanical fixtures. The engines were examined on the mountainside and of course we've got the tail rotor, which thankfully missed the lake.'

'Yeah, that would have been like looking for a grain of rice in there. Put this interference out of your mind. I get the impression that the family think they can buy people, and time. That certainly seems the case with the owner of the Laurie Fell estate.'

They hung up. Kelly relayed the conversation to Kate.

'It's interesting that the Reilly family have been conspicuously absent from all dealings with the newspapers,' Kate said as they walked past the interview suites.

Kelly stopped at the door. 'Not really. They've got the protection of the British government behind them. The Kennedy-Craigs have nothing and no one; they're fighting this alone. By the way, the legal department called me and told me that Bartholomew Kennedy-Craig's will was read this morning and the son gets everything. I wonder if that was a surprise to the mother,' she said.

Kelly went back into the interview room and sat down. They restarted, and Kelly apologised.

'So, where were we? Yes, so Nellie, you were telling me about your relationship with Sasha Granger and Chloe Tate.'

She felt confident that if the woman wasn't going to budge on Bartholomew Kennedy-Craig, then she'd at least catch her out with what she knew about the two girls. But first, she wanted to give her chance to hang herself with her own noose.

It was Rob who'd spotted it. When the girlfriend of one of the pilots had received images from him, excitedly telling her that he was staying in a palatial castle for the weekend, she'd handed them over to the police, and Rob had taken a closer look.

One of them was a selfie taken in the hallway of the grand residence, and in the background were several other people. Kelly had the photograph with her now. There was so much polished glass in the decoration and fixtures of the Laurie Fell house that photos taken almost anywhere would throw back reflections, and the same was true of this particular photo, enlarged and forensically enhanced. Kate knocking on the door had been planned. It was actually to pass Kelly the photo once it had been perfected by Rob to the point where there was no doubt of its contents.

'I've just been handed this,' Kelly said. 'It was found on the phone of one of the deceased pilots. He was staying at Laurie Fell as a guest over the weekend, along with his co-pilot, as their helicopter was hangared next to the maintenance shed. As you can see, the woman standing in the doorway looks familiar doesn't she?'

Nellie Lowther's face became almost human for the first time. It was something she couldn't help and the discipline required to maintain her faceless mask dissolved as she reacted naturally for once. They'd caught a glimpse of Nellie Lowther un-staged, and Kelly pushed her. The lawyer sat forward. She scrutinised the photo and then closed her eyes, defeated.

'It's me,' Nellie said.

'Excuse me?' Kelly said. 'Can I confirm that the witness has identified herself in the photograph, dated Sunday evening, and located inside Laurie Fell house. Nellie, can you identify the two young girls you're stood with?'

'No, sorry, I don't know them,' Nellie said.

Kelly bit her lip. 'I've just showed you their photographs, Nellie.' She pointed to the images. 'This one is Sasha Granger, and this is Chloe Tate. In the photo, you're speaking to them and you look very comfortable. You knew them.'

Rob had done an excellent job with the photograph.

'I don't know them, I'm being polite,' Nellie said.

'But why did you tell us you'd never seen them before?'

'I forgot.'

'And why did you lie to us about not being inside the property at the same time as your guests?' Kelly asked.

'I don't know...'

The lawyer crossed her legs and bounced her foot.

'You can make yourself comfortable, Nellie, and have a think about it. Meanwhile I'm arresting you for making false statements and obstruction of justice, so you have twenty-four hours to have a little think, while the CPS decides if I have enough to charge you. By then, we might be able to add soliciting minors for sexual activity to the list, what do you reckon?'

Kelly looked at the lawyer. 'Maybe you would like to explain the process to your client?' she asked, and left.

Chapter 47

'Mrs Kennedy-Craig, I hope I'm not disturbing you?' Kelly asked. She'd tried several times to reach Bartholomew's widow, and this was the first time she'd actually had the chance to speak directly to her. Kelly wasn't sure what she had expected, but the coldness came as a surprise. She tried to tell herself that it was due to the shock of the woman losing her husband in a violent and dreadful manner. Kelly had yet to work out if the reading of the will or the death of her husband was the worse of the two blows for her. She introduced herself and allowed the woman to process the intrusion.

'Can I say, first of all, how sorry I am for your loss, and give my condolences to the family?' Kelly said. 'I know we've had officers visit you recently, and you turned down the liaison team?' She got straight to it.

'I don't need people in my house telling me what I already know, and I have nothing to add to your investigation. I'm very busy.'

The woman was blunt and Kelly had planned for that. Not everyone wanted to talk to the police after the death of a loved one. Some of them were downright hostile, and that was their prerogative. However, the liaison team wasn't placed with grieving relatives solely for their succour; they were used to gather information on those closest to the victim in case it turned out they were part of the cause of death. Before they were kicked out, the liaison team had already reported that the house was like a mausoleum, with a tense relationship between mother and son, with the lady of the house spending most of the day in bed, and an ever present butler, who watched everything.

The mother and son hadn't been ruled out as suspects. They never were. Bumping off a billionaire and a politician was something that took planning, and the culprit was just as likely to be a relative or a rival as they were to be a climate nutter, or wronged parent of a teenage girl. That was factual context.

The impression she was getting from Mrs Kennedy-Craig was that she was a closed book, and so Kelly decided to go in with the sex with minors angle, to wake her up, if nothing else. If there was anything that rich people disliked more than losing money, it was unwanted and unsolicited attention. Being held to account publicly, when they thought they'd bought their way above that years ago, was their worst nightmare.

If this story got out, the Kennedy-Craigs would be compromised and vulnerable. It could open a can of worms that would likely bring about the collapse of the vast empire of Tactika Enterprises. Kelly wanted to know how far Vivienne Kennedy-Craig would go to make sure that didn't happen.

'If you'll excuse me…' Vivienne said.

'Mrs Kennedy-Craig, let me make myself clearer here. We're investigating the death of your husband and the critical injury of a senior politician. I need to know who the target was: Lord Reilly or your husband.'

'Target?'

'Yes. We have evidence which points to the crash being a result of mechanical sabotage, and that would make your husband's death homicide. I'm being as transparent as I can with you so that you can cooperate with us.' Kelly had made the decision not to mention the specifics about the hydraulic cable to anyone outside the investigation.

Kelly waited. 'Mrs Kennedy-Craig?'

'I'm here. Why would you think that? The crash was an accident, wasn't it?'

Now Kelly had her attention.

'That's what we assumed originally. However, there are certain mechanical issues that have caused the experts to reassess their view. Are you aware of anyone who'd want to harm your husband?' Kelly asked.

'Get in line,' Vivienne said.

'Thank you, but that doesn't really help you or I. I need names. Did he have enemies?'

'The climate fanatics, obviously. Can't you people just do your job?'

'That's the obvious answer, isn't it? We looked into that and it seems unlikely. It's more plausible that your husband and Lord Reilly were targeted because of their arrangements together.'

'Arrangements?'

'Yes. It's come to our attention that your husband was in the habit of using the Lake District property he rented for certain kinds of parties, involving underage girls. Maybe you knew about that?'

Kelly heard a loud intake of breath and braced herself. She wasn't holding back with this woman but she had little choice. She either wanted to know why her husband was dead or not.

'How dare you?' Vivienne said.

'I beg your pardon? I'm simply doing my job, as you've expressed you want me to. The facts are indisputable. We've arrested the housekeeper, Nellie Lowther, you know her? Did you visit the holiday home yourself?'

'Never.'

'Why not? It's beautiful.'

Another sharp inhalation.

'I'll need to talk to your son, who is now in charge of Tactika Enterprises, being your husband's sole heir. Was he aware of the parties?'

'Stay away from my family,' Vivienne said.

Kelly could tell that the woman was losing it.

'I'm afraid that's out of the question until we get some answers and a conclusion to this case. I'm sure you appreciate its high profile in the press currently, and that's unfortunate, but until we conclude the investigation, there's nothing I can do about that for you. Do you have any comment for me?'

'No.'

'That's unfortunate, because this is your opportunity.'

'This conversation is over. If you want to speak to me again then contact my lawyer.'

'The Tactika lawyer with Nellie Lowther? I'll speak to her and explain the nature of your obligations as family of the deceased. I'll look forward to meeting your son.'

'You will not talk to him, I forbid it.'

Kelly was momentarily stunned. The language jarred her senses; this woman thought she could control the outcome of everything. 'Didn't he tell you? He's on his way up here, by helicopter, admittedly a curious choice. Don't worry, we'll take good care of him. And if there's anything you'd like to share with me, then please give me a call. You have my number. But there is actually one thing I meant to ask you before we got side-tracked. Perhaps we've got off on the wrong foot? I was reading your interview with the uniformed police who visited your house after the death of your husband and I want to remind you of what you said.'

'I can't remember what I said, I was in shock,' Vivienne said.

'Let me jog your memory,' Kelly said. 'You asked why your husband was on "the" helicopter. That says to me that you knew he was using one for the weekend. You also said that Lord Reilly wasn't supposed to be on it. You have since said that you had no idea that they were together, so why would you say that?'

'I didn't say that.'

'I've got it written in the statement you gave to police on Monday night,' Kelly said.

'I didn't say that.'

'Did you have any reason to believe that if your husband had a visitor, they wouldn't have got on his helicopter with him?'

'Like I said, I've got nothing more to say to you,' she said and hung up.

Kelly stared at her phone as it buzzed and went dead.

The conversation hadn't been entirely pointless; she'd at least gauged the woman's mettle. The splintering of a family unit because of either money or death was something that usually got messy, and Kelly intended to be there to pick up the pieces.

Next, she called Fabian Kennedy-Craig, praying he answered. She wanted to get to him before his mother, and she'd told a little white lie; she had no idea if he was coming to Cumbria today, she just hoped he was. He answered and she introduced herself, getting a rather different response to that of his mother. He was respectful and interested in the investigation, and asked all sorts of intelligent questions, and it quickly became an amicable conversation.

'Now your father's estate is settled, you're free to come here, when do you think you'll arrive?'

'How do you know about my father's estate?' he asked.

'It's procedure; your lawyers are obligated to notify ours of any outcome from the will, when the death is unnatural. Until the investigation is finalised, your father's death is treated as suspicious. In fact, we've uncovered some information that is pointing that way, I'm afraid. I thought I'd tell you myself.'

'It wasn't an accident?'

'Fabian – do you mind if I use your first name?'

'Not at all, please, tell me.'

'Fabian, it looks very likely that the mechanical failure was due to sabotage.' Again, she purposely didn't mention the hydraulic cable or the spin, or the loss of the tail rotor. They were details that needed to be kept under wraps for now.

'Jesus. I can't believe it. So, the rumours in the papers are true. Does my mother know?'

'I just got off the phone to her and she was angry, of course. If you came up here, you could be closer to the investigation. I did think your mother would want to talk further, but I'm afraid we didn't get along.'

'That doesn't surprise me, she's a stubborn woman. She's also not happy about the will.'

'Ah, that's tricky. She expected everything to go to her?'

'Exactly, but I'm twenty-four years old, for Christ's sake.'

'Old enough to take it on, for sure, and I'm guessing your father prepared you well, from what I've found out about him so far.'

Silence.

'Did you know about the terms of the will?' she asked.

'My dad mentioned it,' he said. 'But I didn't expect...'

'To have the responsibility so soon?' Kelly asked.

Kelly could tell he was reticent. It was probably a father-son conversation that was meant to be a secret. No wonder Vivienne was enraged.

'Listen, you could be here soon if you left right away, assuming you can? The weather up here is pretty bad but you've probably got a couple of hours' window if you get a move on, before the next snow hits. Don't you want to be here? There are certain administrative considerations regarding flying your father's body home. I'm sure your mother didn't want to take that on because she's so grief-stricken.'

Silence.

'Fabian?'

'Yes, sorry. I read the papers of course, but I didn't think it was true, just the usual drama. You really think it was sabotage?'

'That's the angle we're taking at the moment.'

'You think it was climate change protesters targeting Donald?'

'You knew Donald well?'

'Not well, but he and Dad were close once. I didn't think they'd seen each other in years.'

'I'm sorry I can't give you any answers as to who might be responsible for the crash. There are some issues we've come across that are a little sensitive and I know how your family protects its privacy.'

'Sensitive? You mean the articles about my father being a fraud and a disgusting old capitalist?'

'Kind of.'

'Something else?'

'Well, there is actually. Let's talk when you get here. You really need to get going if you're going to make it up here.'

'Did you speak to my mother about it?'

'Yes, and it didn't go well, I'm afraid. I suppose it's to be expected, but I really need some answers.'

'I'll handle her,' Fabian said.

'Before you go, was it you who filed the civil complaint about the AAIB?' she asked.

'No, that was my mother. I told her to wait until after the report is finalised, but she's obsessed with the crash being sabotage by an activist,' he said.

'Really? She seemed surprised when I told her about the sabotage, though she did assume that if it wasn't an accident then it must be climate change activists who did it.'

'And you think it could be someone else?' Fabian asked.

'We're exploring all avenues,' Kelly said. 'Let me know when you arrive, and where you're staying.'

They hung up.

Kelly made her way back to the office, via the lift; she didn't fancy taking the stairs. The lift was empty and she leant against the back of it and felt the gravity pull at her stomach as it lurched upwards. She needed a coffee.

Next on her list was interviewing Paul Edderbridge, and she was going to make sure that she had two large male uniformed officers in the room with her, as well as her wing woman, DS Kate Umshaw, given his background of kicking off, and his violence towards women. The roads had been cleared enough to send a squad car to pick him up and bring him in. At the same time, his girlfriend's place was being searched by forensics, much to the woman's disgust. It was always the kids that were stuck in the middle, and she didn't envy the officers sent to pick him up.

Whatever had gone on at Laurie Fell on Sunday night, and whatever Paul Edderbridge's part in it, Kelly was all ears. Sometimes she wished that the Lake District had a great fence around it, to keep out troublemakers from the capital, but as long as the rich ran out of space in the city, and there was room here to hide, they'd keep coming. But she had to find out why they needed an insider like Paul to become involved, if he was.

Chapter 48

Paul Edderbridge's file made for depressing reading. He was a damaged individual whose addiction to petty crime was predictable enough.

Kelly fixed a coffee and took a call from Chief Constable Andrew Harris. She'd given him an update, but she sensed impatience in his voice.

'How can the AAIB do its job in this snow?' he asked.

She calmly repeated what Zoe had told her about them having already transferred what they needed to the hangar here in Penrith.

'Think of it like a plane that goes down in the Atlantic; they might not retrieve everything, but enough to file a confident report,' she told him.

'Hmmm,' he said. He was doing this a lot. It was a warning that he wasn't happy. And if he wasn't happy then it usually meant that he had someone breathing down his neck.

'And the target?' he'd asked.

'We're not sure, sir.'

'Hmmm. And Lord Reilly's reason for being at the Laurie Fell estate?'

'Unclear, sir.'

'Hmmm. And this local lad, the one identified by the activist as bragging in the pub?'

'I'm just about to interview him, sir.'

'Hmmm.'

She appreciated his frustration but she wasn't in the business of rushing investigations to fit with the media, or the government.

'Sir, I haven't all the answers yet, but I'm getting there. We're analysing the CCTV from the new cameras installed at Aira Force National Trust car park, from Sunday night, to see who travelled along the road to the Laurie Fell.'

'Hmmm. What about the housekeeper?'

'Arrested for obstruction, sir. I haven't enough to arrest her for soliciting underage girls but that's where I'm heading. We're trying to squeeze her for information about the last hours leading up to the crash.'

'Hmmm. This one's a bit tricky. Ex-school teacher, is she?'

'Yes, sir.'

'That's delicate.'

'Why, sir?' Kelly's hackles went up.

'Well, it's distracting for the investigation. I see several threads here, Porter.'

He only called her Porter when he was rattled.

'Sir?'

'I just think your climate activist thread was more convincing, and the Home Office agrees.'

'The Home Office, sir? It really doesn't matter what they think, though, does it? I'm trying to get to the bottom of a very complicated set of circumstances. My final report will follow in due course. If there's been a crime committed then I'll take the necessary action, sir.'

'Do we need all the detritus, though? We need this wrapped up, and quickly; the government is taking a hammering over the scandal. Can you play down the link between Lord Reilly and Kennedy-Craig? Is it really relevant?'

Kelly stirred her coffee vociferously. 'You mean lie, sir?'

'Porter…'

'Sorry, sir. What I meant was *omit*, sir.' She enunciated her words to match her vigorous stirring and found her grasp of the spoon was making it dig into her palm. 'I'm aware of the political pressure, but I can only give you the truth as I find it. If you want me to leave gaps because the government deems some information irrelevant, then why don't I ping you over my report as soon as I wrap up, and you can edit it yourself?'

'Hmmm. Porter, there's no need for that tone, I simply want you to consider how many resources we can plough into this thing before it becomes a media circus and nothing else.'

'That's exactly what I'm doing, sir. With respect, I need to go to an interview.'

'Hmmm.'

They hung up.

Kelly sipped her coffee and leant against the countertop. She was seething. She tried her best to concentrate on what she had to do.

Before turning to a life of intimidating and beating vulnerable women, Edderbridge had led an unsurprising existence right here in Penrith, attending local schools and bombing his GCSEs. Stints in mechanics' workshops and garages preceded pretty minor criminality and thus began a career of latching onto women to pay his rent and feed him, while he roamed around looking for houses to rob.

She walked past Rob's chair and peered over his shoulder at his work.

'Boss?' he said.

'How're you doing?' she asked, more about his sleeping arrangements than the case.

'Making progress. I've identified a few characters that have been on the end of, how shall I put it, unfair deals on behalf of Tactika and might have an axe to grind. I also found this; it's a charitable foundation, one of many set up by Tactika to essentially hide money. It was set up with a million quid, and ostensibly it does decent work, putting kids from unprivileged backgrounds through college – one of whom is Quentin St John, the editor of a respected broadsheet. The same paper that ran the article about Tactika yesterday.'

'Doesn't sound like a man called Quentin would need help with his education,' she said.

'Exactly, so I did a bit of digging. That's his new name; before that he was plain old Paul Stockton.'

'I suppose it makes sense, if you want to overhaul your identity.'

Kelly watched as he brought up Quentin St John's profile on LinkedIn.

'He's not the only one. In fact, many of their alumni went on to successful careers in what you might call *convenient* industries, helpful to a huge company like Tactika: the media, oil, finance, offshore investments and the like. Call me cynical,' Rob said.

'Keep it in the family,' Kelly said suspiciously. 'That explains why he contacted the freelancer about the article. So, they like to control what the press say about them. That's not unusual for the rich and powerful, but why let that particular story run?' she nodded to the article released yesterday.

'To cover up something else?' Rob said.

Kelly nodded. 'Like sex parties with underage girls?' she suggested. It made sense. 'The family gloves are off; let's find out what else they control. I'm assuming the journalist Kate spoke to, the one who blew the lid on the party, wasn't part of the privileged elite?'

'I looked into her. I couldn't get hold of her by phone, but as far as I can tell she has no connections to the family whatsoever.'

'And her article was swiftly deleted. Anything like that isn't going to sit well with either family if they like to control what's said about them. Keep trying her,' she asked Rob. 'By the way, I meant how are *you*? Not the job, the hours you're working?'

He looked embarrassed. 'I'm all right, boss. Nothing to worry about here.'

'Boss?' Kate shouted across the room.

Kelly shook off the conversation with Andrew Harris – the fact that he was Kate's boyfriend was suddenly inconvenient and irritating but she wasn't about to let it show – and went over to her desk.

'The boat that was stolen from Pooley Bridge on Sunday night has been found dumped near the northern shore of Ullswater. The owner was called this morning by a local who recognised it. He's confirmed it's his. He's livid as it's in a bit of a state. We've got the CCTV from Sunday night at Pooley Bridge and have a look: it's a tall Caucasian male, but we can't see the face. I'd wager a guess, though, wouldn't you?' Kate asked.

'Paul Edderbridge,' Kelly said.

Chapter 49

Nellie Lowther's phone had been handed in when she was processed for the pending charges. Kelly doubted she'd get them upheld, but that wasn't the point.

Now she headed in to see Paul Edderbridge, nodding to Kate that she was ready. Kate passed Kelly a fresh coffee from the machine and they headed back downstairs.

Edderbridge had waived his right to legal counsel and he'd arrived alone, with the uniformed officers who'd driven him. He'd been processed as a witness being interviewed under caution, and two officers were inside the room babysitting him, waiting for the interview to begin.

'Did you send a couple of officers down to the dump site of the boat to check for evidence?' Kelly asked Kate.

'Yup. They retrieved a few fag butts on site, as well as a beer can, and forensics have been called to dust for fingerprints, despite them pointing out that we don't stand a cat in hell's chance, because of the snow.'

'They always say that.' Kelly said, smiling. 'Let's do it, shall we?'

They went into the interview suite, and Kelly found a large man, somewhat comfortable and settled, stretched out across his chair, hands behind his back, manspreading his legs, and smiling at her.

'Morning, Paul,' she said breezily. She introduced herself and Kate. He recognised Kate from his one night stay on Sunday night and winked at her.

No one warmed to a witness who made themselves so comfortable in an interview suite. Especially not a woman-beater.

They went through the prelims and Paul yawned a few times.

'Are we keeping you up, Paul?' Kate asked. He smiled at her and nodded.

'You've been skipping your sleep?' Kelly asked.

'It's not very comfortable downstairs in the cells, have you tried it?' he asked cheekily.

Kelly could tell that he liked to think of himself as a charmer; she'd read his notes from Monday night. But he simply made her skin crawl. He was a big bloke, roughly matching the CCTV of the person who'd stolen the boat. She was a small petrol vessel, with a shelter cabin, twelve feet in length, common on Ullswater, which wasn't a busy lake.

'We've got several things to plough through with you, Paul, so let's get cracking, shall we?'

'Whatever,' he said nonchalantly.

'You've heard the news, I assume? About the crash on Scafell?'

'I didn't do it, guv,' he said, laughing and holding his hands up. Neither Kelly nor Kate joined in his fun.

'You recognise this boat, Paul?' Kelly said, pushing a photograph across to him. Kate made notes.

'Nah,' he shook his head. Clearly this was Paul's go-to approach for standard police interviews, but this one wasn't standard and it was about to bite him on the arse.

'And is this you stealing it?' Kelly turned her laptop round and showed him the video of a large man in a dark coat taking the boat from Pooley Bridge.

'Definitely not.'

'So, the cigarette butts and beer can, found where the boat was dumped sometime on Monday, before you went home and a neighbour accused you of beating up your girlfriend, are somebody else's?'

Silence.

'Where did you take the boat, Paul? Was it to the Laurie Fell estate across Ullswater?'

Silence.

'Is it possible that when the shoe prints taken from around one of the sheds there are compared to yours, they'll match?'

Silence.

'Did you visit Green Lead Slate Camp on Sunday night?'

'Nah.'

'Did you try to force your way into the White Lion pub in Patterdale on the same evening?'

Paul sat up and looked slightly uncomfortable for the first time.

'Nah.'

'Did you brag about earning money for taking out rich people?'

Silence.

'Why did you beat up your girlfriend? Did she ask you where you'd been?'

'Fuck off! I didn't do anything!'

One of the male officers stepped forward.

'Mind your language, Paul,' Kelly said. Her constant reference to his girlfriend was having the desired effect.

He sat up and straightened his legs, closing them, to Kelly's relief. He folded his arms across his chest and the smile disappeared from his face.

'Who were you talking to? This man?' She slid a photograph of Neil Hardy across to him.

Silence.

'Why were you bragging about bringing down rich people, Paul?'

'I think I'll have a lawyer now,' he said, going quite pale.

Chapter 50

George sat gloomily staring at his phone. Every time Vivienne called him it was more pressure, more craziness, and the stakes got that bit higher. He'd begun to question just how far he would go to get his daughter back. But he'd gone too far already, and Vivienne knew it.

As an ex-copper, he had a moral code which, over the years, had gone from legitimately pristine like his badge, to distinctly subjective. He'd been kicked off the force for being too heavy-handed with a wife-beater. He'd deserved it. But he'd lost his daughter as a result of his fists. Everything he did was to get her back. Vivienne was equally his saviour and his master.

Paul Edderbridge had been a perfect choice. He was a wife-beater, and a lowlife, so George had no problem suggesting his hands got dirty, rather than his own. Edderbridge had trespassed on the estate before, he was a dropout without a job, he had previous convictions, and he was easily bought. The problem was that it had come to George's attention that Paul Edderbridge was, at the very moment Vivienne called, being hosted downtown in Penrith by Cumbria Constabulary, no doubt over a cup of weak coffee. Paul had called him only an hour before, cocky as anything, and told him casually about it, as if it was the most normal thing in the world. George knew, from his experience, that this wasn't the case at all.

'*Tidy up,*' had been Vivienne's words. He'd said the same to Nellie. The command covered a myriad of actions, which could be masked by euphemism and translation. George looked skyward as he headed away from the flat, leaving the two girls watching some vampire series on Netflix. George knew what he had to do. It wasn't so much what Vivienne had said herself, but what Fabian had told him before he boarded a privately chartered helicopter up here to Cumbria, without telling his mother. The time for playing two masters was coming to an end, and George had some serious decisions to make. Both of his keepers wanted the same thing – to save the family name – but only one knew the truth, and the extent of what they were asking him to do. The other remained in innocent bliss, and George felt as though that could be his last bargaining chip. If he was compromised, then he had at least that to fall back on. It would come at a price, because he was the one up to his neck in it, but the authorities loved a snitch, and that's what he was prepared to do, should he need to.

Things were so much simpler when Bart was alive. He parked the irony at the back of his mind.

Conversations whirred in his head. Bart's words to him, then Vivienne's calls late at night, and more recently, Fabian's demands and worries, bothering his mind like iron mosquitos, never quitting, weaving such a web that was now so big, no one caught in it had any way of escaping.

His phone rang and he looked at the number. It was a landline and he answered, ready to ditch this latest phone once it was used, and replace it. There were only five people who were aware of this number: Fabian, the two girls, Nellie and Vivienne.

'Hello.'

'George, I don't know what to do, I can't breathe, I'm in police custody, they won't let me go, I've been arrested!'

It was Nellie.

'Nellie, slow down, breathe. Jesus Christ. Slowly.'

'I've only got a minute, I can't... I can't...'

'Nellie, don't tell anyone who you called, do you hear me?'

'What do I do?'

'Hold your nerve, calm down. I will sort it,' he said, lying to her. How the hell he'd unpick her from this particular predicament, given her lack of resolve and what she might give away, he had no clue. She hung up, out of time.

The dragline of the web had just got that much tighter and stickier, with similar properties to high grade alloy steel wrapping its long thin strands around his neck. He loosened his collar. He imagined a disgusting flash vision of a spider spinning dense protein out of its swollen abdomen.

The line went dead and he destroyed the phone, walking to the supermarket three streets away, to dispose of it in a wastebin.

He had to get out of the Lake District. The prospect of ever holding his daughter in his arms again was slipping away like the fluttering snowflakes that were freezing everything, stuck in time, like his brain.

He went inside the shop and purchased another pay-as-you-go mobile and inserted a SIM into it as he went to a bench near the recycling area, and called Vivienne.

'Why have you sent Fabian up here?' he asked. George figured that attack was the best form of defence at this stage.

'I haven't,' she replied, somewhat irritably. 'Anyway, how do you know?'

'He called me.'

'He's letting his new position go to his head and making stupid decisions,' she said.

'What does he hope to gain from being up here?' George asked.

'Well, ostensibly, he's collecting the body of his late father. Of course, you know as well as I do that Fabian has his own agenda.'

George was tempted to come clean there and then about how unilaterally Fabian had acted, and how she should perhaps keep a closer eye on him, but he held off, sensing that it might be wise to hold on to that information for now, and play mother against son. He had to save some leverage, should he need it, for when the time came, and he was stuck in between these two toxic partners who pretended to love each other. Fabian fawned over his mother, and Vivienne loved to play the doting matriarch, but George knew them both too well.

Neither would take a moment to choose to save their kin when the time came, and George would be stuck in the middle. And he'd still never see his girl.

'Tidy up.'

He sighed and they ended their call.

Fat flakes of ice landed on his nose, and he wiped them away with one of his hands. The melting water trickled through his fingers. His hands were clean but, like Lady Macbeth, he could see spots on them that could never be erased. This was what Vivienne held over him. It was how Bart had controlled him. It was the same reason that he'd eventually gone over to Vivienne's side in the first place. It wasn't money that lured him, or the promise of women and cars, though Vivienne had tried. Only one thing could make him rich beyond his wildest dreams and that was getting his daughter back. For that, he'd do anything, or so he'd told Bart.

That was until he'd seen what his boss did at Laurie Fell. To girls the age of his daughter.

And now he had to make it all better. He had to make it go away; the trails and tendrils of deals done in pubs and on corners of parole buildings, with men of questionable character.

He'd first met Paul Edderbridge in the grounds of Laurie Fell, prowling one night, peeping through windows, and nosing through the sheds. The stupid fucking idiot had been stealing tyres. Of all things to bet the rest of your life on. Fucking tyres. Anyway, that was how thin the connection was between choosing a way out and a way down. Paul Edderbridge was the type of man to choose to make his life shittier than it was already. George knew that the first time they'd met.

Now, the time had come to end their business ties.

George wiped his large hand on his jeans and stood up, straightening his hat. Something told him that even if he tidied up for Vivienne and Fabian this afternoon, there would always be one more thing to do to secure the future of his daughter.

Chapter 51

Kelly replaced the phone and went to Kate's desk.

'Zoe just confirmed that the AAIB are accepting sabotage as the cause of the crash, having found no evidence to the contrary. However, it'll take weeks to say exactly how it happened. We can inform the families,' she said. They all knew that the final report could take months, but preliminary findings were legally binding at this stage.

'They can kiss goodbye to insurance payouts, then,' Kate said.

Kelly nodded. 'I'm heading over to the mortuary to meet Fabian Kennedy-Craig.'

'Is there much of his father left to say farewell to?' Kate asked. It was a serious question. Bartholomew Kennedy-Craig had suffered terrible blunt force trauma, mostly to his trunk, and it was difficult to say what killed him first: the internal bleeding or the flames. He was burned to a crisp. So Ted had told her.

'The coroner's team has cleaned him up as best they can, and I've been told that he's ready to be viewed by the family.'

'Good luck in this weather; it looks like it's getting worse again,' Kate said.

'Ah, it'll be fine.' She walked to the window and peered out. She checked her watch and glanced at the whiteboard, connected to the laptop on the desk, ready for the brief about the CCTV, newly installed at Aira Force car park. A spate of robberies of the parking machine had resulted in the National Trust's decision to pay for CCTV in several car parks, and as always, it worked to the advantage of the police. That stretch of road along Ullswater was dark and narrow. At least they stood a chance of catching some number plates off vehicles travelling towards or away from Laurie Fell on Sunday night and Monday morning. Kelly sat down to study the footage that had been ploughed through by a uniform downstairs, over the last few days. As she sat studying the list of VRNs, members of her team drifted towards the large conference table and placed mugs of coffee and bottles of water down, alongside pens and pads. When she was happy everybody was ready, she drew their attention to the stills isolated by the technical team.

'Of course, the CCTV here on the A592 only captures traffic travelling east and west from this point; it doesn't tell us who might have arrived from the Pooley Bridge end of the lake. However, we've got some interesting hits, as you can see. Kate, can you get the lights?' she asked.

Kate flicked the lights off and the team waited in silence.

'Here, we've got a taxi coming from the west, and we've identified one of the pilots in the passenger seat. The taxi firm has been contacted, and they've confirmed there were two passengers, another male,' she said. The team watched as she played footage from Saturday.

'The time is one forty-three p.m. so this fits with the WhatsApp messages sent to the girlfriends. We have to assume that they weren't worried about the helicopter being hangared outside overnight, else they would've flagged it up. The AAIB have also confirmed that it's normal practice, as long as the correct equipment is used, and they've established that it was.'

Kelly went on. 'This is Lord Reilly, travelling east from Glenridding towards Laurie Fell, at seven twenty-three p.m. on Saturday, in the passenger seat of a government vehicle. This is the same car returning Sunday morning, presumably for conference engagements, which we have confirmed he attended, then here he is travelling back again. There is no footage of him travelling back to Glenridding on Sunday night. So we have him present at Laurie Fell on Monday morning for the helicopter flight.'

She allowed people to get their heads around the details. 'Now, this one is the most insightful, I think.' She flicked another slide up onto the interactive board and enlarged the image. She saw Rob and Dan squint and lean forward. 'Is that Chloe Granger?' Dan asked.

'It most certainly is. And that's an unidentified male at the wheel. It's a private car, and a VRN check has it registered to Tactika Enterprises. A phone call to their transport section has it logged out to George Fellows, who is on Tactika's payroll as an administrator. Fellows is also an ex-copper. He was discharged following a question mark over his temper. Moving on, the car was found by the forensic team, parked in one of the garages at Laurie Fell, and they've swept it for prints and DNA. It confirms that if Chloe and Sasha were posting about arriving at Laurie Fell – as if going to some kind of gathering, on Sunday night – it wasn't their first trip there either, over the weekend.

'On that note, the press office are hammering the details all over the papers, and it's gone national like we were hoping. The media have picked up on it and I'm delighted to say they've caught on to the sleaze angle and are assuming we want to speak to the girls because they were there and they're underage.'

'That'll infuriate Mrs Kennedy-Craig,' Dan said.

'Won't it just?' Kelly agreed. 'If there's one thing guaranteed to get under her skin, it's the truth about her husband coming out in the press in a manner not controlled by her family. Let's see what happens when I meet her son later. He's flying up as we speak, and staying at the Glenridding hotel.'

Kelly closed the screen and opened another file. 'The information from the six phones found at the crash site is in and the tech people have found a few red flags. One is this number,' she said. 'It's on one of the phones found inside the helicopter, as well as on Nellie Lowther's phone. Unfortunately, we can't hold Nellie beyond tomorrow morning, when she'll have to be released, pending charges and under the condition that she helps with inquiries. Dan and Emma, I want you to keep a close eye on Nellie when she leaves. I want to know where she goes and who she talks to. The number, by the way, is one listed to Tactika. Checks have traced it to a work-issued phone, and it was registered in the name of none other than our George Fellows. I don't need to tell you how important it is that we find this man,' she said, flicking the screen to a close-up of an image of the man from the CCTV footage, driving the girls. It wasn't fantastically clear, and Tactika couldn't, or wouldn't, provide them with a work photo, so it was all they had.

'Fellows has worked for the family for twelve years. He was denied custody of his daughter, based on the mother dragging up his termination from the police, and she's in foster care in London. He hasn't been allowed to see her for four years. The mother died of a heroin overdose in 2015. The girl is fifteen.'

'And just like that another poor sod is orphaned,' Dan said. 'What was an ex-copper doing with a heroin addict?'

'Maybe he thought he could get her off it,' Kelly said. 'We have to narrow down our inquiry to who we know for sure was on site at Laurie Fell. They are, to our knowledge, the only people who had access to the sheds adjacent to the hangared helicopter on Sunday night. So we have Lord Reilly, Bartholomew Kennedy-Craig and the pilots, and we can rule them out. Murder–suicide is a real threat but not in this case, I don't think. That leaves Nellie Lowther, the two schoolgirls, and George Fellows. It's also feasible that Paul Edderbridge could have taken that stolen boat to Laurie Fell and dumped it back at Pooley Bridge before returning to his girlfriend's pad to beat her up and spend the night in here. They're our options,' she said.

The room fell silent. The obvious choice was Paul Edderbridge, of course, but they had to prove he was there beyond reasonable doubt, and they had to find George Fellows and the two schoolgirls.

'It's obvious that somebody with George Fellows's past connections and skills, as well as having an axe to grind and a critical weakness, might be in the family's pocket. It's just a theory, but it's become obvious to me that the whole climate activist theory is a red herring. The true perpetrator is much closer to the family,' she said.

Chapter 52

The drive over to the Penrith and Lakes was short. Kelly could have walked, but even in the snow it was quicker to queue in traffic. A light covering of snow was settling on the streets and the temperature gauge hadn't changed. The sky was a moody grey and the hills in the distance were fat with snow, like iced fairy cakes. She'd taken another dose of tablets, and the two coffees she'd had already were keeping her going. Kennedy-Craig had got permission to land on the rooftop helipad. She wondered how he'd managed that, but at the same time knew that money bought everything, especially privilege. Rob had worked out Bartholomew Kennedy-Craig's net worth when he died; after the shares in Tactika had recovered yesterday afternoon following an article about the company's philanthropic work around the world, his estate was worth 17 billion dollars.

They had photographs of the families of the deceased up on the incident board back at Eden House, and Kelly had become familiar with the sultry good looks of Fabian Kennedy-Craig over the last few days. She was interested to meet this young man in his twenties with all that power at his disposal, now his father was out of the way. There was one thing she was sure of. If Paul Edderbridge had anything to do with the plan to sabotage the helicopter – and this she found unlikely, given Paul's known substance abuse and volatility, as well as his glaring lack of intelligence – then he had no obvious motive. Which only left one suggestion: that it was somebody else's plan, and he was paid to carry it out.

She parked her car and slid her thick coat on to walk to the hospital entrance, where Fabian had said he'd wait for her in the hospital cafe. She spotted him straight away. He jarred against his surroundings, like a shiny new penny in a shitpile. He was pristine in his long wool coat, with its turned up and tailored collar, snugly fitting his broad shoulders like a second skin. His shoes were shiny and unwrinkled and his hair was lush and strong, glinting auburn like her own. He spotted her too, and she noticed his dark eyes kept their gaze on her, unwavering in any other direction. He was tall and Kelly looked up to him when they got close enough. He held out his hand and smiled, but Kelly saw pain behind his eyes. She'd met enough criminals to know that acting was a close bedfellow to breaking the law, and she reserved judgement of the young man who took her breath away.

He could be a killer, based on 17 billion reasons.

'Kelly, it's a pleasure. I know you've been working tirelessly to investigate my father's death. You seem to be the only one in the country who cares,' he said, smiling broadly, maintaining iron-clad eye contact.

She reciprocated, not looking away. 'You're welcome. We've made much progress. I see you've got a coffee and a pastry, shall we sit and talk?'

Kelly noticed stares from other patrons of the small cafe, and she realised they must stand out. They were well dressed, businesslike, and healthy.

'Let me at least buy you a coffee first,' he said.

'Latte, please, one sugar, thanks,' she said. She sat down while he went to the counter, and took off her coat. Snow that had settled on her now melted and created a puddle under the table. The cafe was warm and she could feel her cheeks burning. It might be considered odd that after coming all this way, Fabian wanted to share a coffee before visiting his dead father, but then the body was going nowhere. She had no idea as to their relationship in life, or the one he had with his mother, though she'd got the impression over the phone that Vivienne irritated him, like most mothers who fuss too much. She thought of her own and the incessant questions about her life. She realised now that it was a mother's job to be a pain in the arse, and she fully intended to do the same with Lizzie.

He came back with her drink and sat down.

He was incredibly relaxed for his age, though still cocky, and she thought back to how highly strung she'd been in her twenties, when she worked in London and thought she could save the world, one dickhead in prison at a time.

'How have you been?' she asked.

He looked away finally, and it gave her space to breathe.

'I was doing okay before we got the bombshell about the accident. At first, it was easy to take in the press because they lie about everything, but now you've confirmed it was sabotage, I just don't know what to say. That's why I'm here, because I hired a private detective to do some digging and it seemed more important to be here now. Before you ask, I have no idea who might want my father dead.'

'If he was the target,' she said.

He looked at her and took a bite of his pastry. He chewed slowly, wiping his mouth with a paper napkin. 'You think the target was Donald?'

'How much do you know about him?' she asked.

He sucked in his breath and finished the pastry in one last mouthful. He liked to take his time.

'From my point of view, my mother hated his association with my dad. The two families had a falling-out a few years back and I'm afraid I was not well behaved. My mother informed me that Donald was a drain on my father, and extorted money out of him in return for keeping quiet about certain business deals – perfectly legal, might I add – and protecting him, if you like, from close scrutiny.'

'Why would that offend your mother so much?' Kelly thought about the Polaroids from Laurie Fell, and doubted that Vivienne's distaste for Donald was based on their financial arrangements.

'You're after something else? Something sordid, like they're saying in the press?' he asked.

'I'm putting it out there. Is there any truth in it?'

'What, that my father liked sex parties?' He shrugged and smirked. 'I guess everyone does, don't they? I have no idea, but what I do know is that it would be more damaging to the family for that to get out than, say, stories on our finances.'

'So, you think it's a set-up? Who has the kind of influence to dictate to domestic media?' she let the question hang.

'I didn't say that. I'm trying to answer your questions, not solve your puzzle,' he said.

'Fair enough,' she said. 'You are aware that these parties that are alleged to have happened involved underage girls?'

His comment about everybody somehow being free and at liberty to enjoy a good old sex party had annoyed her.

'You have proof?' he asked. 'Because if that was the case, then I want to know.'

'This private investigator, what has he, or she, unearthed?'

'He. Not a lot so far, I have to say. I assumed your lot would be too busy pampering Donald's family to get to the bottom of my father's death, so that's why he's up here. I underestimated you.'

'Can I meet him?' Kelly asked.

'I don't see why not. George has been with the family for years; he's meticulous.'

Pieces, absent in her head until a few moments ago, slotted into place, and she cast her gaze over Fabian's shoulder, as her mind fitted George Fellows into the role of PI, to see if that would explain his movements as they knew them so far. It was a possibility.

'George Fellows?'

'How do you know?'

'He's popped up on some CCTV, and we'd like to talk to him,' she said.

'Well, that makes sense. At least I know he's been earning his money,' he said and smiled. 'I'll give him a call when we're done. Can I see my father now?'

'You're ready?' she asked.

'No. But I need to see him.'

'Of course. Follow me.' She got up and he followed her to the corridor that led down to the mortuary, via a lift.

'What can I expect?' Fabian asked.

Kelly liked his directness.

'The coroner is my father; he's treated your father with respect. His body will be covered by a sheet but you can see his face and neck. He has bruising on his jaw, and some trauma to his temple, and his skin is discoloured from the fire, but apart from that, he looks at peace.'

'You've seen him?'

'Being present at autopsies is part of my job sometimes,' she said.

'How did he die?'

Kelly could tell that this question weighed heavy on his mind.

'He suffered trauma to his internal organs from the impact of the crash.'

Fabian fell silent.

They exited the lift and Kelly took him to meet Ted, who was the picture of professionalism, as he always was when he met traumatised relatives. She loved him for his sensitivity. He explained to Fabian how the process worked and Fabian said he was ready.

'I'll wait here,' Kelly said.

Fabian turned to her, as if to plead with her to accompany him, but thought against it, and disappeared with Ted.

Chapter 53

Kelly went back to the cafe and bought a bottle of water and some tissues. She was beginning to feel as though her sinuses were clogging again and she imagined curling up in front of the fire at home, and going into a deep sleep. She tried to concentrate, expecting Fabian to come out of the mortuary soon, and for Ted to call her, but, after half an hour, he hadn't, so she packed up her things and went back to the lift.

Updates on the case were steady and she'd been able to read more phone printouts from the crash site. Of the six mobile phones discovered in the helicopter, two of them had been confirmed as belonging to the pilots, another had been Donald's private mobile, and another his work mobile. That left two, which they assumed were Bart's. George Fellows's number had appeared a total of twenty-three times on one of them, and the other was used solely for one single number: an untraceable pay-as-you-go. It wasn't uncommon for somebody in Bart's position to use several phones, and to be calling hundreds of people each day, all over the world. What they needed to do, though, was find out who he'd been speaking to in the hours before his death. One thing was for sure; he'd been talking to George Fellows.

Kelly made a note to ask Fabian why his father might be contacting his firm's private investigator while he was attending meetings in the Lake District, and enjoying leisure time. Perhaps George Fellows was the fixer she assumed him to be. If Fabian could secure a meeting with him this afternoon, then many of her questions would be answered.

When she got to the mortuary, Ted looked at her oddly.

'He left ages ago,' he said.

'Where did he go?' Kelly asked.

Ted shrugged. 'I assumed he was free to go,' he said.

'Don't worry, it's no problem, it's just he was supposed to do something for me before he left.'

'It looks like this snow is settling again. I'll head over to yours when I'm done if that's all right with you?' he asked.

She nodded, and went to kiss him. They were in his private changing area, and so she felt able to show him the affection she felt for him. She would love to go for a pint with him right now, and tell him all the woes of the case, but it would have to wait for tonight. Johnny had said he was cooking again, and it fell into her plans, so she hadn't objected. She'd enjoyed the presence of his body next to hers last night, and despite feeling rotten with a cold, she'd slept better than she had in two whole months. She felt a flutter of excitement hit her tummy as she looked forward to the evening that lay ahead.

She felt lethargic as she left Ted's offices and yawned as she answered a work call.

She stopped in the middle of the corridor and leant against the wall. She nodded and ended the call, realising that a hit of adrenalin had revitalised her senses. She broke into a sprint and took the stairs up to the intensive care unit.

Lord Donald Reilly was awake.

She got to the ICU breathless, and saw to her horror that Fabian Kennedy-Craig was already there, and she could hear a shouting match between him and Elaine Reilly. She rang the security buzzer furiously and was let in by an irate nurse, who recognised her police lanyard.

The nurse was fuming speaking into a ward phone, asking for security.

Kelly could see Fabian, but it was only Elaine's voice that identified his adversary. They were shouting at full volume now, and Kelly marched towards them and held Elaine back.

'Fabian! You need to leave! This is the family's private space, you shouldn't be here.' She had to shout over them to be heard. They both ignored her. Kelly caught snippets of the tempestuous exchange, from the middle of the battleground between them. Fabian was accusing Elaine of dragging his father to his death by association with her husband. In return, Elaine was doing the same.

'Jesus, Fabian, leave now or I'll have you arrested!' Kelly shouted, still holding on to Elaine, who was red-faced and incandescent with rage. The daughter, Abigail Reilly, hovered about behind the spectacle, and pleaded with her mother to calm down. Kelly noticed that she showed no ill will towards Fabian Kennedy-Craig.

Fabian retreated and left the ward, his long coat wafting behind him like a cape of defiance. Kelly looked at Elaine, who was shaking. Abigail's eyes followed Fabian.

'What happened?' Kelly asked.

'*He* happened!' Elaine said. 'What is he doing here?' she shouted.

Kelly felt the full impact of the woman's scorn. 'He was here visiting his father,' she said, sobering Elaine a little. 'What is it with you two?' Kelly asked. 'I heard good news, that your husband is awake, and I get here to a screaming match.'

'The last time I saw that man, he told Donald he'd kill him if he didn't leave his father alone, and now look. You do the detective work!' she spat, and walked away.

Kelly was left in the middle of the corridor, with three nurses going about their business having heard the exchange. She stood in the hallway, with her bag and coat discarded on the floor, wondering what it all meant. If she'd heard Elaine correctly, then Fabian had lied to her about many things. One of the nurses looked at her with sympathy. She gathered her things off the floor and stood up to see Abigail still loitering.

'What happened?' Kelly asked her.

'He just appeared,' she said.

'You know one another?' Kelly asked. 'It was quite obvious that you do.'

Abigail looked down.

'You won't find the answer down there; you either do or don't,' Kelly reminded her.

'Yes, we were close. After he threatened my dad, we stopped seeing each other.'

The girl was timid and, Kelly thought, sad about the fact. There was affection there. She turned to a nurse.

'I had come to check on Lord Reilly, how is he?' she asked.

'He's scoring well on the Glasgow scale, and he's breathing on his own, which is fantastic, but he's too tired to talk, if that's what you want,' she added.

Kelly nodded and passed the nurse a card. 'Call me the minute he starts speaking,' she said. The nurse nodded.

'And please let the next shift know,' she added. She turned around to speak to Abigail, but she'd disappeared.

She left and went to the lifts. By the time she got out of the hospital and called Fabian's phone, he was already in his limousine heading to his hotel in Glenridding, and telling her that he'd forgotten about his promise to introduce her to George.

'Just give me his current phone number and I'll call him myself. He's not using the same phone as the one your father used,' she said. 'I've tried, it's off.'

'Of course, let me get back to you,' he said.

She had to leave it; there was nothing she could do. 'What was that all about with Elaine Reilly?' she asked.

'I told you, our families fell out. Elaine hates my mother and the feeling is reciprocal. I heard Donald was awake and I wanted to speak to him. I assume that's why you turned up?' he asked.

'Yes, but how did you find out?' she asked.

'Abigail called me, we keep in touch,' he said.

'You two are close? I could tell.'

'We're just two people who have bothersome parents, detective,' he said.

'Why did your mothers really fall out, Fabian?'

'That'll be a conversation over dinner, detective. I've had enough today. I'm going to my hotel to get drunk,' he said. 'Unless you want to join me?'

Kelly was intrigued. The last thing she should be doing was socialising with a person of interest in a case, but it didn't need to be like that; she could just listen. And the one thing she wanted, that Fabian could give her, was the whereabouts of George Fellows.

'I'm on my way,' she said, and left the ward.

Chapter 54

As Kelly turned out of the Penrith and Lakes, she got a call from Kate back at Eden House.

'What's up?' Kelly asked.

'The tech department have come back with the results from the electrical equipment seized from Laurie Fell.'

'And?' Kelly waited. She drove through town, intending to take the A592 all the way along Ullswater's north shore to Glenridding, where the climate conference had been held, and where Donald Reilly should have stayed. Now she'd met Fabian Kennedy-Craig, she realised that it was in his character to have chosen the hotel on purpose. She got the impression that everything he did was planned. Maybe he was meeting his private detective there.

'George Fellows beat up a perp, when he was serving in the Met – pretty badly, as well,' Kate said.

'Okay, so he's a martyr to the cause,' Kelly said. It was what they called overzealous coppers who liked to take things into their own hands, and deal with criminals in their own way. A lot of the time they got away with it, especially in the huge constabularies in the cities.

'He was picked up on CCTV at Penrith station accessing an Amazon deposit point yesterday,' Kate added.

'Good, we'll find him. I thought you were calling me about the seized computers?' Kelly asked. It was as if Kate was avoiding something. She could hear it in her voice.

'They confirmed that the CCTV from Laurie Fell was wiped off the server on Monday morning. They retrieved all memory from before then and it would appear that Nellie was telling the truth; there's no footage of the graffiti. However, they did tell me that there was footage from another occasion last week, when there is evidence of a trespasser in the sheds.'

Kelly processed the information and appreciated the gravity of it: somebody snooping around Laurie Fell, especially inside the outhouses, might be pivotal, but she also couldn't help thinking that Kate was stalling for time.

'Okay, Kate, what are you really calling me about? I'm on my way to Glenridding, do I have to turn around?'

Kate sucked in her breath. 'The technical team have found hundreds of child porn images and videos, and some of them are Category A,' Kate said.

'Jesus,' Kelly said. She pulled into a service station on the outskirts of Penrith. Indecent images of children were graded into three levels, A being the most offensive material.

'That's not all,' Kate said.

Kelly's stomach turned over. 'I'm turning round, I'll be there in ten minutes,' she said.

'Sasha Granger and Chloe Tate have been identified in some of them,' Kate said.

'God, I feel sick,' Kelly said. She did a three-point turn. Whatever Fabian Kennedy-Craig could tell her about George Fellows, or his mother, could wait. News like this had the effect of turning a department upside-down. It made officers sick to their stomachs. This was a whole side to the case that no one had expected; the sheer volume and nature of the findings threw up hundreds of other possible explanations as to why somebody might want to take revenge against Kennedy-Craig and his friends. She saw a case like this growing exponentially until they were sucked down a hole that could span years. They could be looking at thousands of arrests and an infinite number of leads to hand over to Europol, who gathered information like this on paedophiles all the time. Nowadays, images and videos containing child porn were rarely kept private. They were worth so much on the dark web. But Kennedy-Craig didn't need money. She was back to motive again, and came up with only one sickening conclusion.

A deduction that Kate confirmed.

'Kennedy-Craig and Lord Reilly have been identified in some of the footage,' Kate said.

'Have you got the child abuse unit on board?' Kelly asked.

'Yes. Done,' Kate replied.

'Good; ask them if this changes how long we can hold Nellie Lowther,' Kelly asked.

'I've already done that,' Kate said. 'Highly unlikely, because we have no more evidence that she is involved directly than we did this morning. Even though the evidence was found on her property.'

'Fuck,' Kelly said.

'I know,' Kate said.

'I'll be twenty minutes,' she said, and ended the call.

Chapter 55

Kelly returned to the office to receive more bad news. The CPS had refused the charges of soliciting minors against Nellie Lowther on lack of evidence and also dismissed the charges of boat theft against Paul Edderbridge. Until they had his DNA from something like the cigarette end or beer can, they weren't interested. Both were free to go.

Meanwhile, Kelly called a briefing meeting with the child abuse team, which was based on another floor at Eden House.

A certain hush fell when they got involved. It was as if by behaving as quietly as possible, some of the pain they dealt with might go away. It was a curious human trait. Kelly could never get her head around why anyone would want to work in the child abuse team. They watched the worst child porn and graded hideous images, from all over the world, all day long, every day. She had no idea how they did it.

Four members of the team arrived and they were shown into the incident room. It would have to be a separate inquiry, because they possessed certain specialist skills and resources that a regular crime team simply didn't have the time or experience to process. All the images had been handed over, including the video footage. It would all have to be trawled through and matched to the child abuse image database (CAID), which aided police with grading images and identifying children.

They'd look for things like carpet patterns, bedspread fabrics, door sizes, points of interest out of windows or on reflections, and of course, the children's faces. It was harrowing.

'They've already identified, after a cursory scroll though, several other pupils at Sasha and Chloe's school,' Kate said as they walked into the incident room together.

Kelly shook her head. It made her blood boil. They were only touching the edge of a sordid world that she could never understand, and she had huge respect for the members of the team who sat waiting for them. They looked like ordinary coppers. They drank coffee, wrote notes and chatted about the snow storms. But what they saw must change them, Kelly thought.

She invited the team to talk them through what they intended to do with the images and files. Then she filled them in on her perspective from the ongoing case.

'It looks like your list of potential saboteurs just got bigger,' one said. It was no surprise that another department in the building was following the high-profile case of the helicopter crash.

Kelly acknowledged this as the case. It was not uncommon for parents and relatives of missing children, who suspected their child was taken by organised groups involved in the dark web, to start their own investigations and go after perps, vigilante style.

She had to consider everything.

She thought about Fabian Kennedy-Craig and Abigail Reilly. Did they know? Was this why their families had fallen out, but the two youngsters kept in touch? Equal amounts of shame and disgust binding them together?

She was under no illusion that somebody must know about the men's proclivities, and that list included, in her mind, Elaine Reilly and Vivienne Kennedy-Craig. Before the meeting, she'd requested Vivienne Kennedy-Craig be brought in for questioning on the matter, and her closest station was Mayfair and St James. How civilised, Kelly thought. The rich even have their crimes examined in style. Meanwhile, Elaine Reilly was being brought from the Penrith and Lakes and should be arriving downstairs shortly. She didn't give a damn that the press might get hold of such information, and Andrew Harris had no leg to stand on if he wanted to moralise to her about doing the right thing. It was now indisputable that Reilly and Kennedy-Craig were together over the weekend in the Lake District to commit horrific crimes. Laurie Fell, it would appear, was their secret playground, and Kelly didn't believe for one minute that Nellie Lowther didn't know about it. It was a constant vexation in police work that, without evidence, no one could progress a case that simply couldn't stand up in court. For that, they had to piece together information, painstakingly gathered over time, to present to the CPS before they'd take a bite. The CPS, or Her Majesty's government lawyers, weren't going to prosecute cases they might lose. Right and wrong didn't come into it.

It was why a lot of coppers left the force.

Kelly couldn't bring herself to be anywhere near the cells downstairs when Nellie Lowther and Paul Edderbridge were released, albeit pending further inquiry, which was standard. Of course, Elaine Reilly would more than likely refuse to be accompanied to Eden House to help police with their inquiries simply because she could, and she'd no doubt insist on a lawyer flying in from London. But Kelly reminded the coppers tasked with driving her from the hospital that the press was still camping on the hospital doorstep and they could either go out the front or the back.

As the meeting started with the child abuse team, they spread out a huge file of notes on the table between them. Kelly threw a glance to Kate.

'What's this?' Kelly asked.

'As you know, part of our job is sharing information with the international community and policing the dark web. It's come to our attention that several of the images and videos, found on electrical equipment at Laurie Fell, have duplicated hits all over Europe. The database has matched the few we inputted on a tentative trial basis, as standard, just in case, if you will. And they've flagged links to a ring that is being investigated out of South America. It's run by a web domain called The Chief.'

Chapter 56

Nellie put on her coat slowly. She felt as though everybody's eyes were on her. The police woman behind the desk, who reissued her private belongings, seemed to be smirking at her. The officer who opened the door for her, and offered to call a cab, seemed to mock her and watch as she walked down the steps. She felt dirty and very alone. The lawyer from Tactika had already gone.

Her father would have known what to do, but then she realised that he would also have been angry with her for failing to follow basic rules. It had been so easy. Her instructions from George were abundantly clear, and he'd even started to tidy up with her, helping to carry bags and cart equipment to outhouses. He'd spent hours going through Bart's computers and deleting things. She could guess what he was getting rid of. She was under no illusion what would happen next.

But no one would understand that it wasn't her fault.

When faced with no choice, what does a person do? She didn't feel sorry for any of the girls. They had to accept their position in life and get on with it, just like she had. She knew that everybody would feel sorry for the girls, and everybody would point their fingers at her. Bart was safe; he'd escaped. He would never be brought to justice. Donald would be better off dying in the hospital. So she was the one who'd be held accountable. These things had been done on her property, and she'd allowed them. She'd found the girls. She'd helped set up introductions, she'd taken money and enjoyed the lifestyle, all so it stopped happening to her.

Her father and Donald had known each other all her life, they'd virtually grown up together. One thing she'd learned over time was that this was a life that one could never escape. You either survived or you became a victim, and she wasn't willing to give in. When the time came, it was her choice to supply girls to replenish the reservoir of children who no one cared about or missed. Her role as head of the English department gave her a unique insight into which children were the most vulnerable, and therefore most likely to succumb to her offer of quick rewards, and they were plentiful. But most importantly, when she fulfilled the need for a steady cache of ideal candidates – in other words, ones who wouldn't talk or brag; the children who were already written off in life and had no desire to draw even more attention to themselves – her father had stopped using her.

She wrapped her coat around her thin, tired body and stared up at the dark sky. She'd spent around eight hours in the police station, freezing and humiliated, and her bones ached. Snowflakes, fat with perfection, floated down from the blackness and were illuminated by street lights. The vision mesmerised her. As the tiny crystals settled on her face and melted, they mingled with her tears and she felt a strange sensation as warm mixed with cold and had the effect of cleansing her mind somewhat.

She walked to the taxi rank near the station and jumped into the back of a car.

'Laurie Fell estate, please,' she said.

'Why're you going there at this time of night? Are you working for the BBC or something?' the cabbie asked, laughing at his clever joke.

'No, I live there,' she said.

That shut him up. No doubt he'd call all of his friends after he'd dropped her off. And soon he'd know the extent of the monster he'd had in his back seat. She didn't say another word. The man drove in silence and Nellie knew that she'd shocked him into quiet, which was just how she wanted it. He couldn't know the truth of course, but she imagined he did, and it crushed her chest.

As they drove along the north shore of Ullswater, she had to tell him exactly where the entrance was. People always got it muddled up, and that was one of the reasons that her father had liked it so much. It was about as isolated as you could hope for. There was no viability in this sort of thing in the cities any more. Tip-offs, nosy neighbours, confident delivery people and everybody thinking they were the new Inspector Morse, all contrived to make it hell for the private investor looking for seclusion. The Lake District was perfect.

She asked him to drop her at the gate. The last thing she needed was him getting out his mobile phone and filming the raiding of her private property by the forensic lab team in white plastic suits, with their blue tents set up all over her lawn, giving the impression that innocents had been murdered there. He wasn't to know that actually what had come to pass on her land was much, much worse.

She watched as he drove off, and she did it on purpose because she knew that what he really wanted to do was send a live film of her walking away from his cab and hashtag it, to be snapped up by a national newspaper for a couple of quid. She was adamant that she was at least allowed to avoid this final humiliation.

She watched his tail lights disappear and went inside the gates, arguing with the officer on the gate about who she was, and walking the final three hundred metres or so in silence, listening to the wind and snow, watching the trees become burdened with the weight of nature, and occasionally hearing the loud dump of a large pile of a fresh drift landing on the ground with a whooshing sound.

Most of the forensic vans had packed up and gone, and only three remained on the gravel driveway. She avoided them and went around the back, crossing the grass without detection. When she arrived in her cottage, which she knew would soon come under the same warrant as the main house, she closed the door behind her and stood dripping in the entrance. She no longer felt the cold, and she didn't bother taking off her coat. She went to the back of the house, without turning on any lights, and got a stool from the utility room. Next she went back outside, towards an outhouse building, tutting as she entered it and found it virtually empty. Things were knocked over and items in disarray. She noted that it summed up her life. She was like an empty storage unit standing in the middle of a vast lawn, open to the elements, stripped of her contents and left bare. She'd tried her best to do what George had asked but she'd been overwhelmed. The shock of losing Bart, who'd looked after her ever since her father's death, even though he was so much younger than she was, had been a terrible blow, and she felt rudderless and lethargic. George's instructions were simply too much. She'd told him she needed no help with all the equipment. She'd known she was lying to him but it had got rid of him, for the time being.

She rooted around and found what she was looking for: a length of sturdy rope. She went back to her cottage and still flicked on no lights to help her. She needed none. Her hands worked expertly. Even though she'd known her father was a monster, she'd still sought his approval and affection. Growing up in Cumbria, this had meant being his willing helper on fishing boat trips, where he'd taught her how to tie the best knots. She never forgot because it was about the only pure thing he ever gave her, and had requested nothing in return. Even child molesters have other hobbies.

The slip knot was the simplest form, and she'd tied it a thousand times. Her fingers grasped the rough fibres of the rope but her brain didn't register the potential violence the material could cause and she acted like an automaton, her brain having long since abandoned the idea of survival.

Her cold fingers warmed up as she worked the rope and a smile appeared at the corners of her mouth. The beam across the pantry ceiling was perfect, she thought. Once she'd looped the rope a few times and she was satisfied, after tugging on it, she took the small stool, went in to the pantry, and closed the door behind her.

Chapter 57

George spotted Paul Edderbridge leaving the red stone Penrith police station, and waved. The young man swaggered over the road and got in to the passenger side of the car. George had saved the vehicle from a dump yard for five hundred quid.

'Pint?' Paul asked.

George smiled and pulled away. 'We need to tie up a few loose ends,' he said.

'Jesus Christ, George, you're always so serious. Let's go and celebrate,' Paul said.

'Celebrate what?' George asked.

'They've got nothing on me,' he laughed.

George concentrated on the road, which was becoming difficult to navigate in the worsening blizzard. They approached a crossing and the lights turned amber, but George carried on. A woman stepped out into the road as the light turned red and George hammered his foot on the brakes. They both flew forward in the car, and the woman jumped back in horror.

'Fuck's sake, George!' Paul shouted at him and waved to the woman to cross. Passers-by helped the woman to her feet and they pointed at the car as George carried on and simply drove around them.

They left the town's lights and headed across the M6. Paul lit a cigarette. George sat brooding and silent in the driver's seat.

'Where we going?' Paul asked.

'That boat you stole, it was sloppy, and now we have to remove it. I'm getting tired of tidying up after you, Paul,' George said.

Paul blew smoke into the car and it filled the tiny space. George undid his window and snow came in and blew all over the two men.

'I was wearing a hat and large coat like you said, and I had my back to the CCTV camera,' Paul said. 'Can you shut the fucking window?'

George gripped the steering wheel and put his foot on the accelerator. They drove on in silence, with the windows open. By the time George came to a small jetty at the end of a private road on Ullswater's southern shore, they were both covered in snow.

'You're a miserable bastard, George,' Paul said.

George smiled at him as he parked the car and got out. He walked to the jetty and indicated to Paul that they were going for a boat ride in a small aluminium dinghy with a motor attached. Paul hung back.

'It won't take long,' George reassured him.

'This isn't the boat, I dumped it over there,' Paul said, pointing in the vague direction of Pooley Bridge, in the pitch blackness.

'I know. It needs towing, you idiot.'

'I thought the police had it?' Paul said.

'They couldn't move it, so we're going to beat them to it,' George said.

Paul shrugged and got into the flimsy vessel. He sat on one of the benches, and smelled the faint whiff of fishing paraphernalia. He looked across the lake.

'How long will this take, George? It's fucking freezing,' Paul said.

'Not long,' George said.

As they headed out to the middle of the lake, George handled the steering and Paul sat in the tiny open cabin, huddled away from the snow, and stared dead ahead.

George took a wrench out of his pocket and left the steering control. The purr of the small engine didn't change and the first blow to Paul's head was almost silent, like the humming thump of the propeller hitting the water. He kept hitting, as hard as he could, and when the wrench became slippery, he stopped. Paul's body slumped into the centre of the boat and George kicked it away as he went back to the controls and turned the boat around, to head across to a different boathouse, which he knew was unused. The lake was littered with them. Some of them were seasonal, like this one, so by the time the holiday makers came swarming back in the spring, he'd have moved the body.

George manoeuvred the small boat under the shelter of the old stone work in silence, and turned off the engine. He jumped out and closed the gates to the dark night. He worked quickly, taking the material he'd stored there out of a large container on the covered jetty. He wrapped Paul's body tightly and placed various items inside the package with him. There was an anvil, some large concrete blocks and various metal beams. He worked right at the edge of the enclosed jetty and so each item was fairly easy to manoeuvre; however, when it came to rolling the body into the deep water, it took all his might to pull it off. Finally, Paul plopped over the edge and sank straight to the bottom. A metal grate at the foot of the jetty would prevent the body from floating away, and he'd deal with the problem of what to do with it another day. But for now, the problem of Paul Edderbridge had just disappeared.

He felt nothing.

He'd dispatched a wife-beater who also harmed his kids. Like Bart had harmed kids. And this, he told himself, was why he was doing all of this: to save *his* child. He knew he'd crossed a line a long time ago, and there was no turning back, if he wanted to see his daughter again.

George checked his runaway thoughts. *Stop thinking!* He had shit to get done before he could go back to the apartment. The girls would freak out if they saw bits of brain and guts on his jacket. He pulled a large holdall out of the same container and stripped, packing all of the dirty clothes back into it and stepping into clean ones.

He locked the boathouse put the key in his pocket, and got back into his car. Now he had to decide who to pin his future on and call first: Fabian or Vivienne.

Chapter 58

The snow on Thursday morning was thicker and deeper than yesterday, and it was still snowing. Kelly watched from the window as Johnny dug a pathway for her car. There was nothing she wanted more than to curl up by the fire and write the day off, but she had no choice in the matter. Last night, they'd discussed the case after Lizzie had been put to bed, over dinner. Kelly had watched her father in animated conversation with Johnny, and they'd shared stories of their experience of human disasters – Ted in Northern Ireland and Johnny in the Middle East. They were the only two people she knew who could pull off a full-on debate about political history and not argue.

But the safety net of being surrounded by family she cared about was burst the moment she woke up, because she'd drunk too much red wine. It hadn't helped her sinuses. It also didn't get her any closer to working out how she felt about Johnny, and she knew that welcoming him into her bed for two nights running wasn't the best way to keep a clear head. But maybe that was the point. She heard Kate telling her to just fuck it, and go with her heart. And she knew that Kate would stand by that, even though it was Johnny who had in effect betrayed both of them when he became a witness for the defence in the Burton trial. The Burton family had blood on its hands, but Kelly knew that Kate would say that it was nobody else's fault. Only theirs. Johnny was no more culpable than the lawyers. Kate had reminded her of that when he'd moved out only a couple of months ago. Kelly envied her friend's clarity of thinking.

Whatever she felt right now, she tried to clear her head and concentrate on just today. Wasn't that what Kate always said? Kelly had seen her friend transform into a new woman since she'd kicked Derek out and divorced him. Even her face was different, as her smile and laughter overhauled her whole demeanour.

After showering and waking herself up a little more, she took Lizzie downstairs and put the coffee machine on. It was becoming more and more difficult to keep Lizzie in her chair, because the child was inquisitive and trying to move around, even at four months old. Kelly plopped her inside a playpen Ted had bought, which was in the hallway near to the kitchen. If she kept the doors open, she could see her and hear her talking and singing to herself, as she mimicked the adults around her. Kelly forgot her headache, and made a quick sandwich to eat later, knowing it would be a long day again. She had to catch up with Fabian Kennedy-Craig and try to pin George Fellows down to a meeting at least, if not an interview. The man was inside Bartholomew Kennedy-Craig's inner circle and Kelly reckoned that it was pretty unfeasible that he wouldn't know what his boss had been up to all these years. However, she also had to give him the benefit of the doubt, because in her experience, paedophiles were the most manipulative of highly disturbed narcissists. It was still possible that nobody else knew. Nellie would have to be brought in again. It was a tedious merry-go-round but the only way to get around the CPS's inability to charge everybody on a copper's nose, as they did in the good old days. Yo-yoing to and from interview suites was now the go-to leisure pursuit of the best criminals, until they made a mistake, or got caught. She wanted to ask Nellie again why she called Kennedy-Craig 'The Chief'. Every time she thought of the pet name, she winced.

As was customary during a big case, Kelly's thoughts overtook her perfunctory morning tasks and she was in a dream-like state when Johnny came back inside. Ted was still in bed. Johnny put his arm around her waist and it made her jump.

'In the zone?' he asked.

She nodded.

'No worries, I'm happy to stay here,' he smiled.

It was funny how making love to him was the easiest thing in the world, but facing him and organising the care of their child was somehow awkward. She put it out of her mind and told herself that she was being paranoid. Johnny was a typical bloke and probably not even considering the rights and wrongs of what they'd done over the last couple of days. It felt good, that was all. Times change. People change. More importantly, opinions change.

Ian Burton had gone to prison for possibly the rest of his life. There was no justifiable reason to let his legacy affect her family. No good reason at all.

'I was thinking I might scoot over to the flat today and get some things to bring over,' he said. 'That's if you're okay with that?'

This got her attention.

She finished frothing milk and stirred his coffee, passing him the cup. 'I think I'd like that, and so would Lizzie,' she said.

He smiled and Kelly thought she'd never seen him so nervous. It made her feel deeply conscious of how much Johnny wanted his family back.

'When's Josie back?' he asked.

It was telling of his relationship with his oldest daughter that Kelly knew her plans before he did. Kelly knew that the bad weather wouldn't have stalled the expedition in Borrowdale. Josie had been hiking with her father for as long as they'd been together, and would love the challenge.

'She's back tomorrow. She's not allowed her mobile until then, so it might come as a bit of a shock that you're suddenly around the house. I'll talk to her,' Kelly said.

Johnny nodded and sipped his coffee.

'I need to go,' she said. She went to her daughter and picked her up to kiss her, and the girl squirmed to get her father's attention. Typical of small humans everywhere, she was letting her mother know that she was nailing her allegiance firmly to the parent who was around the most at the moment. Kelly snuggled into her neck and gathered her things.

'Thanks for digging me out,' she said to Johnny. They kissed.

The drop in temperature outside made her rush to the car, and she almost slipped on the fresh snow, which had frozen as soon as it hit the ground. Johnny had cleared the windscreen for her and had the heating running for half an hour. It was cosy inside and she set her Toughpad up with the Bluetooth in the car to occupy her as she queued in traffic to get to Penrith.

Paul Edderbridge, released pending the continuation of his cooperation, was due back in the station this morning, and the forensic report of his girlfriend's place had been sent to her via email. Sat in traffic, she glanced at it and her stomach dropped to her guts. She read that the flat, shared with his girlfriend, who he used as a punch bag, as well as three young children who were terrified of him, was a chaotic tip. Underneath the detritus the team had discovered various items of interest and one of them was a collection of simple diagrams of a helicopter hydraulic system.

She called Kate, who hadn't made it out of Keswick yet. Rob, however, had spent another night at Eden House, and was fired up at his desk already. Kelly spoke to him.

'How many coffees have you had already?' she asked.

'Only one,' he replied. 'A squad car has been sent to Paul Edderbridge's residence, but has reported back that he wasn't home and he didn't come home last night either.'

'Bugger,' she said.

'They found a couple of envelopes of cash too, totalling around ten grand, minus a few quid, which I guess he'd already spent,' Rob said.

'Ten grand for killing someone,' Kelly said.

'One of them, or both of them?' Rob asked.

'Good question,' she said. 'The CPS must change their minds now.'

'You'd think so,' Rob agreed.

'You know George Fellows was seen on CCTV at Penrith station?' Kelly asked.

'Yes, boss,' he replied.

'Can we go over that again and take a closer look at what he was carrying? Did he take something from the deposit box or place something into it? Or both. You can't get ten grand out of a cashpoint,' she said.

'I see where you're going'

'I'll give Fabian Kennedy-Craig an early wake-up call and see if he can tell me where George is,' she said, ending the call.

She dialled and waited. To her surprise, Fabian answered quickly and sounded sprightly.

'Good night's rest?' she asked.

'The hotel is quite nice. I can't imagine Donald being satisfied with it though, his tastes are far more expensive, on somebody else's tab, obviously,' he said.

'And how would you know that?' she asked.

'My father told me that he paid for Donald to stay in the Ritz once, and he complained about the linen being inferior to the Dorchester. He's that type of man. He's not only ungrateful but rude to boot, especially when it concerns other people's money – usually my father's.'

'Fabian, did your father treat Donald so well because he was afraid that he knew too much?' She was careful what she said. The pornographic material had yet to be sorted through, and a case put together. As yet, they'd only scratched the surface. The last thing she wanted was to tip off the families before they'd opened up to her.

'Too much about what?'

'His business.'

'I think we can safely say that it was the other way around. My father could have destroyed Donald's career, but he chose not to.'

'But you said yourself that Donald extorted money from him. Why did your father put up with that if he held Donald's career in his hands?'

Fabian ignored her and Kelly believed his actions to be evasive on purpose.

'On the other hand, Donald was and is still a lying cheat. Which is why I wanted to talk to him yesterday.'

'The man is still critically ill, Fabian. They won't let you see him,' she said. 'And given your antics at the hospital last night, Elaine Reilly has made sure you're not allowed anywhere near him. What's the animosity between you two?' she asked, giving him an opportunity to give her his side of the argument.

'She knows what an oily fucker Donald is, excuse my language,' he said.

'Excused. Oily?' She got the impression that Fabian knew exactly what he was talking about, but she wasn't quite as clear whether he knew how far his father had been Donald's willing accomplice.

'He's a fucking pervert, detective. Don't believe any of her crocodile tears – that's if she ever shed any. I bet she didn't. She hates him. If it got out what Donald was into, the whole family would be ruined, and she knows it, which is why I told her to keep him away from my father,' he said.

'But it didn't work, did it? They were together last weekend.'

'No, it didn't work,' he admitted.

'Elaine Reilly said that the last time she saw you, you threatened to kill Donald,' she said.

'It's true, I did,' he admitted.

'Did you try?'

'What? And sabotage my own father's helicopter?' he asked.

'Maybe it was a last-minute arrangement and he wasn't supposed to be on it; he was expected in Glasgow later on,' she said.

'Nice try, detective,' he said.

'But you did know about your father changing his will,' she said. 'Your mother didn't.'

Silence engulfed the car and she thought he'd hung up, but he was still there.

'Where is George? I need to speak to him urgently,' she said.

'I don't know.'

'What? Really? As in, you've lost communication?'

'He's in the business of discretion, detective. He'll call me when he's ready,' he said.

Kelly's blood boiled.

'If he was your father's right-hand man, as you indicate, his problem-solver, or fixer, and it was well known in the family circle that Donald was an embarrassment at least, and at most a liability, why wasn't George on the helicopter with them?'

He didn't answer.

'Let me know as soon as you hear from him,' she said, ending the call. Next, she called Nellie Lowther's landline number. It made sense to Kelly that the woman had lied about knowing what was going on inside Laurie Fell, and thus it followed that she'd lied about seeing George Fellows there. It sounded like the man was Bart's sidekick and go-to person, and so he'd have watched his back, given what went on inside the mansion. It was impossible that Nellie didn't know he was there. Dan and Emma had reported that after leaving Eden House, Nellie had gone home and not left.

The number rang out.

The queue of traffic was laborious but steady, and she had at least half an hour to go before she hit Penrith. It made her antsy, and she put a call through to the duty officer at Eden House, asking if the forensic team had finished up at Laurie Fell.

She soon received a return call informing her that a few officers were still on site and, of course, they could go and check to see if Nellie Lowther was in residence at her private cottage. Kelly was hoping that, armed with the terrible revelations of yesterday, and Nellie Lowther's close connection to the property and the two men, she'd have a warrant in her hand for her private residence by lunchtime.

She tapped the steering wheel, thinking of what she could do next as she sat stuck in the queue for the next half an hour. She ate her sandwich out of boredom, and closed her eyes when the traffic stopped. At least her sinuses seemed to have cleared a little, despite the red wine last night.

As she approached the M6 roundabout, Rob called her.

'Boss, a member of the public has identified Sasha Granger and Chloe Tate from their photographs on the evening news last night, and has called in with information,' he told her.

'Go on,' she told him.

'They've given an address right here in Penrith, where they say they saw the girls hanging out of a flat window, smoking,' he said. She could hear the adrenalin in his voice.

'Jesus, get everyone ready who has made it in, plus the night shift, and get me the address, and alert armed response,' she said.

Chapter 59

The last fifteen minutes of her commute were pure hell. Kelly was itching to get things moving and raid the address in Penrith. The warrant came through under emergency orders and three armed response units were assigned to the job. It was in a civilian area, heavily occupied and thus extremely high risk for weapons-bearing officers. There were multiple entry and exit points to and from the building, and so three units were needed as a minimum requirement. The firearms commander was in constant communication with Eden House and they arranged to liaise on site, to coordinate their arrival. As per procedure, Kelly would have to wait until the ART had gone in to enter the flat herself, and after all that, it might be a false alarm. The public was notoriously fickle when it came to tip-offs. Out of every ten thousand calls, they might get lucky and strike gold, but it was more likely to be a mistaken identity. Then they would stand down and wait again. It happened. Police didn't become firearms officers to shoot people; they spent more time managing highly dangerous situations and allocating resources than firing lethal weapons, but that was the point.

A few ART members had worked alongside Kelly on the mountainside on Monday, and she listened, comforted by their familiar voices. Armed divisions were relatively small in constabularies, and Kelly had got to know most of the personnel in recent years, during various raids. She had every confidence in them, and they in her. They used blues and twos, as was standard procedure when vulnerable children were involved with any crime. The hunt for the girls had taken an unexpected and sinister twist since yesterday, and Kelly was now more immediately worried for their physical safety. They were material witnesses to serious crimes, and it was quite certain that whoever killed Bartholomew Kennedy-Craig wasn't messing around: what difference would killing a couple of schoolgirls make?

It was on the way to the address that Kelly was notified by Eden House that Nellie Lowther had been found hanged from a beam in her house, by a forensic officer who'd gone in through the open back door to search for her when she didn't answer the knocking at the front.

'Jesus,' she whispered. Kelly's first thought was homicide. Nellie was a major witness in her investigation and, after yesterday's findings, could have been pivotal to her case. But the forensic officer was also a crime scene officer, and an experienced one at that, and he said he reckoned that from the burn marks on her neck, and the set-up of the rope and stool, it looked to him like suicide. Kelly wasn't willing to rule anything out and it would take Ted to convince her either way. Until then, she was unhappy to discount anything. It also put a menacing twist on the fact that they were failing to locate Paul Edderbridge.

As they travelled to the address across town, a short distance from Eden House, squad cars had been sent to put a perimeter in place around the apartment block. Officers stood on corners, banged on doors above and below the floor they were heading for, and the transit of pedestrians was closed off. Kelly was informed that the line of sight to the flat in question was as secure as logistics and geography allowed.

This was it.

She'd jumped into the front of a squad car and held on to the hand strap attached to the ceiling. The speed of the cars, as well as the lights and sirens, startled members of the public, who stopped and stared; kids ran away, and cars let them through. Kelly was in constant communication with the three ARTs and she heard when they'd arrived at their separate locations at the front and rear of the flat.

'Get me as close as you can,' she ordered the driver, who nodded and concentrated on the traffic. Driving high speed through any built-up area required a set of skills acquired by many months of training. The hazards were immense. Occasionally, an ambulance or squad car collided with a member of the public, and it made the news. It was horrific for all involved. Kelly held on tight, her adrenalin keeping her mind off such occurrences.

They arrived at the block of flats. It was four floors high and they were aiming for the third floor. The ARTs were already advancing from pre-planned positions, and Kelly could see a few residents back off in the opposite directions. Uniformed police from the advance squad cars were holding others back and asking them to keep to the perimeter, but as in all such situations, they didn't have enough boots on the ground to make sure all civilians in the area were doing as they were told. It was quite obvious to anyone who had no criminal intention that the police were asking the public to follow simple instructions. Only have-a-go idiots and those involved might get in the way. So far, they were managing to keep the approaches clear and when the ARTs reached the third floor, all was deathly quiet.

Kelly's phone buzzed and she reached for it, staying on the ground floor, waiting for the all-clear from the ARTs, who were seconds away from the door. The call was from Fabian Kennedy-Craig. She answered it.

'George is in there with the girls, detective,' he told her breathlessly. At first, she was puzzled and couldn't quite work out what she was hearing. It seemed an alien call, but then she realised that he was talking about the flat they were headed directly to.

She shouted into her radio at the ART commander, telling him to pause. She ran to the front of the building and peered up at the balcony, watching as one ART came to a halt. Another was around the other side, and the third was on the stairs. In less than a second, she had to make her mind up over whether to send six heavily armed men into a potential hostage situation and face two dead teenagers, or rethink and strategise, calling off something that was in full momentum, and risk her reputation.

There was no contest.

The ART commander waited for her instructions. She spoke into her phone.

'Talk to me, Fabian. I'm about to send armed officers into the address, are you telling me that George will harm the girls?'

'Talk to him, detective.'

'Talk? Fabian, have you any idea what I'm dealing with here? You have five seconds to convince me,' she said. 'And that's before we even begin to talk about how you know he's in there. And how the hell you know where I am.'

Time seemed to stop and the wind disappear, and with it the last of the snowflakes, as if they too were giving up. The day, having never really woken up, was retiring already, and the sky was in full retreat.

'I need a sign that he is in there, and I need to know that the girls are okay,' she said. 'That is non-negotiable.'

'I'm putting you on to the girls, now,' Fabian said.

'Fabian! What? Are you in there?'

But before he could answer, she was talking to a quiet and very scared female, who confirmed her identity as Chloe Tate. Kelly thought quickly and calmed her breathing.

'Chloe, are you all right?' she asked.

'Yes,' the girl said. She sounded even younger than fifteen, Kelly thought.

'Is Sasha with you?'

'Yes.'

'And is George there?'

'Yes.'

'And anyone else, Chloe?'

'Yes.'

'Can you tell me?'

'No, I don't know him,' she replied.

'I need to speak to Sasha,' she said. There was a muffled sound and another girl came on the line, and confirmed her identity as Sasha Granger. Kelly chatted to the girl in a similar way and tried to buy some time, as well as calm the girl. She had proof of life.

'Can I speak to George?' Kelly asked.

A man's voice came on the phone and it wasn't Fabian she was speaking to. Wherever Fabian was calling from, if it was indeed inside the flat, then he had with him the two girls and another man that may very well be George Fellows.

'How do I know you're who you say you are, and how do I know that you're in the flat I'm looking at, George?' she asked.

'I'm going to tap loudly on the window above you. I can see you, and I can see your officers with guns,' he said. 'I'm not going to hurt anyone.'

She was in no position to trust him or otherwise.

A tapping could be heard above her head and she twisted her head upwards to the sky.

'Stand down and regroup,' she advised the ART commander, and he gave the order. She kept George on the line and asked him what he intended to do with the girls. She was buying time to keep them safe because, in this situation, when the person inside a building surrounded by police had nothing left to bargain with, they had nothing left to lose. And when that happened, people got hurt.

Kelly spoke calmly and tried to reassure George, as well as keeping him alert and focused on her, and not on the outside world.

'Can I speak to Fabian?' she asked.

She heard the phone being handed over.

'Detective?' Fabian asked.

'You have thirty seconds to explain to me what the hell you are doing in there,' she said. She watched as one ART made its way to the ground floor. The other two stayed in position: one to the front and the other to the rear of the address. George was surrounded, and Kelly couldn't work out what he wanted. There was no way out for him, but he had the girls.

'I called him and he asked to meet here. I had no idea he had these girls here,' Fabian said to her. Now wasn't the time to search her soul to see if she thought she believed him or not. Her priority was making sure the two teenagers walked out of the flat unharmed.

'I need Chloe and Sasha out here,' Kelly said.

'I'm trying to do just that,' Fabian said.

'What's stopping you?' she asked. 'And what's stopping me sending in armed police?'

'Well I'm trying to help you, detective, and you won't send armed police in here until you are a hundred per cent sure that no one is going to get injured,' he said.

'Is he armed?' she asked.

'Yes,' Fabian replied.

Kelly closed her eyes and rubbed them. She walked back to the ART that had retreated down to the car park and they looked at her, their expressions expectant yet patient. They were used to being deployed at short notice, only to stand down. They were also ready to repeat the whole process at any moment.

Kelly heard a female voice behind her and then a scuffle. She turned around and watched as a reporter, with a camera operator behind her, was trying to get through to speak to her and take footage.

'Dear God,' she said to one of the officers. 'Get rid of them.' She turned back to the concrete building.

'Fabian, are you there?' she said into her phone.

'Yes,' he replied.

'Have you managed to talk to him? About why he has the girls?'

'Yes,' he replied.

Kelly heard his voice change and her stomach twisted in knots. 'Fabian, you know why he has the girls, don't you?' she asked.

'Yes,' he replied, and he let out a sob.

Kelly's hand shook slightly as she held her phone. 'Is he trying to protect them? Or is he using them to protect himself?' she asked.

'Both,' Fabian said.

'I don't understand,' she said. 'I need to speak to George, and I need him to tell me the truth about what he's done. But that can wait. I have to see those girls. Are they hurt?'

'No, George wouldn't do that. He has the same view of what my father did as I do,' he said.

'You mean you're appalled by what he did and let down by him?' she asked.

'Yes,' he said.

'So you arranged for George to pay somebody local, who wouldn't get caught, to sabotage your father's helicopter?' she asked.

'No! What? No, wait, you have that totally wrong,' Fabian said to her. 'I didn't pay him.'

She could hear the desperation in his voice and didn't know if to believe him or not, but at the moment it was irrelevant because all she wanted was those two girls out of there.

'I believe you, Fabian. And I believe that George only took the girls because of the awful things your father did,' she said. She was going out on a limb because she had no time to call in a professional negotiating team. She was relying on the experience she had as an officer who'd dealt with hundreds of criminal minds, and innocent victims, and hoping she could tell the difference. She was out of her depth, but she had no other option. Her conversation was private, and, until she could get Fabian on a police radio frequency, then she was on her own.

'He had no choice,' Fabian said. It was almost a whisper, but it was an admission.

'Why doesn't he come in and talk about it?' she asked.

'He knows it's over,' Fabian said. 'Donald wasn't supposed to be on the helicopter.'

'Was that the plan?' she asked. 'Just your father was supposed to be on it?'

'We all know that he would have got away with it, too,' Fabian said.

She listened carefully. He was ranting, and she had to let him, but there was also a resigned melancholy she could hear in his voice. It sounded as though he was crying, and she worried for his stability. Was he about to admit that he had killed his own father?

'Got away with it?' she asked.

'If Donald hadn't been on the helicopter, then everybody would have just said that another rich guy was dead, and no one would have bothered investigating,' he said.

'That's not true, Fabian; investigations into crashes are serious, every time it happens, no matter who is on board,' she said, only half believing it herself, and mulling over the distinctly convincing possibility that he was speaking the truth.

'She almost got away with it,' he said.

'Wait, Fabian – *she?*'

'My mother,' he said.

'Your mother is behind this?' she asked.

She heard him wipe his nose as well as the build-up of intense pain in his throat.

'I need to go now,' he said.

'Wait! Fabian, don't do anything stupid, please, I'm begging you. Let me come in; we'll take George in and he can explain everything.' As she was talking, she indicated to the ART in front of her that he should get on to his commander and make preparations for going in. She used common signals learned by all commanders to communicate. They were military in origin, and universal. He nodded and got on his radio. Meanwhile, she tried to keep Fabian on the phone. She was aware of the danger, and communicated to the ART her belief that at least one of the men inside the flat was armed. He walked to his colleague and they spoke into their jackets. She tried to shut the noise of the radio out of her head and concentrated on keeping Fabian talking.

She racked her brain to try to piece together the facts of what she knew to see if she'd missed the opportunity to arrest Vivienne Kennedy-Craig, and she also considered the possibility that Fabian was lying.

'Why did he agree to it?' she asked him. She already knew the answer.

'His daughter,' he said.

Fabian told her about Vivienne's promise. She understood. Vivienne had manipulated a desperate father. 'Did you know?' she whispered.

There was a pause and she barely heard his answer.

'No,' he breathed.

Either he was an extremely good liar, or he was telling the truth. This time she couldn't tell the difference. Usually she took great pride in reading people's body signals when she was looking for clues they weren't being truthful. But she couldn't see his body. She watched as the ARTs advanced back up the stairs and held her breath.

The radio crackled and she held her hand over the mouthpiece of her phone.

The line went dead as she heard the splintering of wood and the breaking of a heavy plastic door, and the shouts of six men as they threatened those inside with lethal force if they didn't cooperate.

Kelly swallowed. It was times like these that were potentially career-ending moments. All she could do was pace from foot to foot as the noises drew a small crowd together behind her and she retreated to the stairwell, away from the journalist who was refusing to leave, but continuing to film the fuss.

A single shot rang out in the dead grey sky and Kelly's attention zoned upwards, towards the balcony, from where it had come.

Chapter 60

Inside the flat, George lay on the floor, on his front, prone and tied by the hands. Blood poured from his leg and he cried in pain. One officer went to the two girls and tried to stop them screaming, another arrested Fabian Kennedy-Craig and read him his rights. Kelly ran along the balcony and entered the flat, surveying the scene and assessing the status of the two girls.

'Fucking hell!' one of them screamed.

'That laptop was new, you pigs!' the other howled.

Kelly didn't know whether to laugh or cry. She'd saved two exploited young women who had been subjected to horrific ordeals, presumably for cash reward, but they didn't show any display of relief, or even some indication that they wanted to leave the flat. It was a strange sensation and one she'd come across before. It was similar to Stockholm syndrome, where captives form real relationships with their captors. It would appear that Chloe and Sasha saw what they did as legitimate work, and Kelly had just blown it for them. She stood back as the ART members, trained in the highest paramedic aid, assessed them.

'Fucking get off!' one barked.

'Get off, you pervert!' the other kicked out.

'Let me,' she said gently, ignoring the irony, and the officers stood back. She approached the two girls, as Fabian was walked past her and out into the open, to be taken to Eden House. George would have to wait for an ambulance, but he'd spend the night strapped to a bed with a police guard outside his room. She spoke softly to the girls, and explained what was happening, after establishing that they were unharmed.

'You can go home as soon as you've been assessed by our team,' she said.

'Assessed for what?' one asked.

'I'm not going fucking home,' the other said.

Kelly had no idea, yet, which girl was which. She hoped that, by now, the child protection team had arrived and the girls would be taken by them. She knew it was quite normal for victims to lash out at those taking them away from a familiar situation. She looked around the pokey flat. There was evidence of takeaways, TV, new phones, and the girls had been sprawled in a leisurely manner across the bed when they'd been apprehended. There was no evidence they'd been held against their will. The sad truth was that they saw this life as their future, not something to be rescued from.

There was no point explaining to the two girls why George had been arrested – not yet, at least. That would unfold all in good time. Her job, starting right away, was to figure out the relationship between Vivienne Kennedy-Craig and George Fellows. How much Fabian knew remained to be seen. Three child protection officers arrived, as George was receiving emergency care, and howling in the meantime, and got the same welcome she had.

'Get your fucking hands off me!' one girl shouted.

'Who the fuck are you?' the other said.

Kelly walked out of the flat, along the balcony, and down the steps. The forensic team would be next in. The call had already been put into motion to send teams to the London residence of Vivienne Kennedy-Craig to arrest her and soon, Kelly hoped she would have all the answers she needed to understand who was ultimately responsible for the crash. She believed that the perpetrator was in custody, and that it was either the wife or the son of the deceased who was behind it. Maybe she'd never know. Maybe it would be a jury who decided.

George was carried out of the flat as an ambulance arrived and this time, Kelly didn't stop the journalist poking his nose into George's face as he was carried to the waiting crew. Before he was bundled into the vehicle, Kelly approached as the small crowd of people was held back. George's face was contorted in pain.

'Who told you to do it, George?' she asked.

He opened his eyes and stared at her. He reached into his pocket and took out a phone, and gave it to her.

'It's all on there. I recorded her. Fabian has nothing to do with it; he worshipped his father, even after he found out what a monster he was,' he said.

Kelly nodded. She could see that he knew he'd never see his daughter again.

She watched as he was loaded into the back of the vehicle and stood in the middle of the car park as it pulled away, sirens blazing, and people parted to allow it through. She walked through the crowd and around a tall wall, where she found a grit bin to sit on, away from prying eyes.

Melted snow soaked through her jacket and she put up her hood.

Finally, she got up and took a cut-through to Penrith town, stopping at the first coffee shop she found. The warm liquid made her feel slightly human again and she made her way back to Eden House. It wasn't far. By the time she got there, she was sodden and Kate asked where the hell she'd been.

'You had perfectly good squad cars in full working order and you decide to walk?' Kate said.

Kelly nodded. She took off her coat and water dripped all over the floor.

'You okay?' Kate asked. 'Vivienne Kennedy-Craig is in custody in London.'

Kelly sat down. 'She's behind it all,' she said. She put the mobile phone given to her by George Fellows on the table and Kate picked it up.

'Have you looked at it?' Kate asked.

Kelly shook her head.

Kate picked it up and turned it on. It was unlocked – George's final act of quick thinking, so desperate was he to reveal the woman who'd used him. He'd probably worked out at some point that she'd never had any intention to help him get custody of his daughter back. Kate quickly found the home page and searched around inside the apps on the screen. She played something and set it down on the table. Kelly listened.

It was Vivienne Kennedy-Craig's voice.

> *'Fabian can never know. Find some dropout up there wherever you are, and make sure you tidy up.'*

Kate fiddled with the phone and found another recording.

> *'Tidy up, George. Nellie is, and always has been, a liability, I cannot have her coming back to me.'*

In just two statements, recorded by a forward-thinking man who was technically a murderer, but useful to them as a pivotal witness, Kelly realised that the whole case had rested upon the fact that Vivienne Kennedy-Craig never knew that Lord Donald Reilly would get into that helicopter, and thus spark an intense investigation. Kelly would like to think that if it had been Bart alone who'd been harmed, then the AAIB would have found the cut hydraulic line anyway, but she'd never know for sure if quite so much fuss would have been made if Lance Tatterall hadn't happened to have been on the mountainside in the first place.

By the time Kate and Kelly had finished listening to the recordings on George's phone, the sky outside was fully dark and Paul Edderbridge had still not been located. They had a fairly straightforward picture of how the murder and attempted murder had taken place, and they had George Fellows willing to testify. He just kept talking. Strapped to a bed at the Penrith and Lakes hospital, he wouldn't shut up, giving them fact after fact, hoping that it would ultimately reduce his sentence. Maybe it would, Kelly thought, but it wouldn't get his daughter back. The CPS were notorious for making such deals. It was why she was a copper and not a lawyer.

Before they left for the evening, Kelly took a call from her father, who'd been driven by Johnny to the hospital to take a look at the body of Nellie Lowther. It was a grim ride to give, especially with their four-month-old daughter strapped into her car seat, but Johnny wouldn't hear of Ted driving himself. The plan was that Kelly would collect him, and they'd eat together as a family tonight, after Josie got back from her Duke of Edinburgh expedition.

'What do you think?' Kelly asked Ted.

'The slip knot came in with her,' he said.

As she listened, Kate put a cup of coffee on her desk. She'd warmed up but hadn't really thawed out in her bones. A fresh box of tissues sat on the table and she used two or three to blow her nose.

'It's well done, and very effective. The friction burns on her skin are oblique and above the thyroid, indicative of a full hanging, which is incredibly hard to manufacture. Her skin is displaced and heaped in part and she's already been to radiology, who've confirmed that she had hyoid damage but her cervical, cricoid and thyroid cartilage are intact. She died from a violent transverse tear to her carotid artery caused by the rupturing of her sternocleidomastoid muscle. It was suicide, Kelly, I'm pretty sure.'

'Hmmm,' she said. She almost laughed out loud as she caught herself doing exactly what irritated her about Andrew Harris.

'You okay?' Ted asked.

'Yes. Thank you. I'll pick you up in about fifteen minutes,' she said, and rang off. She yawned loudly and Kate threw her the look of a concerned parent.

'Any news on Chloe and Sasha?' Kelly asked her.

'They're denying involvement in any wrongdoing,' Kate said.

'What about the videos?' Kelly asked.

'They're saying it was a laugh, and they weren't coerced,' Kate said.

'Jesus, so it'll be the CPS prosecuting without their supporting testimony,' Kelly said. 'I hope they have better luck with some of the other victims they've identified from the school. Maybe after some supportive intervention, they might begin to realise that what they've been through is a crime.'

'Or it might take the rest of their lives,' Kate said.

'At the moment, they're holding on to the idea that they were paid well for their efforts. It's chilling.'

'I think it's time you went home,' Kate said.

'Do we know how Lord Reilly is doing?' Kelly asked, putting on her still wet coat.

'He took a turn for the worse,' Kate said.

Chapter 61

The room was dark and only the flashes of blue and red from the monitors cast an eerie shadow on the hospital bed.

Abigail looked at her father and a tear slipped down her face. She'd been briefed by her mother. They were under no doubt, now, that a full case would be brought against the peer. Not even the PM could protect him now. She'd carried the burden for four long years, looking into his face at times, and begging him to tell her it was a lie. Fabian knew it wasn't a fiction, and so did she. She'd believed at one time that he was sick. After all, he'd never touched her in that way. Her mother had asked her. It had been the worst conversation of her life. No. He hadn't, she'd told her. But this didn't excuse what he did to others. The test she applied to his behaviour was the fact that he did it in secret. Shame was the barometer she used to judge her father's word.

The phone call from Fabian was the final confirmation.

She reached out and touched her father's face and he rallied a little. Since waking up, he was breathing on his own but he was still in a great deal of pain as a result of the burns he'd sustained.

His eyes flickered open and he seemed to recognise her, but love soon turned to the familiar glow of burning shame as he realised that his daughter knew exactly why he'd been with Bart on that helicopter. He'd promised he'd get help. He'd pledged to stop. Forever.

He'd lied.

She rested her hand on his forehead and he winced in pain. Her hand pressed against the dressings and he tried to make a sound, but the tubes sticking out of his mouth and nose prevented him.

Abigail stared at him and his grimace of pain turned to fear. She could see in his eyes that he knew what she was about to do. He was defenceless. All he could do was force his eyes this way and that, as beads of sweat formed on his face, and Abigail wiped her tears away.

She leant over him and took a pillow, careful not to knock the nurse's alarm.

She laid it over his head and pressed as hard as she could. The exertion made her breath shallow and her muscles ache. She was shocked at the effort it took. His body quivered and vibrated under her hands but he was trapped like a fly in a spider's web, his limbs suspended to save his life, and to allow his skin to heal from the terrible trauma he'd suffered up on the mountain. Abigail felt her body fatigue from the stiffness of her force, and she'd lost track of time. She looked down at her father and realised that he was no longer moving. Over the last few days, he'd had such little movement in his body that she had to check herself. She removed the pillow. The beeps and machines were silent.

His face was contorted in a ghastly scream, as though he'd tried his very best to take a gasp of air at the last moment, but Abigail didn't feel guilty, just tremendously sad.

It was best for them all.

She replaced the pillow by his head and straightened the sheets. Gently wiping off some of his sweat from his face, she closed his eyes and his mouth. He looked strangely at peace. She turned around and walked out of the room, checking that the nurse's alarm remained off, as she'd set it earlier. She closed the door quietly and walked along the silent corridor. As she emerged from the bowels of the ICU, where she'd cried her last tears, she felt liberated from the hell she'd lived under for four long years, knowing that her father was a monster.

She called Fabian so she could hear his voice. She wanted connection with the one person who understood. But he didn't answer and his phone went to voicemail.

Chapter 62

Kelly stood opposite Andrew Harris, who was seated comfortably. He'd requested an update, first thing Monday morning.

'Kelly, the report into the crash has to meet certain criteria to satisfy the AAIB and the public inquiry,' Andrew said.

'Certain criteria? You mean an abridged version of the truth? Stop short? Is that what you're asking?'

'I'm not asking, Kelly.'

'You're threatening me?'

She stood in his office, having refused a chair, or a coffee. And sneezed.

'Excuse me,' she said.

He passed her a tissue but she took one out of her bag instead of taking one from him.

'Have you finished?' he asked her.

She nodded tersely.

'Write your final report, Kelly, and submit it to the AAIB. The investigation into *why* Bartholomew Kennedy-Craig and Lord Donald Reilly were together before they were murdered is for the child abuse unit to bring to justice.'

'Don't muddy the waters?' she snapped.

He grinned at her. 'Our job, Kelly, was to investigate what brought that helicopter down, and you've done that.

It was a cut hydraulic line, tampered with, we believe by Paul Edderbridge, who is now missing, and has been for five days. He was paid ten thousand pounds by Vivienne Kennedy-Craig to do the job, via George Fellows. That is it. You have done your job. The wheres, whys and wherefores are for the CPS to take up. Yes, meet with them. Yes, give them your findings. Yes, keep looking for Edderbridge, and build the case against him.'

Kelly went to interrupt and he held up his hand.

'If you're not going to apply for a transfer to child protection, then I suggest you put your effort where it's best served, Kelly, and make the case against Vivienne Kennedy-Craig watertight. It'll come out in court. That will be the day you get your reward for uncovering all of this.'

She didn't have anything else to say. In the last week, since the death of Lord Reilly, and the arrest of Vivienne, Kelly had worked fourteen-hour days, and so had the rest of her team.

Fabian would stand against his mother as a witness for the prosecution. It was a massive win for the CPS, thanks to Kelly. George Fellows's lawyers, paid for by Fabian, had managed to negotiate a reduced sentence for a guilty plea to the charge of transferred malice. He could get five years and serve two. Paul Edderbridge couldn't be arrested or charged until he was found, and Kelly was more sure with each passing day that he was dead, either dispatched by George Fellows or somebody else hired by Vivienne. In interview, when asked about Edderbridge, George had stuck to his story that he'd last seen Edderbridge when he was caught trespassing at Laurie Fell. Kelly thought he was lying but couldn't prove it. They had footage of him collecting something at an Amazon drop box but they couldn't prove that was payment for a hit. All their evidence against him was circumstantial.

Vivienne was charged with murder, and with the absence of Edderbridge, it would be she who faced the full force of the trial by jury, because she'd pleaded not guilty. The woman was arrogant. She was also lacking in any form of integrity. She had pointed the finger at her manservant, giving a statement against him under caution, that he was the one who'd dealt with George Fellows and plotted the death of her husband. The employee, Terrance Over, denied all involvement with the plot, and was released on bail pending further inquiry. The case probably wouldn't come to trial for a good year. The AAIB report was expected in the New Year.

'So, to be clear, sir, my report will omit the details of the world-wide paedophile ring, actively contributed to by the deceased, as well as the fact that either Bartholomew Kennedy-Craig or a peer of the realm was in fact The Chief, sought by child abuse specialists on three, or more, continents.'

She stood straight and fast. She knew it was easy details to him but to her, it was fundamental. However, a conversation with both Ted and Johnny had enabled her to at least accept in her own conscience that justice would get its day, even if she couldn't shout it from the rooftops. She had to settle for the kind of payback that most victims have to wait for: a vengeance on paper. And this was the precise loyalty to procedure that she'd begged Johnny to waver from. During his testimony for Ian Burton, she realised that he'd given the serial killer the basic right to be heard. Without that, no person working in the field of law could hold their head up high and say, in public or private, that they acted in full justice carved out to protect the rights of the accused. In other words, the very fabric of the way they held citizens accountable. The same was true of Bartholomew Kennedy-Craig and Lord Donald Reilly. They'd have their time in court, posthumously, but the law had to be followed to the letter, otherwise, in years to come, their families could appeal and question the charges and the procedure. She knew that this was right. The integrity of the judicial system had to be protected. Ian Burton was in prison for the rest of his life because his case had been watertight and heard in open court, with all the rights in place that would be given to any citizen, innocent or guilty.

It stuck in her throat. She wanted to go after the memory of Bartholomew Kennedy-Craig and Lord Donald Reilly, bringing the government that had protected him to account. She also wanted to reveal the role played by Nellie Lowther. But to uphold the integrity of her profession, she had to proceed with accuracy and legality. Otherwise, she might as well leave the force and take George Fellows's old job.

Besides, she had to stay focused for her team. They took their lead from her and it was her responsibility to err on the right side of the law. She couldn't bend it to her advantage because she felt the harm done to those children, some of whom they'd never identify or save. She had to shelve her desire to rip up the rule book and obliterate the dark web and what it stood for, and how the two men in the helicopter had bolstered it with their cash and their deceit.

Fabian Kennedy-Craig was the hope for the future of Tactika, and it was one way for him to atone for the wrongs of his father.

The death of Lord Reilly had been unexpected, and the staff of the intensive care unit took it badly. Losing a patient, despite their best efforts and his being given such positive prognosis after he woke up, was a shock. Kelly found it hard to find it inside herself to pass on her condolences to his family, but Abigail had surprised her with her commitment to the future. Regardless of whether her father's actions were denounced and exposed in public, Abigail, alongside Fabian, was cooperating with the inquiry in full transparency.

Kelly waited for Chief Constable Harris's answer. He sat back.

'That's correct, and you know it will all come out at trial,' he said.

'Sir,' she said.

'Have a good day, Kelly, and take some time off, for God's sake. You're sneezing your germs all over the place! Take the rest of the week off, at least, I insist,' he said.

'I'm heading home now, sir,' she said.

She left his office and went back to her car. A week off was just what she needed, never mind an afternoon. Besides, she had a few things to wrap up — not least her telephone conversation, off the record, with Quentin St John, to finalise her account of why a member of Her Majesty's cabinet used the opportunity of a climate conference to stay at the mansion of a paedophile. It was uncustomary for her to go against authority but she was sure that it was what she had to do. It wasn't as if she hadn't warned Andrew that the story would eventually break. After all, she could control the AAIB investigation, but not the British press.

Some things, in this game, were just out of her hands.

Chapter 63

It was the first time Kelly had been out in the *Wendy* for months. The small yacht was usually taken to dry dock inside a boathouse on the shores of either Ullswater or Derwent Water for the winter. Johnny had decided that this year, she'd be spending her hibernation at the sailing club at Ullswater's southern point, near Glenridding. He'd unveiled her this morning and checked her over, making sure she was worthy of a short outing across the lake. It was cold but clear: one of the Lake District's finest days.

It was Christmas Eve and Josie was busy wrapping presents and making mince pies at home, ready for the big day tomorrow. Ted was with her and would spend the night with them. It was as if Kelly's life had come full circle. She had a family who loved her and waited at home, in the warmth, by the fire, for her return. Johnny would spend Christmas with them too. When she'd moved back to the Lakes six years ago, she'd had no idea that this was where she would end up. This was her home now. London was not only geographically a world away, it was also behind her in terms of what she wanted. She'd come back in a kind of personal resignation of hope, and to hide from the life she'd created there. This new one took her by surprise.

Kelly parked her car and got out, looking over at the lake, which was serenely calm. The steamers had yet to start up, and there would only be a couple today, allowing the staff to get home early to their families for the festivities. In fact, the lake looked empty. It was perfect. The southernmost point of the great lake was tucked inside a curve that was overlooked by Place Fell, and she tried to remember the happy times she'd spent up there chasing her breath, rather than suspects. She knew that just because it was Christmas Eve, crime wouldn't suddenly halt and allow good will to all men, women and children. No. She knew better than that. It was a habit of hers that she saw potential in all hidden corners to harbour darkness, but she concentrated on her day off and pushed the thoughts aside. There'd be plenty of time for that when she returned to work.

Johnny waved at her and pointed over to the jetty. She got a bag out of the car and went to him. She'd packed a flask of hot soup, some cheese and biscuits and a favourite bottle of red wine. The *Wendy* was stocked with everything else they'd need, including blankets should the sky turn grey. There was no other place that Kelly could think of that presented all four seasons in just one day so brazenly.

He held her hand as she walked across the gangway he'd put out for her.

'I feel like royalty,' she said. 'Should I be offended that you think I need this?'

He laughed. 'I just wanted you to be comfortable. I know you don't need it. Besides, you're getting old, Kel, I don't want you falling in.'

She went to hit him playfully and lost her balance.

'See!' he said, smirking.

She stepped onboard and went to put away the food and drink, as Johnny readied to depart. They waved to staff at the boathouse who they knew. Everybody here now knew the true story behind the helicopter crash on Scafell Pike. News travelled quickly when mountains kept gossip in tight corners.

Johnny set off and he gently manoeuvred the boat out into the centre, easing her across to where the lake bent around to reveal her main trunk. They passed the Glenridding hotel, where Lord Reilly had been egged and hounded, and they passed Glencoyne Wood, pulling slowly away from the shoreline, to reveal the foothills of Helvellyn behind them as they headed east. Johnny sped up now and the wind caught Kelly's hair. They had the lake to themselves. She went to the tiny galley kitchen and got two beers from the cooler. Sitting next to him, she handed him one. They clinked their tins together. They passed Aira point and Kelly sipped her beer.

They could have brought the whole family. They could have just brought their daughter. There were many things Kelly could or should do, but not today. A five-month-old wasn't exactly the ideal backdrop to healing a relationship that had come so close to ending – not because they fell out of love, she realised now, but because they'd both allowed something on the outside to creep inside, and it had been a mistake. Because if they were unable to withstand what came at them from time to time, just because that was life, and her job, then what chance did they have?

Johnny wore a huge knitted jumper, but still had on shorts, and she smiled, putting her sunglasses on. There was little warmth in the sun but it was as bright as any day Kelly could remember in the Lakes. The water was so clear that she could see the contours of the lake bed as they passed shallow water to make their way into the centre of the lake, where it was darker, but still blue. Johnny eased back and set a steady pace. There was no rush, and no traffic to navigate. Cloud clung to some of the features on the south shore, as they were the tallest hills, though the peak of Gowbarrow on their left was clear.

They spotted a few tiny orange and pink forms on the top and realised that five people were waving at them. They waved back.

They planned to spend tomorrow at home, in front of the fire, and then take Ted for a pint later. Johnny had moved some of his belongings back.

Her phone buzzed and she eyed Johnny. The only reason she would answer it was if Josie was trying to reach them because Lizzie needed something. She took it out of her pocket to check. It was Josie; she'd sent a picture of Lizzie and Ted in front of the Christmas tree, sitting opposite one another, seemingly in pretend conversation.

'Maybe he's taking her through what Grandpa does for a living,' Johnny said.

Kelly rolled her eyes. Her father also deserved this break. No matter how much she wanted him to retire, and concentrate on the things that he enjoyed for himself, as well as spend more time with Lizzie, he always found himself dragged back in to the job that he loved. He just couldn't stay away.

She went to put her phone away but it buzzed again and she saw that it was a notification from Emma, who'd volunteered to cover the Christmas shift.

Kelly checked the message.

'Shit,' she said as gently as she could.

'What is it?'

'It looks like the Penrith and Lakes is opening a private tribunal into the death of Lord Reilly. The coroner suspected foul play. The coroner as in my dad. He didn't tell me.'

She looked at Johnny and he concentrated on the boat.

'You knew, didn't you?' she asked him.

'Sort of,' he replied.

'Sort of?'

'He made me promise not to tell you until after Christmas at least. He doesn't want you to worry. Why is work texting you, anyway?'

'You know why,' she said. 'But you're right; there's nothing I can do about it today.' She put her phone away in the bag.

'Apart from think about it all day, which is exactly why he didn't tell you,' Johnny said.

But it wasn't an accusation, or a complaint. He was smiling.

'And that's what you'll do,' he added. 'Because that mind never stops. If I could just get another beer, though, that'd be great.'

She left him and got him another beer from the cooler and decided that, today, work could stay on land. Meanwhile, right now, she belonged out here, on the water. With him.

Acknowledgements

As always, the expert knowledge of certain individuals was invaluable when writing this book. Especially Ali Mack, whose infinite and fascinating knowledge of helicopters kept me on my toes, and Paul Stanbridge, for his practiced authority on emergency response. Special thanks goes to Adrian Priestley who is always on hand to answer tricky questions, any time.

Thanks also to Jack Oliver from Adventuring for the shared stories on our way up Scafell Pike.

Thank you to my agent, Peter, for his encouragement and unstinting loyalty to the Kelly series, and the whole team at Canelo, especially Louise and Siân.

To my home team: Mike, Tilly, Freddie, and Poppy the Wonderdog, for keeping me grounded and happy. I couldn't wish for a better posse.

Do you love crime fiction and are always on the lookout for brilliant authors?

Canelo Crime is home to some of the most exciting novels around. Thousands of readers are already enjoying our compulsive stories. Are you ready to find your new favourite writer?

Find out more and sign up to our newsletter at canelocrime.com